TIM SHOEMAKER

EVERY HIDDEN THING

A HIGH WATER™ NOVEL

FOCUS ON THE FAMILY®

A Focus on the Family Resource
Published by Tyndale House Publishers

Every Hidden Thing

A Focus on the Family book published by Tyndale House Publishers, Carol Stream, Illinois 60188

Cover design by Michael Harrigan

The author is represented by the Cyle Young Hartline Literary Agency.

ISBN 978-1-64607-060-2

Printed in the United States of America

28 27 26 25 24 23 22
7 6 5 4 3 2 1

To my daughters-in-law—

Laura, Sarah, and Beth.

A writer's deepest loves can be found

between the lines of their stories.

You will always be there.

For God will bring
every deed into judgment,
including every hidden thing,
whether it is good or evil.

—

ECCLESIASTES 12:14

CHAPTER 1

Rockport, Massachusetts
Monday, May 2, 11:35 p.m.

PARKER BUCKMAN TOLD HIMSELF that he wasn't afraid of the dark. Technically, it was just the things he couldn't see *because* of the dark that had him on edge.

Imagined things, mostly. Impossible things. Like that creep, Clayton Kingman, bent on revenge, suddenly crawling through Parker's window. Or the skull of the giant alligator Goliath somehow dropping to the floor and growing the rest of its body back, reforming muscle and bone and a nearly bulletproof hide until its full fifteen-foot length was restored right there in his bedroom. Just waiting to snap at Parker if he swung his legs off the bed.

Ridiculous, Parker thought. Ghosts from his past. He'd left those things far behind.

Clayton Kingman had earned himself a lifetime membership at the Everglades Correctional Institution, just outside of Miami.

Locked up in prison, he would never threaten Parker again. And Goliath was dead. The gator stick Parker had used to kill the beast—thrusting it right down its throat—was propped in the corner of his bedroom as a good reminder of that. And if he needed actual proof, the gator's skull sitting on the bookshelf provided that.

Parker had faced this uneasy feeling before, but it felt stronger tonight. He resisted the urge to turn on his bedroom light. *I am not afraid of the dark.* He cracked open his second story window instead, filling his lungs with damp, salty air. The rhythmic sound of waves battering the rocky shore of the nearby Headlands was always a comfort. If the massive swells couldn't get past the rocks—not in high tide or hurricane—the ghosts from his past couldn't reach him here either. The pounding surf was one more reminder that he didn't live in swampy southern Florida anymore. He was over 1,500 miles north—in the town of Rockport, Massachusetts.

He was safe here, right? What was it with all the spooky thoughts?

His phone vibrated next to his bed, the screen casting a pale glow on his bedroom wall.

Who'd be texting me now?

It had to be Jelly. Angelica Malnatti—the best friend he'd had to leave behind in Everglades City. Maybe her dad finally got the transfer, and she wanted Parker to be the first to know. *But why would she be telling me now?* It had to be close to midnight.

He snatched up his phone and stared at the name on the display: *Devin Catsakis.* Instantly Parker wished he hadn't given this guy his number.

`You awake?`

He pecked out a quick reply.

`No.`

`Ha ha! Make sure your ringer is off so I don't wake your parents when I call in 5, 4, 3 . . .`

Parker had barely toggled the ringer off before the thing vibrated in his hand. He answered before the second buzz.

"Something crazy is going on here, Parker," Devin whispered. He sounded out of breath. "Somebody—no, make that some-*thing*—just came out of our neighbors' house. The one they rent out."

"That doesn't sound so cra—"

"He's holding some kind of green light, like a humongous glow stick. It's probably radioactive or something. Maybe some kind of laser."

Radioactive? Now he was really regretting giving out his number. Because Devin Catsakis wasn't living in the real world. That's what Ella Houston said, anyway. Devin was a huge sci-fi fan, but he was totally convinced that a lot of the crazy things he read about actually existed. Parallel universes. Time travel. Aliens. He'd talked Parker's head off about how those things were absolutely real.

"I'm trying to record a video, but it's so stinkin' dark that I can't get a decent shot of him."

"He's still at your neighbors'? Well, call the police or something."

Devin was breathing heavy—like he needed a hit from his inhaler. "Can't do that. He's on the move now."

"Wait . . . are you *following* him?"

"Just until I get a good shot—and you get out here. You've got to see this."

Sneaking out in the middle of the night—to chase a burglar carrying some kind of light saber? "Don't be stupid," Parker said. "You need to go home. Where are you?"

"Rowe Avenue. Almost to Parker's Pit."

The long-abandoned granite quarry on the edge of town. Filled with water, it was a favorite place for Parker to go—and not just because of its name. But at night—*in the dark?* He wouldn't be caught dead there. "Devin, get *out* of there. If you get in trouble, nobody will even hear you cry for help."

"This thing is like a big shadow. A shadow-man. I think the green light is his energy source."

Parker suspected that Devin wanted all these crazy theories to be true so bad that he might stretch the truth.

"Devin—go home."

"Not until I catch a decent image of this Shadow-man. C'mon. Hop on your bike. I'm going to show you this thing is for real."

"You're insane if you think I'd sneak out of the house. Not a chance." It would totally mess up all the trust he'd built with his parents.

"What if this is some sort of paranormal sighting I'm looking at—can you imagine what that would be worth if I could capture it on my phone?"

"As in a ghost?" Parker didn't really want to burst the guy's bubble, but come *on.* "No such thing."

"Listen, Parker." Devin's voice sounded muffled, like he had his hand cupped over the phone to keep from being heard. "Get your tail out here and I'll prove it to you."

If he was still living in Florida, and it was Jelly—or even Wilson—on the phone, would he do it? Would he sneak out? He'd be tempted, for sure. How could he leave Jelly out there, alone? But this wasn't Jelly—and she wouldn't do a stupid thing like this anyway. Would anybody? *What if Devin was making this all up?*

Likely this whole thing was some kind of dumb stunt Devin

was pulling. His friend Ella had said something about that, too. That Devin was always doing goofy things to get people to buy into his theories.

"Are you coming?" Devin whispered. "This is your chance to see a real ghost—or maybe an alien."

"Nice try," Parker said. "Not going to happen."

Suddenly Devin sucked in his breath. "He just turned and looked my way—but I can't even see a face. Maybe he doesn't *have* a face." Devin started talking faster. "This is the second time he's done that. Stopped to look my way. Like he's making sure I'm keeping up."

Devin actually sounded scared. *Was this all part of the act? What did he mean when he said the guy had no face?* "Are you out of your mind? Turn around. It's a trap. Run!"

"I need to record this first."

If even half of what Devin said was true, he was getting in way over his head.

"I'm calling the police," Parker said. "Exactly where are you?"

"I'm off Rowe now, on the road running alongside the quarry. But no police—I don't want to scare this thing away."

"Does he *look* scared?"

Devin gave a quick laugh. "No—but he should be. He doesn't know who he's messing with."

Devin is crazier than I thought! Parker stared out his window. The fog was thick tonight. No stars visible. No moon. The patio light below him was just a brighter smudge. Was the quarry fog-bound like this, too? How close would Devin have to get just to see this Shadow-man? Too close.

"I'm making the call," Parker said. He had to, right?

"No—don't," Devin said. "They'll tell my parents and I'll get grounded for life. They don't know I snuck out. Come on, promise me—no cops."

There was no way he was going to promise that.

"Parker, the thing climbed out on Humpback Rock now." The little peninsula jutting out from the south side of the quarry. Devin was talking so fast—and so soft—that Parker could barely make out what he was saying. "Some kind of ritual, I think. He's raising the energy source over his head with both hands and—"

"That's it," Parker said. "Leave now—or I call 9-1-1."

"Holy donuts, Parker—the thing just did a Peter Pan right off the edge of Humpback!"

"Into the water?"

"It disappeared below the surface. I can see a big green glow in the water!"

For several seconds the only things Parker heard were wind and scuffling noises. "Devin—what's going on? You okay?"

"This is *incredible.*" Devin was back—and even more out of breath. "I'm standing at the edge of Humpback Rock—right where Shadow-man was ten seconds ago. He's gone, Parker. *Gone.*"

"What? You got closer?"

"I still see the green light—way down deep in the water. It's getting fainter."

"Get *out* of there."

"And I didn't even get any footage of this thing." Devin groaned. "Who's going to believe me?"

Nobody. Parker wasn't sure he believed a word of it himself.

"The light is completely gone now. There aren't even any bubbles. Parker—I wish you'd been here. The thing vanished—poof—just totally disappeared."

"Well, it's time for you to disappear, too." Maybe he was home right now—and this whole thing was a hoax.

"I gotta know what this was. An alien being? Some paranormal presence?"

Or his imagination—seeing the very things in the dark that he obsessed over. Parker knew a little of what that was about. "If it dropped into the water, and you see no bubbles, whatever it was is dead now. Go home."

"Dead? Parker, you don't know a thing about this kind of stuff. These things don't die."

"Thanks for that mind-picture, Devin." That was going to make it a whole lot easier for him to sleep tonight. "I'm hanging up now. Promise me you're going home—right now—or I promise you I'm calling the police."

"Yeah, yeah. I'll leave. No need for cops. You and Ella save me a seat at the lunch table tomorrow. I want to see her face when she hears about this."

Devin disconnected, just like that. He'd make a big deal of the whole thing at school tomorrow. Parker was sure of it. He'd point to Parker as his star witness, but what had Parker seen? Nothing. And that was about how much of Devin's story that he believed, too.

Still, a little part of him wondered if Devin was actually hanging out at Parker's Pit at this moment. Some of the rocks there were covered with moss. And they'd be drenched in mist from the fog. Not to mention how dark it would be. Crawling around the rim of the quarry would be stupid-dangerous—even without this supposed Shadow-man. Not that the drop to the water was high at Parker's Pit, but this early in May, the water would be knock-the-wind-out-of-you freezing.

He pecked out a quick text and reread it. If Devin truly *was* at the quarry, he'd need to know Parker was ready to call the police. And if it was all a hoax? Devin would just think Parker was buying the whole thing—which would make tomorrow more interesting, for sure.

`Do what you promised—or I'll do what I warned you I'd do. No more stalling. Do it now.`

Parker smiled. The text sounded strong—like Parker was actually going to phone the police. If Devin really was by Parker's Pit, maybe this would get him moving. He sent it—and stared out the window again.

He'd never seen the fog thicker. Denser. Parker raised the window higher and reached outside with his gimpy arm. The darkness hovered closer to the freaky side of the spectrum. Nobody in his right mind would go out on a night like this. Even the man-in-the-moon wasn't showing his face. Parker could barely see the scars crisscrossing his forearm. He opened and closed his fist. Was sure he could feel the weight of the fog. The presence. Like it was some creature rising from the sea and creeping ashore to do some unholy task. The uneasy feeling gained mass. Size.

Get a grip, Parker. Where was all that coming from? He shook off the dark thoughts.

It wasn't two minutes later before Parker's phone vibrated with an incoming.

`Ok, ok. Could have sworn I heard bubbles coming up. Spooky. You'll get the full report tomorrow. Don't worry, by the time you get this text I'll already be on the move.`

Good. If he was trying to bamboozle Parker about this Shadowman thing, his little scam was over for the night. And if he really had gone out to the quarry, he was on his way home now. Either way, Devin wasn't in any danger.

And neither was Parker. He swiped on the flashlight app and checked his room. Goliath's skull was still on the shelf where it belonged. Nobody was climbing through his open window. Dad and Mom were just down the hall in their bedroom. And most importantly, God was always with him, right?

Which all boiled down to one thing. He was safe here. *Safe.* The things he couldn't see in the dark were all about his imagination—like Devin's Shadow-man with the green light.

He sat on the edge of his bed and stared at the fog again. Yes, he was safe. That was logical—and he got that. But somewhere between his head and his heart there was a disconnect. Because here, in the darkness of his own room . . . for the first time since he'd moved to Rockport, Parker didn't feel safe at all.

CHAPTER 2

Rockport High School
Tuesday, May 3

WHEN PARKER STRODE INTO THE CAFETERIA FOR LUNCH, he still hadn't seen Devin all morning. Which wasn't all that unusual. He was the kind of guy nobody really saw. Still, Parker figured Devin would've caught him in the hallway before this. Suddenly tailgating Parker between classes. Gushing out every detail of the mysterious events at the quarry—and how Parker had missed it.

He dropped onto the blue molded chair at his usual table in the cafeteria—all the way in the back and right next to the windows. Ella Houston took a seat opposite him. She was the only girl in the whole school who wore a dress. And she did every day. Loose. Free-flowing. Falling just below her knees. She probably didn't even own a pair of jeans. Sometimes she wore sandals, but today it was the cowgirl boots. "Weird that Devin isn't here yet," Ella said. "I figured he'd be champing at the bit to tell us about the Shadow-man."

Parker had already caught her up to speed before school—and she'd asked more questions between classes. Honestly? He'd expected her to laugh it off—but she hadn't. She didn't make even one snarky comment about what Devin had claimed to see. It was weird.

"So," she said, "there's a good chance Devin just made this all up. A way of sucking you into his world of paranormal paranoia." The sun filtering through the window gave her skin a rich glow—a dead-ringer match to her brown eyes. "Is that how you see it?"

"Don't you?"

Ella gave a one-shouldered shrug. "I dunno. I definitely want to hear his story."

This from the girl who usually referred to Devin as the "sci-fi freak." Sometimes El was impossible to figure out. She was like Jelly that way—and she wore her hair in two braids like her, too, but that's where the similarities ended. And it wasn't just the obvious things—like El's jet-black hair to Jelly's red, or the way they dressed. It was the way they acted—and reacted. The things they said, and the things they really liked to do.

If Jelly were living in Rockport instead of still back in the Everglades City area, she'd hike the rocky shoreline from Gloucester to Rockport and beyond. She wouldn't stop longer than it would take to retie her shoe. Ella would find a rock that made a perfect chair. She'd kick off her boots and read or just watch the waves and the lobster boats troll by.

Jelly would look for a remote corner to set up her wildlife camera. El would find the perfect spot to set up her easel and watercolors.

Jelly's dad had to get the transfer north soon. And when Jelly moved up here, even as different as the two girls were, Parker still figured they'd become great friends. Hoped they would. And maybe Jelly could help him figure El out.

Parker definitely didn't get her sometimes. "Are you telling me that you believe there was a Shadow-man holding some kind of glowing energy source—and he jumped into the quarry and disappeared?"

Again that one-shouldered thing. "There've been some really eerie things happening lately. Whenever a heavy fog comes in. I've seen things that look a lot like what you're talking about." There was a haunted look in Ella's eyes. "My Grams has seen things."

Grams. Mercedes Houston—but she went by Mercy. "What kind of things?"

She shook her head. "I can't talk about it. But this Shadow-man thing . . . there's something to this."

Harley Davidson Lotitto and Bryce Scorza sauntered toward their table. Some of Rockport High's football jocks. Harley played running back. Scorza first string quarterback. Both of them really good for freshmen—and they knew it.

Ella let out a groan—like she knew exactly who they were coming to see. Harley, anyway. "Don't look at them. Maybe they'll pass by."

Their trays were loaded with pizza slices, chips, and enough milk cartons to build a set of bleachers. Parker had never seen Harley wear anything but motorcycle T-shirts—and the guy must have had a couple dozen different ones from dealerships all over the country. This one was from a shop somewhere in Chicago.

The way Ella told the story, Harley's parents had been bikers to the core. They actually gave him the middle name of Davidson. Parker guessed that made it easier to find personalized T-shirts that way.

While some might have seen his name alone as unfortunate, his family life was a complete tragedy. Born in Tennessee. His mom went MIA before Harley could walk. Left his dad for a guy with a bigger Harley—or so went the story. Ella had no idea what happened to his mom. She never came back . . . and that was all that mattered.

Harley's dad cleaned up his act, got a decent job as a mechanic, and became a great dad. How Ella knew all that, Parker had no idea. But according to her, Harley's dad even stopped drinking so he'd be a better father. Ironically, drinking still did him in. A drunk driver crossed the centerline on a two-lane bridge—right into Harley's dad. His Ford Falcon crashed through the guardrail and made its first—and last—flight . . . right into the flooded river below. At twelve years old, Harley was an orphan.

His next of kin was his dad's brother—living in Rockport, Massachusetts. Harley had been living with his Uncle Ray ever since—and it didn't sound like much of a picnic.

"Don't look now, El . . . but they're still headed this way."

Scorza wore his Rockport High School Vikings jersey with his number 8 on it—like usual. A football was tucked under one arm. Parker had never seen him without it. Like he wanted the ball to become part of him. According to El, Scorza said it was all part of his personal training. He totally believed he'd never fumble the ball in a game.

They slid their trays on the table and stood there for a second. Harley gave Ella a glance like he was waiting for an invitation to sit.

She had the ignoring-him-thing down to a science and focused on the star quarterback instead. "What brings you two to our table, Eight-ball?"

Scorza thumped the number on his jersey. "Eight-ball. I *like* that." He pantomimed a desperate throw to an imaginary receiver. "Scorza throws his legendary eight-ball . . . and a fantastic catch by Lotitto—for the game-winning touchdown!" He raised both hands over his head—like he was basking in cheers from the sidelines. "Eight-ball. I'm going to use that."

He dropped onto the chair next to Ella and stared at her for a sec. He picked up one of her braids and felt it. "Huh."

Ella smacked his hand away and glared at him. "What are you *doing*?"

Exactly what Parker was thinking.

"It's actually . . . soft." Scorza looked surprised.

She scooted her chair farther away from him. "What makes you think you can just touch my hair without asking?"

"What?" Scorza had a cocky smirk going. "I'm the first one who wondered what your hair felt like?"

"No. You're just one more in a long line of stupid people who think girls like me don't mind. Or maybe you're just ignorant enough to think you have the right to do it—without even asking permission."

"She's right." Harley slid into one of the last two open chairs at the table. "You should apologize, dude."

"And *you*," Ella pointed at Harley, "should get new friends—unless you like hanging out with idiots." She gestured with her thumb to Scorza beside her.

Her comment didn't seem to faze Scorza. He leaned closer to El. "Kinda touchy, aren't you?"

"*Me* . . . touchy?" Ella shook her head. "You're the one feeling my hair. So tell me, do you do that to all the girls," she swept her hand across half the cafeteria, "or am I the only one?"

Scorza's face was getting red. "It's just that I never—"

"And you'd better never again." Ella poked her finger at him.

"Hey, what's your problem?" Scorza looked at her like she was pathetic. "I was giving you a compliment, that's all. I said your hair was soft. I thought it would be scratchy like steel wool or s—"

"Next time you have the urge to feel wool—soft *or* steely—find some little lamb at a petting zoo. Touch my hair again and I'll break every finger on your precious passing hand."

Harley snickered.

Parker smiled. She definitely didn't need his help defending herself.

"I mean it, Eight-ball," Ella said. "Fair warning."

Harley cleared his throat. "Miss Houston." It was like he needed permission to call her by her first name—which she never gave.

"Harley Davidson Lotitto." She raised her chin at him. "You want to touch my hair, too?"

"No . . . I was just going to say, um, I like your braids."

Ella tossed both of them over her shoulders. "They're just like any other braids."

"No," Harley said. "Nobody in the entire school has braids like you. They're kind of thick—and poufy."

"Poufy?" She shook her head. "You really know how to compliment a girl." She fished inside her backpack and pulled out a bag lunch.

She gave off a definite vibe that the conversation was over and she wanted to eat in peace.

Scorza dug into the pantry piled on his tray. "Don't take this wrong, because I'm just stating a fact. But most girls in this room would die if I sat at their table. You should be happy I'm sitting with you."

"Why?" Ella stared at him. "Because you're white—and I'm not?"

"Because I'm the quarterback—and you're not," Scorza said. "Some think that's a big deal."

"Especially you. To me it just means you'll need both knees replaced before you're forty."

Scorza looked really annoyed now. "Sounds like you have a problem with football, girlie."

"*I* have a problem? This is May, Mr. Scorza. Football season was over last fall, yet you still wear your jersey. You don't think that sounds just a teensy bit"—she circled one ear with her finger —"unbalanced?"

"You see this?" Scorza pointed at the number eight sewn on his jersey.

"Is that your age?"

"Ha, ha. That number tells everyone who I am."

Ella angled her head to one side. "I just see a zero—twisted in the middle to form an eight. So that's who you are . . . a twisted zero?"

Scorza looked at Harley in disbelief. "Are you hearing this?"

"And by the way," Ella said, "you don't need a number plastered on your chest, Mr. Scorza. You could wear a bag over your head and everybody would know who you are."

"I'll take that as a compliment."

"I'm not surprised." Ella turned to Harley. "You seriously need new friends."

Harley didn't seem to know how to respond to that. He turned to Parker instead—like he was noticing him there for the first time.

Terrific.

"Hey, Gatorade." Harley still seemed to get a kick out of the name he'd given Parker the first day they'd met. "So Scorza and I want to hear the *real* scoop about your Frankenstein arm."

It was days like this Parker wished he'd worn a long-sleeved shirt.

"There's way too many stories floating around," Harley said. "We want to get it straight from the man."

Parker had been here for nearly eight months. And now suddenly they wanted to hear his story? Right. This was about Harley wanting to be near El—but having no idea of how to talk to her.

"That's right. So what's the story, Gatorade?" Scorza hiked one leg up and tucked the football underneath so it was pinned between his thigh and the chair. *Did he really think someone was going to try to peel it from him in the cafeteria?*

Parker liked keeping a little mystery floating around. He'd told El a shortened version—but even she didn't know the whole story. "What have you heard?"

"You went to some alligator farm, or something," Scorza said. "You climbed over a fence on a dare to feed one of the things—and it decided to feed on you instead."

Parker shook his head. "I've never fed alligators."

Harley leaned in. "The way I heard it, some massive man-eating gator ripped your arm off. A cop grabbed the arm before the gator got away, though. He pulled it out of his jaws, beat the alligator over the head with it, and then got you to a hospital where they sewed your arm back on. Which explains why the thing looks like it got caught in a wood chipper."

Parker was having fun with this. "Not even close to the truth. Maybe sometime I'll show you the skull of the gator that did this . . . and tell you the real story. But I'm warning you, after you hear it—you may have a really hard time sleeping."

Harley laughed like that was the most ridiculous thing ever.

A thumping tap sounded over the speakers—the thing some

people do just before making an announcement. "Attention, students . . . faculty." Mrs. Whiting's voice. She waited—as if she thought that students would actually stop talking and listen. Clearly, that wasn't happening. The noise level rose even higher . . . students talking over each other . . . guessing what the interruption was all about.

Parker had only talked with the principal a few times, but he liked her. It was the way she reacted to his arm when he met her for the orientation appointment—a couple of months after all the other students had started. Meet the principal. Get a tour. Start classes. That's how his first day at the new school was to be. He'd deliberately worn short sleeves—just to get the gawking over with.

"Tell me about this." She'd said it so quiet—and in a voice that Parker could only describe as kind. She'd reached over and touched his arm—but not like Scorza touched Ella's braid. There was something in her touch that made it clear she really cared. A mom-touch.

The moment she did, Parker froze. Like suddenly he got an instant case of full-body lockjaw or something. People stared at his arm all the time. Others looked away like they didn't want to be caught staring. But nobody touched the arm—or the scars. Mrs. Whiting did both.

And that was it. Next thing Parker knew, he opened up to her like he was a can of tuna with an easy-open tab.

Mrs. Whiting had probably heard more sob stories from kids than Parker would in his entire lifetime. Still, she'd teared up when he told her how he'd lost a ton of blood and had technically died—before the paramedics jump-started his heart again. "So that's how my arm got so messed up."

"This," she'd tapped his scarred forearm, "isn't just a messed-up arm." Her voice was a little shaky—and softer. Like she was on the edge of losing it—and didn't want that to happen. "It's a badge of honor. It shows you're a survivor. A fighter. And I guarantee you, your arm is a tool."

Yeah, maybe it could be used like a club.

"Mark my words," she'd said. "This will get you lots of attention from girls—and respect from the boys. And if you become the man I think you will, it will keep you humble. And grateful. That arm of yours is a gift."

He'd seen his arm as a lot of things. Messed up, gimpy, 60 percent functional. But never as a *gift*.

The mic-tapping was back. "Students, I have a very . . . very heartbreaking announcement to make."

Her voice had that choked-up sound—like that day in her office when she learned about his arm. Parker strained to hear. Found himself looking up at the speakers mounted in the corner of the cafeteria. The noise decibel level took an immediate nose-dive. Even Harley and Scorza shut their traps.

Bad news has a way of doing that. Everybody's in a hurry to hear something bad—as long as it doesn't really hurt them somehow.

"One of your fellow students was involved in a tragic accident last night."

An audible gasp swept through the cafeteria. El's eyes showed a sense of alarm. Harley and Scorza stared at each other, like they wanted to be the first to see the other's reaction when Mrs. Whiting dropped the bomb and revealed the name. Students scanned the room—as if looking for who was missing. Parker was doing the same. Mrs. Whiting had used the word *tragic*—likely not a word she'd use if she was talking about a broken leg. *Devin—tell me you're here. Tell me—*

"I'm so sorry to inform you," Mrs. Whiting choked the words out, "that there's been a drowning."

Hysterical shrieks pierced the cafeteria—and countless students shushed them. Nobody wanted to miss hearing the name. Harley's eyes got a dead look to them. His face turned about the color of the paper plate sitting in front of him. "Drowning," he whispered.

Parker had already heard too much. His heart rate must have doubled since the start of her announcement.

The principal cleared her throat, like she was trying to pull herself together. "Devin Catsakis . . ."

His heart rate tripled. *No. No. No!* Parker stared at the speakers, but he didn't catch more than a word here or there from then on. A rushing noise filled his ears—almost like the wind when he was skimming along the water in his boat.

"Counselors will be here . . . if you need help . . . talk about your feelings . . ."

It wasn't making any sense. Parker couldn't get his head wrapped around this. Devin? Gone? *God, please . . . no.*

The speakers went silent. Fifteen long seconds passed like maybe everyone wanted to see if there was more—and then the room erupted. Harley sat there staring at Scorza, shaking his head in a look of pure disbelief.

El's head was buried in her open hands.

Parker wanted to bury himself somewhere—far from here.

"How did the guy drown?" Scorza asked the question of no one in particular. "I mean, only an idiot would swim in May. The water is way too cold—right?"

Ella fixed her eyes on Parker. Like she knew whatever had happened to Devin had something to do with the phone call the night before.

"Where do you think he went down?" Scorza was already speculating. Like he wanted to go there himself. "Front Beach? Back Beach? There's a million places around here."

At least.

Harley looked from Ella to Parker. His eyes turned suspicious. "What do you think, Gatorade?"

Parker shook his head. He was pretty sure he knew exactly where Devin had drowned, but he wasn't going to say a word.

CHAPTER 3

ELLA WAS BEYOND STUNNED. Devin—*gone?* It couldn't be real. She stared at the empty seat at their table. There had to be a mistake, right? Instantly her mind flashed back to the conversation with Parker earlier. He'd totally brushed off the possibility that whatever Devin had chased the night before could have been otherworldly. He was probably rethinking that right about now. Shadow-man was real. She knew it. And now maybe Parker did, too.

She watched him react to the mayhem in the cafeteria. She was pretty sure Parker sank lower in the chair. Like Earth's gravity had doubled down on him.

His lunch bag sat in front of him—its mouth gaping open like the mouths of half the student body at this moment.

Harley looked like he was in a daze. Scorza kept rattling on and on—speculating where Devin might have drowned. Each theory was crazier than the last one. Now he was suggesting that Devin had drowned after falling off the Bearskin Neck breakwater, the massive wall of boulders that protected Rockport Harbor from the ocean's waves.

"Probably watching for UFOs on the end of the Neck," Scorza said. "Slipped on a slab of granite, smacked his head—and boom—lights out. Tumbled right into the water."

Harley sat staring at the table . . . shaking his head so slightly that probably nobody else noticed. Was it that he couldn't believe Devin was gone—or was he thinking about the accident that took his dad?

Parker didn't look much better. His eyes darted around the room. His fist clenched and unclenched in a rhythm that probably matched his pulse.

A ripple went through the cafeteria. Volume up—volume down. The type of thing that happens when something big changes in the room—and the students figure it out in a wave of realization instead of all at once. Ella resisted the urge to look for the source of the commotion—but kept her eyes on Parker's reaction instead. He did a quick scan of the cafeteria and locked on to something.

Ella followed his gaze. Mrs. Whiting was in the lunchroom. All eyes were Gorilla-Glued to her—like maybe she had some other detail she was going to give that she hadn't over the PA.

Mrs. Whiting was up on her tiptoes, doing a visual sweep of the room.

"Wonder who she's looking for." Scorza gripped his football at the laces. What was he going to do, pass her the ball?

Ella's eyes flicked to Parker for just a millisecond. The guy looked like he was ready to hurl or something.

Mrs. Whiting was on the move again. Walking by tables quicker now—clearly on the prowl for someone.

Parker wasn't watching the principal. His eyes were on the exit doors. *Was he thinking of running?* That would be insane. A cop stood in the hallway just outside the glass doors. A big dude for sure. Hands on hips in an impatient, trigger-happy way. Like he was itching to be in the cafeteria himself—and didn't like being asked to wait in the hall. What was going on?

Mrs. Whiting glanced their way, and her shoulders dropped just a bit. She angled directly toward them.

Parker's lips were moving slightly. *Was he praying?*

Mrs. Whiting looked almost apologetic when she stopped at their table. "Parker?"

Like she couldn't believe he was somehow involved in this. Like her heart was breaking for him. She squatted down low so she was out of the line of sight of the rubberneckers. But it didn't matter. Kids stood all around the lunchroom now, stretching for a better view.

"Follow me to the office, would you?" Again, that pained look on her face. "Somebody needs to ask you some questions." Parker nodded.

How did they know Parker had talked to Devin last night?

Harley seemed to shake off the funk he'd been in. He leaned in—his face dark. Eyes narrowing just a bit. "What did you do, Gatorade?"

"Nothing." But he said it a little too fast. A little too defensively. It made him sound guilty as sin. "Honest, Mrs. Whiting."

"We just want to talk." Mrs. Whiting patted his arm. *The* arm. "Your dad is on his way."

Ella groaned inside. Principals don't call parents into the office for nothing. Obviously Parker must have left out some critical detail when he gave her the lowdown about last night. Parker balled up his lunch bag—sandwich still inside—and stood.

"He comes here—to *our* town," Harley growled, "and look what happens."

"Harley—zip it." Mrs. Whiting gave him the I-mean-business look.

"It's going to be okay, Parker. One step at a time." The principal took Parker by the elbow and led him away from the table. Every set of eyes in the room locked on him.

"Did *he* have something to do with Devin's accident, Mrs. Whiting?" Somebody shouted the question—Ella had no idea who. But it didn't matter; by the looks on the faces of those she could see, they were all thinking it.

"What did he do?" Again, another random call from the crowd. "Did he hurt Devin?"

The principal acted like she never heard the questions, but she leaned in close and said something to Parker. He nodded, and they both picked up the pace.

Scorza watched them leave—still gripping the ball. "Would I love to see Gatorade getting grilled by the cops."

"Yeah, and when they're done with him," Harley said, "I got a few questions for him myself."

CHAPTER 4

THE PRINCIPAL GUIDED GATORADE through the maze of tables toward the cop. Harley hoped the cop would barge into the cafeteria and slap cuffs on Gatorade. He'd pay money to see that. He couldn't think of a better reward for the guy who swooped in from the swamplands—monopolizing all of Ella's time and attention. From the very beginning he thought Rockport would be better off without Gatorade—and now maybe he'd have proof.

He stared at Ella. She definitely looked worried. She only hung around two people in the entire school. Devin and Gatorade. In the amount of time it would take to run a couple plays on the field, her whole world changed. She'd lost Devin for sure. And with a cop waiting for Gatorade? Hopefully she'd lose him, too. Harley wasn't the one who needed new friends. Ella might soon need a new friend too. "What did Gatorade do?"

"Nothing." But that wasn't what her eyes said.

"Right. You don't get a police escort for doing *nothing*."

Scorza was instantly on his feet and hotfooting it to the exit—football tucked tight to his ribs. Harley jumped up and sprinted after Scorza.

By the time Harley got to the doors, bunches of others had crowded behind him. Pressing in—trying to get a better look. The cop towered over Parker. Honestly, it looked like he'd have to duck if he walked through the cafeteria doors. He had that ex-military, I-can-handle-myself-in-any-situation look about him. A slight gut—but not enough to slow him down if this turned into a chase. The cop said something to Parker and steered him up the stairs and into the school's main entranceway. Harley watched until they walked out of sight—just in case Parker made things more exciting by trying to run.

"Nothing more to see here." Harley ran blocker and cleared a path for him and Scorza back to Ella's table. She was packing her stuff up in a hurry. Had the new kid gotten Ella messed up in this? Would the principal be coming for her next?

"Accidental drowning, my eye," Harley said. "Gatorade is mixed up in this somehow."

Ella burned him a fiery look. "You don't know that. Parker was always decent to Devin—which is a lot more than you two ever were."

"Police don't show up to arrest innocent people," Harley said.

"So you already have Parker judged—yet you've never bothered to find out what he's really like, and you have no idea what really went down with Devin. None of us do. What happened to *innocent until proven guilty*?"

"I can read people pretty good." On the field he'd learned to size a player up just by the way they lined up opposite him. "And Parker *looks* guilty. He's hiding something."

"Are you really that stupid . . . that you judge others based only on what you see? Where they come from, the scars from their past, or maybe even the color of their skin? That's classic injustice—and that stinks, Harley." She balled up her bag of chips with the fierceness of a defensive tackle.

That wasn't it at all. "So you're telling me how to think? I thought we lived in a free country." Okay, even he knew that sounded bad. Right now he wished he couldn't read people so well, because it looked like Ella was totally disgusted with him.

"A free country—do you ever wonder what that really means? You've said the Pledge of Allegiance a million times—but do you think about the words? 'With liberty and *justice* for all,' Harley. *That's* what we're to be about in this country—and I honestly feel such pain when I recite that line—because it's not true."

"Whoa," Scorza said. "Somebody needs an anger management class."

"I've got a right to be angry. I get so sick of injustice in this *free* country of ours. And I get sick of people who—"

"Stop." Scorza was glaring at her now. "It would be a whole lot easier to listen if you said things a little nicer—you ever think about *that*?"

"So now you're the tone police?" Ella glared right back. "I have to say things just right so *you* aren't offended? You're soooo out of touch with reality, Mr. Scorza. You've lived with privilege for so long you have no idea what it's like for others who are different from you—just because they're new to the school or have a different skin color. You don't feel a bit of fear, or grief, or anger about injustice around you—but you want to get all up in my grill because the way I express my pain makes you *uncomfortable*?"

Scorza looked a whole lot more than uncomfortable right now. He looked like he wanted to rip her head off.

Some of what she said made sense. But honestly, wasn't she overreacting—just a little? Harley had to end this. Get the conversation going in a good direction. "All I'm saying is when cops come to question a guy, it doesn't look good. That's all."

Ella stuffed what was left of her lunch into her pack and stood.

"You're leaving?" Harley was finally sitting with Ella without Gatorade—and he got into an argument with her? *You're an idiot, Harley.*

"As fast as I can." Her voice actually shook. Was she about to cry—or just hopping mad?

"Stay, okay?" Devin was gone. Gatorade was in trouble. Wouldn't she need somebody to talk to? "Seems like you're the one who could use a new friend about now."

She stared at him—her head angling slightly like he'd just said the craziest thing. "I'm not going to find that at this table." She hustled away—just like that.

"Little miss high-and-mighty." Scorza's face still had that windburned look. "Walks out like she's queen of the cafeteria or something. Well *that's* going to change."

"Lay off her, Scorza. Gatorade is the one we need to focus on. He's hiding something," Harley said. "And I'm going to find out what it is."

CHAPTER 5

Cape Ann Funeral Home
May 5, 6:30 p.m.

PARKER PRESSED HIMSELF AGAINST THE WALL in the back of the funeral parlor and watched the mass of students file past the body of Devin Catsakis.

Devin had been a loner. Off on his own planet somewhere most of the time—and nobody seemed to be into space travel. Everybody knew him—yet nobody was close. But at a funeral, most acted like they'd lost their best friend.

Devin's death rocked Parker, too—because he wasn't so sure it was accidental. Had he kept looking for that Shadow-man? Had he slipped on the granite lip of the quarry . . . smacked his head on the way down? Had he hit the water unconscious—sealing his fate—or was there more to the story?

Everybody had a theory about his death—and somehow stories of Shadow-man with the green light surfaced. Except for El,

Parker was pretty sure nobody believed the tales any more than he did when Devin called him.

"Dear God," Parker whispered. "What if it was me in that casket?" The room wouldn't be in the "standing room only" state it was in now. There'd be no lines out the doors. School wouldn't have closed for the day. Sure, Parker's mom and dad would've been devastated. Jelly would have been wrecked—she and her ranger dad, Uncle Sammy, would have flown up from the Everglades. Wilson Stillwaters would have made it up to the funeral from southern Florida too, for sure. El was likely the only one local who would've shown up. If it were Parker in that box, it wouldn't have hit the community . . . not like this.

There must have been close to a hundred students from Rockport High School in line waiting to walk past the casket. It was all about paying their last respects—even though most of them hadn't shown Devin much respect when he was alive. No, the line was all about the drama of the whole thing. Suddenly everybody had a story to tell about Devin. Parker had one, too—but besides the police, his parents, El, and Jelly . . . he wasn't telling another soul. If others knew how he'd refused to meet him that night, they'd treat him as even more of an outsider than he already was.

Based on the turnout, the news crew up from Boston probably thought Devin was one of the most popular guys around.

Parker couldn't bring himself to line up with the others. He couldn't face Devin, even though he was dead. He pictured Devin blinking open his eyes and accusing him. "Why didn't you come with me? You could have kept this from happening."

Parker hated funeral homes. Hated the smell of flowers in those big, ugly arrangements. Hated the mockingly impersonal ribbons hoisted across them saying things like *Beloved Son*, *Loving Brother*, or *Best Friend in the World*.

He picked up the sound of an organ—playing too quietly and hanging on each note way too long. Whether it was live or recorded—Parker had no idea. The room was too crowded to tell. But even the music sounded dead in this place.

Kids stood in small clusters. Some girls sobbed. Everyone's cheeks were wet. Even Harley and Scorza looked busted up about Devin's death. This was the first time Parker had seen Harley without a motorcycle T-shirt. He was even wearing a tie. Scorza, on the other hand, wore his jersey under a sport coat. He'd left the football at home, but it looked like he wished he'd brought it. He kept fidgeting with his hands. Jamming them in his back pockets. Massaging his knuckles like he was warming up for a game.

The funeral home was like a super-spreader event for the shock and horror of a classmate dying. Death wasn't supposed to happen to someone their age, right? Guys slung their arms around each other's shoulders. Girls clung to each other. But nobody was hanging onto Parker for comfort. Did they think that maybe Parker could have kept Devin from drowning?

The local newspaper article revealed bits of the conversation Parker had with Devin just before the accident—something they'd picked up from the police report. Since Parker was a minor, they'd left his name out of it when they'd written the story, but thanks to the cop showing up at school to ask Parker questions, everybody pieced together who Devin had called that night.

"Hey." El slid up beside him. She wore her gypsy dress . . . that's what Parker called it anyway. Her cowgirl boots looked like they had a fresh coat of polish. It was the first time he'd seen her hair without braids. It was full—with tiny little waves that ran just past her shoulders. She met his eyes. "Unreal, right?"

To see somebody his same age—in a casket? "Beyond that."

"What did Jelly say?" Ella said it casually enough, but he couldn't help but feel she was watching his reaction a bit too closely.

"A lot of the same things you've been saying." But she'd asked a ton more questions. Tried to get him to make promises too—like staying away from Parker's Pit or any of the dozens of abandoned granite quarries that pockmarked the face of Cape Ann.

"So . . . you going up there?" Ella nodded toward Devin's casket.

"Maybe later." And that was a *slim* maybe. About as likely as him being elected most popular student before summer break started next month.

Ella raised up on her tiptoes and leaned in close. "It's bad luck not to pay your last respects."

That was a new one to Parker. She was definitely the most superstitious person he'd ever met. Even more than Wilson, his half-Miccosukee friend back in Florida.

Ella waved her hand in front of his eyes. "You doing okay?"

No. He wasn't. Devin had been convinced something strange was going on in Rockport. He'd been determined to get to the bottom of it. Instead, he'd ended up on the bottom of the quarry. "I wasn't a believer in all his weird theories."

"Nobody was," Ella said. "Me included—at least at first. But lately . . ."

Did this have to do with the strange things she'd hinted at the other day in the cafeteria?

"Everybody got so tired of his wild stories," Ella said. "They pretty much ignored him. Then he started getting to you."

"I should have gone with him."

"Don't go there, Parker."

"I didn't. Which is why he's in that box."

"That's ridiculous." Ella glared at him. "Don't go blaming yourself. You could have gone out there and had the same thing happen to you!"

Parker shrugged. "It still feels like this is on me somehow," he said. "I was the last person he talked to before he died."

"Look, you're not the kind of guy who'd sneak out of the house while his parents slept, right?"

She had him pegged right on that one.

"And what would they've said if you woke them and asked for a ride to the quarry?"

Parker hadn't even thought of doing that at the time. "They definitely wouldn't have wanted me out at midnight—and probably would have told me Devin was just making this stuff up."

"Devin *told* you he was going home," Ella said. "Whatever happened to Devin, it's on him. Not you."

Technically, El was right. But he should have guessed Devin was still going to nose around the edge of the quarry—hoping for something to video. "If I'd gone with Devin, I would have made sure he got home."

"There was nothing you could have done," Ella said. "He slipped and fell. Hit his head. Dropped into the quarry. End of story."

More like end of life. Of course, nobody knew exactly what happened because Devin was alone—thanks to Parker. But the "slipped and fell" angle was the official story going around. "I could have pulled him out."

"Not if he whacked his head before he hit the water," Ella said. "He'd have dropped like a stone."

Even if Devin was unconscious, Parker could have saved him. "I could have jumped in after him."

Ella stared at him. "Have you ever been by that quarry at night? It's as dark as a basement closet. And at that icy temperature? You'd go into shock—or get some kind of brain-freeze and wouldn't be able to pull yourself out of there. Once he hit those black waters, he was gone."

Until his body floated to the surface.

"That whole green light thing," Parker said. "Sometimes I think he was making it all up—just to get me to buy in. But what if . . ."

"What if what?"

"What if Devin actually saw something he shouldn't have—"

"Aliens? Parallel universe bunk?" Ella shook her head.

"You think he was making it up?"

"No. I think he saw something even more terrifying. I believe that with all my heart. Something otherworldly. Paranormal. Something from the spirit world."

Parker studied her face for a moment. "You're saying Shadow-man is a ghost?"

Ella didn't answer for a moment. "I'm not ruling it out. And if that's what Devin was chasing?" She hugged herself. "I don't even want to think about that."

Exactly what happened to Devin that night was a mystery that would probably never get solved—but it cost him his life. "All he wanted to do was get close enough to film that thing."

"Following that Shadow-man—or whatever he saw—was stupid," Ella said. "And sometimes doing stupid things gets people killed."

Parker motioned for her to keep her voice down. "We're at his funeral, for Pete's sake."

"Exactly."

But she had a point. How many stupid things had Parker done—especially when his dad had been posted in the Florida Everglades? He should have been dead and buried months ago. If not for God, he would have been.

"I need to know what happened to Devin."

"It won't change anything," Ella said. "Life is full of mysteries, right? Things that happen in the dark—when nobody is around—stay hidden, like, forever."

"God sees. God knows. Nothing is hidden to Him." Why he said that aloud, he wasn't sure. Except maybe Devin's death had Parker thinking about that kind of stuff a whole lot more than he ever would normally. He'd even called his grandpa about it. Wondering why God would allow the truth to stay hidden.

Ella snapped her fingers in front of his eyes. "Get this in your head. Devin was in the wrong place at the wrong time. He was following some mysterious being. He would have walked right past the Old First Parish Burying Ground—at night. Totally a bad idea. It was bad karma. Which is why you need to get in that line so something freaky doesn't happen to you."

Okay, her superstitions were way out there. "Do you think his death was an accident?"

"What did that big cop say?"

"Rankin. His name is Officer Rankin."

"And he said . . ." She motioned, like she was coaxing him to tell more.

Rankin had found Devin's phone—and Parker's text. `Do what you promised—or I'll do what I warned you I'd do. No more stalling. Do it now.` He'd had more than a few questions about that. He seemed to think Parker had dared—or bullied—Devin to go to the quarry that night to do something dangerous.

It took some fast talking to convince Rankin the truth about the text. And even in the end, Parker wasn't sure Rankin fully bought it. But he finally seemed to come around. "He said there are drownings in the quarry every year."

"So he thinks it was a freak accident," Ella said.

"But I asked what *you* think." It didn't *feel* like this was an accident. "What if . . ." Did he even want to go here?

"What if *what*?"

Parker took her arm and led her around the corner to the drinking fountain. "What if he saw something he shouldn't have seen—and it got him killed?" That was it, wasn't it? The question he absolutely needed to answer. But how was he going to find out what really happened to Devin?

Ella stared at him. "You're talking about *murder*?" Her eyes searched his to see if he was serious. "Okay. You really want my opinion? Something evil happened at that quarry. Something unspeakable. I think at the very least something scared the living daylights out of him—which may have caused him to slip and fall into the quarry. And at worst . . . Shadow-man ambushed him."

Pretty much what Parker was feeling. "Maybe I could have helped him fight off whoever—or whatever—attacked him."

Ella looked like she was processing that one. "Stop blaming yourself, Parker. If Shadow-man is what I think it is, what makes you think you could have done anything to help?"

Parker shrugged. "I just can't help but feel today would have been different if I'd gone with him."

"Yeah," Ella said. "A lot different. This would have been a double funeral."

CHAPTER 6

HARLEY COULDN'T GET THE IMAGE OF THE CASKET out of his head. That stinkin' body box was a dead ringer for the one they'd buried his dad in. If he'd known the funeral home was going to trigger all these dark memories, he'd have skipped the thing completely. He could have come up with some excuse—and Scorza would have bought it. There were always things Uncle Ray was grousing for him to do at the dive shop.

He made his way down the hall to the narrow staircase. He didn't bother tiptoeing. Uncle Ray would never hear him—not after the number of beers he put down before he went to bed. He paused at the top of the stairs leading to the dive shop on the first floor. Even with the bedroom door shut tight, his uncle's snoring could raise the dead.

If only it was that easy to bring his dad back.

His dad would have loved Rockport. The two-lane roads that

hugged the coastline of Cape Ann were perfect for riding. Dad would be tooling around in his '96 Harley Dyna Wide Glide motorcycle. Harley wouldn't be slaving for Uncle Ray at the Rockport Dive Company. He'd be cruising with his dad—straddling the seat right behind him. He'd never ride on the back with anyone else. It would be terrifying not to see the road ahead—unless you had absolute trust in the guy holding the handlebars. And there'd only been one man he could trust like that.

He imagined cruising Cape Ann for a moment. Remembering the tug and power as Dad ran through the gears. The smell of his dad's leather jacket. Yeah, if Dad were here, they'd go out cruising every night.

And maybe Dad would have biker friends along and Harley would get to ride in a pack again. He missed the sound coming out of those straight pipes at 70 miles per hour. Loud. Throaty. Riding in a mob of Harleys was like being surrounded by an orchestra. He didn't hear the wind. Nothing. Just the music from those pipes . . . every bike a slightly different tone. Some would call it noise. Obnoxious. But to Harley? It was like beautiful music. Soothing. Strong. A sweet sound.

His dad might have been just about the smartest parent in the world. That's what Harley thought when Dad trailered home a 1999 XL 1200 Sportster for Harley's tenth birthday. Used, but in great shape in all the places that really counted. Who else had a dad who bought a used Harley to restore as a father-son project? When they weren't out riding on Dad's bike, they were getting Harley's ready for the day he'd have a license. Just two years after Dad wheeled it into the garage, they'd finished the complete refurbish job. Spring of his seventh-grade year . . . months before the accident.

"If only you were here, Dad," Harley whispered. "I'd ride

behind you until I was old enough to ride the 1200. Then we'd cruise side by side." If only.

They'd have their own place in town, too. Somewhere near Ella's home would be nice. Not that he needed more space than his little room above the shop, but he didn't belong here. Uncle Ray reminded him of that little fact every time he had a bellyful of beers in him—which was pretty much every night.

Harley shook off his thoughts and headed down the stairs to the dive shop. The smell of neoprene wet suits hit him before he got to the bottom. New suits up front. Rentals in the back. The smell was familiar—and comforting in its own way.

Harley knew the layout of the dive shop well enough to get around with just the light drifting in through the windows—and the neon. Uncle Ray left the illuminated signs on all night. Aqua Lung. Mares. The vintage Dacor neon was Harley's favorite, even though the dive equipment company had gone out of business a zillion years ago. The first time Harley had stepped close to check it out, Uncle Ray warned him not to touch it. "It's a collector's item." And it had collected a lot of dust, too. Harley only cleaned it when Uncle Ray wasn't around.

Right above it was a sign with the Rockport Dive Company logo and the brain-dead slogan Uncle Ray had come up with. *Don't Drink and Dive.* In small print just below that? *First Stow Your Gear—Then Hit the Beer!* He'd paid big bucks to have the logo and slogan professionally designed. A pirate skeleton—decked out with mask, fins, and scuba tank—sat on a treasure chest, holding up a bottle of rum. His uncle thought it was hilarious.

Harley hated it.

The stupid slogan constantly reminded Harley of the drunk who'd stolen his dad from him. Uncle Ray never seemed to put that one together. How this guy could for real be his dad's brother was a total mystery. Maybe there'd been a mix-up at the hospital or something.

Harley scooted around the register counter and displays of masks, fins, snorkels, and wet suits. A small assortment of tanks lined up along one wall, with regulator sets hanging above them. A wall rack showcasing dive knives was just to one side of that, then a select group of buoyancy compensating devices—or BCDs. The shop was no wider than a typical one-car garage—but definitely deeper. The things that really clogged up the floor space were the T-shirt displays. Each one jammed with Rockport Dive Company T-shirts—every size and color—and all of them with the stupid logo. Tourists loved them—and the shop probably sold fifty T's for every empty dive tank that came in for a refill.

Harley rarely wore a company shirt—not even when he was working the shop. He snagged up every Harley T-shirt that came into the Rockport thrift store—and wore one pretty much every day. Uncle Ray accused him of living in the past. That wasn't it at all. It was about making sure he never forgot where he came from—and whose son he was.

Harley worked his way to the back room where the tanks were filled. The actual door had been removed long before Harley's time. This was where he spent most of his time when he was manning the shop—which would be more and more once school was out in another month.

Four things dominated this room. The fill station. Rows of scuba tanks—rentals and customer cylinders that had been filled. Uncle Ray's beer can collection. And a sixteen-pane window that gave a killer view of Rockport Harbor.

The fill station was a massive unit as big as an oversized

vending machine. Uncle Ray's name for it? The Blast Chamber. The thing was built like a battleship—and in the unlikely event a tank exploded while getting filled, the fill chamber could handle the force of its impact. The quarter-inch hardened steel surrounding the filling bays made sure of that. The unit weighed some eight hundred pounds . . . probably as much as a decked-out Harley touring bike. Uncle Ray rarely filled tanks anymore. He left that to Harley. But Harley didn't mind.

The station had parallel bays so he could fill three tanks at a time. Oxygen and nitrogen were fed to the unit from a small concrete shed attached to the side of the building through aluminum piping. Honestly, the shed was like a mini bomb shelter. Overall it was a sweet setup, and definitely one thing Uncle Ray had done right—except for the fact that he hadn't used his own money to do it.

The money came from his dad's accounts when Uncle Ray took over everything after the accident. Uncle Ray said he was entitled to the cash for all the trouble it would be to take Harley in—which was no trouble at all. The state of Massachusetts gave nearly a thousand bucks to foster parents every month—along with a quarterly clothing allowance and even money for birthday and Christmas presents. Harley had looked it up online, and he saw the envelopes from the state come in the mail. But he never saw the money—and never once a present for Christmas or birthday.

Harley kept the rental and customer tanks lined up in neat rows. He even had the valves all facing the same direction. He was proud of that.

Uncle Ray's empty beer can collection? Not so proud of that. It was the one thing Harley wished he could haul out of the store and deep-six somewhere. Uncle Ray called it his "Wasted Wall." It was Uncle Ray's treasure—and he'd been building the collection for years. No two cans were alike. Whenever Uncle Ray found a new beer company, he made a spot on the already overcrowded shelves to squeeze it in. The whole *Don't Drink and Dive* slogan was a total joke. Back when he'd had a decent boat, Uncle Ray did plenty of drinking on the dive tours he led. He claimed a few beers kept him more steady.

A sign hung over the beer can collection—hand-painted by Uncle Ray, of course. "If you want something done right—do it yourself." His motto when it came to drinking beer—and building his collection. Definitely a do-it-yourselfer. The motto didn't apply when it came to cleaning up the place. Pretty much all the real work around the shop he left to Harley.

Harley's dad had been a boozer at one time, but that all changed when Harley was just a kid. When his mom left. His dad finally "found his way out of the keg," as he called it. And he'd expressed over and over how much he wanted his boy to stay clear. "Don't worry, Dad," Harley had promised. "I'll never touch the stuff." And after what happened to his dad? Uncle Ray could have his treasure. Harley wanted no part of it.

The window was the real treasure in the room—because of the view. This was Harley's spot, especially after the shop was closed and Uncle Ray was asleep. Harley opened the canvas deck chair he kept stashed in the corner and sat back. There wasn't a smudge on the windows—inside or out. It was as if there was no glass in the panes at all. Harley was proud of that, too. Uncle Ray didn't notice the effort, but that was okay. Good, really. Next thing Harley would know, Uncle Ray would be sitting *here* at night, adding cans to his collection. Then Harley would have to find a new spot.

Rockport Harbor was bordered on the north by Bearskin Neck, a peninsula loaded with tourist shops. A huge breakwater of massive granite blocks jutted from the end of the Neck, protecting Rockport Harbor from behemoth waves that rolled in with the storms. A signal light was at the end of the breakwater to guide fisherman into the safety of the harbor.

Dozens of huge sailboats moored in the outer harbor, with only the breakwater separating them from the fury of the ocean. A large wharf divided the south harbor—with its floating docks, the yacht club, and the harbormaster's office—from the north harbor, where mostly lobster boats were moored. Shielded on four sides, this northern section was the most protected spot in Rockport Harbor.

The famed fishing shack, Motif Number 1, stood on the granite dock. Dark and strong. And to Harley, a friendly sight. Close enough that Harley could step out the back door and punt a football over it if he wanted to.

But the best sight out this window was something nobody else would notice. A plain wooden shed. It didn't look like much, but it was all his. Paid for by money Dad had left him. Money Uncle Ray hadn't gotten his hands on, anyway. He bought the heavy-duty padlock he'd slapped on the door. Harley bought the extension cord running to the shed—and the trickle charger plugged into it. Uncle Ray could have his beer can collection, but Harley's treasure was in that shed—and someday that Sportster would be his ticket to freedom. Dad named it *Kemosabe*—a nickname he'd sometimes called Harley.

"We'll get this thing looking absolutely killer before we're done, Kemosabe." And Dad made good on his promise. They replaced a million parts. Added pounds of custom chrome to give it a streamlined look. Yeah, the bike totally did look killer.

Harley felt his T-shirt for the keys hanging around his neck. One for the shed lock. One for Kemosabe. They were there—like always. And in a way, it was like his dad was always with him, too. Part of him anyway. Even when Harley had a game, the keys always hung under his jersey.

Did Uncle Ray ever look for the shed keys? Harley would bet money on it. Did he guess that Harley didn't trust him? Harley didn't really care. The truth was, Uncle Ray would sell Kemosabe if he was drunk enough and needed the beer money. That was the real reason why Harley didn't keep the title in his room upstairs. He'd made a great hiding spot for that in the shed.

He stared at the harbor. The more he tried not to think about that funeral home tonight . . . and that coffin, the more he couldn't stop himself. He saw the thing silhouetted in the piles of lobster traps stacked by the Motif fishing shack. Saw it plain as day on the back of one of the lobster boats. It was amazing how many things resembled a coffin in the dark dead of night.

Devin Catsakis was gone. He was a weird bird, for sure. But still, it was creepy to think of him as dead. Gatorade had been "cleared." At least that's what he'd heard. He wasn't guilty of anything more than not letting himself get sucked into Devin's crazy scheme. Kind of a shame, really. When Gatorade got hauled out of the cafeteria the other day, for one glorious moment Harley hoped the guy might get shipped back to the Everglades or something.

The guy bugged him. Why was Ella always hanging around him? The guy didn't have a jersey—and he sure as shootin' didn't score touchdowns in full view of bleachers packed with fans.

Devin had shadowed Ella all the time, but that was different—and it never bothered Harley. Devin was no threat. And not *really* Ella's friend. Catsakis was kind of a leech-friend. Hanging too close. Clinging too tight. Draining everyone he latched onto with all his talk of theories and sci-fi things that didn't even make sense.

Harley was pretty sure Ella only put up with the guy because she was nice that way. Actually, it was one of the things he really liked about her.

She acted different with Gatorade. There was a light in her eyes—and it flicked on whenever she talked to that Everglades outsider. But when Harley said hi to Ella? It was a total blackout. Would she even come to the games once the season started? Did she even care about football? Sometimes when he stretched for the catch, he'd imagine her watching. Jumping to her feet like most of the fans on the home bleachers.

Harley's problem was that he was just *hoping* something would happen—or change.

If you want something done right, do it yourself.

Maybe that was Harley's problem. He'd been waiting for a hole to appear instead of blasting through and making an opening. He just needed to find a way to get Gatorade to move on—or move away. Maybe he'd run it past Scorza, and they'd make their own playbook.

The way Harley saw it, the inner part of Rockport Harbor was about the most calming place on earth. There was something about the way the town lights played on the water's surface at this time of the night. But even the harbor couldn't keep his mind from going back to Devin—the way he looked in the box tonight. His face . . . it didn't even look like him. More like some kind of bad wax figure. A mannequin that only slightly resembled Catsakis. Harley pushed the image out of his mind. Swapped his face out, really. Now it was Gatorade in the box. And honestly? He looked pretty good in there.

One way or another, it was time for Gatorade to move on. Harley just had to figure out how to put that play in motion.

CHAPTER 7

Friday, June 3, 8:30 p.m.

PARKER STOOD AT THE TIP OF THE BREAKWATER. He could actually be alone here—a full 660 feet from where the street crawling up Bearskin Neck ended. The sun had already set, and the sky absolutely glowed over the town he loved calling *home*.

"Thank You, God, that I'm here." Of all the places his dad had been stationed with the National Park Service, this was his favorite. The Grand Canyon. Rocky Mountain National Park. No comparison. Not even close. And this was heaven compared to Everglades National Park—where Dad's last assignment had been.

Devin's funeral seemed a whole lot more than just four weeks earlier. The official cause of death was still a drowning accident. Parker called the police department every week to see if they had changed their opinion on that. It didn't take an Einstein to know they weren't going to tell him anything, but that wasn't the point of the calls. He didn't want them to forget what had happened to Devin. Parker never would. Parker wanted to make sure they didn't stop checking into Devin's death . . . to make sure there wasn't something to Devin's Shadow-man stuff, as crazy as it all sounded. Parker felt a growing restlessness to learn the truth, but the case seemed as cold as the quarry where Devin had died.

Both Mom and Dad had spent more time at home these last weeks than usual—and although they never said why, Parker was pretty certain it was all about making sure he was okay. Sometimes even Parker wasn't sure. If Devin's death wasn't accidental, why did God allow such a supreme injustice to go unanswered?

A couple months before Devin's death, Dad had signed the two of them up for scuba classes—something they'd been talking about ever since the move up from Florida. They'd taken their checkout dive in Folly Cove a week before the funeral and were both officially certified. They'd taken two dives since—and had the next one on the calendar. Back when they were in the classes they'd talked about diving the quarry. There was no way that was going to happen now—or ever.

His boat, the *Boy's Bomb*, wasn't the best craft for exploring the coast and inlets along Cape Ann. The bow wasn't high enough, and the motor was too small. But he made it work, watching the weather and staying off the water when the swells got too big.

Parker was in charge of getting the tanks filled, and he loved the cool factor of hefting the tanks around. The only downside? The dive shop was owned by Harley Lotitto's uncle. And every time Parker went there, Harley was the guy filling tanks. Lotitto had never exactly been friendly—but since Devin's death he'd been worse.

Parker sat on a granite slab. Pulled out his phone. Time for his call to Jelly. They texted all the time, but at least once a week they did a FaceTime call.

His phone rang before he dialed her—and *The BOSS* came up on the screen. Mr. Steadman, the guy who'd given Parker a job. The guy was "driven," as Dad liked to say. Twenty years in the military—a Navy Seal. And no family. He'd hung up his sailor cap and reentered civilian life with a boatload of cash. And he invested it well. Had some kind of gift for turning any kind of business deal into a win-win. He owned two vacation rental homes in Rockport besides the house he lived in.

It was amazing what people would pay to rent a touristy fishing village home for a week. Steadman's Navy Seal background landed him a part-time job with the Rockport Fire Department—and about two seconds later the chief made him the commander of the rescue dive team.

Parker answered the phone. "Hey, Boss." Not many guys would hire a fifteen-year-old. Parker liked the idea of having a job—even if he didn't earn a dime doing it. Steadman gave him something better than cash: a mooring at the Rockport Yacht Club for his skiff. It sounded a lot fancier than it was. Steadman had a double-wide dock slip where he kept a gorgeous twenty-five-foot Boston Whaler Dauntless with a hardtop over the console and a 400-horsepower Merc on the transom. But there was just enough room for the *Boy's Bomb* to float next to it like an outrigger or something. Cleaning, odd jobs, and mowing at Steadman's rental homes in exchange for a slip in Rockport Harbor? Oh, yeah . . . it was more than a simple win-win. It was an insanely good deal—and Parker was not going to mess it up. Actually, he'd been to one of the houses earlier today. Was there a problem?

"Swabbie?" Steadman had been calling him that from the day he hired him. "You busy?"

"How can I help?"

Mr. Steadman laughed. "Good answer. Hey, tomorrow's rental is taking both houses for a family reunion, and he wants to come in tonight. But it'll be late—twenty-two hundred hours at least. I know you already did some work at Bayport today. I need a couple more things done. I was thinking maybe you'd get one of the houses ready while I get the other."

The guy named the houses—which was smart. Tourists loved it. "I'm on it. Which one?"

"Take your pick."

"I'm on the Neck. I can get back to Bayport in ten minutes, easy." If he moved fast. He'd need twice that for the other rental.

"Roger that," Steadman said. "Mostly need you to turn on lights. Make it look welcoming. We need the business. Then check the kitchen sink—and garbage, while you're at it. The plumber was there today. Make sure he didn't leave a mess."

Parker took one last look at the harbor and hustled across the uneven rocks toward town. "Consider it done."

"And test the faucet. Make sure we're getting cold *and* hot water. If not, call me pronto. I'll get his tail back over there. I've got a dryer full of sheets and towels at Bayview to fold and put away before our guests arrive."

The call to Jelly would have to wait. Parker jogged down Bearskin Neck—picking up the pace as he passed Rockport Dive Company. No Harley Lotitto in sight.

Parker headed up Main the moment he left the Neck. He hustled across Beach Street and cut through the Old First Parish Burying Ground instead. It was uphill all the way, but he poured on the afterburners and left the weathered tombstones behind in record time. He zigzagged his way through Mill Pond Park, between houses, and over stone fences to the house on Mills in a few short minutes.

Gray-shiplap siding. Two-story. Red shutters. Red door. A typical New England home—and just what tourists looked for, it seemed. Rockport was advertised as a "quaint fishing community," but fishing wasn't the big business in town. Renting vacation homes was where the real money was. That's what Mr. Steadman told him, anyway.

He slowed to a walk by the time he hit the driveway. Even in the growing darkness he could still tell he'd cleaned the windows earlier in the week. It wasn't on the boss's list—but he'd done it anyway. Two blocks off the ocean, the windows picked up a film and sometimes a crusty deposit from the salt air. The place was listed online as a "charming vacation stay in the heart of Rockport." There was nothing charming about dirty windows. Sooner or later the boss would notice. He hoped Mr. Steadman would appreciate the extra effort.

Something swung past the window. Had he just seen a light from inside? It was only an instant—and not like the beam of a flashlight sweeping by. It was more of a glow. Green.

Instinctively Parker crouched—and moved closer to the window. Inside, the house was black. *Was he imagining things?* He stood there for a full minute, straining to see any flicker of light—and hoping he wouldn't at the same time. Is this what Devin had seen the night he ended up in the quarry?

He gave a quick shoulder-check to see if the green could have been some kind of reflection. But there was no green light shining from any of the surrounding homes. And there was no traffic light in town—or anything else nearby—that gave off a green glow.

Maybe he'd imagined the whole thing. With El and so many others talking about Devin's "spirit" still being around, Parker's mind was just doing a little overtime on the creepy side of things, right? He cupped his hands against the window and stared through them into the dark house. Outlines of furniture were barely visible. There was no movement. No green glow. Okay, he *had* imagined the light. But now he couldn't get it out of his head, either.

The idea of going in alone sounded like a way bigger deal than he'd thought when Steadman called him.

Just turn on the lights, check the kitchen, and get out of here. Keeping an eye on the window, Parker backed away from the glass and hustled around the side of the house and up the steps to the back door. He reached for the knob—and the thing turned in his hand. Had Parker left it unlocked when he'd cleaned the windows? He was an idiot. Or was it the plumber?

This wasn't going to be as simple as flipping on lights and checking the plumber's work now that he'd found an unlocked door. He'd have to check the whole house to be sure nobody was inside, right? Every room. Every closet. That would be the right thing to do. But just the idea of doing that made some unnamed fear crawl up his throat. He gave the backyard a quick scan. Everything looked normal. How did it get so dark so fast?

He could call Mr. Steadman. *And tell him what? "I might have left the door unlocked earlier. Would you go through the house with me?"* Steadman would think he was a wimp. Or that he wasn't responsible enough. Maybe he'd get someone else for the job. Parker pictured his skiff in Rockport Harbor. It was the best mooring he'd ever had. There was no way he was going to lose it that easy.

What he'd really like was to call his dad and have him go through the house with him. And his dad would be glad to do it. But once Parker started down that path, where would it end? He'd always be looking over his shoulder—and needing someone to bail him out. No thanks.

"Get a grip, Parker," he whispered. "There's nothing going on here—just your overactive imagination. Nothing more."

He opened the door a few inches, reached for the wall switch—and stopped halfway. A green glow trailed into the kitchen from the den. Not the light directly, but more of a reflection off the kitchen tile—bright enough to cast faint shadows behind the legs of the chairs.

Get out. Call the police. The thought was as clear and strong in his head as if somebody had said it out loud. But he didn't move. He held his breath. Listened.

Call the police. And tell them what? He'd seen a green glowing light?

A muffled crash came from the living room. Parker's heart slammed around inside his chest like it was looking for an exit. A heavy thump echoed off the wood floor like someone had dumped the recliner on its side. Was somebody trashing the place? Parker would be crazy to call the police right here where whoever was in the house could jump him. He needed to make the call from a safe distance away. Three blocks sounded about right. But by the time he did that—and the police came—whoever was inside would destroy the rental, and all because of an unlocked door. It wouldn't be right.

Parker had to do something. He eyed the rock wall separating

Steadman's property from a wooded section next to it—and made his decision. He'd call the police. But first he had to get whoever—or *whatever*—was inside to stop.

CHAPTER 8

PARKER CLUTCHED HIS PHONE IN ONE HAND and the door handle to Steadman's rental home in the other. He took a couple of deep breaths—keeping his eye out for any signs of the green light moving into the kitchen.

Another crash—and a pop at the end with the tinkling sound of glass. Definitely a lamp.

Put a scare into the guy so he stops—then fly like a bat out of a cave. Once he got on the other side of the stone wall, he'd call the police. Not much of a plan, but it just might stop the rental from getting demolished any worse. What else could he do?

Parker tensed. Crouched on the top step, inched open the door, and leaned inside. "Hey!" he yelled in the deepest roar he could conjure up. "I'm calling the cops! Get outta here!"

Parker slammed the door and leaped down the stairs. He

dashed across the yard, vaulted the stone wall, and dropped down on the other side. He pressed his shaking body up against the cold granite. Tiny gaps between the stones gave him a perfect view of the back door.

Call the police. He dimmed the screen brightness down to almost nothing.

He punched in 9-1-1—and the back door yawned outward. It didn't burst open like he'd expected. And it wasn't so slow as to say whoever was inside was being extra cautious. More like the intruder wasn't intimidated by Parker's warning at all. Like the guy was making an entrance on stage.

Parker held his breath. A dark form appeared in the doorway—arms hanging at its sides and slightly slump-shouldered. He held the biggest glow stick Parker had ever seen. At least twenty inches long—and as thick as a closet pole. The stick had a handle on one end, almost like some kind of Star Wars lightsaber. Was that what Devin Catsakis had seen? *Dear God . . . Shadow-man.*

A chill flashed through him, despite the warm night air. It was just like Devin had said. He hadn't exaggerated a thing.

The guy wore a hoodie, but other than that Parker couldn't make out a single detail. He couldn't even estimate the guy's height. He was way bigger than Parker—and that's all that mattered.

"9-1-1 operator. What is the nature of the emer—"

Too loud. Parker clamped his hand over the speaker and disconnected—afraid whoever—or *whatever*—was standing on Steadman's steps would hear. Why had Parker stopped behind the wall? He should have kept running. Put more distance between him and the house before making the call.

The hooded figure stared his way—like he knew exactly where Parker hid.

Had he heard—or seen the light from Parker's screen? But there was no way, right? Parker crouched lower, just in case. Turned off the ringer.

Parker's screen lit up again. A text from Jelly.

`You okay? Still want to talk? Is Ella there?`

Not now, Jelly. Not now.

The hooded man stepped down the wooden stairway. One step. Two. Deliberate. Slow. Maybe he was deciding exactly how to play this. But his pace seemed robotic. Zombie-like. As if he was controlled by a remote.

Run, Parker. Run. He wanted to. But something froze him to the spot. Terror? Fascination? Definitely some twisted mix of both.

Sweat trickled down Parker's spine.

The wood gasped and groaned under the figure's weight—like the steps themselves were petrified, just as unable to move as Parker. There was an evil that clung to the figure like Parker hadn't felt since leaving the Everglades. An invisible aura—but just as real as the green glow that surrounded him. Shadow-man was unlike anything Parker had ever seen. Darker somehow. Shadow of evil.

Shadow-man stopped at the bottom of the stairs—and by the direction of his hood, he was still looking Parker's way.

Parker tensed, crouching behind the stone wall on the balls of his feet. Hands on the ground like he was ready to spring off the blocks in the hundred-yard dash. *You can outrun this guy, Parker. You can do it.* There was what, thirty feet between them? Twenty-five? And one stone wall for Shadow-man to hurdle.

What was he waiting for? The only thing worse than watching the figure in front of him was turning tail and running. At least this way he knew there was a margin of distance between them. Once he started running, there'd be the terror of feeling

Shadow-man was gaining on him. *Turn away, Shadow-man. Crawl back into whatever hole you climbed out of. You can't be sure I'm behind the wall. Check the other side of the house.*

Wishful thinking.

Parker skimmed his hand along the ground, feeling for a small rock. Anything he could toss away from him. A diversion.

For a moment, Shadow-man didn't move. He didn't step closer, but didn't turn away either. Slowly—so insanely slow—the thing deliberately raised the glow stick toward his hood, like he actually intended to show Parker who he was. Why would a burglar do that—unless he was dead-sure Parker would never get away to ID him.

Parker didn't want to see—but couldn't look away either. He peered between the rocks forming the wall as Shadow-man raised the glow stick to the rim of his hood.

Dear God in heaven. There was nothing to see. No face—only blackness inside the hoodie.

CHAPTER 9

ELLA HOUSTON SAT ON THE WRAPAROUND PORCH of her grandma's place and watched the fog bank advance. Like an invading army—in total stealth mode. There was something almost otherworldly about it. Like it was alive. Had a soul. And some dark purpose for coming ashore.

Parker wouldn't see the fog as a sign of something coming. He'd see the fog as nothing more than a product of humidity and temperature. Part of nature. Like many boys, he couldn't see beyond the obvious.

Ella raised the collar of her canvas jacket and drove her hands deep in its pockets.

"Ella-girl?" Grams's voice. "What are you doing outside?" She slipped out of her button-down sweater and handed it to Ella. "There's not enough meat on your bones to keep you warm without a little lamb's wool."

The sweater would wrap around Ella twice—at least. Grams had always said she wouldn't trust a skinny cook—or baker. And Grams was terrific at both.

"Unless you'd rather just come inside," Grams said.

Ella rose up on her tiptoes and kissed Grams on the cheek. "I just need a little time to think."

"The sea smoke . . ." Grams motioned toward the misty tentacles of the approaching fog. "It's bad luck, dear."

Like the angel of death creeping through Egypt before the Exodus, slaying the firstborn of man and beast. Grams had unusual taste in the bedtime stories she'd told Ella as a girl. The Bible account had both fascinated and terrified her—yet she'd loved hearing it over and over. Even all these years later the fog always brought back those haunting memories.

"The fog never slinks back to sea empty-handed," Grams said. "As sure as the fog is silent, somewhere within the reach of its clutches some unsuspecting soul will meet the angel of death tonight."

The last time Ella had seen fog this dense was the night Devin Catsakis died.

"Why don't you come and do your thinking inside?" Grams wasn't very good at hiding her uneasiness. "Where it's warm."

Fog could be so mesmerizing though. Hypnotic. "In a minute."

Grams looked down the street, likely gauging the time before the dense mass would ghost up the porch steps. "One minute. No longer." She hesitated a moment, then slipped a necklace made with small chunks of turquoise and silver beads from around her neck. An large silver cross hung from the other end. Grams held it out. "Wear this."

Ella studied the cross. Grams had told her years ago that it was handmade by a Navajo craftsman. She'd never seen it off Grams's neck—and never this close. Grams always kept the cross tucked beneath her shirt. This necklace was for protection, not fashion.

The cross looked ancient, like it had been in the family for generations. A chunk of turquoise was mounted dead center, with Navajo symbols etched deep in the silver all around. Absolutely gorgeous. "But *you* need this."

Grams wasn't religious in the way some people were. Not a regular churchgoer, for sure. But she kept a Bible in the family room—and Ella found her reading it at the strangest times. She referred to Bible verses often, but it was what some would call superstition that truly guided her. Her own blend of beliefs and experiences. Somehow the cross necklace fit into all that—and she never took it off. Not even when she went to bed.

"I'm too old and ornery for the spirits to bother me. But you're young." Grams's eyes darted toward the street again. "I'll be inside anyway. Take it, child." She gave the necklace a gentle shake. The cross spun in a slow spiral, revealing for an instant a deeply engraved inscription on the back side. Grams kissed the cross and shook it again. "Don't dawdle, now."

Ella reached for it with a reverence she'd never quite felt before. She took the turquoise and silver necklace in one hand and cradled the cross in the other. It felt warm from where it had been against Grams's skin. The thing fit neatly in Ella's palm, but just barely.

"On with it."

Ella slid it over her neck. The cross itself hung just inches above her belly button.

"Tuck it inside your shirt, Ella-girl," Grams said. "Close to your heart."

Ella stretched her T-shirt from her neckline and dropped the cross inside.

"There, now." Grams checked the street again. "I feel better already. You?"

Ella patted her shirt. "Much." She'd wear an anchor around her neck if it would keep Grams from worrying. And she had real things to fear. Things Grams wouldn't bring to the police and had made her swear not to talk about—to anybody. Ella desperately wanted to download the whole thing to someone she could trust. She needed to talk to somebody other than Grams. And right now, Parker was the only somebody she had. "I'll give it back as soon as I get inside."

Grams ran a hand across Ella's cheek. Kissed her on the forehead. "It's yours now, sugar."

Hers? "But, Grams, you need this." Especially with the strange things that had been going on recently. "You always—"

"You keep it—and don't ever take it off."

"Seriously? Grams . . . I love it."

Grams pulled her close. "Ever since the poor boy died in the quarry my heart has been telling me you'll be needing this—and it troubles me to no end to think what that might mean."

Something in Ella spiked. Excitement? Fear? It was impossible to tell. But she wasn't about to discount what Grams was feeling. She hugged Grams back—and felt her shudder ever so slightly.

Grams took her by the shoulders, held her at arm's length, and looked her in the eyes. "You've been spared many a hard thing in this life. But don't be reckless with the good sense God gave you. Come in before the vapors climb the porch steps." Without a word Grams slipped back inside the house. Other grandmas might have a problem with Ella being up late, but Grams's protective ways were rooted in her superstitions. Even now, Grams would be all about shutting their windows and locking them tight. She'd paint a swath of blood over the front door if she truly thought it would help.

The vapors. Mysterious. And getting closer. Ella loved how Grams didn't smother her. She gave Ella space to think for herself—and make decisions—even when Grams surely feared the consequences.

The fog had crossed Clark Street now. Normally she could see Parker's house from her bedroom window. But even if she was in her room at this moment, she knew the vapors had already completely shrouded Parker's home from view. They were barely a block apart, but the fog isolated him in another world right now.

Parker.

She had the oddest feeling . . . like he was in danger. For a moment she shook it off, but the sense of foreboding thickened like the sea's breath creeping toward her. Was he still out on the breakwater, talking to Jelly? With vapors this thick, it would look like he was on an island, held under siege by the fog. She'd been caught out there herself when painting. She'd heard the motors of boats out in Sandy Bay, even though she couldn't see them. At the time, it seemed they were looking for shore—or for the entrance to Rockport Harbor, but had been unable to find it.

Ella grabbed her phone and dialed. Heard it ring. And ring. And ring. "Pick up, Parker. Pick up." Her stomach tightened and throbbed with the rhythm of her heart.

The fog enveloped the house, strangling the streetlight to a mere smudge of light as it did.

Angel of death.

Ella slid one hand inside the sweater. She clutched her shirt—and the cross beneath it. Not for herself, though.

She did it for Parker.

CHAPTER 10

HE DOESN'T SEE YOU. There was no way he could. But if Parker moved, he was pretty sure Shadow-man would be all over him. Shadow-man stretched out his arm and pointed the glow stick directly at Parker like the empty hood was equipped with night vision.

Okay—he sees you. But how?

It didn't matter how. Parker just had to get away. But he couldn't move. *God help me!*

Shadow-man stepped toward him—the glow stick still outstretched, leading the way like some kind of divining rod.

But it worked more like a cattle prod. Instantly Parker was up—and running. Through the brush. Trees. Branches whipping his face. Briars tugging at his pants like they were Shadow-man's minions. Parker crashed through the stand of trees and across the neighbor's open yard. A dog barked from somewhere inside the house like the thing was rabid. Was it warning Parker of the thing chasing him? He didn't dare look back.

Over another rock wall, and Parker tore through a second yard. He vaulted himself over a cedar fence, landed on a driveway—and plowed into the side of a parked F-150. His knee slammed into the passenger door hard.

A man stood there, unloading the bed. "Hey! What are you *doing*?"

Parker spun away from the pickup and took off around the front end. Too winded to answer the man—and too scared to stop. His knee felt like it might buckle, but he hobbled on at maybe 60 percent speedwise.

"Get back here, punk! If you damaged my truck—you're dead!"

If Parker stopped, he'd be dead before he found out if he'd damaged the pickup or not.

"Stop! I'm calling the police!"

Good. Parker should have done that himself the moment he found Steadman's door unlocked. With any luck the police would show and grab him—before Shadow-man did.

CHAPTER 11

Chokoloskee, Southern Florida

ANGELICA STARED AT HER PHONE. Willed it to ring. But the screen was as dark as her own thoughts had turned. He never missed calling her at their set time. And he hadn't answered the text she'd sent either.

She tucked a stray hair behind her ear. Flipped her braids over her shoulder. Adjusted the Wooten's Airboat Tours cap on her head. Parker's hat.

Was something wrong—or was she being replaced? He talked about Ella more and more, it seemed. Unless she asked him a direct question about her. Then he turned into a regular Sphinx.

She retucked her "tour guide" shirt, as Parker called it, to smooth out the wrinkles. He teased her about it—but that was because he liked it, right?

Was Parker with Ella? Is that why he'd forgotten their call? The more she thought about it, the more sure she was. That's *exactly* what had happened.

Angelica had biked all the way to the docks at Wooten's for this call. She liked making Parker guess where she was at—and had hoped to see if he'd get a tiny bit protective when he realized she was this close to the water of the Everglades. She checked the time again. It was even later than she'd feared.

After pacing another ten minutes, she took off Parker's cap and strapped it to her handlebars. She grabbed her helmet and snapped the chin strap. She flipped on her lights, untucked her shirt, and mounted her bike for the long ride home. Her backpack seemed a lot heavier than it did on the ride to Wooten's.

Angelica hadn't biked a quarter mile before sweat plastered her shirt to her back. The temperature had swelled into the upper nineties today in southern Florida—and the humidity seemed just as high. Even in the dark it felt like she had a wet, hot towel over her shoulders. She had to get to Rockport. Transfer or no transfer.

And not just because of the weather.

She watched Parker's cap swing to the rhythm of her pedaling. When she took the hat from him all those months ago—promising to give it back to him when she moved to Rockport—she pictured he'd be wearing it long before this.

Did he have a new hat now?

The truth was, Parker needed her. He didn't exactly have people lining up to be his friend in Rockport—except Ella. And she seemed a little too anxious. Angelica had been keeping her antenna up about that girl ever since Parker first mentioned her name.

Angelica kept a spiral notebook in her pack with a list she'd never show Parker. Things I know about Ella Houston. Just bits and pieces she'd picked up from Parker. And even more she'd dug up with her own detective work. Still, she didn't know enough. Even as she pedaled, she reviewed the list in her head.

Native to Rockport—and supposedly knows everything about the town.

Seems to have appointed herself as Parker's personal tour guide. She'd drawn a little emoji next to it. The eyes were crossed and its tongue was sticking out. Definitely primitive as far as artistic talent went—which brought her to another thing about Ella that bugged Angelica. The next item on her list.

Paints watercolor scenes of Rockport—and she's good. Angelica could barely even draw stick figures.

Lives with grandma—less than a block from Parker. Bio-mom got pregnant freshman year of college in Boston. Didn't want baby—but Grams wouldn't allow an abortion. After Ella was born, bio-mom left for a job or a boy (or both) in New York City—and left Ella with her grandma. Eventually Grams adopted Ella. Bio-mom more of a totally messed-up big sister now—who Ella rarely sees. Dad was never in the picture—and only bio-mom knows who he was. Totally MIA now.

Apparently has no curfew. Her grandma goes to bed early—and once the hearing aids hit the dresser she wouldn't know if an elephant entered the house—or if Ella left.

Probably cute—though Parker won't say. But doesn't the fact that he only gave sketchy details about Ella prove she's cute—and that he liked her? Angelica had tried to find a picture of Ella, but no luck. Ella posted plenty of pictures of her watercolors—and lately even pictures of Parker—but not even one selfie. Either the girl wasn't stuck on herself, or more likely she was careful, knowing Angelica would check her out.

Fifteen years old—just like Parker.

Finished freshman year at Rockport High School—just like Parker.

Loves hanging out at the end of breakwater at Bearskin Neck—just like Parker.

Or maybe she likes hanging out there just because she *likes* Parker? Of course she would like him. He was the most decent guy Angelica had ever met. Loyal. A protector. Would do anything for a friend. What wasn't to like?

How loyal had Parker become to Ella, and where did that leave Angelica? Was he taking on that "big brother protector" role with Ella now, too?

Angelica still didn't have nearly enough information on this girl—and yet it was way too much. What kind of girl has the last name of Houston? Shouldn't she be living in Texas somewhere instead of in a coastal fishing town northeast of Boston?

Angelica wished Ella *did* live in Texas. She pictured her wearing a cowboy hat. Riding a horse. Falling from it into a pile of—

Get a grip, Angelica. Now she was imagining bad things happening to Ella? "You're ridiculous, Angelica," she said aloud. "Totally pitiful."

Just like the situation with Dad's transfer. *What was holding it up?*

She neared the outskirts of Everglades City. A car hadn't passed her the entire time she'd been biking toward town. And why would they? This was the kind of place people wanted to escape . . . not the place they came to visit.

What else had she written down about Ella?

Superstitious. Believes in ghosts—unlike Parker.

Finally something about Ella, besides the watercoloring, that was truly different from Parker. But what made her believe ghosts were real? Had she been spooked somehow? And the fact that Ella was superstitious—could Angelica use that somehow?

But she'd have to get to Rockport first. And she had to get there soon. She had the strangest sense that Parker needed her. Or was it that she *needed* him to need her? Whatever.

The calls with Parker were supposed to help them stay close. Keep them caught up with each other. But it seemed lately that the FaceTime calls ended up piling up more questions than they did answers. Questions she couldn't ask over the phone. Things she'd have to find out for herself when she got there.

Had Parker gotten a new hat? Of course he had. But had Parker found a replacement for *her*? *C'mon, Angelica, you're being ridiculous.* Parker hadn't replaced her with Ella. Nothing had changed. He cared.

But why hadn't he called tonight?

She pictured Ella sitting on the rocks painting. And Parker there, too. Watching the scene come to life on the canvas while the tide crept in. Angelica didn't even know what color Ella's hair was. Was it red like hers? She imagined Parker's new friend laughing and talking with him. But Ella Houston wasn't wearing a cowboy hat. It was a baseball cap . . . and it was Parker's.

Angelica had worked and schemed to get him out of this area. Far away from the alligators. She'd been just naive enough to believe everything would be perfect after that. But in some ways this was worse. There was a different kind of gator stalking him in Rockport, she feared. And Angelica was going to have to figure out how to keep it away from him. But this wasn't just any gator.

This was an Ella-gator. Jelly smiled at her own joke. Wished she could share it with Parker. Wished she could share lots of things with Parker. Which meant she'd need to find a way to get to Rockport—and soon—whether her Dad's transfer came in or not.

CHAPTER 12

WAS SHADOW-MAN STILL ON HIS TAIL? Parker didn't dare look. Not yet. There was no way he was going to lead whoever was wearing that hoodie straight to his house—even if he could make it that far. The safest place was smack-dab in the most public spot he could find.

Bearskin Neck.

Tourists were always out walking the Neck at night. And he'd take the most direct route—right through the Old First Parish Burying Ground. Ella would kill him if she knew he was taking this shortcut right now.

Parker's phone vibrated in his pocket. Again. No way was he going to pick up—not until he was on the Neck.

His knee seemed to loosen up with every stride. He raced up the hill, past the iron fencing, and through a gap in the stone wall.

By the time he dashed into the cemetery he wasn't limping at all. He chanced a look over his shoulder, even though he couldn't see more than thirty yards behind him in the dark. Nobody. No Shadow-man in a hoodie. No angry pickup owner. But that didn't mean they weren't coming.

Parker crested the hill overlooking Sandy Bay. Seeing lights along the shoreline jutting out to Bearskin Neck gave him a surge of energy. A curtain of fog was drawing across town. The fogbank would work in Parker's favor, wouldn't it? Parker hauled right for the smoky edge. Shadow-man or Mr. Angry F-150. Would they both come looking for him in town? Neither of them would have gotten more than a quick glimpse of him, would they?

Parker needed to change his appearance somehow—without breaking his stride. He'd doubled up on T-shirts tonight—short sleeve over long. He peeled off his outer T-shirt and hat on the run, pitching them behind a gravestone. He'd come back for them tomorrow.

Parker nearly stumbled in his rush downhill. He'd cross Beach Street, and then he'd have to make a decision. Slip onto Front Beach and take the shoreline rocks to Bearskin, or stick with the sidewalk?

The beach would almost guarantee the guy with the pickup wouldn't find him, but if Shadow-man was still following—did he really want to chance meeting him all alone out on the rocks? No thanks.

Parker booked it out of the cemetery and across Beach Street, checking over his shoulder as he did. No green glow. Not a soul in the cemetery. Not living anyway.

"You did it, Parker," he whispered. "You lost him."

CHAPTER 13

THE GHOST WATCHED THE KID, still trying to figure out why he'd shouted inside the house. It was a risky move. Was the kid just stupid that way?

Keeping up with the boy had been easy—and he hadn't even broken a sweat doing it. He'd tucked the glow stick into his waistband under his hoodie and did one of the things he did best: dropped into ghost mode. He'd stuck with the shadows, anticipated where the kid would run, and found a more efficient way to get there. *Rolling anticipation,* the ability to plan and adjust in real time—he'd always had a knack for that. And once again his abilities hadn't let him down.

At first, the kid had taken off like a scared rabbit. By the time he got to the cemetery the panic seemed to be gone. Even from a distance, he could tell the kid kept his head. He was thinking.

Which meant the kid *wasn't* stupid—and shouting inside the house had been a calculated risk. What made him do it?

And he hadn't called 9-1-1. If he had, there would have been sirens by now.

So if the kid wasn't stupid, that meant he had some steel in his spine. The kid intrigued him. There wasn't one kid in a hundred who'd be gutsy enough to chance scaring a burglar away before calling for help. They'd slink off to a safe place, call 9-1-1, and let the real men do the work. Obviously the kid had been scared—but he'd mastered his fear enough to stick his head inside the house. Impressive.

Which was the real reason he'd followed the kid. Something inside him said this kid wasn't to be underestimated. The kid could think on his feet—and had his own code of conduct . . . even if that meant doing something absolutely out of his league. Not that the kid could possibly slow him down, but getting a little intel on your adversary was never a bad idea. If he played this right, the kid might even be turned into an asset.

Shouting inside the house wasn't an impulsive thing. It wasn't done for the same reason that a kid might take a dare. The kid did it because he was trying to stop the place from getting trashed—which would have definitely happened if he'd waited to get help. It was the same character trait that made a stranger on the beach rush out into the surf to save a drowning victim instead of searching for a lifeguard first. The kid was a do-gooder. A regular Dudley Do-Right.

The Ghost smiled. That was it. *That* was the kid's motive for getting involved. Once he'd locked on to an adversary's motivation, it was only a matter of time until he'd find a way to use that to defeat him—or lure him into a trap. The results would be the same either way. The kid's greatest strength was something inside that drove him to do the right thing. And there was always a way of turning a strength into a definite weakness if the kid didn't let this go.

The Ghost stood on the hill of the Old First Parish Burying Ground and watched the kid pause on Beach Street long enough to look behind him. Obviously Dudley Do-Right didn't see him. But he *felt* him, didn't he? He had taken the most direct route to get to the most public place possible. He kind of admired the kid's instincts. And shedding his T-shirt like that showed the boy was thinking ahead—probably to throw off the irate neighbor who might go looking for him. "Nicely done, Mr. Do-Right."

There was no need to follow Do-Right anymore tonight. He'd seen enough—and learned plenty. There was no way the Ghost was just going to walk into the busiest part of town. It wouldn't be hard to find the kid later if he needed to. "See you later, Do-Right."

The Ghost hustled inland, staying with the shadows. Right now, there were a couple of other things he needed to get done. Maybe he'd use Do-Right's T-shirt somehow to mix things up a little. To send the kid a little message.

Anticipating what his opponent would do—and staying one step ahead. That was the Ghost's way. So the next question was whether the kid would let this go or not. Clearly Do-Right was a do-gooder, and he'd keep poking his sniffer into this—trying to do the next right thing. Which meant he may get in the way again.

And if he got too close? That was the million-dollar question, wasn't it? But there really was no decision to make. He'd laid out his battle strategy months ago. If anyone got too close . . . he'd deal with it. So if Mr. Do-Right got too warm . . . the Ghost would put him on ice.

Do-Right would have an unfortunate accident—just like that kid at the quarry.

CHAPTER 14

PARKER GULPED IN DEEP BREATHS—the cramp in his side stabbing deep each time. He heard his own heartbeat pounding in his ears. Staying right there on the sidewalk at the entrance to Front Beach was stupid. Too visible—and with nobody around to help if he needed it. Parker jogged up the sidewalk to the corner of Beach and Main. There were more lights, and with them came a feeling of safety.

The entrance to Bearskin Neck was shrouded in fog. Shop lights were no more than a dim haze. He needed to change his plans. How smart would it be to go out on the Neck where he could easily get trapped? What he really needed was to call for help. Now.

He glanced over his shoulder. No hooded pursuer carrying a glow stick. And no pickup barreling down the road with an angry Mr. F-150 at the wheel.

Thank you, God. Parker doubled over, hands on his knees, trying to catch his breath. He drove a fist in his side to ease the cramp. "It's over, Parker. You made it." Saying it aloud helped. Sort of. But it didn't feel like it was over. The thought nagged at him like the stitch in his side. Maybe it was just beginning.

From this vantage point he could see anyone approaching from all directions. And window-shoppers strolled along the sidewalk on Main less than half a block away. This was the perfect place to make a call.

Parker pulled out his phone and dialed Dad. It immediately went to voicemail. He left a quick message and hung up. He should be calling 9-1-1, right? Or Mom? But what was the point? Shadow-man was gone. He knew exactly who he should call—and dialed Mr. Steadman. His boss answered on the second ring.

"Swabbie?" he said, the smile obvious in his voice. "Got the place shipshape for the renters?"

He gave Steadman a twenty-second recap—including where he was hiding out.

"Are *you* okay?" Steadman's tone completely changed. "Are you still being followed?"

Just hearing Steadman's voice made Parker feel safer. "Nobody is chasing me—at least not that I can see—not anymore." He watched down Beach Street—just in case. "Except for a nasty side ache, I'm fine. I'm sorry about your place—"

"I'll pick you up—and call the police on the way," Steadman said. "Stay put. I'll be there in two minutes."

Parker pressed himself against the building and waited. He checked down Main Street to make sure tourists were still around. Just knowing people were close helped. He shook the antsy feeling out of his hands. Bounced on the balls of his feet. Stretched his calves. His gimpy arm. And watched. He didn't take his eyes off the street for one second.

True to his word, Boss roared up Main from the direction of Bearskin Neck a couple of minutes later. He pulled over to the curb, his passenger window down. "Hop in."

Mr. Steadman kept scanning the street like he expected Shadow-man to materialize somehow. Parker climbed in, locked the door, and rolled up his window. For the first time since Parker saw the glow inside the house, he allowed himself to truly relax. Even if Shadow-man showed up in front of them, he couldn't get at Parker inside the truck. And nobody in his right mind would mess with Boss. El said he'd been a Navy Seal—and Parker believed it. The guy had a quiet confidence about him. Not arrogant, or anything like that. But Parker just picked up a vibe that the guy could handle himself if a situation got dicey.

Steadman pulled a 9mm Glock from a belt holster and laid it on the console between them. "Don't touch this, okay? I've got one in the chamber. And don't worry, I'm totally legal. Got my concealed carry permit—although I'd carry even if I didn't have one. A man's got to do what's right for himself. You remember that."

Right now Parker didn't care if Steadman had a permit or not. Seeing the gun there was reassuring. "You always carry?"

"Always. Police are on their way to check the rental," Mr. Steadman said, "although I'm sure the perp is long gone." He eyed his rearview mirror, then the side mirrors. "Keep your eyes peeled. You see this green light guy—you give me an o'clock." He pointed straight down the center of the road. "Twelve o'clock." Jerked his thumb behind him. "Six o'clock. Got it?"

Parker nodded. "Thanks for picking me up, Boss—and so quick."

"Roger that." Steadman smiled. "I may have broken the speed limit—just a bit. But you're okay—right? He didn't touch you?"

"Thank God he never got that close."

"Well, I'd like to get close to *him*," Mr. Steadman said. "Close enough to rearrange his face."

Parker would love to see that. But rearranging his face was impossible—even for an ex–Navy Seal. Shadow-man *had* no face.

CHAPTER 15

PARKER DIALED HIS DAD AGAIN. Still no answer. Where *was* he?

For an instant he thought about calling his mom, but quickly ditched the idea. *Excuse me, Mr. ex–Navy Seal guy, while I call my mommy.* No thanks. Parker could wait until he was alone before trying her.

Steadman pulled away from the curb. "The police told me to bring you to the station for questioning. Want me to swing by your house first—see if your mom or dad is there?"

Parker didn't want to tie Steadman up longer than he needed to. "That's okay. I'll keep trying to call. I figure you're in a hurry to check the rental yourself."

Steadman growled. "Exactly what I'd like—but Officer *Rankin* made it pretty clear he wants to investigate—alone."

"Rankin?"

Steadman glanced at Parker. "You know him?"

Parker shook his head. "Not really. It's just that he, uh, talked to me before." Interrogated him was more like it.

Steadman cut him a look. "Don't like the guy, huh?"

Parker shrugged. "I don't think he likes *me*."

"If it makes you feel any better, I've actually talked with him before tonight." Steadman glanced at Parker. "And there was something about him I didn't like." Steadman gripped the wheel and rolled his hands a bit, like he was revving a motorcycle. "Anyway, Rankin said he'll go through the place with his gun drawn. If I show up, he might accidently put a couple rounds in me." The frustration in his voice was obvious. "I don't think he was kidding, either."

Was this all Parker's fault? Had he left the back door unlocked after he'd cleaned the windows earlier? Is that how Shadow-man got inside? Parker had worked so hard to be a person of integrity. He'd have to tell Mr. Steadman, wouldn't he?

Steadman checked his rearview and side mirrors. "You mind if we take the roundabout way to the station? I just have to make sure of something."

Parker shook his head. It would give him more time to build his nerve to tell Boss the whole truth. *He had to tell him, right?* Telling someone only half the truth was pretty much telling them a lie.

A minute later Steadman pulled onto Mills Street—a half block from Bayport. The police cruiser was out front, lights flashing—but siren off. Steadman pulled to the side of the road and watched for a moment. He loosened his grip on the wheel. "At least he's there. I guess I can relax a bit."

And Parker wouldn't relax until he spilled that one little detail. "Boss?"

He told him about the back door being unlocked. The very one he'd left the house from after he'd finished with the windows in the morning. "So I'm afraid this is my fault."

Steadman looked at him for a long moment. Like he was trying to figure him out. But there was no anger there, that was clear. "You don't know that, Swabbie. The plumber may have left it open. And how do you know the burglar didn't jimmy the door? Don't strap on a pack that's not yours to carry."

Which made Parker feel a little bit better. And Steadman was right. Parker couldn't be sure if he'd left the door open or not. Or maybe the guy got in another way. "I just wanted to be up front."

Steadman smiled and shook his head. "Even if you did leave it unlocked, it was an honest mistake. Don't beat yourself up, Parker. The person who *trespassed* is the criminal here—not you. That guy targeted my rental—and he was going to get in whether a door was locked or not. Maybe the burglar unlocked it himself for a quick getaway if he needed it. I'm just glad the guy didn't get his hands on you."

Parker couldn't agree more.

"And I'm glad you called me when you did. But next time, I'll check the house myself first, *then* call the police."

Parker hoped there wouldn't be a next time.

The boss shifted the truck back into gear and pulled away. "Nothing more to see here, I guess."

Steadman made it to the police station in record time. Probably because he never came to a complete stop for any stop sign. He paced outside in front of the station. Checked his watch. Called the renter—who backed out of the deal by the way it sounded to Parker. Boss looked totally frustrated when he pocketed his phone.

Which didn't make Parker feel any better.

"My place gets burglarized, and I'm not allowed to even go there to check it out. How do you like that?"

Parker was pretty sure he wasn't expecting an answer. Parker kept his mouth shut and tried dialing his dad again. Still no answer.

Steadman eyed Parker. "How are you processing all this? Doing okay?"

The truth was, Parker was still a little numb. But even now he felt a seismic shift had happened inside. He told Steadman about the night Devin Catsakis drowned—and about the mysterious Shadow-man he was following. "I'd always hoped that Shadow-man thing was just something Devin made up. Which meant his drowning was a freak accident. But deep down I think I knew Devin saw something. And after what I saw tonight?" Parker shook his head.

"You're thinking the drowning wasn't an accident."

"I'm sure of it now. Which means I have to figure this out. I can't let whoever—or whatever—did this to Devin get away with it."

Steadman gave him a look that was kind of, well, parental. "Well, I hope you're wrong, Swabbie. Because if you start poking into this—and you're right about what happened to Devin?"

He didn't need to finish. "Right. I'll have to be careful."

Steadman laughed. "I was going to say, stay away from the quarry. But being careful works, too."

A police SUV rolled into sight and pulled into the lot. A big man swung out of the driver's seat. Steadman hustled over with Parker right on his heels.

Parker recognized him immediately—even before he saw the name *RANKIN* stamped on his brass nameplate. It was definitely the same cop who'd questioned him after Devin's accident.

Rankin stood nearly two inches taller than Steadman—which put him at what, six foot three? Steadman seemed a little more compact, but Rankin still looked plenty strong—and intimidating.

"Nobody at the house," Rankin said. "But someone definitely was there. You'll have one nasty mess to clean up."

Steadman ran his hands through his hair like he just wanted to get to Bayport and see it for himself.

"TV, appliances—everything is still there. But you'll need to do a full inventory to see if anything is missing," Rankin said. "Back door lock busted—like the thing had been forced."

Instantly Parker felt a tiny bit of relief.

Steadman reached over and clapped him on the back. "See?"

Rankin gave Parker a once-over. "You the one who spotted the burglar?"

"Yes, sir."

"Did you call your mom or dad?" Rankin motioned them toward the building. "I'd like to ask you a few questions, but it's probably best if your parents are here."

Parker explained the trouble he'd had reaching his dad. "I'll keep trying to get them, but I can answer a few questions without my mom or dad here." He didn't think he had anything to hide.

They followed Rankin to a cramped office in the station. Rankin shifted stacks of paper and mail from chairs.

"Officer Rankin," Steadman said, "any idea who did this?"

Rankin glanced at Parker for an instant with a curious look on his face. Like he recognized Parker, but couldn't place him. If Parker's sleeves were rolled up, Rankin would have made the connection the instant he saw the scars. "No clues, if that's what you mean. I'll be checking for prints later, but I wouldn't be too optimistic about that. There were none at the other places."

Parker looked from Rankin to Steadman, and back. "Other places?"

Rankin got an annoyed look on his face, like he'd said something he hadn't intended Parker to hear.

"There've been other burglaries," Steadman said. "All of them in the last month or so, right?"

Rankin hesitated.

"Officer, c'mon," Steadman said. "It's not like people don't know. Word gets around."

But not to Parker. Obviously he wasn't that well connected.

"Yes." Rankin kept his eyes on Parker, like he was still trying to pull up his file. "All in the last month."

"Every one of them since Devin's—" Parker caught himself too late.

"For the most part, yes." Rankin gave him a suspicious look like the system in his head to remember names and faces had just made the connection. He looked at Parker with total recognition. For an instant his eyes darted to Parker's arm. "Funny you should bring that up."

Not funny at all—but definitely stupid. What was he thinking?

"And all of them," Rankin said, "rental homes."

Steadman stared at him. "*That* I didn't know. You're saying not *one* of them was a regular home?"

"Rentals," Rankin said. "Just like yours."

Steadman looked stunned. "That can't be a coincidence. What are the odds?"

Rankin didn't comment.

"And the same MO, right?" Steadman stared at the ground, like he was putting something together in his head. "Things get messed up—but not stolen?"

Rankin nodded. "But it still scares the living daylights out of renters—and owners . . . even if nobody is home when the break-in occurs."

"This changes everything," Steadman said. "If it's only rental homes—"

Rankin held up one hand. "Let's not jump to conclusions, Mr. Steadman." He turned back to Parker. "Now I want to hear everything. *Every*thing. From the moment you got to the house."

Parker spilled it all—while Rankin listened and took notes. Twice he interrupted, asking for details about the faceless guy. He seemed frustrated Parker couldn't describe him in more detail. Parker was getting the idea that he was the first one to have seen the burglar at all—other than Devin, of course. So that made Parker the only *living* eyewitness?

Rankin looked over his notes. Parker waited, figuring another question was coming.

"How tall, can you tell us that?" Steadman must have figured the moment of silence was his chance to get more info. "Any distinguishing marks? Scars? Tattoos?"

Rankin shot him a look like he was the only one who should be doing the questioning—and investigating.

"The guy wore all black—even his hoodie," Parker said. "Like a walking shadow." No wonder Devin called him Shadow-man. "He could have been a green-skinned alien from Mars for all I know."

Steadman nodded like he understood, but Parker couldn't help feeling he was letting his boss down.

"You mentioned Devin Catsakis," Rankin said. "You're the friend who says he didn't go with him the night he drowned."

Said he didn't go with him? Was that a really poor choice of words, or did Rankin deliberately say it to shake him up? And why would the cop do that? "Yeah, that was me."

Rankin nodded like he was just adding some mental notes to Parker's file. "Green light. Isn't that what you claim Catsakis was chasing?"

Claim? "That's what Devin Catsakis *said* he saw. I never saw a green light—until tonight."

Rankin tapped his notebook with the pen. "Some kind of coincidence, wouldn't you say? I mean, you told us Catsakis was chasing a green light—and now *you* were chased by one. In the twelve years I've been on the force I've heard a lot of strange goings-on. Only twice did they involve green lights—and both reports made by you. Anybody else see the lights?"

For a moment he thought about the man with the pickup. Maybe he saw the guy chasing Parker. He hated to bring it up. What if he *had* damaged the guy's truck? But if he didn't—

"Taking a long time to answer a simple question, boy," Rankin said. "Any other witnesses?"

"Not exactly."

Rankin looked up from his notes, his eyes drilling into Parker.

Parker explained about broadsiding the pickup and Mr. F-150 yelling at him to stop. "Maybe he saw something."

"Maybe we can take a ride out there once your dad gets here," Rankin said, "retrace your steps, and I'll have a chat with him."

Right now Parker just wanted to go home.

"Let's go back to the rental thing," Steadman said. "What's your take on the significance of every burglary taking place at a rental home?"

Rankin shrugged. "To me that can only mean one thing." His eyes flicked toward Parker for a millisecond. "Kids."

An uneasiness knotted Parker's gut. He did *not* like the way Rankin looked at him.

"Kids?" Steadman shook his head. "Why would they only hit rentals? That makes no sense."

"A druggie would have stolen things that he could turn into fast cash," Rankin said. "But all kinds of things of value haven't been touched. Computers. Cameras. Smartphones. Every house, same thing. So this isn't about money," Rankin said. "Trust me—this has 'kids' written all over it. By the number of homes hit, I'd say there's a group of them."

"But what's the point?" Steadman looked at Parker—but not in an accusing way. More like he was just trying to get his head wrapped around this.

Parker was no expert on what kids in town thought. Maybe if he understood them a little better he'd have more than just El as a friend. "I have no idea."

"Really?" Rankin gave Parker a long, hard look. "You have *no* idea?"

What was it with the tone in Rankin's voice? Parker wanted to call Dad again. Maybe he'd gotten Parker's message and was on his way.

"Maybe kids don't need a good reason," Rankin said. "Maybe they're bored. Maybe this is their way of having fun—being the total idiots that they are. Like this is one big game."

Steadman didn't look like he was buying that. "Maybe if it were more random. Like if there were some regular homes in the mix—but all rentals? That seems too deliberate."

"Rentals are easy," Rankin said. "Almost zero chance of an angry homeowner walking in on them—with a firearm or baseball bat."

Which made some sense.

"Kids got spring fever . . . and the break-ins started. Once school got out, they're upping their game a little." Rankin gave Parker the side-eye again. "Kids. Trying to prove themselves. Getting their kicks. It's as simple as that."

Steadman shrugged. "I still say there's something more."

"What I want right now," Rankin said, "are more details." He looked right through Parker. "Let's go over this one more time. You're going to tell me everything that happened. Again."

Parker told Rankin every detail. Be honest—that was the right thing to do. Parker focused on the massive light stick. And he went into more detail on the chase and how he'd shed his cap and T-shirt in the cemetery.

Rankin jotted down notes on a pad now and then—but didn't exactly look overjoyed at the lack of details Parker shared. "Anything else?"

Parker pictured the faceless Shadow-man. Looking his way. Pointing the glow stick at him. "That was about it. Except . . ."

Rankin clicked and unclicked his gel pen in a steady rhythm.

"Don't you think this means maybe Devin Catsakis's drowning *wasn't* so accidental? He described the same Shadow-man that I saw. Now we know he wasn't making that up. You've got to open the case and find out what really happened to him."

Rankin looked at him with eyes that could do laser surgery. "Do I?" He did the pen thing like he was priming a pump to fuel his brain or something. "Every week I hear that some kid calls to say we've got to look into Catsakis's death again. That you making the calls?"

Parker nodded.

"This is making a whole lot more sense now." Rankin chuckled. "How's this for a theory? There's something you haven't been quite honest with Officer Rankin about in regards to that boy's drowning. You egged him on. Dared him. Did something. You cooked up that story about Catsakis seeing the light and Shadow-man. But the police didn't buy it. Maybe kids at school are suspicious too. Giving you a hard time. So you keep calling, hoping the police start looking for a ghost—so maybe the kids at school get off your back. But that isn't working for you either. Suddenly *you* see Shadow-man yourself. Nobody else in town . . . just you. Fits pretty nicely into your agenda, wouldn't you say?"

Parker stood. He had to get out of here. Needed to talk to Dad. Or El. And definitely Jelly. Somebody who at least acted like they believed him. "Look, I really need to go. I hope you find whoever broke into Mr. Steadman's house."

Rankin tapped his pad and smiled at Parker. One of those polite smiles that have nothing to do with being friendly. His eyes narrowed slightly. "Oh, I'll get him. Count on it."

A knock on the door startled Parker. A cop stuck his head inside the room and held up a scrap of paper. "Got a Ted Borker here who says he got a good look at the burglar. Says he can ID him in a lineup."

"Yes!" Steadman stood. "Now we're getting somewhere."

Finally, somebody else Rankin could grill. Parker excused himself and brushed by the cop at the door. The moment he stepped into the hallway—he saw the eyewitness. The guy with the pickup truck.

"That's him." Mr. F-150 pointed directly at Parker. "There's your burglar."

CHAPTER 16

Saturday, June 4, 7:35 a.m.

ELLA KEPT IN STEP ALONGSIDE PARKER as he walked through town and filled her in on the crazy things that had happened the night before. He'd insisted they meet early, but she was okay with that the instant he described Shadow-man. Whether Parker would admit it or not, it was just possible he'd seen his first ghost.

Two questions were playing tag in her head. First, how much did she dare tell Parker about *her* encounter with this Shadow-man character? Second, had Parker already talked to Jelly this morning—or was he actually confiding in Ella first? She'd have to find that out somehow—without him catching on. Ella didn't have friends, and she wanted to be careful not to get her hopes too high. Was she just someone Parker was hanging out with until Jelly moved to town? Or was there really room in his life for more than one close friend?

"I'll bet your parents were a little worked up."

He gave her a sideways glance. "I think my dad was more upset with himself—that he missed my calls."

"And your mom?"

"Definitely ticked at me."

Ella didn't blame her. "Because you stuck your head inside the house and yelled—or that you were so worried about looking like a wimp that you never phoned her?"

Parker laughed. "It's a toss-up. But she sure was upset."

She could imagine it. Having a real mom and dad who stayed with you? Sounded like heaven to her—even if they did get worked up at times. At least that would mean they cared, right? That they were there.

"What did Jelly say when you told her about your creepy adventure last night?" She tried to make the question sound casual.

"She wasn't happy."

Ella should have known he would've talked to Jelly first—no matter how early in the morning. "You probably woke her up. I'm sure she loved that."

"She wasn't asleep yet. I called her last night."

Oh. Of course he did. That's what you do with really good friends.

"She just wishes she were here."

"No transfer for her dad yet?"

"Not a word."

That was something, anyway. Once Jelly moved north, Ella feared she'd see a whole lot less of Parker. She'd be alone again. "Tell me again everything you can remember about Shadow-man."

Grams's cross necklace tapped gently against her with every

step. It brought an unexplainable comfort when Parker talked about the faceless man.

She actually laughed when he mentioned the neighbor guy who'd identified him as the burglar. "You—Mr. Total Boy Scout—a burglar? And Rankin bought it?"

"He let me go—so that must count for something. But Rankin will be keeping an eye on me—he made that pretty clear." Parker walked past the wharf without even looking out at the harbor—which was totally unlike him. "The neighbor—with the pickup—insisted I was wearing a hoodie."

Ella studied his face. "Were you?"

"No." Parker looked annoyed that she'd asked. "Just a short-sleeved T-shirt over a long-sleeved one."

"The one you peeled off to disguise yourself?"

Parker nodded.

"I can't believe you went through the Old First Parish Burying Ground—at night."

"I was being chased—by a *faceless* man," Parker said.

"Exactly. And you thought it was a good idea to take a shortcut through a cemetery?" Ella tapped her head. "Get a brain, Parker. You were on its home turf."

Parker laughed. "*Its?* You're saying the burglar isn't human?"

"It had no *face*," Ella said. "How many humans do you know without a face?"

"None. But—"

"Thank you," Ella said. "Now you're talking sense. Next time you're being chased, avoid the graveyard, okay? It's bad luck."

"Bad luck?" Parker took a couple quick steps to get ahead, then walked backward in front of her. "I got away, didn't I?"

"For the *moment*," Ella said. "But that's the spooky thing about bad luck. It's like a relentless stalker. It follows you at a distance, but you have to stop sometime. You rest. Think you're safe. You let down your guard—and bad luck catches up. It always does." If she was going to tell him what she knew about Shadow-man, this was the time. But she couldn't, could she?

Parker fell in step alongside her and made an exaggerated show of looking over his shoulder.

Obviously Parker had no idea what he was messing with. "Make fun of me all you like, wise guy. I'd have still gone *around* the cemetery," Ella said, "even if I were being chased by an angry mob."

They passed the entrance to Bearskin Neck and headed uphill along Main Street. "Anyway, the shirt I ditched was my favorite one from Wooten's Airboat Tours."

She knew the shirt. "What a shame to lose that ratty old thing. You're lucky that's all you lost—running through that old burial ground at night."

"I'm not going to lose it." Parker grinned. "We're going to the cemetery to find it—along with my cap. That's why I wanted to get going early—before somebody grabs my stuff."

"Nobody in their right mind would pick up anything lying on a grave," Ella said, "especially that disgusting shirt."

He gave her a look like he thought she was joking.

"I'm serious," Ella said. "Just leave the stuff there. It's bad luck—and no shirt is worth that."

"Bad luck to run through a cemetery. Bad luck to pick something up in a cemetery." Parker laughed. "You are *sooo* superstitious."

"No—I'm *careful*. There's a difference," Ella said. "My Grams is the superstitious one. She believes the first person to step inside your home on New Year's Day makes all the difference as to what kind of year you'll have. If it's a man, you'll have a year of good luck."

"So if Shadow-man burglarized your place on New Year's Day—that would be a good thing? Hey, come on in. Have a seat. So glad you could stop in."

She so did not want to think of Shadow-man at their place . . . again. "Be careful, Buckman, or the next watercolor I do will be of you—and you'll be holding a Teddy Bear. A big one. I'll title it *Parker Buckman with His Only Friend*—and I'll sell it at the Farmer's Market."

Parker laughed like the events of last night—and even Devin's death—were behind him. Ella knew him better than that.

"Anyway, if you insist on going to the Old First Parish Burying Ground, you're on your own." She was half-bluffing, but he didn't need to know that. The truth was, she wouldn't let any friend go there alone, even in daylight. "I'll just wait for you at Brothers Brew." The coffee shop door was propped open, and the aroma of fresh-baked donuts beckoned.

Parker hooked his arm through hers and walked her right past the place. "How about we stop in *after* I get my stuff? I'll buy."

The guy was definitely on a mission—and clearly she wasn't going to talk him out of it. "I'll walk you to the edge, but I'm *not* going in."

He laughed again. "Seriously? What's your problem?"

She wanted to tell him what she knew of Shadow-man. But what would Grams say? Wouldn't she see that as a betrayal? "Walking through a burial ground is reckless. And the fact that you even ask that question shows just how naive you are, Parker." Even the thought of waiting at the foot of the cemetery while he went in made her uneasy. She didn't want to think about it—or hear Parker tease her about it, either.

"What I don't understand is why Officer Rankin let you go,"

Ella said. "After that eyewitness neighbor, how did you convince him you weren't the burglar?"

"I didn't. Steadman vouched for me," Parker said. "Said the theory of me doing it was insane. Rankin had nothing to hold me on—so that ended it."

"You're a dangerous friend to have, Parker," Ella said. "I mean, hey, you went through some pretty intense things in Florida . . . and now trouble seems to be finding you here."

"There's a cheery thought."

If he'd have looked her way when she was talking—instead of at the shop windows—he'd have known she was dead serious. The way she'd heard the story, Parker definitely had some bad luck in the Everglades. Had it found him here? Maybe it had come in with the fog. Ella needed to keep the conversation light. Waiting for the right moment to talk more about Shadow-man.

They turned onto Beach Street and headed for the Old First Parish Burying Ground. The road sloped downhill. If a kid dropped a ball on the street it would roll all the way to the foot of the graveyard before stopping. And the graveyard seemed to be drawing Parker to it just as easily. Just seeing the cemetery creeped her out—which is why she never swam at Front Beach. Every time she'd turn her back to the water, she'd see gravestones. No thanks.

Parker's mood changed, too, the closer he got to the base of the hill. He got quiet, and Ella guessed he was reliving the chase from last night. There was no traffic, and they walked down the center of the narrow street side by side. This might be the best opportunity she was going to get. "What if Devin wasn't the only one who has seen Shadow-man—besides you now? Ever think of that?"

Parker shook his head. "The police would have heard."

"Unless those other witnesses were too scared to talk about it." Maybe she'd said too much. "So he really had no face?"

He gave her a sideways glance. "I didn't *see* a face. That's different from not having a face."

"You said all you saw was black inside that hood," Ella said.

"Right," Parker said. "I've been thinking about that. His hood must have shadowed his face."

"But you said he was holding up a glow stick. A big one. And right in front of his hood." She let that little fact hang out there for a second. "So your shadow theory has a hole in it."

Parker didn't answer.

"If there was a face, you'd have seen his eyes." Ella was sure of it. "I know you're a Christian, so you probably don't believe in ghosts, but honestly . . ." There. She'd cracked open the door to the topic—and she wasn't going to say any more unless he walked through it.

Maybe Parker was processing the idea of a supernatural element. Or picturing the faceless hoodie-man all over again. But he angled across the street toward the cemetery without another word on the subject. The guy just couldn't admit the obvious.

She stayed on the street until after they'd passed the small garage-like building at the foot of the cemetery. Entombed inside the granite structure sat the hearse that had been used to carry the dead back to the burial ground back in the 1800s. It had been restored and displayed in the windowed shed like it was some kind of tourist attraction. It was sick. Tasteless. She lifted the necklace from under her collar and held it out to him. "Take this when you go in, okay?"

"A cross?" He gave her a look like he thought she was joking. "You expecting a vampire to jump out at me?"

"Just carry it, idiot. I'm trying to do you a favor."

He reached for it. Turned it over. He ran his finger over the inscription:

Deliver us from evil. "From the Lord's Prayer, right?"

"Don't ask me. You're the Christian."

He handed it back. "True. And that means God is always with me. So you hang onto this. I'm really okay . . . trust me on that."

Besides Grams, trusting others didn't come as easily as putting color on a canvas. Obviously Parker's life experiences were way different than hers. She shook the necklace. "Last chance."

Parker laughed. "No, you keep it—in case a boogeyman shows up."

So much for him taking her seriously. She slipped the Navajo cross back over her neck. "Make all the fun of me that you like, Parker Buckman, but it doesn't hurt to be a little cautious." Apparently something Parker knew absolutely nothing about.

Set on a steep hill, the Old First Parish Burying Ground overlooked Front Beach, Sandy Bay, and beyond that, the Atlantic. And weirdly enough, so many whose names were etched on those gravestones had died in the ocean. The graves of sea captains and fishermen lost at sea were empty. Had to be. Grams said some of the spirits of the dead came in with the vapors—because they'd never been buried.

The sidewalk in front of the cemetery had been cut from the base of the hill, and a retaining wall had the job of holding the whole thing from sliding into Sandy Bay. The Old First Parish Burying Ground had an iron fence on two sides, not completely surrounding it like lots of other cemeteries. Fences around graveyards made no sense to Ella. There was no need to keep people out. Only an idiot would go in after dark. And a fence definitely couldn't keep a spirit in.

Parker took several steps into the cemetery and turned back. "You really aren't coming with?"

Ella stood on the sidewalk and folded her arms. "Absolutely not. And if you were smart, you wouldn't either. This place is messed up." Okay, so maybe she had a thing about cemeteries—and the Old First Parish Burying Ground in particular. Tourists were always climbing around, taking pictures—like it was some kind of attraction. But it was a tragic place—and one she didn't take lightly. Especially with the things that had been going on lately.

"What if I had a hundred bucks," Parker said, "and offered it to you just to walk through this place?"

"I wouldn't do it for a thousand."

"*You*—are crazy," Parker said.

Yet he was the one claiming he'd been chased by a faceless person. But she wasn't going to go there. "Did you know," Ella said, "that graves are supposed to run east and west?"

He glanced up the hill—and back at her. "And these do."

"The heads should be to the west—and the feet to the east," she said. "They did it opposite here. It's not a good sign."

"They're *dead*," Parker said. "So why on earth would it matter?"

"Forget I ever mentioned it." If he was going to do this, he should do it quickly and get out of there. She clutched the cross, just in case. Not for herself, but for him. "You can be pretty pigheaded, did you know that?"

"Oink-oink." He grinned like he thought *she* was acting like a kid. Without another word, he turned and headed up the incline.

The first lonely hill of the Old First Parish Burying Ground had weathered countless storms pounding in from the Atlantic. Maybe that's why they buried everybody the wrong way. If the gravestones faced the ocean, likely every trace of etching on the faces would have worn away decades ago. But still, the burial ground was laid out all wrong. That had to be bad luck, right?

Parker swept his head left and right—looking down each row of headstones like he wasn't sure where he'd dropped his stuff.

"Do *not* step on a grave, Parker," she said. "Be careful."

He didn't turn, but raised one hand over his head—and deliberately walked across a grave with a small, white tombstone. Probably a child or an infant. Desecrating the grave of an innocent? He clearly had no idea what he was doing—or messing with. "Very mature, Parker. Wow."

He did some kind of lame dance move on another grave. Obviously trying to warn him had an opposite effect.

A police cruiser crept toward her and pulled over to the curb. The cop who'd met Parker at school the day after Devin died. Rankin. The big cop swung out, hiked up his belt, and strode toward her.

Her pulse must have gone off the canvas, fearing she looked guilty—even though she'd done nothing wrong.

Instinctively she wanted to run—and warn Parker—but he hadn't done anything wrong either, except for the way he moved through the graveyard. He zigzagged between headstones like he was on a playground. If he noticed the police car, he didn't let on.

Be polite. Look the officer in the eyes. Smile. Say "sir." Grams's voice was in her head. Coaching her.

The slightest chill tickled her arms, like a cold breeze had been lurking behind a row of gravestones, waiting for her. Or maybe some of the vapors from last night. Since she refused to step within the bounds of the cemetery, some invisible wisp had come in search of her. She clutched the cross with both hands, rubbing the chunk of turquoise mounted in the center.

Do not look at his gun. Keep your hands in plain sight. Do not reach in your purse—for anything. Do not even think about running—he'll see in your eyes and think you're guilty. Don't hesitate when he tells you to do something. It was like Grams had recorded a checklist in Ella's brain, and seeing the cop triggered the playback.

The cop strolled over—putting a finger to his lips like he didn't want her tipping Parker off that he was there. The brass name tag confirmed what she'd guessed. Parker definitely should have borrowed her cross.

"Now I've got my bearings," Parker called over his shoulder without looking back. "Right over there—behind those monuments—is where I ditched my gear." He hustled toward a pair of slate gray headstones—leaning in toward each other like they were huddling for warmth or comfort. The instant Parker rounded the headstones, he stopped dead.

He stretched one leg forward and nudged something on the ground. "You won't believe this," he said.

"Maybe you should get out of there," Ella said. She felt the edges of the cross dig deeper into her hands.

He bent over and gathered something in his arms, then held them up to show her.

The cap. The T-shirt. And a black hooded sweatshirt. Parker's expression fell when he saw Rankin.

"Well, well, well." Rankin motioned Parker down the hill. "Let's have a look at those, boy."

CHAPTER 17

ELLA SHOULD HAVE WARNED HIM the moment she saw the cop car pull up—but she'd locked up. What was it about the police that made her freeze like that?

Parker stood there, just staring for a moment. His hands dropped to his sides like all the strength had suddenly drained out of them. He trudged down the hill.

"I come out to do a little early morning investigating," the cop said. "Imagine my surprise to see you here."

"I just came to get the things I dropped last night."

"Is that the hoodie," Rankin pointed, "that you *weren't* wearing?"

"It isn't mine." Parker dropped the sweatshirt on the granite retaining wall.

"What about the hat," Rankin said, "and the T-shirt? You telling me they aren't yours either?"

"*They're* mine—but not the hoodie." Parker shrugged. "The burglar must have shed his hoodie while he was chasing me."

Officer Rankin smiled like he wasn't buying it. "You realize you're the only one who saw this mysterious burglar, right? The neighbor only saw *you* running from Steadman's house. And that eyewitness swore *you* were wearing a hoodie."

Say something, Ella. Help Parker out.

Parker shook his head. "The faceless guy—he was there."

"But you never actually *saw* him chase you into the burial ground here, right?" Rankin eyed him. "I mean, that's what you said last night."

Parker nodded. "Last I saw him, he was still in Mr. Steadman's yard—but coming right at me. But this sweatshirt proves I was telling the truth. There *was* somebody following me. He must have ditched his hoodie just like I dumped my stuff."

Rankin chuckled. "So let me get this straight. You believe the mystery man chased you—even though you didn't actually see him behind you, and neither did the eyewitness neighbor. But somehow, in the black of night—and a foggy one—this ghost of a burglar just happened to lose his hoodie right here, at the exact same spot you did?"

Even Ella had to admit Officer Rankin made Parker's story sound ridiculous. Cops could do that—no matter how innocent a person was. Would it do any good to try to defend him? *Explain yourself. Fine. Defend yourself? Never.* Grams's lessons about how to act around police started as far back as Ella could remember.

Rankin swept his hand across the burial ground. "Over a hundred grave markers here—and plenty more that are missing a headstone. What are the odds that this Shadow-man picked the same headstone as you did—in the dark?"

Parker shrugged. "Well, he did." He nodded toward the sweatshirt. "There's your proof."

"Proof?" Rankin laughed so hard that it morphed into a short coughing fit. "Why don't you just admit it, boy? For some juvenile reason you trashed Mr. Steadman's place. You got spotted on your way out, so you ran. You dumped your stuff in the cemetery here—and made up some cockeyed story about a ghost with a light saber. It all fits with what I said last night."

Parker took a step back, and Rankin moved closer.

"Which is why you decided to come out here so early today," Rankin said. "You had to get rid of the evidence."

"Hold on." Parker raised both hands in the air like he thought the cop might draw his gun. "I can explain. Sort of."

And Parker did, though he was pretty much just repeating the same things he'd already said. In the end, the cop let Parker go. But Rankin took the hoodie and stuffed it in an oversized evidence bag first. What . . . did the guy think he'd find traces of DNA—*from a ghost?* He took Parker's hat and T-shirt, too. What was he going to prove with those?

Ella stood beside Parker, watching Officer Rankin pull away.

"He doesn't even know me—but it's like he's made up his mind. He doesn't trust me." Parker said it like he couldn't quite get his head wrapped around that.

"You act like this is the first time a cop looked at you like you were as guilty as sin—without doing a bit of investigating first. Welcome to my world." Ella was usually shocked when somebody *did* trust her.

Parker drifted across the street and leaned on the iron rail overlooking Front Beach and Sandy Bay. "It's just not right."

"There is no justice in this world, Parker." She pictured the massive statue of Lady Justice she'd seen on the eighth-grade field trip. Lady J held the scales of guilt and innocence. A blindfold across her eyes so she wouldn't be swayed by the looks of the people in front of her court. "Lady Justice peeks sometimes. She sees color—I can tell you that."

"What are you talking about?"

She wasn't going to get into it. Not now. "I'm just saying 'liberty and justice for all' doesn't really exist. For some, maybe. Not for all. And the real kicker? Most people don't really care."

"God cares. And He's all about justice."

Leave it to Parker to bring up God in the conversation. "Is He?" Okay, maybe calling out God—right out loud—was a really great way to get zapped by lightning. But holy mackerel, if he really believed God was truly just, Parker was the one wearing a blindfold. "It's been a month since Devin's drowning—which *you* believe deep down was murder. Where's the justice? If God sees—and cares—why doesn't He do something about it? There won't ever be justice for Devin Catsakis."

Parker shook his head. "Payday someday. Justice doesn't always happen when we'd like it to . . . but it will happen."

"Sounds like a Sunday school answer, Parker. How can I even debate that?"

"Is that what you want to do? Prove me wrong?"

She reached over and grabbed him around the neck in a mock attempt to throttle him. "I'm saying I wish you were right—but you're just not, okay? I'm *saying* you need to open your eyes. Face the truth. There'll be no justice for Devin. Just like there'll be no justice for . . ." This was pointless.

Parker looked at her like he actually wanted to understand. "For . . . ?"

She wasn't going to go down that path. "For people who have had their rental broken into by Shadow-man, for example. Devin saw the guy coming out of his neighbors' rental. Was Shadow-man caught? No. Obviously he's still on the prowl. Who knows how many places he's hit now." She had to be careful until she got Grams's permission to say more. What could Parker do to really change their situation anyway? Nothing.

"Sometimes God doesn't give us the answer key. He allows mysteries. But that doesn't mean they'll stay that way. He sees everything. Even the hidden things. At the right time, when—"

"And don't you think the *right time* would have happened by now? If God really has all the answers, if He really cares, what on earth is He waiting for? And if you say the right timing again, you will so wish you hadn't."

Parker raised both hands in mock surrender. "I'll change the topic. Rankin says nothing ever seems to be missing from the break-ins, so that's something."

"Rankin doesn't have a clue."

"You mean, he doesn't have any leads, or—"

"Shadow-man has been stealing *renters*, Parker. Rankin doesn't get it—and obviously neither do you. A renter posts a nasty review, and word gets out about a ghost . . . the Shadow-man breaking into rentals. And what do you think that does for other potential renters planning a nice little visit to Rockport? They become ghosts themselves."

"Mr. Steadman lost his renters—for both houses," Parker said. "That's tough. I get it."

"No. You don't. Not the half of it. *Think*, Parker." Was she saying too much? Tipping her hand?

She had to end this. "Look . . . imagine decent people take out a massive loan to fix up a place to rent, and not because they're greedy. It's a gamble they took, believing the rental business will one day provide a college education for someone they love. They *need* that rental money to pay off the loan before they can start that college fund. But with no renters, the hopes and dreams of a better life drift off to sea like the morning fog. With no renters, they can't make their payments. Then what happens?"

Parker stared off into the bay. "They lose their home."

"Doggone right they do. Police say nothing's been stolen? Nothing *in* the house, maybe. But homes are going to be stolen right out from underneath decent people if this God of hidden things doesn't get off His throne and start pulling back the curtain—and soon. You said it yourself. There's been a whole slew of break-ins—maybe more than the police know. This isn't going to end well if this doesn't stop. It may already be too late."

That got Parker's attention. "Too late for what?"

Ella realized that she'd probably said too much. "Never mind. I'm just saying there's something bigger at work here. This is definitely not the end of it." But it would be the end of everything she loved and cared about if the break-ins didn't stop . . . if something didn't change. In her heart, she knew this wasn't blowing over—not in time, anyway. It was a lot more likely to blow up first.

"Is there something you aren't telling me? Do you know something?"

And he was just figuring this out now? "Yes . . . and yes."

There was no smile on his face now. "Are you going to tell me?"

"I'm not supposed to."

Parker thought about that for a second. "Want to play *twenty questions*?"

"Can't."

"Okay . . . one question, then. Just one. Are you in some kind of trouble—or danger or something?"

"I can't say."

Parker looked totally frustrated now. "I want to help you—but how am I supposed to do that if you won't tell me what's wrong?"

"If you're so sure God cares so much—and He knows every hidden thing—why don't you ask Him to tell you?"

CHAPTER 18

Monday, June 6, 3:05 p.m.

PARKER LOCKED HIS BIKE TO A POST and hustled down the ramp to the floating docks below. Sometimes taking the *Boy's Bomb* for a run in the harbor was what he needed to help him think. He hadn't even made it to the skiff before he got a text from his dad.

`Grandpa sent something for you. FedEx package on table.`

He unlocked his bike from the post and tore home. He shot up a prayer on the way. "God . . . El is hurting. Help her . . . and show me how I can help You do that." How many times had he prayed that since their conversation on Saturday? Plenty. But it was kind of like playing ping-pong alone. Nothing ever came back.

Mom was working from home today, and she greeted him with a smile like she'd been waiting for him. "Record time, Parker. Now I know how fast you can really get home from the wharf if you're motivated."

He dashed into the kitchen and grabbed the bulging letter pack. Inside he found a package wrapped in plain brown paper—along with two sealed envelopes. READ FIRST was printed in letters across one of them.

Parker smiled. "Okay, Grandpa. Definitely liking this so far."

He pulled open the refrigerator and grabbed the chocolate milk—giving the carton a good shaking before pouring. He filled a glass right up to the rim. Too high to lift it to his mouth without spilling. He bent over and slurped off the foam and first half-inch of the cool deliciousness.

The letter was short.

Grab the second note—and the package. Go to the quarry where your classmate drowned. We need to talk—and that's where we need to do it. The next letter will explain. Trust me.

Parker's gut twisted. Why *there*?

After Devin's death he'd purposely steered clear of the place. He hadn't been there in over a month.

Parker sipped on the chocolate milk, hoping it would help calm his stomach. He studied the package. Maybe ten inches long. He tested the weight in his hands. Lighter than the glass of chocolate milk. Heavier than the empty glass. He squeezed the package, but all he could tell was there was something solid inside. Grandpa had used enough bubble wrap inside to keep Parker from feeling any detail that would give a clue as to what he'd sent. The thing was taped up good and tied with twine.

He held the second letter up to the light—but couldn't make out a thing. He wandered up to his bedroom. Found himself looking at Goliath's skull. Facing a gator in the Everglades was definitely a lot worse than the quarry, right? But he'd had Wilson in the Glades with him back then.

Parker would have been happy avoiding the quarry forever, thank you very much. Was Grandpa trying to get him to face his fears? Probably. But knowing him, there was something more to it. And that package definitely had him intrigued.

"Buck up, Buckman. You can do this." And just like that, he made the decision.

He slapped his cap on his head. Grabbed a pocketknife. Stuffed the letter and package in his pack. Slung it over his shoulder and bounded down the stairs.

"You going to be okay?" Mom had an apologetic look on her face like she knew where Grandpa had asked him to go. "I could drive you."

"I'll be fine." If it had been dark out, that would have been a different story. There was no way he'd go to the quarry at night. Not for a thousand packages. He hustled for the door.

"Not so fast, buster." She motioned him over for a hug.

"Mom." He tried to make his voice sound annoyed, but it didn't come out all that convincing. He gave her a quick one.

"You be careful." Mom slapped him on the behind on his way out.

His legs felt like concrete by the time he pedaled to the quarry. For a moment he sat there, straddling the bike, feet on the gravel road. Listening. Scanning. Ready to stand on the pedals and peel out if he saw or heard anything out of the ordinary.

Then again, there was nothing exactly ordinary about a quarry. Parker's Pit was sort of split into two sections—with a granite peninsula jutting out from one shoreline dividing the smaller front section from the back like a breakwater. Ella called the thing Humpback Rock, and with a little imagination it did resemble the back of a whale in look and size.

Parker's Pit was definitely one of the smaller quarries in the area, but that didn't mean it was tiny. From the eastern lip to Humpback Rock had to be fifty yards or so. From Humpback to the western edge, maybe another thirty yards. Dense forest surrounded most of the quarry, except for the gravel road, likely the same route used generations earlier to haul the rock from the quarry to the railroad. The southeast corner of the quarry had a large shelf just below the surface—a perfect entry spot for swimmers. The quarry had a bit of a curve to it, so a swimmer had to leave the safety of the ledge by a few strokes before they'd see Humpback Rock. Last fall Parker and Ella never thought twice about swimming it. But now?

How deep was it? Sixty? Seventy feet? Like a giant, flooded elevator shaft. Who knew what was on the bottom of the thing? Parker never intended to find out.

"Are you going to do this, Buckman?" Hearing his own voice boosted his confidence a bit. Yeah, he was going to do this. But he wanted to be out in the open. A high point where he could see someone coming. Humpback Rock.

He leaned his bike against a tree and walked the perimeter of the quarry, careful not to get too close to the edge. A high ridge spine ran nearly the entire length of Humpback, standing a good six feet above the dark water. The further the better.

He sat nearly halfway out on the rock, gave a careful scan of the area from his perch, and pulled out the package and note. If Mom was here, she'd remind him to open the card before the package. But Mom wasn't here.

He pulled out his pocketknife and sliced through the packing tape. He tore off the brown paper and unrolled a couple of layers of fine bubble wrap. A dive knife.

And a great brand.

Aqua Lung. In a sheath with a quick-release. Black, easy-grip handle with deep blue accents. Gorgeous. No straps for his calf—which was perfect. He already had a dive knife with leg straps. This one was big enough to do serious work, but small enough to fit in his BCD vest pocket.

He slid the knife from the sheath. Double-sided four-and-a-half-inch titanium blade with the Aqua Lung logo laser-etched on the flat. Hair-splitting edge along one side. A wicked-long serrated edge along the entire length of the other. There were times a diver could get hung up in fishing lines that had become snagged on the bottom. This was definitely the kind of tool that could saw a guy free from any line—from buoy ropes to lobster traps—fast.

"Nicely done, Grandpa," he whispered. "I love it."

He flipped the knife over. A dark charcoal-colored, laser-etched inscription ran along the flat part of the blade just below the spine.

"He reveals deep and hidden things;
he knows what lies in darkness."

DANIEL 2:22

Cool. And kind of creepy.

Parker ripped open the envelope and read Grandpa's note.

Dear Parker,

A knife is meant to cut through entanglements that hold you back. And a knife can slice through packaging to reveal what's inside a mystery box. I bought this knife for you as a congratulations on passing your dive certification test. I'd planned to bring it when I visit in August.

After the loss of your classmate and hearing how you struggled with all the unanswered questions, I had the blade laser-etched with a Bible verse. May this knife remind you that we serve a God who is the great revealer of mysteries and secrets. A God who brings wrongs done in darkness to light.

Your dad filled me in on the incident this past weekend with the burglar, or Shadow-man as you've named him. Another verse came to mind. I felt I should overnight this to you. Especially now, when you're wondering where the justice is.

"For God will bring every deed into judgment, including every hidden thing, whether it is good or evil." Ecclesiastes 12:14

He knows all the dark secrets, and will bring them to light in His timing. Trust Him in all this, Parker. Sorry I had you come to this spot to open this . . . in a place that is probably creeping you out about now. I tend to learn lessons better when my heart is racing a bit. I think you probably do, too . . . and this is a life lesson I want to be sure you really hang onto.

Love you like crazy!

Grandpa

PS . . . I got the knife at Sea Level Diving—the place you loved visiting when you were in town. Remember Art, the owner? He said this was a good choice. I hope it serves you well.

Parker smiled. Oh yeah, the knife would serve him really well. And he loved the verse on the blade, and in the letter. But if God was so big on justice—and revealing the hidden things—shouldn't He have done something about Devin Catsakis's murder by now?

The sound of a twig snapping caused Parker to jerk his head up and look around. It had come from somewhere off in the dense woods. Parker listened. Scanned.

Nothing.

But it didn't *feel* like nothing. He picked up the note and envelope. The wrapping. Dropped them all in his pack—still keeping a close eye on the thick brush. *Was he being watched?*

He slid his new knife in his back pocket. An easy grab. He fought the urge to run for his bike. He eased his way off Humpback, all his senses on high alert.

"Okay, Grandpa," he whispered, "my heart rate is definitely racing—just like you hoped it would be. Now I'm going to get out of here."

CHAPTER 19

Tuesday, June 7

PARKER SAW RANKIN no fewer than three times from when they talked by the cemetery Saturday morning until Tuesday afternoon. The first time, he thought it was a coincidence. Rankin just happened to walk into Brothers Brew for coffee and donuts minutes after Parker and El sat down. He chose a table right next to theirs—even though there were plenty of empty tables closer to the ordering counter.

Rankin cruised past Parker's house minutes after he'd arrived home after church Sunday. Actually *cruised* was the wrong word. *Crawled* was more like it. Monday, when he was mowing the lawn at Bayport, there he was again. He did a roll-by, with the windows down. The cop actually tapped the horn and waved—like he wanted to be sure Parker didn't miss the fact that he was there.

Every time Parker saw him, Rankin was staring his way. Maybe

Rankin thought the whole stalking technique would intimidate Parker. And honestly, it kind of did. But if the cop really had anything on Parker, he'd haul him in, right? Still, he couldn't shake the way Rankin's obvious mistrust bothered him.

But the thing that really bothered him was the way El acted ever since he'd told her about Shadow-man. Like the end of the world was coming. That was the only way Parker could describe it. She was distant. Distracted. Spent a little more time just looking out over Rockport Harbor—or doing a watercolor of one of the classic views.

Whatever was on her mind, she was keeping it to herself. How could he help her if he didn't know what was wrong? *Show me how to help, God.* He'd prayed something like that every time he thought about it.

He'd see her tonight. Somehow, he needed to get her to open up. But first he had another problem. The scuba tanks needed a fill—and that meant going to the Rockport Dive Company . . . and likely seeing Harley Lotitto.

CHAPTER 20

HARLEY SLIPPED THE BINOCULARS out from where he'd stashed them in the back room. He focused on the figure sitting on the granite breakwater that shielded the harbor from the fury of the Atlantic.

Ella.

She had her easel set up nearly all the way out at the end of the jetty—close to the base of the signal light. The canvas itself blocked most of her from view, but it was her. Barefoot, with her cowgirl boots lounging on a granite block a few feet away.

"I should be out there." And if Uncle Ray hadn't told him he needed to work until closing at six, he would be. *What would he say to her anyway?* That was always messing him up. He'd think of something this time, though—and she'd smile. He could picture it. He smiled back.

The front door opened—and the spell was broken. Seconds later Bryce Scorza stepped into the back room, football gripped at the stitching.

Harley slid the binoculars back in their case. "Hey."

Bryce glanced at the binoculars—and scanned the harbor. Grinning, he pointed the ball toward Ella. "Bird-watching, Lotitto?"

"Shut up."

Bryce grabbed the binoculars, set down the football, and homed in on the breakwater. "You're pitiful, you know that? Harley Davidson Lotitto, the star running back, is hiding in his uncle's shop—afraid to go out on the field and talk to the girl. Why don't you get off the bench?"

Right. Talking to girls came easy to Scorza.

"You almost never drop the ball on the field," Scorza said. "But with girls, man, you can't make a catch for nothing."

Harley slugged him in the arm—hard enough to know Bryce wouldn't be lying on that side when he went to bed that night.

Scorza laughed it off. "You're ridiculous. I don't know what's worse . . . you even wanting this girl for your friend, or the fact you don't do anything to get Gatorade out of the picture. You're double dumb. And while you're pacing the sidelines? Gatorade is racking up first downs."

Harley balled his fist—but Scorza was ready. He stepped back and picked up the football again. "I'm just saying, you need to do something."

The front door opened, and a customer stepped in. Harley stretched to see into the front room. "Speak of the devil. Guess who's here?"

Ever since Gatorade finished the dive class, he'd been in the shop for fill-ups nearly every week.

The ship's bell clanged from where it hung near the cash register. Uncle Ray rang it whenever he wanted Harley—even if he was only in the back room. Truth was, Harley could hear the thing even if he was out in the shed.

"Barista!" Uncle Ray loved calling him that, probably because he knew how much Harley hated it. "Need a couple of tall ones." The way he referred to fills for 80-cubic-feet air tanks. "Nitrox 32."

Gatorade and his dad always got the Nitrox mix. It definitely allowed a diver to stay deep longer without the need to decompress on the ascent. Great for multiple dives in the same day, too.

Harley squared his chest and brushed past Scorza. Sure enough, Gatorade stood there—towing a suitcase with rollers behind him. He looked like a total tourist with that thing, but it was actually a clever way to carry two tanks all the way back to his house.

Normally Harley would've taken the cylinders and brought them to the back himself. He just didn't like the idea of feeling like Gatorade's hired hand. He motioned for the outsider to follow him.

Immediately after seeing Gatorade step into the back room and unzip the suitcase, Harley regretted his choice. This was *his* home field—and Gatorade didn't belong here. Without a word, he took the tanks from Gatorade and gave them a quick inspection. Checked the neck just below the valve stem for micro-cracks. Double-checked the date of the last hydrostatic test and visual, even though he knew they were both well within specs. Harley didn't take shortcuts—which meant he'd never make a mistake that could result in the filling station becoming a for-real blast chamber.

Harley grabbed the clipboard and marked the serial numbers, tank size, pressure limit for each tank, and "Buckman" on the log sheet—although he almost wrote Gatorade. Even after only filling these tanks a handful of times before, Harley could easily pick them out of a lineup of twenty tanks—all the same size and color.

Most people would probably think it was lame, but Harley made a game out of knowing the tanks for each of his customers. It was the little things. The letters and numbers stamped right into the crown of the aluminum tank. The last three digits of the serial number. The tank manufacture date. But mostly it was the stickers. Not just tank brand-name stickers, but the personalized things the divers did to make their own tank stand out in a group. Sports team stickers. Bands. Coffee shops.

"Work like a captain, play like a pirate." Gatorade read Uncle Ray's sign above the doorway. "Looks like you do the work here."

"Got that right," Harley said. "And Uncle Ray definitely plays the pirate." Honestly? He didn't care if his uncle overheard him.

"So, Gatorade," Scorza said. "Still working for Steadman?"

"For now, unless the rentals die out completely."

"How much does he pay you?"

Gatorade hesitated just long enough for Harley to know he was weighing whether or not to give the information. Harley could have told Gatorade not to tell him anything he wouldn't want blabbed.

"Nothing. But he lets me share his slip for my skiff—and that's totally worth it. Otherwise I'd have to trailer the boat every time I wanted to ride . . . and most days my dad wouldn't be home from work early enough for me to go out at all."

"Let me get this right," Scorza said. "You work for no pay—and you think you're getting a good deal? You take stupid to a whole new level."

Gatorade's face turned red. He kept quiet, though. Probably

smart. There never seemed to be a way to win an argument with Bryce Scorza.

On the control panel of the fill station, Harley dialed in the big black regulator knob to 3,000 pounds per square inch to match the limits on Gatorade's tanks. He slid the tanks into two of the open bays in the fill station drawer. He connected the fill whips, opened the tank valves, and opened the fill station valves. He gave it all one quick recheck, and closed the bay door.

"Should be about ten minutes." He hoped Gatorade would get the hint and go back up front. But he just hung there watching Harley do his thing—like the whole filling station was fascinating. Which, of course, it was. In a way, it was kind of nice knowing the guy watching you seemed totally impressed.

Scorza, on the other hand, couldn't have looked less interested in the mechanics of the fill. He inspected the laces on his football, placing each finger carefully in its designated spot.

It was too quiet—which felt weird. "Where you diving this time, Gatorade?"

"Folly's Cove."

"With your dad?"

Gatorade nodded. "How about you, Harley. Dive much?"

What, was he looking for a new dive buddy? Dream on. Some people had to work. Besides, if God in heaven wanted people to swim underwater, He'd have given them gills, right? "I don't have much use for scuba gear."

Scorza snickered. "I'm surrounded by idiots. One works for no pay, and the other works a dive shop but doesn't dive. Great advertisement you are for your uncle's dive shop."

Gatorade looked to Scorza and back—like he wasn't sure he should believe it. "You don't like diving?"

Right now he'd seriously like to slug Scorza in the other arm. "Not unless there's nitrous oxide in the tank."

Gatorade grinned. "Laughing gas?"

Okay, the guy was smarter than he looked.

"But seriously, you don't like diving?"

"I'd rather wear cleats than fins. Big deal."

Scorza snickered again. "Harley avoids water like the Wicked Witch of the West."

Harley flashed the quarterback a glare—and there was no way Scorza didn't know *exactly* what he meant by it.

"Gatorade." Scorza made sure he had the guy's attention. "That's how Harley's dad died, you know—underwater—so don't give him a hard time about it."

Scorza talked like Harley wasn't there. And making like he was sticking up for Harley? That was an act. It was a way of putting Harley down. Reminding Harley that Scorza had something he didn't. In this case, a dad. And that wasn't the first time. Scorza was all about having more than anyone else. Harley wished he'd never told Scorza a word about how it all happened. He had no right to—

"Drunk driver slammed into him." Scorza held the football up high. "Pushed his beater right off the bridge into the water." He dropped the ball to his other hand. "Harley made it out of the car—and his dad didn't."

"Shut. Up." Dad had *pushed* him out of the car. Forced him out—even though Harley wanted to keep trying to get Dad's belt unbuckled. But it was dark and water was pouring in—and he couldn't find the stinkin' buckle. His dad was hurt bad. Blood everywhere.

"Won't do any good." Harley could still hear his dad's voice. Strong. Desperate. Yet somehow calm. "I'm pinned, Harley. My legs. I'm not getting out—but you have to. I love you, son. I'm proud of you."

Somehow Dad still had enough strength to shove Harley through the missing window before the car disappeared into the black waters.

Harley shook his head as if that could shake the memory right out of his head.

"The way Harley told me—"

"Stop." Harley would hit him. He'd do it. "One more word and you won't have enough teeth left to hold your mouth guard in place."

"What?" Scorza stepped back out of easy reach. "Gatorade would probably be afraid of water, too, if that happened to him."

Harley wasn't afraid of water—or anything—except maybe how he was going to explain why he knocked the stuffing out of the star quarterback.

"I am so sorry," Gatorade said. He actually looked like he cared. "That had to be incredibly hard. I can't imagine."

No. He couldn't. Nobody could. Especially not some scuba-diving, gator-wrestling, Ella-monopolizing outsider with a dad who was there for him all the time. A mom, too. What would he know about "hard" things?

The whole room got kind of quiet—like Gatorade didn't know what to say—and maybe Scorza knew he'd pushed things too far and didn't want to risk another slug to the arm.

"Great view from here." Gatorade looked out over the bay. "Nice spot to work."

Yeah, until Gatorade walked into the place. And Harley didn't need any more small talk right now. "Pay up front. We still have a few minutes."

Gatorade got the hint this time.

The tanks were filled and standing in a row with others by the time Gatorade stepped back into the fill room. Harley had Gatorade sign off on the log sheet, reminded him it was a Nitrox 32 fill, then pointed to the cluster of tanks. "All set for you to grab and go."

Gatorade squatted down to check which tanks were his. "You ever get mixed on whose is whose? I mean, without the BCD vest, they all pretty much look the same."

"I can recognize any tank I've filled," Harley said, "and can tell you who it belongs to." Okay, that was a little bit of a stretch. But not much.

"Really. What is it about my tank—or my dad's?"

Harley smiled. "Last two numbers on your tank serial number? Forty-two. Same as my jersey number. And both of you have Wooten's Airboat Tours stickers down by the boot. Nobody else has those."

Gatorade turned the tanks to reveal the stickers. "Nicely done." A minute later he had the tanks packed up, and he disappeared out the door.

Right now all Harley wanted to do was get out himself. Go to the shed—or maybe the breakwater. He'd be closing the store in minutes. But with Scorza hanging around, they'd probably just go to Front Beach or someplace and run pass patterns. He resisted the urge to check if Ella was still working on her painting.

"You should have seen your face when Gatorade walked in," Scorza said—like he hadn't just betrayed Harley by spilling all that information. "Absolutely green."

"You're delusional. Why would I be jealous of *him*?"

Scorza grinned—like he saw right through him. "I say we do something about the guy."

Harley casually hung the clipboard on the side of the fill station—like he wasn't taking Scorza seriously. Like Gatorade didn't really bother him.

"You and me. We run ourselves a play that will take him out."

Harley gave him the side-eye. "Take him *out*?"

"Get him to know he shouldn't stay in Rockport. Get him to convince his park ranger dad to get another transfer."

"Or at least get him to back away from Ella?" Harley immediately regretted saying it. Clearly Scorza wasn't one to trust with secrets.

"Exactly! You've wanted this for weeks—but you never do anything about it." He was at the window now. He held out the ball, pointing to the jetty. "Got your binoculars?"

Harley looked where Scorza was pointing the ball. He didn't need binoculars to see what was going on. Gatorade was on the breakwater, running from granite block to block toward Ella. He must have stashed the tanks somewhere, because the suitcase was gone.

Ella waved—no—she was motioning him over. She'd never called Harley over like that. Whenever Harley got close, everything about Ella said she wanted him to back off.

"You're never going to get her attention with him around," Scorza said. "That's the weird thing about you. You're a madman on the field. Off it? You're a total marshmallow."

Harley felt his face grow hot.

"So let's make a game out of this." Scorza acted like he didn't give all his blabbing about Harley's dad a second thought. Probably he didn't. "I'm going to work out a couple plays in my special little playbook. And by the time we're done with Gatorade?" Scorza winked in his totally cocky way. "There won't be anybody motioning him anywhere—but away."

CHAPTER 21

PARKER SLOWED AS HE NEARED ELLA. She sat on a folding camp stool, facing town. She must have been there a couple of hours before he got there, based on how the scene on the canvas was taking shape. The tip of granite rocks in the foreground. Then the harbor, with the town watching over it from behind.

"Another one to sell at the Farmer's Market?"

"That's the plan." She looked at her canvas, then surveyed the view in front of her. "They've all sold so far—which is a miracle. There's others at the market whose work is better than mine."

"Maybe you've got a fan out there."

Ella Laughed. "Not likely."

She'd picked a gorgeous view. As great as the harbor looked on the surface, Parker would love to strap on his tank and explore the bottom. To see things that many people totally miss. "I'd like to dive the harbor sometime."

Ella shook her head. "Can't see the appeal in that."

"Exploring, for one. Finding lost things. And gliding around weightless . . . the freedom of it. There's no gravity . . . it's almost like being on the moon."

"You can't breathe on the moon, Parker."

"That's why you need an air tank when you dive."

Ella rinsed her brush in a cup of water at her feet. "I have an aunt in Connecticut who drags an oxygen tank everywhere she goes. Not my idea of freedom."

Parker laughed. "Okay, I get it. You don't want to talk about diving. What would you like to talk about instead?"

"So exactly what *do* you believe about ghosts?"

"Not this again."

She didn't look away from her canvas. "You don't believe they exist?"

"The guy I saw was flesh and blood." Parker saw Shadow-man in his mind again. "He didn't pass through the door. He opened it—just like you or I would."

"Okay, forget about what you saw at Steadman's place. Just answer the question," she said. "Ghosts. Real—or not?"

The funeral for Devin had been, what, a month ago? "Tell me this isn't about Devin Catsakis." Other kids claimed to have "felt his presence" since he'd been buried. The only thing Parker had felt? His death wasn't an accident.

She shook her head. "Forget it."

"Now you're not even going to give me a chance to answer?"

Ella rinsed her brush and flicked off the excess water at Parker. "You already told me everything I need to know when you dodged the question. So let's drop it."

One thing he'd learned about Ella Houston was that when she

made up her mind, there was no sense trying to change it. She looked out over the harbor and reached for the silver cross necklace. She tucked it in her palm, closed her fingers over it, and just held it over her heart.

For an instant he thought about Wilson, still living down in the Everglades, and all his Miccosukee superstitions. Like the alligator tooth necklace he'd given Parker just before the move north. The thing was hanging over the bedpost in Parker's room. He'd said it was for luck or something. Parker wasn't a believer in luck, but sometimes he wore the thing just to feel a connection to a friend who'd always had his back.

"Something's going on in Rockport," Ella said—but more like she was talking to the canvas than to Parker.

"There's always something going on." Parker grinned. "Farmer's markets. Craft fairs. All the kinds of stuff that I avoid. That's why tourists like it here so much."

"You know what I mean." Her eyes got wide and her voice dropped to a whisper. "I'm being serious here."

Parker had learned not to tease El about her crazy superstitions—most of the time. "Is this about that thing you were talking about earlier but you couldn't tell me?"

"Something is going on with this Shadow-man thing—and it's bigger than you know. But what if Shadow-man is really a spirit-being?"

An icy flash zinged up his back and down his arms. "A ghost?"

"Just don't be so quick to rule it out, okay? Ghost or no ghost, this much I do know." She looked across the narrow harbor inlet channel separating them from the rocky outcroppings of the Headlands. "If something doesn't change—really soon—I'm going to lose the place I love more than anyplace in the world."

Suddenly some pieces of their other conversation dropped into place. "Wait, I know you haven't had renters in a while. How bad is it . . . I mean, are you and your Grams going to be okay?"

If she heard him, she didn't act like it.

"So." Ella turned and looked directly at him. "Ghosts?"

Hey, he was going to be honest. "No such thing." But he did believe in demons—which was exponentially worse. Probably not what she'd want to hear.

She looked at him for a long moment. "Well, that's your opinion." She rinsed her brush again. "But you're still kind of new here."

"New?" Honestly, if one more person hit him with that newbie thing he was going to—

"Your family has been here what, seven months?"

"Eight," Parker said. "Since last October—and don't tell me you didn't know that."

She gave a little one-shouldered shrug. "All I'm saying is that you haven't lived here long enough to know if something feels"—she stroked the air with her brush—"different. You're like a baby."

Parker smacked his forehead with the heel of his hand. "So *that's* why I've been sucking my thumb at night."

"You can be annoying, you know that?" Ella stared toward the heart of town just past the harbor, "Seriously, though. Shadowman at Bayport wasn't the only otherworldly thing that's happened. Strange things have been going on—especially since the funeral."

So this *was* about Devin. "Define *strange*." The last year of Parker's life—everything that led up to his park ranger dad getting transferred out of the Glades could be summed up with the word "strange."

Ella stood and brushed off her dress. Slid her bare feet into her cowgirl boots. "I forgot. You don't believe. And I've got to head back." She collapsed her easel and stool and tucked them inside a duffle.

Was she baiting him? "El, come on. What kind of strange things?"

Ella emptied the water container and packed her brushes away. "You don't believe in ghosts—so what's the point of talking about it?"

Oh, yeah. She was definitely baiting him.

Without another word, she handed Parker her bag with the watercolor gear. She picked her way across the massive rocks toward the paved turnaround of Bearskin Neck where he'd left the luggage with the two tanks inside.

Parker fell in step beside her, long-stepping from rock to rock. "You *want* to tell me. You know you do. So what's this all about?"

"The day you admit that ghosts could be real," she said, "is the day I'll tell you everything."

Which meant, like, never. "I told you, I don't—"

Ella put a finger to her lips. "I heard you the first time. You don't believe."

Right. But that didn't mean Parker wasn't up for a good ghost story. "Just tell me what's going on."

"So you can discount what I believe?" She shook her head. "I don't think so."

"Look," Parker said. "I'll listen—and I promise not to downplay or criticize or make fun of anything you tell me."

She skirted around the north side of the turnaround at the end of Bearskin Neck, keeping to the rocks just above the waterline.

She was taking the long way back. That meant deep down she was hoping to talk, right?

He eyed the piece of luggage—right where he'd parked it. And nobody was likely to bother it there until he got back. People would think a tourist left it so they could climb down closer to the water for pictures. He'd hustle back for it later—but right now he needed to find out what El was talking about. Especially that earlier bit about losing the place she loved most. She had to be talking about her and her grandma's place. Were they thinking of moving?

The tide was creeping in—and along with it a wall of fog that silently moved shoreward from the sea. Parker slowed his pace to match hers. "So, you going to tell me or what?"

Ella stopped and scanned the shoreline north of Bearskin Neck. Parker wasn't sure if she was looking at Front Beach—or at the old graveyard on the hill directly behind it.

"At first I passed it off as random weirdness," Ella said. "But now I know better."

He fought the urge to interrupt. Sometimes *not* asking a question was the way to learn more.

"It's not just Steadman's place. And those other rentals in town that have been hit. Bad things have been happening at our rental home."

The small, barn-shaped building on the south end of their lot. Back in the day when a for-real sea captain owned the place, that had been his sail-making shop. It had been nothing more than a great storage garage for all those years until El's grandma turned it into a rental cottage that made even Steadman's rentals seem drab.

"Three times in the last month." Suddenly she clammed

up—and just by the look on her face Parker figured she'd already said more than she wanted to.

"What happened?"

She gave him a long look, like she was making a decision of whether or not to trust him. "Things I can't explain any other way—other than to say something paranormal is going on. Patio chairs and table upside down in the morning—more times than I can count. Three different renters were terrified by some "presence" in their room. No, they didn't see the green light, but everything else they described? It was Shadow-man. Grams said I can't say more right now . . . but it's bad."

Again, that zing up his back and down his arms. But there was always an explanation, wasn't there? Even for Shadow-man. "Ever watch Scooby-Doo as a kid?" He wouldn't trade the hours he'd spent watching those episodes with his grandpa for anything.

She gave him a sideways glance. "Don't you dare compare what's going on here with that mindless cartoon."

"Mindless?" Parker shook his head. "Hey, they were solving mysteries—you had to use your brain when you watched that show."

"Yeah, about this much of my brain." Ella held up her thumb and forefinger with barely enough space to squeeze a paintbrush between them. "And even that was overkill. What's going on here has nothing to do with some stupid old TV show."

Obviously she didn't *get* the show, so there was absolutely no sense arguing with her. "All I'm saying, is that sometimes what *looks* supernatural—or paranormal—is just an illusion. There's usually a reasonable explanation."

"Yeah," Ella said. "Like ghosts."

As if there were no other way to account for what was going on.

"I gotta go. Grams is still kind of rattled. I need to be back before dark." She took the duffle of watercolor supplies from Parker. "And I'm guessing you're going to stay right here and call Jelly. It's about that time."

But first he'd hustle back and retrieve the tanks. "Tell me more about the strange things going on—and maybe I can come up with a different theory."

Ella started toward Front Beach again. "Other than ghosts?"

Parker shrugged. "I told you. I don't believe in ghosts."

Ella walked backward for a moment. "Stick around here long enough . . . and you will."

CHAPTER 22

BUGS. SNAKES. GATORS. Humidity that sucked the sweat—and the life—right out of him. Those were all on the highlights reel for the Everglades. The place gave him an overall bad feeling in the creepiest kind of way. The Glades was a place of death—and when Dad got the transfer to the Boston area, Parker was totally on board with the move. When he thought back to his life there, he missed some of his adventures with Wilson, for sure. But even all these months later he honestly couldn't think of a single thing he truly missed about Everglades City.

Just a single some*one*.

Angelica Malnatti. *Jelly*. A park ranger's kid just like Parker. Their dads were best friends—and had somehow managed to finagle things to work at the same National Parks at the same time since before Parker and Angelica were born. Until this move, that is. Parker had called him Uncle Sammy for as long as he could remember, even though they weren't blood relatives. After Dad got the transfer to the Boston area, Jelly's dad turned in his paperwork for the same. At first, it sounded like Uncle Sammy would get the transfer quickly. Jelly wanted out of Everglades City as much as he had. But the months dragged by—and still no moving truck.

Something was different about Jelly lately. He'd noticed it on the last couple of calls, but then second-guessed himself on it. It seemed that the more he adjusted to life in Rockport, the more desperate Jelly seemed to get out of Everglades City. She asked a million questions about El. Even asked Parker to send a picture—which he never did. How weird would it be to take a picture of El—to send to Jelly?

He'd have never guessed Jelly and her dad wouldn't be living here by this time. Who knew what her sister, Maria, was doing. Parker never asked Jelly about Maria—and thankfully, he didn't really care. Not like he used to.

Parker went back for the luggage with the tanks, rolled it down Bearskin Neck, and dragged it onto Front Beach. He sat on the rocks with a killer view of Sandy Bay and propped his phone on a nearby boulder to give Jelly more of the full effect of the spot.

She answered on the first ring.

"Parker!"

He could hear the smile in her voice—even before he saw her face on the screen.

She wore his Wooten's Airboat Tours cap—like she did for every phone call. "Guess where I am," she said.

It was a little game they'd played every week. He usually called from a different spot as a way of letting her explore Rockport and the surrounding area before she even moved into town. And somehow Jelly never managed to be at the same place twice in a row herself. Even though he couldn't see much of the background, it wasn't hard to figure out where she was today. "The Marina. On Chokoloskee." The sun had already dipped below the horizon and the sky was ablaze with orange.

"Oooh," she said. "Very good. But *where* at the Marina?" She swept the phone in a quick arc like she was giving him a hint.

"On the dock." Where Clayton Kingman had threatened him. Oh yeah, Parker knew the spot. He hoped the sicko never got out of jail.

"And I'm sitting," Jelly said, "right at the end."

Sitting? "Show me your feet."

Jelly trained the lens at the water—with her feet dangling just below the surface.

Parker's heart slammed into high gear—and instinct kicked in. He looked for bubbles. Approaching ripples. The terrifying black snout of an alligator. "Sheesh, Jelly. Get your feet out of the water."

Instead she swished them back and forth, creating just the kind of disturbance that would attract gators. Of course she wasn't about to listen to him. And if he said any more, she'd get just what she was likely fishing for: proof that he still worried about her.

He wasn't going to give her the satisfaction of taking the bait. "I'm at Front Beach—looking over Sandy Bay. Behind me is the Captain's Bounty on the Beach motel and the Old First Parish Burying Ground."

"All I see are rocks," Jelly said.

Which was one of the best things about the coastline here. Massive rocks, power-eroded from tides and squalls that gave the shoreline a beating. The rocks appeared smooth from a distance—but if you took a tumble on them? The coarse surface would peel away your skin faster than fifty-grain sandpaper on a belt sander.

"What's with the suitcase? Are you thinking of moving back down here," Jelly pointed at the screen, "or are you running away from home?"

"Hilarious. I got the tanks filled. It's easier to roll them home this way. Any word on a transfer?"

Jelly smiled. "Soon."

But she didn't say it like she believed it anymore.

"You've been saying that for months."

Jelly moved her head from one side of the screen to the other—like she was trying to see past Parker. "Ella there with you?"

Her question sounded innocent enough—but Parker wasn't that stupid. He shook his head.

"That's a shame," Jelly said. "I just thought I'd say hi."

Drop dead was more likely what she wanted to say. Jelly was careful enough not to show her colors, but Parker wasn't exactly color-blind either. "You two will really like each other. I know it."

"Why wouldn't I? Did you see her today?"

Here we go. "Actually, she just left."

"Really." The camera was on her feet again. "Too bad I missed her."

"Too bad you're going to be missing a foot soon," Parker said. "Are you going to get your feet out of the water or what?"

Jelly reversed the camera—and smiled. "What did you and Ella talk about?"

"I thought this call was for you and *I* to catch up," Parker said.

"That's exactly what I'm doing," Jelly said. "So what did you two talk about today?"

The thing of it was, he'd already sent Jelly a picture of the knife from his grandpa. Texted her about the note—and how things were at a complete standstill as far as anything new about Devin Catsakis. The only things he hadn't told her about were the things he and El had talked about. Like the strange things going on at their place. He gave Jelly the whole rundown—including the weird questions about ghosts.

"She's right about Scooby-Doo," Jelly said.

"Don't even start."

Jelly laughed in that musical way she did that made everything in the world seem right. Talked to him about how often things seem worse than they are. The kind of fluff-talk that makes you fool yourself into believing maybe everything will be okay.

"So does Ella dive?"

Back to El again? "Nope."

"Perfect. I was thinking of taking a class when we move up. Maybe we can take one together. Then Ella and I could be dive buddies."

What's with the obsession with Ella? "She likes to *paint* water—not swim in it. You can dive with me—unless you lose your legs to a gator first."

She whirled the camera down to show her feet tucked under her on the dock. "See? Crisscross applesauce. Way ahead of you. Like usual."

"Terrific. And do me a favor. Don't let Wilson talk you into any adventures out in the wilds, okay? Just stay away from the Glades."

"Deal . . . cross my heart. And you stay away from—" Jelly stopped abruptly and smiled.

"Stay away from *what*?"

"Actually," Jelly said, "it was more of a *who*."

He had her cornered. Now he'd finally get her to admit she was jealous of El. "And *who* should I stay away from?"

She laughed again. "Ghosts."

CHAPTER 23

THE ROCKPORT DIVE COMPANY closed at six on weekdays. Now that summer was here, Uncle Ray had Harley working the shop from open to close—but kept his pay at five bucks an hour. There had to be a law against that.

"Gotta earn your keep, boy." Those were his uncle's exact words. And what did that even mean? Harley bought most of his own food. Loaves of bread and peanut butter for lunch and dinner. Cereal and milk for breakfast. Not that Uncle Ray didn't offer him mac and cheese when he felt like cooking, but Harley never took it. It was bad enough his uncle said Harley "owed" him for the room he slept in. He didn't want to feel he owed him for food, too.

Uncle Ray flipped the *Open* sign on the door window to the other side where he'd handwritten *Gone Diving*. The only place

Uncle Ray would be diving tonight? Into a bottle with his drinking buddies in Gloucester. Lately he'd been going out almost every night. He never said where, but he definitely came back smelling like a bar. Friday was Uncle Ray's official "party night" as he called it—and that meant he'd be so drunk he'd have to climb the stairs on all fours.

Uncle Ray grabbed the whiteboard he kept propped in the front window. Erased the last dumb thing he'd written, and pulled out a marker. *RAY'S RULES OF DIVING: THINK like a fish. DRINK like a fish.* Uncle Ray read his new slogan aloud and grinned. "I think I'll put this on some T-shirts. What d'ya think?"

He never waited for an answer, but set it back up in the display window. "Yeah, I think I'll do that."

Harley straightened the Rockport Dive Company T-shirts on the merchandise racks and grabbed a broom to sweep up. Uncle Ray popped open the register and pulled out all the cash. He peeled off two Jacksons and dropped them on the counter for Harley. The rest he stacked into a bundle, folded it in half, and stuffed it in his jeans pocket. "For party night." He motioned his chin toward the door. "Lock her up after I go."

Like Harley always did. He pocketed the twenties.

The bundle of cash bulged in Uncle's pocket, and he slipped out the door without a goodbye or a look back. The guy robbed his own store—then went to the bar and got robbed himself. He probably wouldn't have a dollar in his pocket by the time he staggered home.

Twenty minutes later Harley had the counters wiped, floor mopped, and the dry-erase marker in his hand. He picked up Uncle Ray's new sign . . . *THINK Like a Fish. DRINK Like a Fish.* He added one line: *STINK Like a Fish.* He put the sign exactly back where he'd found it. "Put *that* on a T-shirt, Uncle Ray." How long would it take for Uncle Ray to notice? Harley hoped he'd be around to see his reaction.

Harley locked the front door and slipped out the back. He picked his way around lobster traps to the shed—or the Hangar, as he'd started calling it. And Hangar was the right word. Inside were the set of wings that would fly him out of here someday . . . away from Uncle Ray.

The Hangar was bigger—and way nicer inside—than it looked from the outside. Harley was careful not to go in the shed when Uncle Ray was around. The last thing Harley needed was for his uncle to remember what was in there—and how much cash it would bring if he sold it.

The double-door entrance to the shed was wide enough to roll Kemosabe in and out easily—especially with the small ramp he'd built. He took a careful look over both shoulders before fishing the key from around his neck. He opened the padlock and let both it and the chain thud to the ground.

He liked the sound of walking across the wood plank floor inside the shed. Like he was on the boardwalk of some western town. Harley closed the shed doors and slid the 2×4 crossbeam in place to secure them—locking himself inside. It reminded him of something pioneers would do to their log cabin doors to protect their families from wild animals or war parties. A red light glowed from the switch on the power strip. He toggled it on, and the Hangar came to life with an incredibly bright shop light suspended from the shed rafters. The light drove out every shadow in the shed and made working on the bike a dream. His dad would have loved that light.

The inside walls had several scavenged road signs hanging

throughout. ONE WAY. DEAD END. NO PASSING. WRONG WAY. DETOUR. SPEED LIMIT 70. In the spaces between metal signs he'd hung watercolor paintings and old license plates. Cars mostly. Some motorcycle tags. But all of them from states he'd been to with his dad—or hoped to ride to someday on his own.

The shed had only one window, and he'd coated the inside of the glass with white spray paint. He didn't want anyone peeking in to see the bike or tools stored there. Still, he'd wanted a view. He'd solved that problem by secretly sending someone in to buy Ella's watercolors at the Farmer's Market. Every place he hung a painting was its own kind of window.

He'd made a table out of an upended lobster trap, and a five-gallon pail made a pretty decent chair. Cereal boxes were lined up on the mini-fridge sitting in the far corner. He'd picked the thing up at the curb on garbage day nearly a year ago—and the thing still worked. It kept the chocolate milk cold for his cereal. Harley made two quick PB sandwiches.

His dad's thirty-six-inch, seven-drawer tool cabinet sat at the far end of the shed. Uncle Ray had tried to get his mitts on it. To sell, of course. But the tools went with the bike—and Harley pushed back. If it wasn't for the lawyer who worked out the whole custody thing, Harley would have lost the tools *and* the bike. Dad had bought the tools so they could work on Kemosabe together—and nobody was going to take them away from Harley. He'd kept them locked tight in a storage container until the Hangar was ready.

Harley grabbed a screwdriver from the drawer, removed the screw from the bottom corner of the NO PASSING sign, and slid it to one side. He'd made hidden shelves between the studs behind the sign—which fit a couple of plastic food storage containers perfectly. One held the extra set of keys for Kemosabe—and the title—along with other treasures from his dad. The other was the cash stash.

He took the twenties out of his pocket and tucked them away inside—and screwed the sign back in place. Money he'd hidden in his room early on had a way of disappearing, so now everything with value went to the Hangar. If his uncle had any idea how much money was squirreled away in this shed, he'd tear it apart board by board until he found it. Uncle Ray was still trying to get at the money from Dad's life insurance policy. The lawyer said it was locked up tight in a trust. Harley hoped so, because locks didn't mean much to his uncle.

Kemosabe sat in the middle of the Hangar, under the softest blanket Harley could find at the thrift store. Even hidden under that covering, the strength of the bike showed. Like it was hunkered down in its own set position, ready to fire off the line of scrimmage.

Harley lifted the blanket corner, then pulled it back far enough to expose the drag bars Dad had bought to replace the straight handlebars. They'd swapped out the original banana seat with a Badlander. Thinner—but still comfortable. The original gas tank was way too boxy. Dad picked up a stretch tank that followed the shape of the motor. The thing had dual chrome gas caps. Dad had it custom painted—with the name *Kemosabe* added below the Harley logo.

They'd pulled off the stock air cleaner and replaced it with a side-draft model. Sold the front wheel and bought an eighty-spoke wheel instead. It was a nightmare to keep clean, but it totally changed the look of the bike.

Together they'd put a bobtail fender above the rear wheel, and chopped and shaped the front fender to about a third of the size of the original.

Except for the name Kemosabe in deep red, every painted part on the bike was black. The rest was chrome.

The best part about Kemosabe was the exhaust. Dad had said the last thing a guy wants to do is ride a Harley with a stock exhaust. They ended up outfitting it with one-and-three-quarter-inch straight pipes. No muffler. No baffles. Nothing to slow—or quiet—the bike down.

When Kemosabe was finished, and they took it on rides, other bikers noticed the chromed plates that filled in gaps between the motor and other parts on the bike. They'd ask Dad where they could buy them for their bike. "You can't," Dad had said. And he was right. Together they'd picked up mild steel at the hardware store. They'd cut, ground, filed, and chromed plate after plate to give Kemosabe a streamlined look like no other bike on the road.

Kemosabe wasn't flashy in a foo-foo way . . . but the thing would turn heads.

Harley wolfed down the last bite and brushed the crumbs off his palms. He opened the shed doors wide and swung one leg over Kemosabe like he was mounting a horse. He wrapped his hands around the grips and checked the clock. He still had plenty of time to fire it up and get it covered again before Scorza showed up.

He reached for the second key around his neck and slid it into the ignition. Kemosabe fired up immediately, like it had been waiting all week for this. Another benefit of nights when Uncle Ray was gone. The last thing Harley wanted was to remind his uncle that the motorcycle even existed. His uncle had sold off everything else his dad owned—including Dad's Dyna Wide Glide. Uncle

Ray kept every dime. Said it was to pay the rent for the piece of ground the Hangar stood on.

It didn't take any imagination at all to picture Kemosabe begging him to back it out of the shed and take a quick run to the end of the harbor and back.

"Soon enough, Kemosabe. Soon enough." He revved the engine. The deep rumble was just about the best sound on earth. The vibrations traveled through his entire body as if showing off its power. And in a way, the thing infused Harley with a strength that made him feel totally invincible. Like his body was a human battering ram. Like he could punch a hole between any guard and tackle and sprint for the end zone.

For a moment he pictured cruising through Rockport. Taking 127A along the coast toward Gloucester. Ella would be riding with him. Holding on for dear life. They'd stop at the Long Beach Dairy Maid. Harley would get a lemon soft serve. What would Ella get? He had no idea, but she'd laugh and smile the way she did when she was with Gatorade.

"Hey, hotshot." Scorza's voice boomed over the music of the engine. He wore a dark hoodie over his jersey, but the game ball was still tucked under one arm. "When are you going to let me take this for a ride?"

Harley cut the motor. *Cold day in hell.*

"What did you name this thing? Kim-something?"

Actually, his dad had named it. "Pronounced Key-moe-sob-ee. It means—"

"It means you're an idiot for giving a nice bike such a lame name. We should rename it. Something in English."

A really cold day in hell. "You're early."

"Yeah, well we've got lots to do." He flashed a wicked smile. "I've worked out a couple of plays to deal with Gatorade. Tonight."

Harley covered the bike. "That was fast."

"I'm a genius." Scorza shrugged. "What can I say? And it doesn't hurt that my favorite little auntie is the dispatcher at Rockport PD."

A fact Harley was well aware of. "But what does that have to do—"

"The burglaries," Scorza said. "There've been a lot of them. And there's a cop who's been hounding Gatorade about the break-in at Steadman's rental. The cop thinks Gatorade is behind it. So we're going to turn the place upside down. One of them, anyway. Who do you think the police will hassle first?"

There was more to winning a football game than which team had the stronger players—or how many passes they completed. It was about keeping the other team guessing—and one step behind. When they expected the run, Scorza would pass the ball. When they guessed he'd pass, he'd hand it off to Harley for a first down. Harley had to admit, Scorza's plan made sense. Nobody would guess what they were going to do tonight. But if Gatorade had been questioned before—and about the Catsakis drowning too—sooner or later the cops would think he had to be involved more than he was admitting, right? "Brilliant."

Scorza gave a slight bow. "By the time we're done with Gatorade, I predict Ella will have a tough time hanging out with him—unless she's visiting him in juvie."

CHAPTER 24

Tuesday, June 7, 9:30 p.m.

PARKER COASTED DOWN BEACH STREET, his bike picking up speed with the steep pitch of the road. The sea air was cooler here, and he was glad he'd taken the time to throw on his hoodie. He hadn't told his mom where he was headed, but he was pretty sure she knew. He just had to do a drive-by past Bayport to make sure everything looked okay. It was pretty much becoming a nightly routine since he'd seen Shadow-man there. And every night he didn't see a green glow coming from inside, he felt just a tiny bit more like maybe things would get back to normal.

What would Ella say if she saw him biking past the Old First Parish Burying Ground . . . after dark? He smiled. She'd probably whip off one of her cowgirl boots and throw it at him.

Bayport sat silent in the dark. Like it was waiting for the guests to arrive. But there were no guests coming this week. Actually, bookings for rental homes in Rockport had dropped to an all-time low—and cancellations were up. All due to properties Shadow-man had hit—and the bad online reviews that followed. That's what Mom had said, anyway. She was doing an article on the situation.

And El was in trouble. But it couldn't be as bad as them losing their place, right? The way Parker saw it, the more he could do to figure out who was behind the Shadow-man thing, the better off everyone would be.

He dropped his bike on the front lawn and walked around the side of the house to the back door. A security light blinked on from the eaves of the house next door. That was new.

Parker shielded his eyes and squinted up at it. The drapes of the window below the new light moved slightly, like someone was watching. Likely all the neighbors were on edge. Who could blame them? He doubled his pace back to the shadows and around the corner to the back door. The quicker he got out of here, the better.

No sooner had he reached the cover of darkness than he wanted to get back in the light. It creeped him out, standing at the base of the stairs where he'd seen Shadow-man just days earlier.

He crept up the back stairway, stood at the back door, and listened. No noise from inside. No green glow. He gripped the doorknob. Tested the lock. All good.

Now get out of here. As much as he wanted to head for the light, he swung around the other side of the house, staying with the shadows . . . checking the windows as he went. Minutes later he wheeled through town and up Atlantic Avenue toward El's. It was a little late to stop by, but they'd still be up.

He spotted her on the porch, even from halfway down the block. Thick sweater. Oversized—like maybe it was her Grams's.

Hands on the rail, she leaned out over the edge like she wanted to be closer to the ocean. He coasted onto her driveway and dumped his bike.

"El."

She turned away from him for a moment and wiped her cheeks before looking his way. She flashed a smile, but it didn't reach her eyes.

"What's wrong?"

She stroked the railing. "It's about our home. Beulah."

It seemed everyone had a name for their home. He bounded up the steps and stood beside her. "What's going on?"

"I asked Grams if I could tell you more than I already did—and she agreed. But you have to promise not to mention this—to anyone."

Parker raised one hand. "I promise."

She looked at him with sad eyes, then stared out into the darkness again. For the longest time she didn't say a thing. "It's worse than I thought. Way worse. We're losing the place. We're losing Beulah."

No. "You *can't* lose this place." It was one of the nicest homes around—his mom had said something like that, hadn't she? And with a rental home on the property, the thing was a gold mine.

"My grandpa and Grams worked so hard to get it. Fix it up. To keep it." Ella wiped at her tears again—and the story gushed out. How Grams had wanted to make sure El got a college education. How the rental they had now was nothing more than an oversized garage up until a year ago. How a local contractor had talked her into converting it to a cozy two-bedroom rental. They'd added a kitchen and bathroom, run all new electric. Basically the works.

The renovation had barely started when Grams needed

unexpected hip surgery, which kept her from working. She'd used some of the loan for medical bills—and the property tax payment. The contractor put a lien against their home for the final payment he never got. They'd missed every one of the loan payments, and the bank threatened foreclosure. When the rental home started bringing in money in April, the banker gave them a thirty-day extension before foreclosing—with Grams promising they wouldn't miss another loan payment.

"We put all our hopes on the rental, but the burglaries have killed that. We haven't made a single payment. I think the bank started the foreclosure process for real this time—and it's getting close, but Grams won't say. I think she's just hoping things work out somehow and this all goes away."

Unless there was some massive change, the only thing going away was their name on the mailbox. "It's like a perfect storm."

"More like a perfect mess. Grams never had a lawyer look over the loan papers. Turns out there's some little nasties in there that make things even worse."

Parker groaned.

"Devin's story got a ton of publicity. And none of it was good for the rental business." She shook her head like she wanted to rid her mind of it all.

Mom had written at least one article about Devin Catsakis's tragic death. Had that made it harder on Ella and her Grams?

Of course it did. It had to.

"Rockport visitors want a beautiful getaway. The perfect little community. Neat little houses as old as the granite quarries. White picket fences." She talked faster and faster—the words gushing out of her. "Hydrangeas—and flower boxes that burst with color and life."

The fence, the flowers . . . Beulah had it all.

"Tourists want the quant little fishing village. They want the craft fairs and farmer's markets and the deliciously schizophrenic collection of shops down Bearskin Neck."

She stopped to take a breath and swallow.

"And none of them—not one—is looking for a place where some unspeakable evil is present. Stalking in the darkness. You may not believe something paranormal is going on—and that Devin's death was unrelated to the burglaries. But some visitors—most visitors—just aren't willing to take that chance. I'm telling you, Parker, when Devin died . . . the ripple effect of that went far and wide."

"Rings of death." Grams stood behind them. Parker hadn't even heard her step out onto the porch. "And they aren't done killing. It looks like my hopes and dreams for my sweet Ella Mae are facing the Grim Reaper as well."

Parker had no idea what to say. It felt like he shouldn't be here. Like he shouldn't have heard that. But he didn't want to go, either.

Grams pulled a rocker closer and sat heavily. "Should have never taken that loan. But rentals had been strong in town for years—so I signed the papers on the bloodline. And the payments were high. So high. We needed the rentals to make it work. Every one of them."

"And we were booked, Grams," Ella said. "Nobody could have known this would happen. It was totally unexpected."

Grams shook her head. "I didn't live this long—or have the fine honor of living in this home with the man I loved for so many years—by expecting everything to go according to my plans. Together, my man and I, we always expected the unexpected. Prepared for it. We never borrowed. Never bought what we didn't have the money to pay for. I let my Gabriel down when I took that loan. Ella Mae too. And this is what comes from it."

Ella rushed over, sat on her Grams's lap, and hugged her like she probably did when she was a little girl. "We'll figure out something, Grams. I promise."

Grams shook her head. "Be careful about making promises you can't deliver, girl. That's the mistake I made that got us into this nightmare."

"The story my mom wrote." Parker had to ask the question. "Did that hurt you?"

"Of course not," Grams said. "It was just one more thing—and when you added them all together it was enough to spook the renters. The thing that did us in was the reviews."

"Our renters . . . the ones who experienced Shadow-man," Ella said. "The week before Devin's funeral, and twice since."

Parker leaned back against the railing, like he needed to brace himself. "Did you actually see him?"

Ella shook her head. "But the renters sleeping in the house when he appeared? They saw him—just like you and Devin described. Big. Black. No face."

As bad as seeing Shadow-man was, Parker had been on the other side of a granite wall. He didn't want to imagine what it would be like being trapped in the same room with Shadow-man. "Was anyone hurt?"

"No, thank the good Lord Almighty," Grams said. "But Shadow-man scared the living daylights out of them. I begged them to take a refund and not give a bad review. One agreed—"

"But the other two?" Ella stood, fire in her eyes. "They blasted us good. Like it was our fault."

"This rental home was our ticket to make Gabriel's and my

dreams for our sweet Ella-girl come true. But we haven't had anything but cancellations since those reviews," Grams said. "We took a shot below the waterline . . . and we can't bail fast enough."

Ella wrapped her sweater around her tighter. "That's why we never reported all this to the police. We were afraid it would make other renters shy away. But we lost the bookings anyway."

How many other homes might have been hit—and the police were clueless? "Can I talk to my parents about this? Maybe they'll have some ideas."

Grams's eyes widened just a bit. "We can't have another newspaper story making things worse."

So the earlier article *had* made things harder for them. *Terrific.* "I promise—they won't say anything if I ask them not to. And what about other rental home owners—like Mr. Steadman? Right now you need reinforcements."

Grams thought about it for a moment. "You do what you want, Parker. I don't see how any of that can help us now. But as long as there's no reporting of this to the police—or anyone else official—I don't see how it could make things worse, either."

Parker's head was already spinning. He had to do something. They couldn't lose this place—*and they wouldn't, right?* "I'll work on it. We'll figure something out. I promise."

"Oh, Parker." Grams gave a half-smile. "Like I told Ella Mae . . . don't promise what you can't deliver."

CHAPTER 25

ELLA HUGGED GRAMS while both of them watched Parker hustle toward his house.

"He's pressing his hands against our wounds, trying to stop the bleeding," Grams said. "I appreciate the efforts, yet I worry for him. He's got a good heart, but . . ."

He was the most decent guy Ella had ever known. Parker once said that the day he moved to Rockport was one of the best days of his whole year. Turns out it was every bit of that for Ella, too. And more. She'd needed a friend more than she knew. "But *what*, Grams?"

Grams shuddered for just an instant under her shawl. "I have a bad feeling about this. Something evil is on the prowl, and I don't want that young man devoured."

CHAPTER 26

Tuesday, June 7, 10:05 p.m.

HARLEY CROUCHED ALONGSIDE SCORZA behind a granite stone wall and scoped out the rental house where Gatorade claimed to have seen the burglar.

"Gloves on," Scorza said.

Harley was way ahead of him.

"We go in the back door. Flip things over—but quiet like—and go right back out." Scorza poked his head above the wall. "When we leave, we split up . . . take different routes . . . and meet behind the dive shop."

Harley couldn't help but grin. "Sounds like the QB is still calling the plays."

"And don't you forget it." Scorza pulled up his hood. "Quarterback sneak. On three."

The count was still rolling in Harley's head when Scorza tucked the football to his ribs and side-vaulted the stone property marker. Harley was only an instant behind him—and pulled up even before Scorza hit the stairs.

Scorza tried the lock. What, did he think the thing would be left open for them? "Hand off." Harley motioned for the ball.

Scorza made the transfer without a question.

Harley grabbed the football with both hands and jabbed the windowpane with the tip of the ball. The glass shattered onto the floor inside. He reached through the opening, found the latch, and an instant later they tiptoed across shards of broken glass.

"That worked." Scorza clapped him on the back. "Let's tear this place apart in sixty seconds." Scorza disappeared into the other room.

Harley set the kitchen table on its side. Nice and easy so as not to make noise—and honestly, he didn't want to wreck anything. Six chairs followed. He spread all the pots and pans on the floor from the cabinet under the stove before joining Scorza.

The QB had the couch upside down and the lamps on the floor. Clearly he had this room under control—and looked like he was having a good time doing it.

Harley slipped into the bedroom. There was just enough light coming through the windows to do what he needed to do.

Scorza had the bathroom roughed up by the time Harley finished the bedroom.

"No more time on the clock," Scorza said. "Let's move."

They hesitated at the back door for a moment—making sure there were no defenders on the field. "I'll go right," Scorza said, "you go left."

Harley handed him back the football. "I'll be waiting for you when you get there."

Scorza grinned. “Not if I get there first.” He bolted down the stairs.

Harley pulled the door closed, raised his hood, and cut around the side of the house. Instantly a light came on from the neighbor’s place—like it was on a motion-detecting sensor, or somebody in the house suspected something and flipped it on.

He sprinted for the shadows—and kept going. If someone spotted him running like that, they’d call the police for sure. Which was okay. Nothing like the thought of someone on your heels to make you run faster. “Good luck beating me, Scorza.”

CHAPTER 27

Tuesday, June 8, 10:20 p.m.

"WE GOTTA DO SOMETHING." Parker sat at the kitchen table with his mom and dad after explaining El's situation.

"I like your idea of getting Mr. Steadman involved," Mom said.

"I've already texted him to see if he'll meet tomorrow night," Parker said, "and he's in."

"Your dad and I will be there, too."

Parker wasn't sure what any of them could do, but it had to be better than El and her Grams facing this on their own.

The doorbell rang—and for an instant they just stared at each other. It was nearly 10:30.

Dad stood and hustled to answer it. "Who'd be stopping by at this hour?"

Exactly Parker's thought. He trotted after his dad. His heart did a face-plant when Dad opened the door.

"Officer Rankin?"

"Saw the lights on." The cop was talking to Dad, but watching Parker—and not in a friendly way. "I hope this is okay."

Parker took a step back. *What did he do wrong now?*

Rankin didn't waste any time. "Parker, did you stop by Steadman's rental tonight?"

He could feel his stomach tightening. "Yeah, at his Bayport rental. I just checked the locks."

"Something Mr. Steadman asked you to do?"

"No, I just—"

"Did you go inside?"

"What? No—"

"What time did you stop by—and how long were you there?" The guy asked the questions like he was a robot or something. Didn't raise his voice. Didn't smile. Didn't show any bit of emotion.

Dad raised one hand. "Slow down, Officer. What's going on here?"

Mom stepped up behind Parker and laid her hand on his shoulder.

Rankin kept his eyes on Parker and explained everything. How the house had been turned upside down. How the neighbor ID'd Parker on his way in. How she'd seen him leave sometime later—at least a half hour.

"I wasn't there more than thirty seconds," Parker said. "I checked the lock—and left. And there's no way she saw me leave. I saw the neighbor's new security light come on, and a curtain moved, so I wondered if someone had seen me. But I went around the other side of the house to check the windows and then left."

Rankin flipped a page in his pocket spiral. "The neighbor says different." The officer said it like he was just repeating what he'd heard. Like he had no personal opinion on the thing. But what he was really thinking was pretty obvious, wasn't it?

"Then it had to be someone else."

"Officer," Dad said, "this neighbor. You said she ID'd him on the way out? But you heard my son. He went around the house the other way. So it had to be someone else she saw."

Rankin studied his notebook again. "I'll ask again. But I showed her your picture. Can you describe what you were wearing?"

Parker pointed at his jeans. "And a black hoodie."

One of Rankin's eyebrows raised slightly. "Hood up—or down?"

Parker didn't have to think hard about that. "Hood down. I wanted to make sure I could hear good—and had my full field of vision."

Rankin tapped his pen on the notebook. "Because you were on the lookout for Mr. Steadman?"

"No, no." What was it with this guy? "It was Shadow-man I was worried about."

"Right." Rankin nodded in a totally exaggerated way. "The mystery guy with the green light."

"When you left the place thirty minutes later . . . hood up or down?"

Parker looked at his dad, then back at Rankin. "I told you, I was gone in thirty *seconds*. Around the other side of the house. And my hood was down the whole time—even riding my bike home."

"Officer," Dad said. "I think we're done here."

Rankin smiled. "Actually, I'm pretty sure we're not." He waggled his notebook. "But I've got what I need for now. I'll see what Mr. Steadman wants to do. Sleep tight, everyone."

The three of them watched the cop pull away.

"Sleep tight? Not likely." Parker looked from his mom to his dad. "You believe me, right?" But he already knew the answer. "What do we do now?"

Dad put his arm around Parker's shoulders. "We'll get this cleared up. The truth always comes out. God's got this, right?"

"For sure." He gave the right answer, but his heart definitely wasn't in it. At this very moment there was only one thing that Parker was absolutely sure of. This whole mess wasn't going away. And he wasn't so sure Officer Rankin was impartial enough to give Parker a fair shake. More likely the cop would keep looking for some way to prove his theory. Rankin had questioned him about Devin's death. About Steadman's break-in. And now Parker was Rankin's go-to guy for tonight's break-in, too. Every time there was a break-in now, would they be getting late-night visits from Officer Rankin?

Parker definitely had to stop counting on the police to get to the bottom of this. To find the truth. And obviously God still wasn't shedding any light on the situation. Maybe Parker would have to clear his own name, and the only way to do that was to mount a little investigation of his own.

CHAPTER 28

Wednesday, June 8, 7:00 p.m.

PARKER WOKE UP TIRED—and still frustrated. The day seemed to drag by, at least until the meeting at El's place started after dinner. Mom. Dad. El. Grams. And even Mr. Steadman made it. Actually, he seemed over-the-top pumped that Parker had invited him.

Parker's mom got a tour before the meeting started. He could tell by the time she came downstairs she loved the place. "Oh, Mercedes. The place is lovely."

"Call me Mercy," Grams said. "That's what family calls me."

They pulled chairs around the kitchen table. Grams had glasses for everyone and a couple of pitchers. Lemonade and sweet tea.

"Tell me about your family." It was just like Mom to want to get the backstory.

Actually Parker wanted to get to the real reason they'd gathered at the Houstons'.

Grams had a voice that was as smooth and rich as maple syrup. She grew up in New York. Queens to be more exact. That's where she met a young man named Gabriel Houston, who wanted something more from life than he'd ever find in Queens . . . which is exactly what Mercy wanted. They married, and after reading an advertisement looking for workers in a fish cannery in Gloucester, Massachusetts, they took a train north.

"We thought we knew what we were getting into," Mercy said, "but there weren't many of our kind in Gloucester."

As in none.

"Gabriel was a hard worker. Clever, too," Grams said. "He made a good friend there—Art Carson—which was no small miracle." She smiled like she was picturing the guy. "Art called my Gabriel a human oil can. There wasn't a production line that he couldn't find a way to make faster. Smoother. More efficient."

She told how Gabriel applied for every supervisory position that opened—and got turned down every time. But eventually it was Art who climbed the fishnet, as they called it. He became production manager—and took Gabriel with him.

"The good Lord granted him favor in the eyes of Art Carson. Art would get a bonus—but he'd always split it with my Gabriel. Art knew he wouldn't be production manager without him. We've got Art to thank for us coming to live here in our own little Beulah land."

"We lived in an apartment in Gloucester worse than a scurvy ship's hold—just saving the money. Gabriel wanted a real home. We made offers on God knows how many—and some sounded like done deals over the phone. But as soon as we'd show up to look at the place, we'd learn the home had just been sold to someone else—or suddenly they were not so sure they wanted to sell after all."

Grams let that one sink in a bit.

"Because you're black?" Mom asked the question—even though Parker was pretty sure everyone in the room knew the answer.

"I suspect." Mercy had one hand on her hip. "Our money was the same color as everyone else's, so I don't know why the color of our skin should've mattered.

"Rockport was the first place we'd seen where there were no fences keeping people apart. At least not the privacy kind that says folk don't want to visit with their neighbors. Just picket fences to keep a puppy from running. Low granite walls. And garden fences. The town was bursting with those. We knew we wanted to live here. Fell in love with the place—even though it was falling apart."

"So here in Rockport," Mom said, "nobody tried to keep you from buying the place?"

"We didn't take any chances. We stayed clear of the place. Never even went inside for a look so nobody would know what we were up to. Art bought the place—then turned right around and sold it to us."

Mom smiled. "Clever. And a good friend."

"I put flowers by his headstone every time I go to Gabriel's grave."

"It's a gorgeous house, Mercy," Mr. Steadman said. "And the house is in wonderful shape now."

"Gabriel was handy that way. And we raised a family here." She smiled at Ella. "Ella's mom got pregnant way too young. She couldn't be a mom—she was practically a baby herself. That girl was a magnet for trouble. Made more messes than a puppy that hasn't been housebroke. She moved back to Queens, of all places, but not before we'd adopted our Ella Mae here. Lord Almighty, Gabriel loved Ella-girl. She'd clomp around the kitchen in his work boots when he got off shift. He bought Ella her first pair of cowgirl boots when she was five so they could tromp around together. Now she's the legal heir to Beulah—Gabriel got the paperwork done proper. He wanted nothing more than to pass on this piece of heaven to her."

Ella stared at her cowgirl boots. Like she knew the chances of that happening were getting slimmer by the day.

"Your husband was a smart buyer," Steadman said. "Beulah is so close to the Headlands. And with the outbuilding as a rental? A great revenue stream."

"Which is why I chanced the renovation after Gabriel passed. I so wanted Ella to get an education like I never did. I let myself get talked into taking a loan to renovate the building.

"The loan manager actually came out to see the place. That banker was so complimentary. Talked about the fine job Gabriel had done with the property. He was very convincing . . . affirming my plan that the rental home would pay for itself and Ella's education in time. I think even then the man was scheming to plug his Crockpot in our kitchen someday—but I saw it too late."

Mercy lowered her head like she was ashamed of how things had turned out. She told of taking a bad fall. Having hip surgery. And lots of medical bills. How she took in extra work where she could.

"By May we were in trouble," she said. "Went to the loan manager. Tried to lower our payments. Spread them out. I told him we were booked all summer and that we were good for the money."

"So he let you refinance?" Mom sounded like a reporter now.

Grams looked at her a few long moments. "It doesn't work

that way for some folk. He advised me to sell the property—even said he knew a potential buyer."

"Which was him," Mom said. "Am I right?"

Grams tilted her head and raised her eyebrows. "I suspect. Or some crony of his."

Parker's dad had been quiet pretty much the whole time. But by the look on his face it wasn't hard to figure out what he was thinking.

"My man worked hard," Grams said. "And if I lose Beulah now, I'd feel like I lost a part of him, that's for certain. And worse, I'd be letting my Ella Mae down, too. This is her home."

Parker couldn't stand the thought, either. He did not want to lose the only friend he had in town. *God . . . are you seeing this? It all seems so wrong. Please, help them . . . and show me how to help them save their place.*

"The loan manager started the foreclosure process. I keep thinking that if I start getting bookings again, he'll call it off," Grams said, "but at times I do wonder. The man seems a little too eager."

Parker's dad pulled an envelope from his back pocket and slipped it to Grams. "I wish we could do more," Dad said. "But I'm hoping this helps."

Grams teared up. Kissed the envelope. Clutched it in her hands.

When Parker looked El's way, it was like she'd been waiting to catch his eye. Her face said it all, but she mouthed "Thank you" anyway.

"Do you mind," Mr. Steadman looked almost apologetic, "if I take a look at your bills? The ones you're behind on."

Grams set a short stack of them on the kitchen table. Steadman leafed through them, stopping now and then to read more carefully. By the time he'd gone through the pile, he'd set three bills aside.

"Okay." He held up the targeted bills. "Consider these paid. I'll send checks to each of these tonight. Get them off your back."

Grams shook her head. "You're good neighbors. Both of you. I'm not sure why you're doing this."

"We're doing more than trying to be good neighbors," Mom said. "We're followers of Jesus . . . and we can't imagine He'd do less."

Steadman raised both hands. "Well, I'm not a believer myself, but I do believe we need to stick together on this. We've got to fight. We've just heard how important the rentals are for your survival. And the truth is, this is how I make my living, too. I don't want to go back to scraping by with dive charters."

"Thank you," Grams said. "I'm grateful for the help."

"You said the bank started the foreclosure process," Steadman said. "Do you have a timeline?"

Grams looked at El—like she wasn't sure she wanted to say more with her granddaughter in the room.

"Hey," Ella said, "don't hold back because I'm here. Actually, that's a question I've been wanting to know, too."

Grams squeezed her eyes shut and gave a deep sigh—like she'd been dreading this moment. "If I don't pay off the entire loan by June 18, they'll take it from us. We'll be evicted June 19."

"What?!" Ella's question came out more like a shriek. "That's in ten days. Only nine days to pay off the loan? Can they do that?"

"Never underestimate the power of a schnook."

Parker looked to his dad, hoping he'd add something that would change how bleak it all looked at this moment. Dad just shook his head. "Looks like we have something to pray about."

Parker wasn't so sure the idea of prayer did anything to relieve Grams—or El.

"Juneteenth?" Ella looked at her Grams as if in disbelief. "It's supposed to be a celebration . . ."

"I'm so sorry, Ella Mae."

"Of all days." Ella's voice shook.

"Hush now, sugar," Grams said. "Let's just leave it at that."

Okay, Parker was clearly missing something, but this didn't seem like the time to ask.

"The banker sounds totally unreasonable," Mom said. She was looking a little steamed, like the investigative reporter was dying to get out. "You'd have to put it on the market right away if you hoped to have paperwork in place—with a deposit big enough to pay off the loan by the nineteenth. This just isn't right."

"We are *not* going to sell this place," Ella said. "I'll chain myself to the porch railing if I have to."

Parker could see her doing exactly that. But Grams didn't say a thing.

"Grams?" Ella's voice had an edge of fear to it. "We're not selling, right?"

"I don't want to, Ella Mae. I surely don't. But I'm not finding any underground railroad on this one. I don't see a path to freedom. For now I'm not selling. I'm hoping that somehow that loan department manager grows a heart between now and then."

Ella scanned the room. "We can't let this happen. We can't."

Dad looked like he was ready to drop on his knees right there to bring it before the throne.

"I have a friend who runs the loan department at Boston Federal—and they have a branch in town," Steadman said. "Lucius Scorza. I'll talk to him. Maybe his bank can do something."

"Scorza," Parker said. "Does he have a son at Rockport High?"

Steadman nodded.

"Ugh," Parker groaned. "Total rich-kid syndrome. The guy's a jerk."

"Well, I've always thought his dad was a decent guy," Steadman said. "I'll see if he can help us."

Grams shook her head. "Don't get your hopes up too high. Mr. Scorza is the loan manager I've been dealing with."

Steadman looked surprised—then smiled. "Well, I'll have a little chat with him. He owes me a favor anyway."

For the first time, Ella looked hopeful. "You hear that, Grams?"

Grams smiled back. "We'll see, sweetie."

"Let me ask you a question," Mr. Steadman said. "And you don't have to answer it if you don't want to. But has anyone offered to buy this place—since this all started, I mean. Besides Scorza hinting at buying it himself."

Grams fidgeted with her sweater. "Yes, sir. I got a call from some big city lawyer—on two occasions."

Ella wailed and threw her hands in the air. "I hope you told them *no*, Grams. Tell me you did."

"I haven't agreed to nothing, Ella Mae. He pitched me a price that was snake-belly low. But I'd be lying if I didn't tell you I'm in a corner here."

Steadman leaned forward. "That lawyer . . . did he represent an outfit out of Boston?"

Grams nodded. "Boston Investors Group."

"This is a conspiracy!" Steadman was on his feet. "Right after my cancellations started, I got calls from them too. Don't you see what's happening here? Somebody is making a power play."

Mom picked up on it. "This organization is using the burglaries—and loss of rental business—to their advantage."

"Or one step worse," Dad said, "this isn't about kids breaking into rentals for the thrill of it—or ghosts," he glanced at El, "but what if all this was a group of investors wanting to get prime properties at bargain prices—and *they've* set up the burglaries—this Shadow-man—to help along their cause?"

Steadman eyed him. "That's a whole lot darker picture than what anybody has suggested before. Including the police."

Scary dark.

"But I think you're on to something." Steadman swore—then saw Grams's face. "Sorry about the language. But this fits. It makes sense."

Could Shadow-man really be somebody hired to put a scare into locals? Is that what happened the night Devin followed the green light?

"There's good money in rentals," Steadman said. "Especially in a town that attracts tourists like Rockport. This is making so much sense now. This Boston Investors Group is trying to muscle in. Take over our business. And if they do? Prices for homes will skyrocket. A normal guy—or grandma and granddaughter—won't be able to afford living here. This investor group will gobble up the prime property. Our town will change—and not for the better."

Parker looked around the table. "So what do we do?"

The room got quiet. Parker searched for options—but if this all came down to a ton of money needed to pay off Grams's loan—what *could* they do? "What about the police? If someone has hired muscle to scare renters away, we'll need the police, right?"

Steadman snorted. "Rankin still thinks this is kids chasing

some kicks—and he still believes you're part of this, Parker. He so much as said he wasn't going to investigate any more break-ins at Bayview or Bayport as long as you still had the keys."

"Gee, thanks, Officer Rankin." Parker couldn't help the sarcasm. He turned to Steadman. "You want my keys, Boss?"

"No." Steadman's voice was firm. "I know this isn't you."

Which was a relief. "But if you need the police to help with the investigation, maybe—"

"You ought to fall on your sword?" Steadman shook his head. "Not going to happen. Besides, we can't wait around for the police to get it in gear. I think we leave the police out of this."

"Which comes back to the question," Ella said. "What do we do now?"

"If some Boston group is trying to take what's ours—we fight back," Steadman said. "This means war."

"Great," Ella said. "I'll just go up to my room and load my bazooka."

Everyone laughed—including Steadman. But the room got serious again—quick. There was something about Steadman's eyes. A determination there. Confidence. "We're not going to let them win. We're going to fight."

"I know this isn't really our fight, but we're in, too," Dad said. "We don't want anyone else to own Mercy's place here. But before we can beat an enemy, we need to know everything we can about them."

"And," Ella said, "how are we going to do that?"

"We look for a weakness," Steadman said. "A blind spot. We already know their objective, and we do all we can to block them."

"And we'll pray God shows us the way," Dad said.

"I don't know beans about God," Steadman said. "But I do

know a thing or two about guerilla warfare. Smaller forces—outmanned and outgunned—have historically held back incredibly more powerful forces. But we need to stick together. Work as a unit—or they'll pick us off one by one. I say we form some kind of Rockport Resistance movement."

Ella nodded. "I like it."

"If there are spirits involved," Grams said, "no amount of resistance on our part is going to make a lick of difference—unless God Almighty fights for us."

Steadman held up one hand. "I'm not going to sit back waiting for miracles. But I have a friend—we served together. I'd trust him with my life. He does investigative work now. I'm going to have him get some intel on this Boston Investors Group."

"I'll check some sources too," Mom said. "Maybe someone at the paper has some info on them."

"And I'll also have a little chat with my banker friend, Scorza," Steadman said. "See if we can't get him to cut you some slack."

To Parker, the thought of Steadman putting a little friendly pressure on Bryce Scorza's dad sounded really promising.

"We stick together on this," Steadman said. "We can't let an outside group get a toehold in Rockport. Agreed?"

Nobody was arguing with him there.

"And Mrs. Houston, please," Steadman said. "Don't go to a realtor about this. And do not sign anything. No papers. No agreement to sell. Nothing."

Grams looked directly at El. "I won't sign a thing—unless I'm absolutely sure there is no other way."

"Okay, let's get back together in a few days," Steadman said. "By then we should know a lot more about this Boston Investors Group."

Ella sucked in her breath. "Boston Investors Group!"

Parker raised his eyebrows and looked at her—along with everyone else.

"It's an acronym. BIG."

Steadman whistled. "I should have caught that."

Parker had a feeling BIG was bigger than any of them might guess. If this group hired muscle to intimidate owners into selling—what might they do if one pushed back?

CHAPTER 29

THE IDEA CAME TO PARKER as he lay in his bed long after the house got quiet. The muffled rumble of waves storming the Headlands sometimes helped him drift off to sleep. Other times it helped him sort out his thoughts. And tonight the ideas were falling into place.

Mr. Steadman and Mom could do the checking into BIG. But Parker wasn't going to sit around and wait. If this was war, then maybe Parker needed to set his own combat strategy.

The pounding surf sort of sounded like a battle, didn't it? Wave upon wave of attack. What if this really was some kind of twisted big business strategy of this investing group? What if they really were mounting some kind of campaign to intimidate rental owners? Could it be that the burglaries weren't random at all? Were they all about eroding the incomes from people like Grams and

Mr. Steadman so they'd sell cheap? And was Mr. Scorza tied into this scheme somehow?

Steadman clearly had deeper pockets than Grams did. Thankfully it seemed like he could ride this storm out—at least for now. But Grams was in over her head. She was drowning—and El was going down with her.

That couldn't happen.

Parker had been worried about losing his job. His boat slip. Not that those things didn't matter, but his issues were no comparison to what El was going to lose if something didn't change—and fast.

The note from his grandpa sat on the small table beside his bed with the dive knife on top. He unsheathed the knife and reread the verse. "God, I'd really appreciate if You'd reveal some hidden things right about now." And honestly, without some kind of miracle, exactly how could Parker ever help El and Grams?

He raised his bedroom window. Felt the sea breeze on his face. Heard the relentless attack on the Headlands shoreline.

"God," he whispered. "Show me what I can do. Help me to help them. Strengthen me for the fight." He stopped, and wondered at his own prayer. *Strengthen me for the fight?* Where did that come from?

But there would be a fight. Somehow, he knew that was coming.

What they really needed to do was solve the mystery of the break-ins. If the burglar was caught—and word spread that it wasn't a ghost and that the threat was gone—wouldn't that change everything? If it happened quick enough, maybe Grams could start booking rentals again—and she could get her loan extended or something. Maybe BIG would move on to another town.

The key would be catching the burglar somehow. Finding his connection to the investors group. Maybe they could do some kind of surveillance on the rental homes. Not all of them, but focus on Grams's place—and Steadman's rentals. Those seemed to be the houses they were after—or the ones they'd made offers on, anyway. If they could catch the guy or get video evidence, that might be all they'd need. If it could be traced back to BIG, the investors would disappear faster than a sandcastle in high tide. Catch whoever was doing the break-ins. That's what he needed to do.

He made some quick mental notes. The more he thought about it, the more sure he was that they needed to act on this—and fast.

Maybe he'd send Jelly a quick text now, just to get her take on it. And he'd definitely run it by El tomorrow. Maybe take her out for a ride in the *Boy's Bomb* and outline his plan. She'd go for it. The only doubt he really had? Himself. How was he supposed to organize a stakeout—and catch Shadow-man?

"God, strengthen me for the fight."

CHAPTER 30

Thursday, June 9

"THIS IS *NOT* HOW I PICTURED THINGS PLAYING OUT," Harley said. He stared out the back window of the Rockport Dive Company with Scorza at his side. On Tuesday night, they'd roughed up Steadman's rental home—and for what? Gatorade still hadn't been hauled off to jail. When the cop stopped at his house barely thirty minutes after the break-in, Harley and Scorza had been doing an end zone victory dance in the shadows. But it didn't last long. Why didn't the guy even haul Gatorade in for questioning?

Harley had a great view of Rockport Harbor—and a lousy view of Gatorade driving his wimpy little skiff around the south side of the yacht club and into deeper water. Ella sat in the bow seat, facing Gatorade at the wheel. She dangled one hand over the side like she hoped to catch some spray. From this distance she was no bigger than a spectator sitting on the top row of the bleachers—but it was still obvious she was happy. For a moment Harley imagined it was him driving the skiff. Would Ella ever look that happy just hanging out with him?

Scorza followed his gaze and pointed the football at Gatorade's boat. "What . . . you didn't figure Gatorade would be taking your sweet little Ella for a ride?"

Harley hauled off and slugged Scorza in the arm—but not the passing arm. "She's not my *sweet little Ella*."

"Got that right, loser. Black Beauty is riding with Gatorade."

"She's not a horse, either."

"Okay . . . how about I just call her Beauty then. Or Black."

Scorza liked getting guys riled up. Finding a bruise and grinding his knuckle into it. But usually he was careful not to step over the line with Harley. Toe over, for sure, but never quite enough to draw a penalty flag. But he was getting close.

"You've got plenty of friends. You don't need *her*."

Plenty of friends? Harley wasn't so sure about that. Kids knew his name, but they didn't know him. If he wasn't on the team, he'd be invisible.

"Anyway, she's the real loser," Scorza said. "She should be thanking her lucky stars you'd even want to be seen hanging around her. And if you ask me, you can do better."

"What's that supposed to mean?"

"Actually, my dad was just talking to me about the Houstons. Here's exactly how my dad put it." Scorza smiled. "He told me to picture my Nike football spikes."

Alpha Menace Elites. The two-hundred-dollar spikes Harley would drool over, but never own.

"The Nikes are me. And you. Got it?"

Harley had no idea where this was going.

"And my dad said the Houstons are dollar-store flip-flops. Ella's not even in the same universe as us."

Harley grabbed two fistfuls of Scorza's jersey and slammed him against Uncle Ray's prized beer can collection. Empties went flying in all directions. "Your dad's an idiot."

Scorza acted totally unfazed. "I'll bet your dad, the big motorcycle dude, was no different than mine."

Harley pushed off and turned away to keep from popping him in his big fat mouth. "You don't know a thing about my dad."

It was moments like this that made him wonder. Was the guy truly his friend, or was it all about what Harley did for him on the field? Did Scorza love hanging around only because Harley caught nearly everything he threw at him in a game? The wobbly balls. The low passes. The ones that were just too far out in front of him—but somehow he caught them anyway?

Outside of football, they really had nothing in common. Scorza's dad wore a suit and drove an Audi to his big man bank job. The only time Harley had seen his own dad wearing a suit was in the coffin. And the suit wasn't even his.

Harley grabbed empty beer cans and restacked them on the shelves as fast as he could, careful to have the labels facing out. Scorza leaned against the doorjamb and watched. If Uncle Ray walked back in the shop at this moment and saw his booze-can bounty scattered the way it was, he'd lighten Harley's pay for the night. Guaranteed.

"I don't get your fascination with her anyway," Scorza said. "What's she got that every other girl at Rockport High doesn't have?"

She was smart—like in a way where she wouldn't take trash talk from anybody. Kind of a fighter that way. She was confident—but not in some proud way like so many girls who knew they were gorgeous. Ella was kind. Saw somebody hurting and said something nice to make their day a tiny bit better. Nobody gave Devin Catsakis a seat at their table. But Ella did. She made space in her life for somebody that none of the others would. Like that stupid Gatorade. And he loved the way she took care of her grandma. He'd seen them walking past the windows of the dive shop on their way to get strudel or something, arm in arm. Who did that kind of thing? Would the girls Scorza talked about even take the time to be with their grandma? "Lots of things."

"Right. And you can't name one."

Harley had the urge to take the Old Milwaukee can in his hand and shove it down Scorza's throat.

"Forget the Houston girl, man. She isn't even in the same league as all the—"

"Shut *up*, okay? I don't want to talk about this."

Scorza snickered like he'd scored an extra point. "Why do you want her for a friend so bad anyway? I just can't figure that out."

If Scorza would take his face out of the mirror long enough to really see who Ella was, he wouldn't be asking dumb questions like that.

"She some kind of charity case for you or something?"

Something inside Harley was rising up. Flexing. Between Harley and Ella? Harley was a lot more likely to be the charity case. He straightened the last of the beer cans.

"You want to be a big brother to her, is that it? If you think she's an only child, you're totally stupid."

"Stop."

Scorza grinned liked he'd found the bruise he was looking for.

"She's probably got twenty half-brothers or something. But you never see them around because they're all in jail."

"Just shut your stinkin' mouth." There were times, just before the hike, where the guy lined up opposite him would start trash-talking. As hard as Harley tried not to let it get under his skin, sometimes it just did. Those were the moments he'd get this angry blood rush he'd feel all the way to his eyeballs. It was a super-charged thing—and whenever it happened he knew he was absolutely going to cream the defender lined up against him.

"Or maybe," Scorza said, "you feel some kind of weird bond with her. She doesn't have a dad—"

"Don't go there. Not another word." The rush was already flowing—and Scorza was deliberately inching his toe over that line of scrimmage. "Final warning."

"Just saying . . . she doesn't have a dad, and you don't have a dad, so—"

HIKE.

Harley whirled and charged. His shoulder slammed into the big 8 on Scorza's jersey. The force of his momentum lifted enough weight off Scorza's feet that Harley drove him easily out of the back room and into a rack of *Don't Drink and Dive* T-shirts. The entire display crashed to the floor—along with Scorza and Harley.

Scorza was on his back, scrambling to roll over, trying to get to his feet. Harley had him pinned good. He balled his fist and—

"HEY!" Uncle Ray rushed through the open door and was on him. Grabbed Harley's T-shirt and yanked him backward. "Not in my store."

The blood rush was gone as quick as it had come over him. He stood. Brushed off his jeans.

"Save it for football camp, fellas."

Harley did not want Scorza to think his comments bothered him as much as they did. It was a little late for that. He offered a hand to Scorza—still on his back—and tangled in Rockport Dive Company gear. Scorza hesitated, then smiled and grabbed his hand with an arm-wrestling grip. Harley gave him a hard yank to his feet.

"Now get this place cleaned up," Uncle Ray said. "Right now. And I'm going to inspect the merchandise after you do." He glared at Harley. "Damages come out of your pay." He fished his Marlboro pack out of his pocket and tapped a cigarette free. "Better look perfect in here when I come back in." Uncle Ray stepped back out the front door and slammed it behind him.

Scorza worked alongside Harley without a word. But probably twenty seconds didn't go by before he started laughing. The real kind, where you can't find the kill switch. It was contagious that way, and soon Harley was doubled over, too. Burning off the excess adrenaline.

"Whatever got into you, I wish we could bottle it for the whole team." Scorza wiped the laugh tears from his cheeks. "We'd have their first-stringers in the hospital by halftime."

And that was that. There was no "Hey, sorry for the stinkin' comments about Ella," and Harley sure wasn't going to apologize for taking him down either. But it was over. For now.

Satisfied with the T-shirt display, Harley made sure the booze-can collection looked perfect before walking to the back room window. Gatorade was nearly out at the entrance of the harbor now. Too far away for Harley to really see anything.

"Okay." Scorza stepped up beside him. "So you want the girl to be your friend—or more than that—which probably won't happen with Gatorade around. So we gotta keep Gatorade from the girl—which ain't gonna happen all by its lonesome. What are we going to do about it?"

Harley shook his head. They'd already tried something. It hadn't gotten them anywhere.

"No game plan, hotshot?"

Harley shrugged. But it seemed to him that if Gatorade got pulled in for questioning—or better yet, arrested—Steadman would fire him for sure this time. Gatorade would lose his boat slip—and there'd be no more rides with Ella. The game wouldn't be over, for sure, but at least Harley would have possession of the ball.

"So let's run the same pattern again."

Harley eyed him. Scorza was serious.

"Listen," he said. "How many times have we run a play, and we don't get past the line of scrimmage or we lose yardage? What do we do?"

They'd execute the same play again—and soon. The other team never expected it, and they'd get a first down easily. Harley smiled. "OK, let's run it again. And maybe we step it up a little. Throw in a couple surprises." The gears were already turning—and meshing in his head. What if they hit *both* of Steadman's rental homes—and planted a little evidence at Gatorade's place?

Scorza backed across the room and absolutely drilled the ball to Harley—like he hoped it might lift him off his feet, too. "And this time, we're going to get some yardage."

"I'm not looking to pick up a couple yards." Harley tossed the ball back. "How about a touchdown attitude here?"

"Even better," Scorza said. "When?"

Harley thought for a moment. "Let's do something quick tonight." And they'd keep doing damage—every night—until

Steadman sent Gatorade to the bench. Until Ella wrote him off as bad blood.

"A quick fix isn't going to cut it," Scorza said. "Not if we're going to step it up."

Harley smiled. "Way ahead of you. Tonight is just the pregame show. The warm-ups."

"Okay." Scorza cocked his arm back like he was throwing a Hail Mary. "When do we *really* start putting points on the scoreboard?"

Harley pictured his uncle doing his Friday after-closing thing at the Gloucester bars. That would give them all the time they needed. "Tomorrow night."

CHAPTER 31

THE SCARS ON PARKER'S ARM INTRIGUED ELLA—in a weird, artsy way. She wanted to duplicate them on a canvas—then take those random, jagged lines and draw something beautiful. Scars always formed an image eventually. Sometimes the worse the scars, the better the picture.

He tooled around the bay, steering around sailboats, constantly looking over the side into the glassy water. It was the diver in him, always interested in what was down in the water, on the bottom of the bay. Ella preferred to focus on what was above the surface.

"So, what's this urgent thing you wanted to talk about?" Whatever it was, he didn't seem to be in a big fat hurry now.

He tossed her the bag of donuts from Brothers Brew. "What's the story with June 19th? When your Grams mentioned that date, it seemed like it was something special. Your Grams's birthday or something?"

She stared at him for a moment. He was serious. "June 19th. It's a huge—as in massive—part of US history. *Juneteenth*."

Parker thought for a moment. "I actually kind of like history—and my memory can be freaky good. But I don't remember that date being mentioned—ever."

"That's because it doesn't make it into the history textbooks, and it isn't taught in the classroom—even though it is a totally legit national holiday."

Clearly he was still drawing a total blank. "Holiday?"

"You are soooo white, you know that?"

"What?" Parker shook his head like *she* was crazy. "What does my skin color have to do with this?"

"Everything. Trust me." She pulled a donut from the bag, perfectly frosted with cinnamon sugar. The confectionary ring of happiness was still warm.

"Okay, so enlighten the ignorant pasty-face. What is Juneteenth?"

She wasn't going to let him off that easy. If he really wanted to know—if he really *cared*—he'd do the homework. "Look it up, Mr. I-kinda-like-history. And tell me you didn't bring me out here just to talk about Juneteenth."

He slowed to an idle. "Actually, that's exactly why we're here. Because if we don't come up with a way to save your place before June 19th, you lose the house, right?"

She *so* didn't want to talk about this. Gulls wheeled and cried overhead like they didn't want her talking about it either. "What we need is for you to find a treasure box on one of your dives. Then we can pay off the loan and keep the bank from taking Beulah away."

"You need your rental business back, and that won't happen until whoever is scaring renters away is caught—or exposed."

Parker had a way of ruling out the possibility of the supernatural. But in this case maybe it was better he was so closed off to those things. She'd hate to hear his plan to catch a ghost.

"Rankin thinks this is kids having a good time," Parker said.

Ella pointed at Parker. "Actually I'm pretty sure he thinks you're the kid."

"The point is, until we can prove it isn't me—and that we've got a serious crime going on here—I don't see him throwing the weight of his badge behind this."

"Gotta plan, big man?"

He was looking down in the water again. Like the answers were somewhere out of reach. "Sort of. But it's a shot in the dark. And kinda risky."

This was the guy who took some incredible chances in the Everglades, from what she'd pieced together. A guy who'd almost got himself killed helping his friends. "How risky are we talking . . . one to ten. One, I might get my cowgirl boots wet. Ten, my arm might end up looking like yours." She clamped her hand over her mouth. "I am so sorry. That just kind of spilled out."

He laughed and waved her off. "I'd put this at a solid five. No more."

"Really, that comment about your arm, I'm so s—"

"El . . . I'm fine. You want to hear the plan or not?"

For the next ten minutes he laid out his scheme for finding out who was behind the burglaries. It was a totally "guy" plan. Surveillance. Traps. All nighttime work. And nothing that would help one lick if this truly was an otherworldly presence at work. How he ranked his plan as a solid five on the one-to-ten risk scale, she had no idea. This felt a lot more like an eight in her opinion.

"You don't seem excited."

"It's dangerous. And I don't think it will work." There. She'd told him right out. Even though she was desperate for a solution, it would be a whole lot easier to get behind this if she honestly thought his idea could actually do any good. "Stick with diving. The odds are higher that you'll find a treasure chest."

He didn't say anything for maybe a half minute. "We have to do something, El. We have to try."

"I agree completely. I'd just like to try something that might actually work."

"It'll work." Parker started the engine and headed out toward the breakwater. Like the thing was decided.

"And when will you implement this plan?"

He had an answer for that, too. He'd have to talk to his parents first. He didn't go into too much of an explanation, but he was all about integrity on this—and that meant not keeping secrets from his parents.

Was Ella staring at him with some stupid expression on her face as he spoke? She hoped not, but honestly? She'd never had a friend like him. Not ever. Most had secrets they didn't want their parents to find out about—and they put a lot of energy into covering up. But Parker was putting effort into being open with them?

"So I'll talk to them tonight," he said. "And we go live tomorrow night."

"I haven't agreed to this yet, you know."

Parker smiled like he knew it was all an act. Like he knew she would do anything to save their home—no matter how insane the plan might seem.

Parker neared the harbor inlet between the Headlands and the granite jetty. Even here the waves felt a lot bigger than they'd looked from back near the Motif. She studied the water outside the protected harbor. The swells rose with angry brows of foam. Ella gripped the sides of the boat.

"Change of plans." Parker swung the boat around and headed toward the T-shaped wharf. "Definitely too rough to chance it."

For a moment Ella wasn't sure if he was talking about the waters out in Sandy Bay, or the crazy idea he had to catch the rental home intruder.

"I probably should get back anyway." Parker got a restless look about him. He flexed the hand of his scarred arm like he was stretching knotted muscles in is forearm. Maybe he was beginning to realize his plan was more dangerous than he'd admitted.

Ella didn't want him to think she was analyzing him like she would a scene before painting it. She focused on the back side of the shops on Bearskin Neck as they came into view. For some reason she looked at the bay window of the Rockport Dive Company. Harley was there, just staring out the window. Ella waved, just to be sure he knew she saw him watching.

Harley suddenly backed out of sight. For just an instant she felt a power rush. Harley could toss her over his shoulder and walk around all day without breaking a sweat—but apparently she had the ability to intimidate him. If only it was that easy to make him disappear every other time she saw him.

Parker motored around the yacht club and eased into the slip next to Steadman's Boston Whaler. There were a few inches of scummy water inside—and it hadn't rained in a couple of weeks.

A police car cruised down the T-wharf, snail speed. There were no cars parked in the spaces along the docks, so the cop drove close to the edge of the granite pier. He stopped dead even with them.

Rankin.

"Parker, you've got company." For an instant she almost

dropped into coaching mode. *Look him in the eye. Be respectful.* But the white in him would think she was paranoid.

The cop leaned toward the open passenger window—like he wanted to make sure Parker saw him. He pointed at his eyes—then back at Parker.

Parker waved. "Yeah, and I'm keeping my eyes on you, too." He didn't say it loud enough for the cop to hear, but even from his body language Rankin had to see he was rattling Parker.

The cop smiled and moved on.

"Don't you worry what he might do when you talk to him like that?"

He gave her a confused look. The guy was totally clueless.

This wasn't the time to go into it. "Let's say your parents do allow you to do this—even though I doubt they will. How are you going to run surveillance without getting spotted? If Officer Rankin sees you scoping out one of the rentals, he'll shadow you closer than a . . ." She grinned. "Closer than a gull follows a fishing boat."

Parker laughed. "Stop worrying. I'll melt into the shadows. I'll move without a sound. Nobody will know I'm there."

"You're the guy who doesn't believe in ghosts." The irony of it hit her. Now it was her turn to laugh. "But to pull this off, it sure sounds like you'll need to become a ghost yourself."

CHAPTER 32

THE FACT THAT SOMEBODY WAS IMITATING HIM was a compliment. It was also a complication. For one, the copycat was an amateur. It wouldn't take much detective work to figure that out. And that would bring the wrong kind of publicity. If people were convinced a punk was behind the break-ins . . . someone out to prove himself or to get his kicks, it would water down everything the Ghost had been doing. Pretty soon rentals would trickle in again.

He wasn't about to let that happen. *Nope. Nopity-nope. Not going to happen.*

So he had his work cut out for him. He'd still keep his eye on Do-Right. And he'd keep his eye out for the impersonator. If the Shadow-man wannabe kept up with the copycat thing, sooner or later that unlucky fool was going to meet the real Ghost, and he'd wish he never did.

Damage assessment? For the moment, no real harm had been done by the impostor's break-in Tuesday night. But the Ghost had to maintain total control. So he'd make more appearances—just to keep everyone a bit more on edge.

People always talked about the "element of surprise" like it was a surefire way to overpower an opponent. "Hey, if you want to be the big winner in a fight, use the element of surprise." Like it was a superpower. A genie lamp that granted unlimited wishes instead of just three. A victory machine that kept paying out.

But *surprise* wasn't it at all. Surprise was the stuff of Hollywood films and bigmouths who didn't know what they were talking about. The element of surprise was a Swiss Army pocketknife. It could probably help in a pinch, but it was never the best tool for the job.

To merely surprise an opponent was weak. It was the same tactic used at a birthday party, for crying out loud. A surprise gave someone a quick jolt—a shot of low-dose adrenaline—and then it was over. Surprise wasn't the type of thing that kept opponents awake at night. It wasn't the type of thing that made them want to check—and recheck—their locks. Surprise had no muscle. No useful lasting side effects.

EOS is what gave a guy the real advantage over an opponent. *Any* opponent. EOS. Not the Element of Surprise . . . but the Element of Shock. And he was good at shock. Really, really good. It was about doing something so horrifyingly unexpected and maniacal that the opponent just might wrestle with PTSD afterward. EOS was about doing something that would come across as absolutely possessed. And if the opponent thought you had a coven of demons in you, even better. They'd surely fear you'd left one behind to haunt them.

Element of Shock. That was the prescription now. That Catsakis kid swallowed a lethal dose of EOS—and missed his chance to run. Shock had that effect on people. After you've hit someone with *that* stun gun, the rest was easy-peasy.

Which brought him back to Do-Right. If he got too close—or got in the way—he would be dealt with. He would OD on shock too.

He checked the time and smiled. Maybe the Ghost would make a little surprise appearance tonight. He laughed at his own choice of words. Not a *surprise* appearance, exactly. But it would be a shock.

CHAPTER 33

Thursday, June 9, 9:45 p.m.

BLACK SWEATS. Black hoodie. Black gloves. Black spandex face-covering. Harley imagined he was some kind of Special Ops commando on a training exercise. Scorza crouched beside him in the shadows, scoping out the Steadman rental on Mills Street while they let their eyes adjust.

"I'll watch your backfield—and meet you at the cemetery," Scorza said. "You ready?"

Oh, yeah. Totally. It made sense that only one went in. If somebody spotted two people inside, that would actually eliminate Gatorade as a suspect, wouldn't it? The guy didn't have a friend—except Ella. And Harley was going to take that one away, too.

Harley tore open the wrapper on the glow stick and balled it up in his fist, saving it for later. He shifted his body into the set position, like he was ready to fire off the line.

"Picture Gatorade at the top of those stairs," Scorza said. "Have fun."

Harley rocketed ahead like he was charging for the end zone. He bounded up the stairs and lowered his shoulder into the back door. The doorjamb shattered, sending frantic splinters in all directions. Enough light crept in the windows—and he remembered the layout well enough. He didn't really need it, but he cracked the glow stick and shook it to life anyway. If a neighbor saw a green glow from inside, it would be perfect. He'd be down by Front Beach before the cops arrived.

He spread out both arms and bowled through the first floor, taking down lamps and chairs like they were helpless defenders. He even flipped the couch, pretending for a moment that it was actually a car. He felt strong enough to do it for real. Ten feet from the front door he tossed the wrapper from the glow stick behind the couch. They'd find it when they cleaned things up. And hopefully they'd find the stick itself, after he planted it at Gatorade's house.

CHAPTER 34

Thursday, June 9, 10:05 p.m.

GRAMS'S SCREAM COULD WAKE THE DEAD. Ella flew out of her room and down the stairs. "Grams!"

She was on the kitchen floor—sprawled out like someone had pulled the rug right out from under her. "Are you o—"

"Down, Ella Mae, and hit the light—don't let him see you."

She hit the switch on the fly and skittered down beside Grams. "You hurt?"

Grams clutched at her. Drew her close. Hugged her like she thought Ella would get ripped away if she didn't. "I saw it. I saw it."

"Saw what, Grams?"

"Where's the cross—the necklace?"

Ella pulled it out from under her shirt. Grams clutched it with both hands and pulled it close. The turquoise chain dug into Ella's neck. "You don't never go nowhere without it, hear?"

"What. Happened."

"I saw it. I *saw* it. Lord Almighty, I saw it." Grams's whole body trembled.

And right then Ella wanted Shadow-man's head on a platter. Grams was the strongest woman Ella had ever known. But that thing had terrified her. "I'm calling the police."

"No." Grams clung tighter. "We got a call for a rental tomorrow night. A for-real booking. No police. No bad publicity."

"Then I'm texting Parker." Her thumbs flew over the screen. Pushed send.

"There was no face."

"Grams." Ella held Grams's face between her hands. "Tell me everything."

"The ghost—right there in the kitchen window—holding a ghastly green light."

Goose bumps rose on Ella's arms.

"He was writing something on the window with his finger." She whispered like she thought the thing was still outside.

Ella raised herself up just enough to see the window. "He's gone, Grams."

"I know," she wailed. "He disappeared—before my eyes!"

Ella's stomach did one of those flip-flop things that happens on the first drop of a roller coaster.

"It was a spirit, Ella Mae. And not a good one."

They clung to each other on the floor. Ella listened. Tried her best to control her breathing. Expected the sound of a window shattering any second. "I should call the police," she said.

"Won't do us no good."

Footsteps pounded up the porch steps and someone banged on the door. Grams and Ella screamed.

"It's me, Parker."

Ella peeled herself from Grams's grip and opened the door a sliver—with her toe wedged at the bottom to keep it from being forced open if the ghost was still out there.

She double-locked the door behind Parker and gave him a twenty-second recap. Together they helped Grams to her feet and onto a kitchen chair.

Parker found a glass in the cupboard and poured her a cup of water. "You've had a nasty shock, Mrs. Houston. Take some water."

She shook her head. "I need sweet tea, Parker, my boy."

He dumped the water and poured some tea instead.

She took a sip, and then another. A few minutes later her breathing steadied, and she retold the entire experience to Parker.

He got a curious look on his face, walked to the window—and stopped dead. "He wasn't just writing with his finger."

Ella could see it now. Words written on the window in black marker—and the ghost must have written them backward, because they were right-reading from inside.

"Lord Almighty," Grams whispered. "What does it say?"

Parker stood in front of the window, back to it, blocking Ella's view. "You sure you want to read this?"

Ella motioned him to move—and he did.

"Read it aloud, Ella Mae," Grams said. "Don't leave a thing out."

Ella moved closer to the window. "GET OUT OF MY HOUSE."

Grams rested her elbows on the table and cradled her head like she didn't have the strength to hold it up.

Parker stood behind her chair, patting her back. "Ghosts don't carry markers in their pocket. Don't you worry, Mrs. Houston. This isn't right—and we're not going to let someone scare you out of your own home."

A nice thought. As if justice was truly available for everyone. But what could he do? And when would he change—like every other person they'd known? The older Ella got, the more people had a way of seeing her as a problem, instead of someone who desperately needed friends and community. They grew suspicious—as if her heart was filled with vicious plans. When Ella started junior high—and stopped looking like a little girl—Grams had "the talk" with her.

And it wasn't about the birds and bees.

It was about how the world really worked. How people would be treating her different around town. Every little girl is cute and innocent—no matter what their skin color. "But when you start looking like a young lady," Grams said, "folks will treat you different." Grams had told her stories of things that happened to others, but in time Ella had her own stories.

When she was just a little girl walking through town with Grams, tourist ladies would smile when they passed. They'd bend down and tell her how cute she was in her dress and tiny cowgirl boots. But as Ella's body changed and she was tall enough to look adults in the eyes, there were no more compliments on her dress. Women tended to hold their purse a little closer. Or they hit the remote clicker on their parked car a second time—making sure the doors were really locked. All because she was growing up—and she wasn't white? *Where was the justice in that?*

Parker assumed justice actually existed. For everyone. Obviously he hadn't experienced suspicious looks from clerks when he strolled down the candy aisle at the mini-mart. They didn't hover—or follow him—or keep asking if they could help him find something. Parker wasn't living in the same world she lived in.

"Why aren't the police here yet?" Parker was back at the window, staring at the message. "You did call the cops, right?"

"We're fine, Parker," Grams said. "You best get home before your parents get worried. Land sakes, you don't even have shoes on."

Ella looked—and sure enough, Grams was right.

Parker shrugged. "El's text scared me half to death. There was no time."

Like it was the most logical explanation in the world. But nobody had ever done something like that for her—or Grams. There was something about him. A strength. Something inside. She glanced at his scarred arm. Maybe whatever happened to him in the Glades had made him into more of a man than any man she knew. And he was only fifteen. Was Parker's dad the same way?

"We don't tell a living soul about this—except your parents and Mr. Steadman," Grams said. "Understood?"

"Not a soul outside the Rockport Resistance," he said. "Except my best friend Jelly—but she still lives in southern Florida. There's nobody for her to tell down there—except alligators."

Naturally he would tell Jelly. Ella was pretty sure he told her *everything*. But that wasn't what bothered her. It was that "best friend" bit. Of course Jelly was his best friend. Why wouldn't she be his best friend? But where did Ella fit? Two's company, three's a crowd, right? She shook off her ridiculous thoughts.

Parker headed for the door. "I'd better get home. G'night, Mrs. Houston."

Ella followed him out onto the porch. A thick fog had left its ocean lair and was creeping around the neighborhood. Fine droplets of mist haloed the streetlight on the corner of Clark Street.

Tears appeared as unannounced as the fog. "I don't know what I'll do if we lose Beulah."

Parker kept his eyes on the plank deck of the porch, pretending he didn't notice her crying. "I'll talk to my dad. I have to do something."

"You're still set on your stakeout idea?"

"More than ever."

She stared at him. "Why are you sticking your neck out like this?"

He gave her a puzzled look, like he couldn't believe she'd even asked the question. "You're my friend—and you're in trouble."

Maybe this was really about him not meeting Devin that night. Maybe he was trying to work off his guilt this way. But she didn't care. She needed help. "You can't do this alone. It's too big." There was no way he was going to catch a ghost.

"So . . . does that mean you'll help?" His face looked hopeful. He held out his hand like he wanted to seal the deal.

Maybe the fog had crept into her head somehow. It must have—because without another ounce of thought about all the things that could go wrong, she found herself grabbing his hand and shaking it. Somebody had to keep him from getting himself killed, right?

"We need God's help on this, El. I need His help."

She gave him a long look. "We've needed His help for a long time. But I haven't seen God show up. And my grandpa needed His help. But a man named Art stepped up instead. Now Grams needs His help—but instead it's me picking her up off the tiles after Shadow-man scared her to the floor like a child. Don't get me wrong, I appreciate your help, Parker. I do. But you'll have to excuse me for not having a whole lot of faith in God here. Seems He's a little too busy to be bothered with my problems—or my Grams's."

"El . . . what if God sent Art? What if He's sending me now?" Parker shrugged like he didn't know what to say.

"I don't know, Parker. I may not be religious, but that doesn't mean I doubt God's existence. Maybe I just doubt . . ." She caught herself. Did she really need to say more? Obviously Parker saw God in a whole different way than she did. She didn't need to rub his nose in it.

"You doubt . . . *what?*"

Honestly, it looked like he really wanted to know. "Maybe I just doubt that He cares."

Parker nodded slowly, but to his credit he didn't try to defend God.

"One question," Parker said. "The cross necklace. If you really don't believe God cares . . . why hold the cross like you do?"

Like she was holding it right now. "Maybe I'm hoping He'll notice. Or maybe I'm hopelessly superstitious. Now get home, Parker Buckman, before that fog gets you." She smiled and tried staging a good front, but deep down couldn't help but think of how sure Grams was about the vapors being deadly. Parker didn't seem like the type that gave up on a friend—no matter how dangerous things got. And by shaking his hand, hadn't she just encouraged him to take the next step—one that was likely to be risky? "Hurry. Grams will be nervous."

"Not until you go inside—and I hear you double-lock that door."

Even ten minutes after he'd left—when she was sitting in her bedroom—she kept thinking about how Parker was so ready to help. He'd run over in his bare feet when she texted him. Who does that?

A really good friend.

But was she as good a friend to him? Even now, was she using Parker? Allowing him to take chances he wouldn't be taking if not for her problems?

There was going to be trouble. She sensed it. Grams knew it, too. Why hadn't she pushed Parker away? Devin Catsakis got too close to Shadow-man. More than ever she believed Parker was right. Whatever happened to Devin was no accident. Why did she shake Parker's hand—likely committing him to take some ridiculous chances for her? What if he did come face-to-faceless with Shadow-man—and something horrible happened? She stared at her hand. "Dear God," she whispered. "What have I done?"

CHAPTER 35

Thursday, June 9, 10:20 p.m.

THE GHOST STOOD IN THE DEEP SHADOWS along the back side of the Houstons' guesthouse. There was a small stand of trees here. A perfect spot to do a little recon.

Somebody less professional, less confident, would have been halfway across town by now, looking to lay low or get out of Dodge. But he'd always found there were things he could learn by sticking around. And honestly? He got more of a buzz this way.

He'd seen Do-Right sprint over. Barefoot. Was the kid just impulsive and stupid? Or did he understand that in battle sometimes the quicker and more decisive the reaction . . . the more sure the victory? He couldn't possibly know that . . . or were his instincts just that good?

Do-Right was one to watch. That much was clear. But once again he'd revealed a weakness. Do-Right would react to help someone else before really weighing out the personal cost. Like running across pavement in bare feet.

It wouldn't be hard to anticipate Do-Right's moves. He'd do whatever was best for protecting someone in trouble—regardless of the personal cost. That was some valuable intel.

And just as valuable was the fact that the Houstons didn't call the police. If they had, he'd have seen lights by now. So instead of calling in the man with a badge and a gun, they called the barefoot neighbor. Classic bad decision-making—but really good to know.

Ten minutes later he watched Do-Right leave and head home. The Ghost had seen enough at the Houston house for now. Moving as silent as the shadows he crept through, he followed Do-Right instead.

Do-Right walked around the back side of his house. His second-story window was wide open, and a thick rope hung from somewhere inside to the ground below. So he'd climbed out the window. *Really* interesting. Why? So his parents wouldn't know he'd left? Or did he think it was faster? Which it surely would be if he did it right. The more important piece of info here was that Do-Right left his home base exposed while he was out trying to save the world. Anybody could have climbed that rope while he was gone. A ghost could have stopped in for a little visit.

Now *that* was a rich thought. To go up to Do-Right's room? The shock value would be worth the extra risk and effort, wouldn't it?

Do-Right shinnied up the rope without a sound, then hand-over-handed the rope inside, like he was pulling up a genuine anchor line. He left the window open though—and there was no screen. Why is it people felt so safe leaving an entrance to their home wide open—just because it was twelve feet off the ground? It might keep an animal out, but not a ghost.

The Ghost sensed someone approaching before he saw him. It was a sixth sense he had. And it wasn't some late-night dog-walker. Instinctively he scanned the area—even though the fog didn't allow for much range.

The figure appeared almost ghost-like at first. Dark hoodie. Face completely covered in the shadows. And in a hurry. Walked right up the road, constantly checking Do-Right's house.

Interesting.

The guy was big, in shape, and young. He carried himself with that teenage sense of immortality—like he could handle anything that dared come his way. The Ghost would see about that.

The guy hesitated, then suddenly turned off the road and streaked across the lawn to Do-Right's backyard—clearly unaware how close that would bring him to the Ghost.

The guy dug a glowing light stick out of his pocket, lifted the lid on one of the trash cans, and dropped it inside.

Really interesting. So this was the guy doing the look-alike burglaries? Total jackpot.

With a look over his shoulder, the guy raced out of the yard again toward the street.

It paid to stick around after completing a mission. Oh, yeah. He almost always learned something he could use later. Something of value. And tonight he was getting pure gold.

Tailing the copycat was easy. Especially since the punk clearly had no idea he was being followed. The Ghost's light stick was inside his sweatshirt—completely out of sight. No matter how many times the kid looked behind him, he'd never spot him. He loved these foggy nights.

The kid moved fast enough. Peeled off his hoodie and tied it around his waist. He walked right into town. He didn't look behind him now—obviously feeling safe. An amateur mistake.

Past the first row of shops, the kid cut down toward the T-wharf—then took a sudden left turn to cut behind the first building at the heel of Rockport Harbor.

The Ghost's rolling anticipation kicked in and knew exactly where the kid was headed—or rather where they were about to meet. The Ghost kept to the front of the building. Sure, there were street lights, but the fog was heavy and the traffic light. He poured on the speed. A quick sprint to the launch ramp and he knew he was far enough ahead of his prey. He dashed halfway down the ramp, crouched at the corner of the building, and waited.

Sure enough. Here came Mr. I-feel-safe-in-town. Picking his way along the rocks just above the high-tide line. The moment the copycat stepped onto the concrete launch ramp, the Ghost bolted for the kid and rammed into him with enough force to send him skittering down the mossy ramp—and headlong into the water.

The kid never saw what hit him. But he sure saw the Ghost when he thrashed back to the surface. The Ghost stood there on the ramp. The light stick out now. Holding it close enough to his face for him to see that he had none.

The kid stood. Water up to his chest. Even in the fog the Ghost could see the kid's chest heaving. If the kid were forty years older, he'd already be dead of a heart attack. The kid didn't move. Didn't dare.

The Ghost stood there for a long moment, just to let the image burn into the kid's retinas. Slowly he shook the light stick at the kid. A silent warning. Without a word the Ghost turned and strode up the ramp.

The instant he was around the corner he buried the light stick under his sweatshirt, circled the building back toward the T-wharf, and crept onto the rocks along the water. He retraced the very route the kid had taken just before the Ghost baptized him. He hunkered in the shadows to watch—not twenty yards behind the kid.

The kid must have stood in the nippy water another ten minutes before he sloshed up the ramp. Real slow. Looking toward the street, like he expected the Ghost would still be there. He wrung out his sweatshirt. Retied it around his waist. Picked his way along the rocks behind the buildings, still heading for Bearskin Neck.

The Ghost kept just far enough behind him not to lose him—although if he did, it wouldn't be a big deal. The kid was leaving a water trail behind him that would be easy enough to track, even as dark as it was.

The instant the kid reached the corner of the harbor, he climbed the granite wall and doubled his pace until he got to the gravel lane behind the shops of Bearskin Neck.

The Ghost had no problem keeping up.

The kid was running now and didn't slow up until he reached the back of one of the buildings. Rockport Dive Company.

The Ghost smiled—and moved in. The kid was still fumbling for his key. Wet pants. Cold hands. It took him a little more time than he'd probably hoped. But it was just perfect for the Ghost. He picked up a piece of gravel. Tossed it at the back of the building.

When the kid wheeled around, the Ghost had the light stick back out. He stood there so the kid would know the Ghost knew exactly where to find him. The kid tore around the building toward the front.

By the time he got inside and dared look out a window, the

Ghost would be halfway to Do-Right's place. This was turning into a perfect night for EOS tactics. First the fat Houston lady. Then the copycat. Two down. One to go. And this next one would prove to be the most challenging—and definitely the most fun. But he would do it. A perfect trifecta. The ultimate hat trick.

And by the time he was done, everyone would know the break-ins weren't a bunch of kids getting their kicks. If any one of them had doubts there was a ghost in Rockport, they wouldn't after tonight.

CHAPTER 36

Thursday, June 9, 10:35 p.m.

AS MUCH AS PARKER DIDN'T BELIEVE IN GHOSTS, the Shadow-man didn't exactly seem human, either. How was he supposed to catch it? He had to do something. He flopped onto his bed and stared out his open window. He couldn't exactly see the ocean from here, but on a night like tonight he could picture the waves crashing against the Headland rocks. The salty air was fresh, like it had been fully filtered as it crossed the Atlantic. The air was perfect, the way God created it to be. So totally different from the heavy air of the Everglades.

His mind seemed to be carried on the breeze. He pulled out his phone. Looked up Juneteenth. Sure enough, a whole slice of history he'd never heard about in school. Yes, Lincoln's Emancipation Proclamation outlawed slavery, but it took the Union Army time to enforce it in remote areas. Texas was one of the final holdouts, and when slaves were finally freed there on the nineteenth of June, 1865, a holiday was born. Jubilee Day. Juneteenth.

Okay, he'd come up with a plan to make that day special for El. Add that to the list of other plans he had to come up with—like catching Shadow-man.

People were always overthinking plans. Over-analyzing. Quicker to take a poll rather than follow their gut. And that often meant little got done.

Just do something. That's the way Parker's dad operated sometimes, too, right? When there was a problem, that's what Buckman men did. They sorted it out on the fly. They attacked—even if the plan wasn't perfect.

And that was exactly what Parker intended to do. He had the start of a plan—or maybe just the first step. Ella didn't seem one bit optimistic about the stakeout. Hopefully Dad would be more encouraging. But the plan, as it was, wasn't likely to be enough. There were too many places to watch. He needed something more—and he knew where to get it. He checked his watch. Almost 11:00, but she'd understand.

He picked up his phone—and texted Jelly.

CHAPTER 37

Chokoloskee, Florida
Thursday, June 9, 11:25 p.m.

ANGELICA READ THE TEXT—AGAIN. He'd sent it what—a half-hour ago? *How had she not noticed it before this?*

Parker was over a thousand miles away from the Everglades, but he was stepping into another type of swamp. And he was going to do it with the Ella-gator this time.

Which annoyed Angelica more than just a little bit. He was likely going to put himself in some kind of danger. Normally Angelica would be there—to be the voice of sanity. To keep him from doing something stupid or too risky. She had no idea if Ella would do that—or how effective she'd be. You couldn't just tell Parker not to do something. If he saw it as an issue of honor or integrity, he'd find a way to do whatever she warned him not to anyway. He was stubborn that way. Did Ella even know him well enough to realize that?

Angelica sat up in bed and stared at the blackness outside her window. But is that what really scared her most?

No.

It was that deep down Angelica was pretty sure Ella *did* know him well enough. And if she did, that meant they were spending a lot more time together than Parker let on. And that could only mean one thing. Angelica definitely *was* being replaced by the Ella-gator.

Sure, she'd suspected it before, but his crazy plan to somehow track down and stop Shadow-man—with Ella's help—was proof, wasn't it?

She read the text again.

OK, I thought about it. I still think catching this Shadow-man is the only way to help El. Then maybe the police can force a hold on the foreclosure while they investigate. I'm still thinking about some kind of stakeout, but I need more eyes on this. I need your help.

Angelica paused. Would Ella losing her home be the worst thing in the world? Maybe by the time Angelica's dad got the transfer, Ella would already be gone from Rockport. Parker and Angelica would pick up right where they left off. She went back to the text.

I've modified my plan to figure out what's really going on here—and maybe we can stop it.

Of course Parker had a plan. He always came up with a plan—and they usually fell somewhere neatly between insane and insanely dangerous.

All I need is your trail camera. Can you UPS that up to me—ASAP? If you get it out tomorrow, I should have it by Monday at the latest. Thanks, Jelly . . . you're the best!

You're the best. "Gee, thanks, Parker." But did he even mean that? It seemed to Angelica that right now Ella was the best.

Obviously he wanted the camera to catch Shadow-man in action. With the infrared feature, he'd catch an image of the thing—even in the darkest night—or more likely with the way Parker described the weather in Rockport—in the thickest fog. Unless it really was a ghost. Then there would be no heat to trigger the infrared sensor.

Angelica tiptoed over to her closet and slid the camera off the shelf. She carried it to her desk, set it down, and stared at it. Could she get it to UPS tomorrow? Sure. Dad was off shift. He'd give her a ride.

But did she really want to send it? Wouldn't that just give Parker another excuse to spend more time with Ella? And likely it would mean slipping out late at night—sneaking around town together. Angelica pictured them somewhere in Rockport, that gorgeous place that she'd already grown to love just by the FaceTime calls with Parker every week.

And if she sent the camera, would that *really* be the best thing? Wouldn't he be in more danger? Which looped her right back to her earlier question. Could Ella really protect him?

That was Angelica's job.

Of course, she'd never say something like that to Parker. He'd hate to think she was trying to be his guardian angel. He'd push her back—right out of his life—and he'd go it alone.

You're exaggerating the danger of this whole thing, Angelica. Or was she? Honestly, the idea of kids being behind all the burglaries—doing it all for thrills—didn't resonate with her. Not a bit. Not that she believed in ghosts, but *somebody* was breaking into those homes. That took guts, planning, and likely a really sick mind. Would somebody like that sit back and do nothing if Parker started poking around, sticking his nose in their business?

How far would Shadow-man go to protect his secret—or to keep out of jail?

Far enough to hurt somebody. And that person would be Parker.

She stared out the window into the blackness of the night. She checked the lock—as if somehow the darkness intended to seep into her room. Into her very soul. She flicked on the light on the stand next to her bed. That's when she noticed her hands trembling. Was she that upset about Ella taking her place? Or that worried about the danger that Parker was getting himself in? Probably both. But there was something else. It was the fresh spark of an idea. A strategy to handle both of her problems.

A light tremor rippled through her—and she knew. Angelica had no intention of being "the best" by dropping that camera off at UPS. But she couldn't let Parker know that. Not yet.

She pecked out a quick message and stared at it after sending it to Parker.

`I'll figure something out.`

She wasn't lying. Not exactly. She *would* figure something out.

Actually, she already had.

Sending that camera would only be enabling him. Allowing him to get himself up to his neck in alligators again, so to speak.

Her phone vibrated—and Parker's response flashed on the screen.

`You're the best.`

"Yes, I am," she whispered. "Don't you ever forget it, Parker Buckman."

She read his text again. `You're the best.`

She hoped he still felt that way when he learned she wasn't going to play his game—at least not without changing the rules.

CHAPTER 38

Friday, June 10, 5:00 a.m.

WHEN PARKER'S ALARM RANG AT FIVE, he silenced it with a single stab and dropped back on his pillow. It had taken him forever to drift off to sleep after the run to El's. But if he didn't get up now, he'd miss his chance to talk to his dad.

One thing Parker had learned in the Everglades was to aim at doing the right thing every time. And right now the right thing was to trust his parents with the truth. But what if they didn't like his plan, and Dad pulled in the reins?

Morning sounds filtered through the house. The muffled thump of the refrigerator. Sounds of a bowl being set on the table. The coffee maker. Parker stretched and rolled out of bed. He trudged to the bathroom like a sleepwalker, his eyes closed pretty much the whole way. He splashed some water on his face, pulled on his jeans and T-shirt, and shuffled to the kitchen.

He stood in the hall for a moment, letting his eyes adjust to the light.

Dad was already in his ranger uniform—ready for the forty-five-minute ride into Boston. Working at the oldest commissioned ship in the United States Navy—the USS *Constitution*—was probably the most unusual post Dad had held as a National Park Ranger. Launched in 1797—and undefeated through 1855—the ship picked up the nickname "Old Ironsides" in the War of 1812 by sailors who'd witnessed cannonballs deflecting off the warship's thick oak hull like the thing was made from cast iron. Dad loved history—and getting to know every scuttle and hold of the floating American icon was like living a dream for him.

Dad admitted to Parker once that he missed the action of the Glades—and working with Jelly's dad—but the transfer to Boston was a welcome change from the armpit of America that the Everglades turned out to be. And the move was a godsend for Mom. Her work with the *Boston Globe* newspaper was an easy commute by train from Rockport.

"Morning, Dad."

"Hey, my son is up before the sun is up." He grinned at his own joke.

Parker groaned. Leave it to Dad to work in a lame dad joke before breakfast. "Got a minute?"

Dad motioned to a chair and listened as Parker gave him a quick sketch of his plan to catch Shadow-man—electronically anyway.

"So." Dad rinsed his bowl and set it in the sink. "You're going to set up Jelly's trail cam at Ella's place?" He pulled his insulated cooler bag holding his lunch from the fridge.

This was the moment of truth. Planting the camera wasn't

risky at all, but the other part of his plan? If he was going to be a person of integrity, he'd have to tell his dad everything—even if that meant taking the risk that Dad would pull the plug on his plan. "That's the plan. Part of it, anyway."

Dad looked toward his bedroom door. "Let's talk by the truck so we don't wake Mom."

Parker followed him outside.

"What else is rolling around in that head of yours?" He opened the driver's door and set his lunch and pack inside.

"Mr. Steadman is checking on that Boston Investors Group through his investigator friend. And he's going to have a talk with that loan guy from the bank—and he's paying some of Mrs. Houston's bills, right?"

Dad nodded.

"Meanwhile Mom is going to do some poking around with her sources at the newspaper to see what she can learn about BIG. And you've already given Mrs. Houston some money for bills."

"Right."

"But I'm not doing anything—and I want to help. I *need* to help. The camera will only cover El's place. But if we want to catch whoever this is, we need to keep an eye on Steadman's rentals, too," Parker said. "But these other places would be more of a recon mission."

Dad raised his eyebrows. "A stakeout?"

"From a safe distance." He held up one hand. "Promise."

Dad stared at the ground. Maybe Dad was mulling it over—or figuring out how to tell Parker he was pulling the plug.

"Look, we want to be good neighbors," Parker said. "And the Houstons are going to lose their home. If some new information doesn't come out that will stop the foreclosure—and if the renters don't return—and fast—Ella and Grams are gone. That just doesn't feel right. The Houstons need help, Dad. Maybe this is one reason God got us this fantastic home—right on this block—so we'd be here to help them when they really need it." Okay, maybe he was laying it on a bit thick, but deep down, he really believed everything he'd just said.

Dad nodded. "I hear you, son. But she *did* take that loan. And she *did* sign that loan agreement. And if she can't pay, the bank has every legal right . . ." He shook his head. "But look, I get it. Something about the whole situation really stinks."

"The only reason she can't make her payments is because somebody—or some organization—is trying to take it from her. That isn't right. And you always taught me—"

"To be a defender of the weak," Dad said. "The oppressed."

"They've had it hard, Dad."

"So, maybe the camera picks up a usable image. Something to help Officer Rankin see this isn't you—or some other kids messing around. So he starts looking for the real criminal here."

"Exactly. But June 19 is coming—and we don't have much time."

"And if the perp is spotted on the stakeout, you're not going to play hero and try catching him, right?"

Parker raised one hand. "Honest. I only want to catch him on my camera—and call the police. If I have images, Rankin's got to believe me then."

Dad looked at the house for a moment like maybe he was thinking about what Mom would say. "There'll be some conditions," Dad said. "Ground rules."

"Of course." He tried not to show a trace of excitement—or shock—at his dad's answer. "Shoot."

"You don't go inside Steadman's house—even if you find the door wide open."

Exactly the kind of thing he'd expect Dad to say. "Easy. I won't go near it."

"You let Mr. Steadman know you'll be there—just in case."

"In case *what*?"

Dad shrugged. "If I were him, I'd be hiding somewhere too. Watching. He has a concealed carry license. We don't want any confusion."

For just a second Parker pictured it. Both of them thinking the other was Shadow-man. "Done. I'll talk to him today."

"And one more thing." Dad swung into the truck and fired it up. "I'm going with you."

Actually, Parker really liked that idea. A minute after Dad pulled out, he slipped back inside the house and tiptoed upstairs. He could still catch a little more sleep before Mom got up. He liked that idea too.

The instant he stepped in his room he saw the green glow coming from under his bed. He couldn't move. Couldn't breathe. *O God . . . help me, God!*

He fumbled for the light switch. Even with the lights blazing, a trace of green still clung to the shadows under his bed. There was nobody under that bed, right? There couldn't be. The storage bin took up most of the space. Still, he grabbed the closest weapon. Amos Moses, the six-foot gator stick with Dad's dive knife strapped to the end. He yanked off the sheath, grabbed the gator stick with both hands like a spear, and bent low to check under his bed.

The glow stick was there. Big. Just like the one from Shadow-man. Parker scanned the rest of the room. Not a soul there.

He stood. Opened his closet door. Used the business end of Amos Moses to separate the shirts, just to make sure nobody was there. And if there was? Shadow-man would be shish kebab.

The closet was clear. Deep down he knew Shadow-man was gone. Not that Parker wouldn't check the rest of the house, just to be sure. There would definitely be no more sleep for him.

How had he gotten in—and when?

The answers fell into place quickly. The window had been open wide. Parker scanned outside. He'd check more closely in daylight, but he'd bet money he'd find indentations on the ground from a ladder.

"Okay, no more window wide open at night." He closed the thing and locked it. And it had to be last night, while he slept. A thought which totally creeped him out. Shadow-man wouldn't have tried pulling this off once Dad had lights blazing, would he? How had Parker not seen the light when he left his room to talk to Dad? Maybe because he'd been half asleep.

It didn't matter when Shadow-man had made his visit. It was the fact that he got in that totally unnerved Parker.

Now it was just the question of why. But that was obvious, wasn't it? It was about letting Parker know that Shadow-man knew where he lived and could get to him anytime he pleased.

Message delivered.

He breathed a prayer of thanks—that God had protected him while he slept. And prayed a whole lot more about God protecting him as he went forward.

"We've got to find this guy. Stop him. Ella can't lose her place. There's got to be a way." It was a for-real prayer, not a pep talk. But saying it aloud made him feel stronger somehow.

The inscription on the knife from Grandpa flashed through

his mind. *He reveals deep and hidden things.* He reached for the knife on the table by his bed—but the thing was gone. Grandpa's letter was still there, but where was the knife?

The eeriness of the whole thing crept over him. He didn't need to search his room for the missing knife. He knew it had been there when he went to bed.

So Shadow-man had climbed through his window. Left his light stick as proof he'd visited, and taken Parker's knife to show how close he could get to Parker. The guy would have been standing right over him as he slept.

This thing was out of control.

Okay, right now he needed to make sure Mom was okay—and check the house. And call Dad. Better yet, he'd call Dad and have him on the phone with him while making sure the house was clear.

And from now on, Parker wouldn't get caught without a knife on him. He'd strap one to his leg—even while he slept. And when he showered. When he went out.

Actually scratch that last one. Whenever he left the house he wouldn't just have one knife on him. He'd have two.

CHAPTER 39

PARKER WAS PRETTY SURE Rankin didn't buy his story. But he went through all the right motions, anway. The police checked his bedroom. Dusted for prints. Took the light stick as evidence. Double-checked the entire house. The truth was Parker could have made the whole thing up and planted the light stick under his own bed to look like an innocent victim.

Ella believed every word of his account. It was obvious by the way she gripped the cross necklace, and the skittish look in her eyes.

He'd texted Jelly with the details of the whole thing. Even without the sound of her voice, her replies betrayed a sense of desperation that he was still going through with the stakeout.

Let the police catch Shadow-man. She did her best to talk him out of it, but it was a losing battle from the start.

An hour before Parker and his dad left for the stakeout, Parker tightened his Gerber survival knife to his calf, using the heavy nylon straps attached to the sheath. Technically, he hadn't had the need to really use the knife in any kind of survival mode since the Everglades—but that didn't mean he didn't strap it on every couple of days. He'd named the knife Jimbo, after Jim Bowie, the inventor of the Bowie knife. Whenever he explored the flooded granite quarries, trekked rocky shorelines, or climbed the massive rocks making up the Headlands, Jimbo kept him company. About the only time he'd unsheathed it was cutting tangled lobster buoys free. He hoped he'd never need it for more than that, but after knowing Shadow-man had been in his bedroom, Jimbo was going to stick with him like a tattoo.

Parker pulled the knife free from its sheath. The black five-inch blade had an absolutely wicked cutting ability. He thumbed the edge—testing the sharpening he'd given it. The thing could slice like a surgeon's scalpel—and a serrated heel near the hilt worked perfect for sawing.

The handle was coated with a black rubber scientifically designed to give a solid grip, even if the handle was wet or muddy. Three holes were strategically drilled through the handle, allowing it to be fastened to a pole or branch with parachute cord to make a spear if you were in a true survival situation. Yeah, a good knife could be a real lifesaver—along with a lot of prayer, of course.

Parker bounced the knife in his open palm, amazed at the perfect balance of it. Every part of the knife was brilliant in its simplicity, ruggedness, and functionality. Even the butt was heavy steel, fashioned to a point perfect for busting open a car window—or somebody's head.

He slid the knife back into the hard plastic sheath until the hilt clicked—locking it in place. He snapped the straps around the handle, and pulled the cuff of his pants back down from his knee to cover it. He stood and looked down at his pants. Nobody would even know it was there.

But Parker would.

He strapped his dive knife to the other calf. This was definitely a two-knife night. If the one from Grandpa hadn't been stolen, he'd have brought that one, too. The weight of them on his legs felt good. Like he was ready for anything. This was just the way it was going to be until the break-ins stopped. Not that he really thought he could use the knife against another human being, but it might be enough to keep someone away.

Steadman was totally revved up for the stakeout. Chafing at the bit. His Bayview rental had been hit again last night—and there was some real damage this time. Shadow-man had been really busy. When Parker told him about his dad helping, he could sense the excitement in Steadman's voice. "Okay, you and your dad watch one place, while I guard the other. Tonight we get some answers. And I'm expecting some intel coming on this BIG outfit," he said. A meeting was already set up at Ella's house for the next day.

He didn't tell Steadman about the trail cam idea. He didn't want to get Steadman's hopes up. Actually, that wasn't it. He didn't want to let Steadman down. *Always deliver more than you promise.* Parker tried living by his grandpa's motto. What if something got messed up and the camera didn't make it?

Then again, what if Jelly hadn't even sent the camera at all? He knew her well enough to know she wasn't wild about the idea. But in the end, she said she'd send it, right?

He replayed the conversation in his head—then pulled out his phone to reread the texts. Had she actually agreed to send it?

No. She hadn't. She'd only said she'd figure something out. What on earth did *that* mean? And if she already did send it, why hadn't she sent him a text letting him know when to expect it for sure?

The more he thought about it, the more he was sure Jelly didn't ship it at all. Parker sent her a quick text.

The trail cam—here tomorrow—or Monday at latest, right? I'll pay you back for the shipping!

He set the phone on the window ledge and looked toward the Headlands. So many places he couldn't wait to show her—if the transfer for her dad ever came through.

His phone dinged, and he opened her response.

Tomorrow. Guaranteed delivery.

Perfect. The question was, where exactly would he strap the camera? He'd have to find the right angle—but if he set the camera too far back, the image would be too small or grainy and wouldn't be of much use. He fired back a response.

Thanks. UPS or FedEx?

He didn't have to wait more than thirty seconds.

Sheesh, Parker . . . what's next—need the tracking number? Stop worrying. You'll get the camera. ADS.

Okay. She sounded a little testy. What was bothering her? Maybe he was asking for too big of a favor. And ADS? Normally she was really particular about typos. He'd take that as UPS.

He waited to see if she'd say anything else—and with every minute that passed, he was sure she was miffed about something. He had no idea what—and wasn't sure he wanted to ask.

Parker read her last text again. Maybe she wasn't upset. Maybe he was imagining it. He could put out a feeler to see.

Thanks again for doing that. I owe you. And how are you doing?

He added that last part as a test.

He watched the dots blinking on the screen while she responded to his text.

`Oh, so you DO care about how I'm doing? I thought you only cared about the camera. But I can't talk now. Let's catch up tomorrow—after you get the trail cam.`

So that was it. Just because he got right down to business without checking to see how she was doing first? And she didn't even have time to talk anyway. Girls could be complicated.

Another text popped up.

`And Parker . . . you're absolutely right.`

He had no idea what she was talking about. Maybe she was baiting him to talk more . . . which was fine with him. He'd bite. Until the stakeout tonight, he had nothing better to do.

`About what?`

The response came back so quick—like she'd been waiting for him to ask.

`You DO owe me—and I'm going to collect.`

Parker laughed—and wasn't even going to try imagining what she had in mind.

Mom knocked on his door and stepped inside his bedroom. "Dad's ready."

She had that look on her face—like she wished she could talk him out of going.

Parker pretty well knew what she needed to hear—and it wasn't that he'd strapped Jimbo to his calf. "I'll be careful, Mom. I won't take any stupid chances. And I'll be with Dad, so everything will be safe."

"Actually, it's Dad I'm worried about." She wagged her finger at him and smiled in her teasing way. "You'd better keep him out of trouble, or I'm going to put the kibosh on this whole thing. You'll both stay home next time—and I'll make you watch Hallmark Christmas movies with me."

Parker groaned. "Not that—anything but that. That's got to be some form of child abuse."

"Then you'd both better come home in one piece, hear?" She wrapped her arms around him.

He could see over her easily now, something he hadn't been able to do when they lived in southern Florida. "It's just a stakeout."

She gave him a squeeze. "That's what I keep telling myself."

CHAPTER 40

Friday, June 10, 9:20 p.m.

HARLEY HAD THE DIVE SHOP SWEPT AND LOCKED UP fifteen minutes after his uncle left for Gloucester to get himself slopping drunk. If his uncle made it home before morning, he'd never notice if Harley was there or not. Perfect. Hopefully he'd be just as undetected by anyone else that night—especially the black-hooded guy who sent him for the swim in Rockport Harbor.

Harley had never been hit like that in any game he could remember. The guy was a human battering ram . . . if he was human at all. Harley had gotten such a creepy feeling when he'd planted the evidence in Parker's garbage. Had Black-hood been watching him, even then? Harley was sure of it.

Harley had tried aborting the plan for tonight. "This Black-hood guy knows where I live. We gotta lay low."

Scorza hadn't let him back down. "Stop whining. This is part of Rockport High's Star Quarterback Summer Football Camp. You be there."

It was the first time Harley had ever detected a threat in Scorza's voice—at least directed at him. Harley wasn't afraid of Scorza, but it moved a "got-your-back" dial in Harley's mind—the wrong way. It seemed that questions about what kind of friend Scorza really was were coming more and more often now.

"You planted the evidence, but the cops didn't haul Buckman in. So we do it again and again until they do," Scorza said. "Gatorade loses his job, his boat slip, and his BFF status with the girl. That's what you said you wanted, Harley, and I'm trying to give you that. But you can't be yo-yoing on this."

He went to the Hangar and sat on Kemosabe, started it up, and wiped it all down again. He was killing time, and he knew it. Maybe if Ella saw him on the Sportster someday she'd let him take her for a ride. Maybe she'd like it so much she'd stop going out on Gatorade's boat, and ride on Kemosabe instead.

He kept an eye on the clock and locked the shed back up again just before the rendezvous time. He grabbed his gear and met Scorza on the rocks at Front Beach, in the shadows of the Captain's Bounty motel. Together they jogged uphill through the Old First Parish Burying Ground and made their way to within fifty yards of Steadman's rental on Mills. They slipped on their hoodies—and full-face nylon masks. They looked like faceless identical twins. Or maybe like a couple of demons. Without a word they stretched their hands into latex gloves. They were getting better at this.

And more aggressive.

This was the last time Harley was going to let himself get talked into this—so he was pulling out all the stops. This time they'd do some damage—and they weren't going to stop at just one house. The plan was to hit both of Steadman's places in the same night—and plant more evidence at Parker's before it was over. And this time, it was going to work.

CHAPTER 41

Friday, June 10, 10:15 p.m.

ELLA WOULD HAVE FELT A WHOLE LOT BETTER being on the stakeout. Everybody was in place. Had been for over an hour. Parker and his dad were hunkered down behind some stone wall by Steadman's rental on Mills Street. Bayport. Steadman himself was doing the stakeout at Bayview, his other rental. She was pretty sure he wasn't hiding outside behind some wall, though. He was inside—just hoping he'd get his hands on whoever was behind the break-ins.

Ella's "post" was her own house. Which made some sense, actually. She didn't want Grams left alone—especially since they had a renter tonight. But she felt out of it here. Like everyone else was out doing something important, while she patrolled the house.

And patrol was the right word for it. Every few minutes she walked the house. Every light upstairs was on—and all the yard lights were blazing. Ella stopped at every window—like a full stop. She used her artist eyes to take in every detail in the yard outside. To be observant. Looking for anything that seemed out of place.

Right now Ella wished she had a weapon. Something that would scare—or stop—an intruder long before they got close to her.

If anybody saw something suspicious, they were to send a text. They were all on the same thread. Ella. Parker. Steadman. Parker's dad and mom.

If Gramps were still alive, he would have been out there too, wouldn't he? For sure. She stared across the patio to the rental. "I miss you, Gramps."

Grams insisted on staying up with Ella until the stakeout was officially over—however long it took. But she'd drifted off in Gramps's recliner downstairs just after ten o'clock. Ella had no intention of waking her. With all the worry about losing the place, Grams hadn't been sleeping much at night.

She finished her rounds on the second floor and tiptoed down the staircase. Grams's hearing wasn't what it once was—so the risk of waking her was remote. But still, Ella didn't want to take the chance. In a house that was over 150 years old, she'd learned the dance of getting down the stairs with minimal squeaking of floorboards.

Every door and window was locked—and double-checked. But still, she gave each one a quick visual as she passed. The kitchen window absolutely gave her the creeps. She'd scrubbed the warning off first thing this morning—every bit of it—but she could still picture it there.

Ella gripped the cross dangling from her necklace like she was some kind of vampire slayer. Shadow-man had gotten into—and out of—Parker's bedroom undetected. Nobody found ladder marks on the ground below his window, either. Why was it so hard for them to believe this thing wasn't from their world?

And with absolute heart-crawling-up-her-throat positivity she knew something else, too. Whatever the thing was, it was going to make another appearance tonight.

CHAPTER 42

Friday, June 10, 10:20 p.m.

PATIENCE WAS THE KEY. Rush into something too fast, and it leads to mistakes. He was staying a safe distance from Steadman's place until he was sure nobody was there—or waiting in ambush.

"Are we going to do this—or are you still building up the guts?"

Harley motioned for Scorza to shut up. On the field the QB called the plays—and everyone moved on his count. But it was getting old off the field.

Scorza signaled for a huddle-up, which Harley ignored. There was no need to talk over anything. They had the whole thing worked out. Harley would be the inside man while Scorza stood guard. It made sense that Harley would be the one to go in. He was the one who wanted to get Gatorade out of the way. He didn't argue with Scorza's plan, but still, it felt a little weird that Scorza wasn't going in with him this time. Again.

"Hey, I agreed to be the one going in. I'm not going until I'm sure this isn't an ambush. Don't rush me." Would Scorza back him up if Harley ran into trouble? Of course he would. Right?

The house was dark, but he could see the windows well enough. If one drape moved, they'd book. There had been enough break-ins to put everyone on the lookout. Every time they did this, they'd be upping their chances of getting caught. So they'd take it slow and careful before going in. If he were Steadman, Harley would park his truck far from the home—and be waiting inside the dark house. Steadman would be at one of the rentals for sure. It was just a question if he was at this one. A fifty-fifty chance.

It was insane to hit this place again. Absolutely crazy. Scorza insisted that this was exactly what made it a brilliant move. Nobody expected the same place to get hit two nights in a row.

A muffled snapping noise drew his attention. Scorza was on the move. In a half crouch, he darted through the shadows on the opposite side of the house from the neighbor with the security lights.

What was he doing? But Harley knew. He was calling the plays again, and he obviously expected Harley to follow his lead. He growled inside. Part of him wanted to ditch Scorza, but that would be missing the whole point, right? He had to try this one more time. Hit Steadman's homes. Pin some evidence on Gatorade. Force the police to take action. Ella wouldn't want to hang around a guy like that. She'd be looking for a new friend—and Harley would be there.

Scorza motioned him over.

Harley climbed over a granite rock wall that looked like it had been in place since the Revolutionary War. He worked his way across the yard silently, with his peripheral "game vision" fully activated. He'd always been able to see a defender rushing toward him from practically any angle except directly behind him. If anyone was around tonight, they'd hidden themselves well. The place seemed as lifeless as the burial ground.

Scorza stood beside a dark window and motioned him to put it in high gear. No going through the back door this time.

"About time." Scorza grinned. "We good?"

No apology for rushing him. Just an expectation that whatever the QB did was okay. Harley gave him a thumbs-up—even though he felt like sacking the QB. He handed Scorza a glow stick and kept one for himself.

"Gatorade is going to lose some serious yardage tonight," Scorza said.

Scorza had left his signature football at home this time, but the first-floor window didn't need more than a jab from Harley's elbow to drop the pane to the floor inside. A moment later he reached inside for the latch and raised the window.

Harley boosted himself inside and dropped into a crouch.

"Go to the kitchen and unlock that back door," Scorza said. "I'll be there, standing guard. If I see anything, I'll duck inside to warn you. Then we'll fly out the front door together."

They'd been over the plan. Harley didn't need a recap except for one little detail Scorza kept ignoring.

"And if Steadman is in here waiting for me?"

"He's not."

Harley put his back to the wall and kept an eye on the dark room. "And what about Shadow-man?"

"Look, I've got your back. You'll find an opening or blow right through him. You always do. Or do you want me to do this?"

Harley shook his head. "Just keep your eyes open." Maybe it was the fact that he was alone in the house. Maybe not. But he had a really bad feeling about being there.

CHAPTER 43

Friday, June 10, 10:28 p.m.

PARKER STRAINED TO SEE THROUGH A GAP between the granite stones. Had he heard glass breaking, or was it his imagination? The wall gave them perfect cover, and they had a clear view of the back of the house. Even though Dad and Parker had agreed they weren't going to play supercop, that didn't mean they wouldn't try to slow down Shadow-man's escape until the police arrived. They'd used 25-pound rated fluorocarbon fishing leader to set up trip wires. One behind them in the woods. The other in front of the house—actually across the street. Each zigzagged from tree to tree, about six inches off the ground. The fishing line was clear—so nobody would know it was there until it took them down.

A hooded figure seemed to materialize from the shadows on the far side of the house. Parker reached over and gripped his dad's arm.

"I see him," Dad whispered.

Parker shifted to a crouching position. Felt the prickling as the blood worked its way back into his numb legs. This was it. What they'd been waiting for. *Thank you, God!*

Dad put a finger to his lips and picked up his phone. "Texting Steadman."

Shadow-man edged his way to the back stairway. He took one step. Then a second. Slowly—and without a sound. He moved different than he did before. More catlike. Way more guarded. The last time Parker saw Shadow-man there, he'd been standing tall like he didn't care who saw him. And he didn't look as big as last time—but maybe that's because Dad was here with him.

Dad's phone vibrated—which sounded way too loud in the dead air. Shadow-man hesitated. Cocked his head.

Could he possibly have heard?

After what seemed like a full ten-count, Shadow-man was on the move again.

Dad tucked his phone back in his pocket. "Steadman's on his way—and he's calling Rankin."

Perfect. *Perfect.* They'd catch the guy—and maybe Grams and Ella would have a fighting chance to keep their place.

Shadow-man was at the top of the stairs. He peered inside. Appeared to be trying the lock.

Dad leaned in close. "Guess that rules out him being a ghost."

It was true. A spirit being would just walk right through the door, right?

Shadow-man fumbled with something in his pocket. A moment later a green glow lit the area.

"The light was way bigger last time, Dad. Honest. Like the one he left in my bedroom." This one looked no bigger than what he'd find in a dollar store.

Dad and Parker instinctively crouched a bit lower. Now all they had to do was hope Rankin got here in time.

CHAPTER 44

Friday, June 10, 10:33 p.m.

HARLEY CROUCHED INSIDE THE BEDROOM and pulled off his hood. It was bad enough that the thing cut out some of his side vision, but it also muffled his hearing. If Steadman was in the house, guarding it, Harley definitely wanted to hear him coming. He stood there in the dark. Letting his eyes adjust a tiny bit more. He turned over a lamp without a sound, then waited.

Nothing.

Harley pulled the bedspread into a heap. As bad as meeting Steadman in the house would be, meeting Shadow-man would be worse. Had he followed him here? And if Shadow-man caught him . . . what would he do this time?

He eyed the closet, balled his hand into a fist, and slid open the door.

Darker than a shadow—but no Shadow-man inside. No Steadman either.

Harley held his breath and reached into the blackness. He felt the back wall. Slid to one corner, then the other. Bumped the closet pole and nearly knocked it from its mounts. He held it in place for a second, then lifted it free. Inch and a quarter thick at least. An easy three feet long. It would make a good defensive weapon. If Shadow-man did show up, Harley would swing for the fence and take off running.

He held the rod like a club and ghosted into the family room.

He upended a chair. A coffee table. Eased the couch onto its face. All with minimal sound.

It was one thing to run the same play in a game—hoping for better yardage. What was the worst that would likely happen? The other team would anticipate the strategy and flatten you before you got past the line of scrimmage. But hitting the same house, for the third time in four nights? It was playing-football-without-a-helmet stupid. The chances were incredibly high that somebody was just waiting for them—and this was a trap.

Just get this done—and get out. Fast.

Even if the cop didn't find the evidence he'd planted at Gatorade's house, Harley was *never* coming back here. If Scorza called this play again, he'd have to find a new receiver.

Harley tiptoed into the kitchen. The green glow from Scorza's light stick silhouetted him slightly against the back door windows. Harley slid the dead bolt open and twisted the lock mechanism on the doorknob. He opened the door a sliver.

"If you see something—let me know. The door is unlocked."

"Yeah, yeah," Scorza whispered. "You're clear."

It didn't take thirty seconds to lay the kitchen chairs on their sides.

Finish the job, Harley, and get out of here.

Positive he was the only one inside, he moved through the house faster now. He dropped the towels on the bathroom floor. Tossed the roll of TP in the toilet.

Good enough. Let Scorza know the job was done—and move out. Once they were clear, he'd tell Scorza he was aborting the plan to hit Steadman's other rental tonight. If Steadman wasn't here, he definitely was at the other one.

Harley picked his way back to the kitchen.

The green glow outside the back door moved. Scorza took the stairs back to ground level and just stood there at the bottom. Was the guy antsy—or did he see something?

Scorza's hood was still up. He seemed to be watching the stone wall holding back the forest beyond. Harley studied it too—and for just a second saw a faint glow blink on, then off just as quick. Either he imagined it—or it was the glow from a phone display screen.

Instead of coming inside to tip off Harley, Scorza slowly backed toward the opposite side of the house from where they'd busted in. Scorza still faced the stone wall like he was trying to figure out if someone was really there—positioning himself for a head start right down the driveway just in case. Would Scorza really leave—without warning him?

Nice team spirit, Scorza. If Harley didn't get out—fast—he'd be trapped. He soundlessly grabbed the back doorknob to join his idiot friend before whoever was behind that wall could ambush them. How many others were surrounding the house?

Suddenly a security light washed over the entire side of the house—and through the window over the sink. Scorza shielded his face, then spun and ran for the street out front. Two figures vaulted the stone wall and tore after him.

They hadn't seen him, had they? They couldn't have. Harley bolted for the bedroom, climbed through the busted window on the dark side of the house, and dropped to the ground below. He stayed low, holding the rod like a baseball bat—ready to swing at the first thing that moved.

CHAPTER 45

"STAY HERE," Dad shouted, "in case he doubles back around the house the other way."

Instinct told Parker to stay with his dad. Honor told him to obey. And Dad may be right. It would be smart for the guy to slingshot around the house and run the other way while Dad was temporarily blinded by the security light. Dad ran for the street. Parker hesitated for a moment, then cut across the backyard toward the dark side of the house. The lousy security light messed with his night vision too, forcing him to slow up.

The horrifying sound of a vehicle braking hard and skidding came from the street out front. Like the treads were going to rip right off the tires. Parker heard a sickening dull thump.

Dad!

Parker bolted through the tunnel-like blackness on the side of

Bayport for the streetlights ahead. Almost immediately he sensed more than saw he wasn't alone. A flash of pain exploded against the side of his face—and Parker wasn't running anymore. He was falling into a pit—or a quarry.

Make that a black hole.

CHAPTER 46

Friday, June 10, 10:39 p.m.

HARLEY STARED AT THE CLOSET POLE IN HIS HANDS—and the crumpled form lying on the ground. Not big enough to be Steadman. Definitely too small to be Shadow-man.

He dropped the makeshift weapon. *What had he done? What should he do?*

"Oh, God." He hesitated. He had never prayed before. Wasn't even sure God would be listening. "Don't let him be dead—whoever it is."

Run. *Run*. Everything inside him screamed—RUN. Who would know, right? But he'd just grand-slammed somebody really good—in the head. Had he smashed their skull—or started a brain bleed? What if they needed help? *How could he leave them to die?*

He took a step closer to the body. Crouched down. Strained to hear breathing. But the shouts and confusion from the street out front weren't helping matters. With whatever was going on there, whoever he'd just bushwhacked may not be discovered until daylight. That might be too late—if it wasn't already.

Scorza has been hit by a car. The screech of the tires. The frenzied voices out front. The awful sound of someone getting hit. It had to be Scorza. He hugged the shadows along the rental home and made his way to the front corner of the house.

Steadman's pickup was nearly sidewise on the street, the front tire up on the curb . . . headlights on. Dust—or smoke—still rising in the beams. A man lay on the ground with Steadman kneeling over him. "Paramedics are on the way, Vaughn. Do not even *try* to move that leg."

Vaughn. Gatorade's dad? A sick feeling dropped its shoulder deep into Harley's stomach. The force drove hard—like Harley's gut was a tackling sled. Scorza got away, but Gatorade's dad got hit? *He* was the one behind the wall? If that was Gatorade's dad, who had he just smacked with the closet pole?

He hustled back to where he'd left the body. Bending over, he pulled the light stick from his pocket, cracked it, and held it close, using his own body to shield the light from street view.

Gatorade. Cheek split wide just below the eye—and bleeding like a stuck pig. Eyes shut. Mouth slightly open. Face white as football laces. He'd wanted the guy out of the area—but not like this. "God. Please."

It was all his fault.

Flashing lights orbited the yard as police cars pulled up. Cops got out of the cruisers, and Harley edged closer, hugging the shadowed side of the house. Nobody in the back seat of either of the cars. Which pretty well confirmed Scorza had slipped by them.

Sirens wailed—but close. Maybe a couple blocks away. Sure

enough, the paramedic van came in hot and stopped right in the middle of the street. Two medics rushed to Parker's dad while a third went to the back of the truck.

Steadman was explaining everything to the cop now—who was taking notes. Steadman didn't look at all like the confident guy who used to come in to get tanks filled for dive charters. He paced like he was in agony, like he wished he hadn't been the driver—but the one who got hit instead.

"It was my fault. I saw the perp run right out in front of me." Steadman used his hands to help the cop visualize the scene. "Braked and swerved. Glanced off Vaughn instead. Never saw him until it was too late."

The paramedic pulled a gurney from the open double doors on the back end of the truck. A small crowd gathered to watch.

There was never a better opportunity to run and hide. Do it right, and nobody would know. But how could he live with that? He crept back to Gatorade's side again. It didn't look like Gatorade had stirred. The guy needed help.

Harley laid the light stick on Gatorade's chest. His face picked up a Frankenstein glow—and with the bloody face and scarred arm, it completed the effect.

The two paramedics were talking to Gatorade's dad again—but the third guy was still messing with some adjustment on the gurney.

Harley moved as close as he dared without leaving the shadows. "Hey, medic." Harley did his best to deepen his voice—and to only speak loud enough for the lone medic to hear him. Hopefully.

The uniformed guy looked directly Harley's way, but there wasn't a chance he could see into the shadows, right?

"Got another guy here. Hurt bad. Better check him out."

The medic hustled toward him. Harley backed up. Stepped around Gatorade. Kept to the shadows. "Make him okay, God," he whispered. "Make him okay."

The medic zeroed in on the glow stick. He dropped down on his knees next to Gatorade. Pulled out his flashlight and leaned close. "Hey, pal. Can you hear me?"

Hear him, Gatorade. Please. Hear him. God . . . do something.

Gatorade groaned.

"Hey, that's better," the medic said. "What's your name?"

Harley backed away. He'd heard enough—and there was nothing more he could do here. Now to get away without being spotted.

CHAPTER 47

Saturday, June 11, 8:00 a.m.

ELLA SET THE BOX OF BROTHERS BREW DONUTS on the center of the kitchen table. The second meeting of the Rockport Resistance was even bleaker than their first one had been.

Grams. Mr. Steadman. Parker. Officer Rankin was there at Steadman's invitation—which probably shouldn't have been such a surprise after the fiasco the night before. Rankin didn't stay longer than it took to hear a quick update from Mr. Steadman—and give everyone a piece of his mind.

Parker's mom and dad missed the meeting. His dad was still in the hospital—and would be for a couple of days, and his mom was making sure he was being taken care of. Ella couldn't imagine how hard he'd been hit to get his femur snapped in two, but it took a late-night surgery, a steel plate, and a handful of screws to put him back together again. He wasn't going to be diving with Parker anytime soon.

And Parker would be getting another scar on his face to complement the one he'd gotten from a gator's tail. Eight stitches didn't sound like much, but right now, his face looked awful. Swollen cheek—already turning a whole palette of colors. As far as she knew, every one of Parker's scars—arm and face—was the direct result of helping a friend. And now one of them existed because of her. He looked so tired, too. He should be in bed recovering, but he seemed determined to be part of things anyway.

Parker said he'd update his parents after the meeting—but admitted he might miss something with the pain-killing meds he'd been given. When she offered to call Parker's mom for him, he looked totally relieved. It was a small thing, but a way she could show her gratitude for all they'd done. Ella jotted some notes down to help her keep the details straight:

Mr. Steadman's investigator friend found that the Boston Investors Group may have organized crime connections. He said BIG had long arms and deep pockets. How deep? Picture the deepest spot of any ocean on earth. The creepy Mariana Trench. That's how deep.

As if that wasn't depressing enough news, there was more. BIG is active from the Carolinas all the way up to Maine—taking over little chunks of lots of towns. The unofficial word? They expand their real estate holdings by putting a scare into owners—getting them to sell cheap. Turns out they put a scare into the big, tough investigator, too. He won't be helping Steadman anymore. Thanks for nothing.

Mr. Steadman's other "friend" (Scorza's dad . . . the loan department manager stealing the home from Grams) was given strict orders to foreclose by the parent bank in Boston. Apparently BIG is a massive customer there in the big city. Scorza is afraid to push back. So it turns out he's a jerk, a traitor, and a coward, too. I think Grams summed up this guy best. "His speech is smoother than butter . . . but war is in his heart. He's in cahoots with the devil himself. That man is as cold as the landlord's heart." Mr. Steadman could use new friends.

Since Mr. Scorza started the foreclosure process, no other bank will even consider giving Grams a loan. They'd see the foreclosure was in motion—and that Grams's payment history was horrible. So a bailout by getting another loan was a total dead end. More terrific news.

BIG called Grams again yesterday, renewing their offer. That was news to me. Really, really bad news.

Incredibly, Officer Rankin still thinks kids are culprits—and he's going to take them down. He made it clear: no more stakeouts. No more chasing Shadow-man. Basically no more doing his job for him. He warned us to stay out of his way—which almost made me laugh out loud. How can we be in his way when he isn't even around?

Mr. Steadman bought security cameras for his rentals, and is having two mounted at Beulah . . . today. He told us this after Officer Rankin left. He hopes it keeps the BIG goons away. That they'll go to easier targets. At Beulah, one camera will be mounted on the rental, the other on the main house. The cameras will give a hi-res image capture of the backyard and patio. All of us can download the app so we can do our next stakeout from inside our own homes—and we can't possibly get in Officer Rankin's way. Mr. Steadman himself is hoping Shadow-man comes to one of his rentals—the one where he'll be inside waiting. And Mr. Steadman made it clear he'd deal with Shadow-man in his own way—and wouldn't call Officer Rankin until it was time to clean up the blood. If only!

Parker believes that catching Shadow-man, or discovering his identity somehow, is the answer. He thinks that could open up a bigger investigation—and stall the foreclosure long enough for rentals to come back. He still seems to believe his God is the great revealer of mysteries—and somehow He will expose what's going on here. Personal sidenote: Parker is the nicest guy I know. He's also the most naive.

Grams and I are still in the minority (ha!) and believe something evil and ghostly is involved. We aren't holding out much hope for a miracle.

Much hope? Ella knew better. There was no hope . . . and to think otherwise would have been completely delusional on her part. Which brought her to the last—and most devastating—part of the update.

Grams blames herself for keeping her head in the sand so long—hoping the bank would stop the moves to take Beulah from her. She has decided to sell—but hopefully not to BIG. Her exact words? "We have to sell. I just wish I didn't have to sell to them."

She's banking on the rental this weekend posting a good review—and that it will bring in other bookings. Not that it will save Beulah. It will just help her get a different buyer—and hopefully a better price than BIG offered.

Mr. Steadman told Grams not to sign anything . . . the fight isn't over yet. But it is over. If Mr. Steadman believes what he says, his head is even deeper in the sand than my Grams's was.

Ella looked at her list. She wanted to run to the Headlands, just stand out there on the rocks and scream where the pounding surf would drown her out.

She appreciated what the neighbors were doing. How they were trying to help. Besides the stories of Art Carson, never in her whole life had Ella heard of a neighbor putting themselves out to help Grams in any real way. The Buckmans were the first neighbors who'd ever treated them like equals. Even Grams told her that. Maybe whatever the Buckmans had was contagious—and Steadman was catching it too. But it was too little.

And way too late.

CHAPTER 48

ROCK-RUNNING. It was one of Harley's little training secrets. The rugged coast gave him the kind of agility drills a coach could never set up on a practice field. His go-to starting point? The granite jetty jutting out like a giant curved finger from the end of Bearskin Neck. He was getting a late start this morning, but the shop wouldn't open for an hour.

He ran the granite gridiron all the way to the beacon light at the end—then around and back on the other side. From rock to rock. Leaping small chasms and spaces between the boulders that would annihilate the strongest ankle with one misstep. Stretching his stride. Staying close to the water where the monster waves rose like linebackers to take him down—and the rocks were wet and slippery like turf on a rainy game day.

Out on the Rockport Harbor side of the breakwater, back on the Sandy Bay side. Basically two football fields out and two back.

Most days he didn't end his training run at the Bearskin Neck turnaround where the shops ended. He kept going all the way to Front Beach. Sometimes he'd push on to Back Beach. He'd time himself, just to be sure he didn't start doggin' it. He never took exactly the same path, yet he knew it so well he didn't have to focus on each step anymore. It was like his feet had a mind of their own—and they were in the mood to fly.

On the field a running back needed super agility to dodge around, jump over, squeeze past, or smash through defenders. Opposing players who wanted to knock him off his feet and plow the field with his face guard—with his head still in the helmet. Rock-running prepared him for that element of the coming football season like nothing else. Some thought his moves on the field just came naturally. Not hardly.

The way Harley saw his secret training method? Out of the box. Others might say he was out of his mind. He'd never even told Scorza about this part of his training regimen.

Scorza.

He hadn't seen the jerk-face since last night—and was in no hurry to. The moment Scorza realized they'd walked into a trap, he'd ditched Harley. *What kind of a friend does that?*

The answer came at him as fast as a rogue wave. A friend doesn't. Not a real one. When things got dicey, Scorza had looked out for number one. Or number eight, actually.

Harley had always been bothered by the way pro quarterbacks would make a run with the ball—when they were out of passing solutions—but as soon as they'd see a defender getting close, they'd drop to the ground like they were sliding into home plate. Harley understood—QBs had to protect themselves. They were valuable to the team and couldn't risk an injury.

But *still.*

Harley saw it as a wimp move—even in the NFL. And what Scorza did was way beyond that. It was pure cowardice. He'd turned tail and run—without giving Harley a warning. Without circling back to help. Without checking to see if the guy chasing him needed help after he'd been hit by Steadman's truck. Without even a late-night text to be sure Harley made it out without getting caught.

Total jerk-face.

It was almost a game to Harley now. How long before Scorza texted—just to see if he was okay? It could take all summer as far as Harley cared. In the meantime, he'd channel his anger into training harder. The burn in his calves and thighs felt good. The balls of his feet were on fire, like maybe his soles would give off a blast of steam if a wave got a lick at them.

Harley had Scorza figured out now, but Gatorade was the mystery. Obviously he'd been helping Steadman. No wonder Harley's plan to get Gatorade fired wasn't working. Gatorade was doing recon for Steadman. Harley had been an idiot.

The bigger mystery was how Gatorade was doing. He was alive, Harley knew that much. The moment he woke up this morning he'd taken an early morning run up by the Headlands and purposely crossed and crisscrossed near Gatorade's house. Finally, he'd seen him from the back walking slowly toward Ella's. At least Gatorade wasn't in the ICU or something. It was a total relief, and at the time, that was all he needed to know. But now Harley wanted to know he was really okay. Maybe then Harley could stop beating himself up for hitting Gatorade with the closet pole.

Harley had worked his way around White Wharf and Old Harbor and was flying across the rocks behind the shops on Main

Street when he spotted Ella on Front Beach. Cowgirl boots standing by themselves up above the last high-tide swash mark, where the sand was dry. She stood barefoot on the hard, wet sand at the water's edge, wearing that powder-blue dress with the swirly design going through it. Head down, like her day was going just as bad as Harley's.

Harley poured on the afterburners and let his feet find their own path. When he got to the sand he kicked off his shoes, peeled off his socks, and left them near Ella's boots. He headed down to the water, taking deep breaths to get his wind back. He briefly wished he'd brought a towel to mop off his face.

Ella stood facing the water, the retreating tide sucking and pulling at her feet like they wanted to take her with.

"Ella!" Did he just call her by her first name?

She turned—a smile with teeth as white as the sea foam swirling around her ankles. Her smile faded slightly, like maybe she'd been expecting someone else. Suddenly he wasn't sure what to say. His feet slipped out of autopilot and suddenly felt big and clumsy.

He waved—and he knew it was lame even as he did. "Hey, Miss Houston." He was a total idiot. Ten feet away and all he can do is wave and say hey?

"Harley Davidson Lotitto. What brings you to Front Beach?"

He wanted to tell her about his routine—and other things he'd never told anybody. Like about the Hangar. Kemosabe. And his lousy Uncle Ray. What was that all about? Her voice alone worked like truth serum on him. He wanted to tell her everything. "I run this way almost every day. I've never seen you here."

"I avoid this place." Her eyes flitted to somewhere distant behind him. The street? Or maybe the Old First Parish Burying Ground. "But it fit my mood today."

Harley was no expert on reading faces, but she definitely didn't look like her I-can-handle-whatever-you-throw-at-me self. "Bad day?"

"Like you care." She turned to face Sandy Bay.

He stepped up alongside her. What if this was about Gatorade? "Maybe I can help." Which probably sounded as stupid to her as it did to him.

"This isn't the kind of thing you can tuck under your arm and run down the field for a quick touchdown."

Actually he loved the fact that she was talking football. "Well, maybe you could just hand off the ball . . . even for a minute . . . and give yourself a breather."

She gave him a sideways glance. There was just the slightest smile—or maybe he was imagining it. "I've seen you and that idiot friend of yours playing catch in the burial ground across the street. Trampling over sacred ground. And you think I should trust you—with anything?"

"We were running pass patterns. 'Go long to Eliza Jewitt's headstone—then cut right. I'll hit you before you reach Captain Thaddeus Brinkman's marker.' Stuff like that."

"You have no respect for the dead—or the living."

"But I want to. I mean, give me a chance, Miss Houston. Toss me the ball."

She looked out to sea again. Maybe she was thinking about it. "I lost a friend in May. Not a great friend, but he was nice to me. Treated me like I wasn't less than him in some way."

Sheesh. She was still thinking about Catsakis?

"And then I almost lost another friend last night."

Gatorade's injury must have been worse than he thought. A beach-hugging wave raced past them, swirling frantically around his shins like it wanted to push him out of the way. Harley felt heavier. Like he was wearing full pads—and a pack with another fifty pounds of free weights to boot. His feet sank lower in the sand as the water rushed by. He had done this. "I'm sorry. Honest. Is your friend going to be okay?"

She nodded. "He got hit in the head. And if the hit was just an inch closer to his eye?"

Ella didn't have to finish the thought. She'd have a one-eyed friend.

"But he's fine, right?"

"Just some stitches. And bruises. Man, his face looks terrible. But this is just the start of worse things. I feel it."

Harley wanted to tell her it wasn't the start of anything. It was the *end.* Harley wasn't going to trash Steadman's rentals anymore. There was no point. "It will be all right."

"Says the guy who knows nothin' about nothin'."

The sand shifted under his feet again as the tide sucked it out from under him. "So educate me."

She looked at him, like she wondered if he was serious. "Parker Buckman is the one who got hurt last night."

He tried to put on a shocked face. "Gatorade? Seriously? How did it happen?"

Ella told him about the break-ins at Steadman's, and how Parker and his dad were helping. "What happened to Parker is all my fault."

Harley could still feel the closet rod in his hands. The sickening smack he felt when he connected with Gatorade's face. "How is it *your* fault?" It made no sense.

Ella shook her head. "I just opened up to you more in the last five minutes than I have in the last two years."

"Hey, I won't talk about this . . . is that what you're worried about? But everybody knows there's been a ton of break-ins. My uncle has me on a sleeping bag in the shop—just in case the burglar decides to branch out and hit businesses." The water racing up the sand seemed more aggressive. More sand below his feet loosened and gave way with the high-speed erosion. His feet sunk a couple of inches closer to the earth's core. The water splashed up to his knees. He wanted to back up, but since she wasn't making a move he didn't either. "You can trust me."

She grabbed his arm to steady herself while she pulled her feet free from the sand. "We'll see."

And she would see. He'd prove to her that he could be trusted. He stood strong—like he wanted her to see that even now, in this small way she could depend on him. Lean on him. "Whatever's wrong . . . let me help make it right."

Having fully caught her balance, she let go of him and backed up toward her boots. "There's more to this—a whole lot—and I really don't want to talk about it. But I'll just say this much. I don't think real justice exists, Harley. Not for people like me."

"Justice?"

"Equality. A level playing field."

Okay, that was making a little more sense. He squared his shoulders. "Is somebody giving you a hard time?" He'd never seen anybody bother her. He wouldn't have let that happen. The truth was, she was pretty much a loner. Except for Gatorade. But if someone was giving her a hard time . . .

"Forget I said anything, okay?"

Like that was going to happen. "Trust me."

She snapped her fingers. "Just like that? It doesn't work that way, Mr. Football Star. You gotta earn it."

Like Gatorade somehow had gained her trust. "How?"

She looked at him long and hard. "You figure it out. And if you do, maybe we'll meet out here another time."

Count on it, Miss Houston. But he had to say something to her. Something more. He couldn't leave the conversation like this. "You don't have to talk at all right now. But can I just say one more thing?"

She kept backing up, but she didn't say no.

"I just think you're being too hard on yourself. Gatorade getting hurt wasn't your fault. Not one bit. I mean, you said it yourself. He was helping Steadman."

She smiled. But no teeth this time. "You've got it all wrong, Mr. Lotitto. Parker was helping *me*."

CHAPTER 49

Saturday, June 11, 10:30 a.m.

PARKER GRIPPED A SCUBA TANK IN EACH HAND by the black knurled knob of the valve. Carrying both kept him balanced, but they'd grown a lot heavier since he left home with them. And lugging the dead weight wasn't helping his headache one bit.

"It's a wonder you didn't get a concussion." Those were the doctor's exact words. As far as Parker was concerned, it was a wonder his head was still attached.

By the time he reached Bearskin Neck, he was really wishing he'd packed the tanks in the wheeled suitcase. But once he dropped them off to get filled, he'd be free. He was in no hurry to pick up the tanks after the fill, and he definitely didn't want to be rolling an empty suitcase around all afternoon.

With Dad in the hospital until tomorrow sometime, or maybe even Monday, there was no rush to get them filled in the first place. Sure, taking care of the tanks was his job. But really this was more about doing something. The stakeouts were over. There wasn't a thing Parker could do to help El until Jelly's trail cam arrived. But even that seemed kind of pointless right now. The multi-camera system Steadman was having installed would probably be all the recording devices they'd need. At least dropping the tanks off was something to keep his mind off the impossible spot El was in.

Parker stepped inside the Rockport Dive Company and let his eyes adjust for a moment. Harley stood behind the counter, palms flat on the wood top, elbows locked. Like he was holding it down or something. Was he staring at Parker's face? Probably. And who wouldn't?

"Gatorade. Where's the luggage?"

Parker couldn't see the smirk, but he was pretty sure it was there. He set the tanks in front of the counter. "Thought I'd carry them today."

Harley gave a single nod. "Better workout that way." He scooted around the barrier and grabbed the valves in an underhanded grip. His big arms curled the aluminum tanks like they were made of aluminum foil as he walked them into the back room. "Gonna wait?"

"No rush. I'll pick them up Monday."

Harley set the tanks down by the fill station and hustled back. "Sorry about your dad. And this." He brushed his own cheek. "Ella told me about it. Actually, the way she described it, I thought it would be worse."

Ella had talked to *Harley*? Parker tried not to show his surprise.

"Hurt much?" Harley jutted his chin toward Parker's cheek.

"Only when I laugh. Or smile. Chewing doesn't feel so great

either. And whenever I yawn, I feel like I'm going to split the stitches."

Harley grinned. "So pretty much don't move your face at all. I get it. Get a Coke at Top Dog when you leave here. A little caffeine will cut the yawning."

"I think I'd need a lot of caffeine." Especially for how little Parker had slept last night.

"Ella told me you've been helping Steadman with the burglary thing."

What was it with the chattiness? "Yeah, and I guess we know how that worked out."

"Hey, you tried, right?"

Okay, this was getting weird. *Harley* was actually being *nice* to him? What was going on? Parker backed toward the door.

"Ella told me you've actually been helping *her* more than Steadman."

Parker stopped. Ella told him about the house?

"Can I tell you something, Gatorade? When that thing happened with Catsakis, I kind of felt it was partially your fault. Like you could have stopped it. I don't know, I was just being stupid, I guess. But after talking to Ella, I guess I'm seeing a different side of you."

What was he supposed to say to that?

"I want to help. What can I do?"

Okay, so Parker couldn't have been more shocked if a shark jumped out of the harbor and through the bay window. "Right now *I* don't even know how to help her anymore."

Harley boosted himself up on the counter. "There's got to be something. She looked miserable. I offered to help, but she didn't seem to know what to do either."

Maybe Ella spilled her guts because she saw no point to keeping the big secret any longer. "What did she tell you?"

Harley shrugged. "Pretty much everything, I think. But I want your opinion. Honestly, how much trouble is she in?"

So she *did* tell him. Unbelievable. "It's bad. The break-ins hurt Steadman's rentals for sure. Probably others in town, too. I have no idea. But the ones who really got crushed in this are Ella and her Grams. They're totally stuck. Did she tell you about the loan?"

Harley nodded. "But I didn't really get it. And it seemed hard for her to talk about it—I didn't want to ask too many questions. She's never really talked like that with me before."

Parker couldn't imagine how desperate she was to do something like that. "Well, your buddy's dad called in their loan."

"Scorza?"

Parker nodded. "They were super-behind in their payments, but hoped some solid rental bookings might change his mind. But the Shadow-man break-ins crushed that option—if it ever was one. So we had stakeouts at both of Steadman's rentals—and Ella was on patrol at her place. We hoped we'd get lucky and catch the guy."

Harley nodded like he wasn't hearing anything he didn't know.

"We catch the burglar, the rentals start booking again . . . and maybe the Houstons catch a break. That was the plan." Parker shrugged. "I think we were fooling ourselves."

"Thinking you could catch the burglar?"

"Yeah—but no . . . that wasn't really the end game. Ella and her Grams were in a corner, you know? And fighting it all on their own. It just wasn't right. But unless we get some kind of miracle, a little rental income won't be enough to help them. She needs to pay off the entire loan." Parker reached for the door. "I'm praying for a miracle."

Harley was on his feet, heading his way, like he was going to walk Parker out. "What's going to happen if she can't pay it off?"

Maybe Harley had as hard a time believing it as Parker did. "What did Ella say?"

Harley jammed his hands in his pockets. Looked at the floor. "Enough. But I was hoping she was just being dramatic."

Parker shook his head. "Scorza's dad put them into foreclosure. They have to pay the entire loan by next Saturday. One week from today—or the police will evict them."

"What?!" Harley looked like he wanted to tear somebody's head off. "Isn't there some way to get the money in time?"

"The only way to pay off the loan is to sell. So either they get kicked out of their home—or they have to sell it. But one way or another, by June 19 El will have to leave Rockport."

CHAPTER 50

Saturday, June 11, 11:30 a.m.

IT AIN'T OVER UNTIL THE FAT LADY SINGS. He had no idea why that old saying kept rolling around in his mind. But he pictured the fat grandma who'd been clinging to the ridiculous hope that she could stop the inevitable.

It was time to deal with those hopes, and tonight was the night. The Ghost was feeling the power. That invincible sense of strength from the core of his soul. A real ghost might walk through walls, sure. But this ghost could *crash* through them. Tonight he'd seal the deal—and then there'd be no stopping him. Zero resistance. Everything else would fall in line.

Tonight would remove all illusions that kids were behind this. They'd know there was a *force* at work. One so totally beyond them that whatever hope they were clinging to would be crushed like a soda can underfoot.

And tonight they'd know the chance of selling to someone other than BIG was slim. Who wants to buy a house that's haunted?

Fear was useful. It was a fire that could do tremendous damage. Perfect if one had the luxury of time to kindle it. But when one didn't have the time or patience for that, the Ghost had learned to take the flames of fear to a whole different level. Stoke it into blazing terror.

First, he'd deal with the unsuspecting family in the rental home. After tonight they'd be gone—along with all hopes the Houstons might have of more rentals. He was going to enjoy that.

Then the really fun part of the night. It was time to teach some hard lessons. The kid from the dive shop. The Ghost had warned him to stay out of things. There was no way the kid didn't get his message. Yet he was pretty sure it was him who'd been out copycatting again last night. It was time to make sure he never ignored a warning again.

And then there was Do-Right. Honestly, he was no threat, but still, he was a wild card. The kid was like one of those inflatable bop bags kids punched at. He'd take a hit and keep coming back. An admirable quality, but there was no telling when he'd show up—and get in the way.

He'd lure the kid into an oven, of sorts. The Oven of Terrors. Let him feel the heat that raw fear could produce. The Ghost would give the kid a warning that would keep him awake at night. A final warning. If he didn't back off this time, Do-Right would have nobody to blame but himself for what would happen next. Scare him away, or put him away. Either worked.

The Ghost was close. Really close. Everything was falling into place perfectly. But that didn't mean he was going to let down his guard or start coasting. He'd keep the full court press going.

It ain't over until the fat lady sings. He pictured the grandma and smiled to himself. Actually, he was going to modify that old saying a bit. Just rearrange two tiny letters. It ain't over until the fat lady *signs*. And she would be signing soon.

CHAPTER 51

ANGELICA STEPPED OFF THE TRAIN and onto the platform, dragging her roll-aboard behind her. She adjusted Parker's cap on her head and surveyed her surroundings. Parking lot. Hardware store. Some kind of small town ballpark—with granite walls around the bleachers. Nothing all that different from any number of train stops across the country, she figured. But something deep inside her stirred. *Leaped* was a better word. She was home.

And there was something about the air. From her first breath outside the train, she knew this was unlike any other place she'd lived. There was the scent of the ocean—but not at all like it smelled in Chokoloskee or Everglades City. She drew in a deep breath and let it out slowly. Even as she did, the shakiness in her breathing was obvious.

C'mon, Angelica. Why the jittery, over-caffeinated nerves? The fact that she was finally in Rockport—after all these months of waiting? Absolutely—that was part of it. The fact that she was going to see Parker in person instead of on a display screen? That was a huge factor. But there was something more, wasn't there?

She marched down the ramp and along Railroad Avenue to Broadway. Her stuffed-to-the-hilt roll-aboard clacked a rhythm on the sidewalk seams behind her.

Angelica wanted to park her suitcase and run straight to the ocean. But she resisted the urge—and tried to absorb everything about the town. She passed the fire department. Rockport Pizza. And some of the biggest hydrangea bushes she'd ever seen. Granite curbs, walls, and fences ran the entire way—reminders of the quarry era long gone.

She stopped at the corner of Broadway and Mt. Pleasant Street to take in the sight in front of her. Harvey Park to her right. Barletta Park to her left. Both of them tinier than she'd imagined. A petite little lighthouse stood right there in the intersection. Angelica wasn't sure what that was all about, but it just added something small-townsy to the place.

Shops lined the other side of Mt. Pleasant Street. Brightly painted wooden buildings with big picture windows displaying T-shirts, souvenirs, or jewelry. But straight ahead was the real jewel. Broadway dead-ended into something called the T-wharf—a massive granite pier jutting out into the most inviting little harbor in the world.

This time she didn't resist the urge to run. Across the street and onto the T-wharf. Public washrooms, the harbormaster's office, and the Sandy Bay Yacht Club off to the right. To the left, a mosaic of lobster boats chained to their moorings. Judging by the dark waterline on the granite, the tide was nearly to its highest point. Floating docks lined the edges of the granite pier with colorful dories tied to them. The far side of the little harbor was rimmed with more wooden buildings—the back side of famous Bearskin Neck. She'd studied it all on the satellite view a million times since Parker had moved. Every time he called, she'd find the spot later on the screen and drop a marker.

The view got even better the farther she walked out on the T-wharf. The deeper part of the Rockport Harbor moored dozens of sailboats—bows nosing into the breeze, as if they couldn't get enough of the fresh sea air either. To the left side of the harbor, Bearskin Neck and a huge granite breakwater sheltered it snugly from Sandy Bay and the Atlantic beyond. On the other side, stunning homes lined the shoreline—and finally the storm-weathered rocks of the Headlands.

"Dear God . . . this has to be one of your masterpieces!"

And just off to the port side of the harbor, nearly in the middle of it all, the whole scene was showcased by Motif Number 1: the barn-red fishing shack that was the most-photographed structure of its kind in the world. How anyone could verify that fact, she had no idea. But she'd read it on a travel site—and as she looked out over the water she believed every word of it.

She stopped at the end of the T-wharf and tried to take it all in. The fresh salt air—tinged with a hint of fishiness here. If somebody could bottle the scent—or capture it in the wax of some candle—she'd definitely be a buyer.

She pulled out her phone and FaceTimed her dad. He answered almost immediately.

"You made it?"

"It was a little scary, but exciting, too." Angelica held the phone high and did a slow 360°. "And can you believe this place? I mean, c'mon. Look at it, Dad!"

"Just like the pictures we saw on the websites."

"Better," she said. "Seeing it in person—smelling the place—it's gorgeous, Dad. Absolutely gorgeous. Thanks for doing this . . . for working this all out with Uncle Vaughn."

Her dad chuckled. "I miss you already. Kinda quiet here, you know?"

He kept his questions about the flight to Boston and the transfer to the train to a minimum. "You find Parker now, okay? And when you see Uncle Vaughn, tell him I'll get up there as soon as I can." Dad grinned. "Somebody's got to keep that guy from killing himself."

She nodded. After getting the text from Parker about the fiasco the night before, her dad probably wasn't that far off. Parker promised more details when he called, but she'd heard enough to know the situation was worse than what he was telling her. For just an instant that jittery feeling was back—and totally in her belly. Not butterflies. They were too light for what was going on inside her. This felt more like panicked crickets hopping around inside her. The crickets jumping off the walls of her tummy kept telling her that something had changed with Parker . . . something she'd never get back.

"Angelica?"

Immediately the crickets went into hiding—and she forced the smile back on her face. "I'll call you tonight."

"I'm on shift, but I'll be waiting for that call. I love you, sweetie."

Angelica kissed her finger and touched the camera phone lens. "And, Dad . . . if I forget to tell you later . . . I really, really love you."

A woman on a nearby bench was staring at her over the top of her book. "I couldn't help but overhear part of your conversation," the woman said. She had a kind face. "Tourists love this spot. But some of us locals never tire of it either."

Angelica would be the same way. She was sure of it. "Actually, I'm not exactly a tourist, though."

"Really?" The woman looked surprised. "My name is Linda. I know a lot of people in town, but not everybody. I saw the suitcase and just—" She thumped her forehead with the heel of her hand. "You've been traveling. So where did you go—and how long were you gone?"

"I've been everywhere—and I've been gone all my life." She gazed over the harbor and drew in a deep breath of the sea air. "But I'm home now."

CHAPTER 52

Saturday, June 11, 1:45 p.m.

MOST OF THE TIME Parker found a new spot to FaceTime Jelly, or at least a new angle. Today he settled for a tried-and-true favorite. He hustled to the end of Bearskin Neck to do another call from out on the granite breakwater. There was something comforting about the ebb and flow as the water gulped and echoed between the massive stones under his feet. And he could use a little comfort right now. He had a lot on his mind.

El was already out there—nearly at the end. Easel up. Boots off. He picked his way across the rocks on the Sandy Bay side of the breakwater. The water was a lazy kind of flat right now—like everything was right in the world.

Except it wasn't.

El had one brush sticking out the corner of her mouth, another in her hand, and a third poked out from the base of one of her braids. He still couldn't picture her opening up to Harley, but then again, was there anything normal about the last twenty-four hours?

"Hey, El."

"Hmmm." She did her best to talk out of one side of her mouth. "Hey to you, too."

The canvas looked amazingly complete—and incomplete all at the same time. Heavy dark clouds hunkered low over the town. Everything was gray or black—except for the Motif fishing shack. "Where's the sun? Blue skies?"

She looked at him, then back at the town. "I paint it the way I see it."

He slid the brush out of her braid and used it as a pointer. "You're definitely seeing something I'm not." Parker looked east over Sandy Bay and the endless Atlantic beyond. "Clear skies, El. Your canvas makes it look like a wicked storm is coming."

She snatched the brush from his hand and tucked it deep in her braid. "It's coming, Parker. Something evil. I sense it. Leaving here is part of it for sure . . . but I feel there's something more. Something dark."

The cross necklace was visible, hanging outside her dress. She clasped it in her free hand. "I feel like everything is going to change—and I can't do anything about it."

Parker didn't even want to think about her moving away.

She pointed at the phone in his hand. "Going to FaceTime Jelly?"

"Yeah, in a few minutes."

El waved him off. "Go have fun. Don't worry about me. I'm going to pack things up, anyway."

"I just had the weirdest conversation with Harley Lotitto." Okay, he was fishing, but maybe she'd give a clue as to why she'd opened up to him like she did.

"Me, too. Very strange. Like he really wanted to be my friend." She rinsed her brush. "Go out to the end and make your call. I'll wait here so we can walk back together afterward."

"You should hop on with me," Parker said. "Get to know each other."

"What's the point? I'll be long gone before she moves up."

"You two would be great friends with each other," Parker said.

Ella turned to face him. "Because *I'm* your friend—and *she's* your friend—you think that'll automatically make Jelly and *I* friends?"

"Yeah, I do," Parker said. "Why wouldn't you be friends?"

Ella shook her head like he'd just asked the most ridiculous question. "Boys." She turned back to her painting.

Parker whipped out his phone and headed toward the signal light. He wasn't even going to try to figure El out.

Jelly picked up on the first ring. Her voice came through perfectly—but that was it.

"The screen is completely dark," he said.

"Weird," Jelly said. "I can see you just fine. You're a mess. Looks like you zigged when you should have zagged. I guess you've got lots to tell me."

"First, guess where I am." Parker held up the phone and gave her a view of Rockport Harbor and the circle drive at the end of Bearskin Neck.

"On the breakwater."

"Ooh," Parker said. "Very good." Over the next fifteen minutes he gave her the total rundown of the stakeout, his dad's leg, how this whole BIG thing was a lot bigger than anyone had imagined, and the fact that the camera still hadn't been delivered yet.

"Is Ella with you?"

What kind of a question was that? "Were you even listening to what I said?"

"I heard every word," Jelly said. "So she's not there?"

Parker sighed. "She's on the breakwater, too. Painting. But there's probably a couple million tons of granite between us now." El had the easel packed away—and just about everything else—except the paintbrush in her hair. The finished watercolor lay flat on a rock, drying. Her boots were still off, and she had her face turned up to the sun, eyes closed, like she wanted to take it all in. "So why all the concern about where El is?"

"I thought I'd say hi—if she was right there," Jelly said.

Girls could be so strange. He'd like to have seen her face when she spoke, but the screen was still black. He was pretty good at reading her voice—and something told him she wasn't being entirely up front with him. She was moving, too—and fast. He could tell by her breathing she hadn't stayed in one spot like she usually did. At least she wasn't sitting somewhere with her feet in the water.

"Now it's your turn," Jelly said. "Guess where I'm calling from. You've got three chances. Get it wrong and you owe me ice cream."

Parker stood and leaned against the rock. "Could be the dark side of the moon—the way the display looks."

"Wrong," Jelly said. "Two more guesses."

Parker laughed. "Give me a hint—what do you see when you look around?"

Jelly paused. "Gulls overhead. Fishing boats."

"That's way too general," Parker said. "There's gulls where I'm at—and fishing boats, too."

"So you think I'm in *Rockport*?" Jelly said. "Is that your second guess?

"No," Parker said, laughing, "that is definitely *not* my guess.

You could be at the crab boats behind Everglades City High. Or by the ranger docks."

"Wrong and wrong," Jelly said. "You owe me ice cream."

Parker smiled. "You cheated." But he let her have her fun. "You going to tell me where you are—or not?"

"Check the screen."

Suddenly the display flashed white, then evened out. Jelly's face dominated the screen. Her teasing smile. His Wooten's Airboat Tours hat she'd snagged from him all those months ago. She kept easing the camera farther from her face. The background was a blur of colors. "See anything you recognize?"

She angled the camera away from her face—and the background snapped into focus. Sailboats, harbor—and the T-wharf all in the distance.

"Jelly—you're *here*?" He lowered his cap visor to shade his eyes and scanned the area. He saw her—standing at the curb where the circle drive and the breakwater met, clutching the handle of a roll-aboard bag. "You *are* here!" He let out a whoop—and ran for her.

"Jelly!" His feet barely touched the rocks as he burned up the distance between them. He pointed to her as he passed El. "Jelly's *here*."

Jelly bounced on the balls of her feet—waving as he ran to her.

He didn't stop for the entire two-hundred-plus yards—not even when he got close. He bowled right into her. Lifted her off her feet and swung her in a full turn before setting her down. "How'd you pull this off—did your dad get the transfer?"

She shook her head and pointed at her bag. "Angelica's Delivery Service—the camera—remember?"

"Oh . . . ADS. I get it now. Yeah—you did say that." His grin made his stitches feel like they were about to split wide open. She was *here*.

"I have something else for you, too." In one smooth move her hand darted up and snatched the hat off his head. She swapped his old Wooten's one on his head before he could even react. Not that he would have stopped her.

He took it off and gave it a quick inspection. "I can't tell you how much I missed you."

She smiled in that teasing way. "Are you talking to me—or your hat?"

They both busted out laughing.

"So *this* is Jelly," El's voice—behind him. She zigzagged lightly across the last few rocks separating them—and stood beside him. "What a surprise!"

But at that moment Jelly was the one who looked surprised. She looked up at Parker—a question in her eyes—but he had no idea what she was asking. The sparkle in her eyes was gone. The smile was still there, but fewer teeth showed.

"I'm Ella."

"Somehow I knew that the moment you called my name."

Jelly smiled—and was all polite—but she was stiff, too. She pressed one hand against her stomach.

"You okay?" Parker said.

She nodded and dropped her gaze.

Ella leaned over to get a better look at Jelly's face. "Seriously, you look like you just swallowed a bug."

Jelly laughed. "Exactly how I feel. I'm pretty sure it was a cricket."

CHAPTER 53

PULL IT TOGETHER, ANGELICA. Get a grip. She looked up and held out her hand. "Nice to meet you."

Ella shook her hand and smiled back. Perfect teeth. Perfect nails. Her hand—so soft—and not at all clammy like Angelica's felt at this moment.

"Nice to meet *you* finally," Ella said. "Parker has a million stories about you."

Parker never would tell Jelly much about Ella, though. And now she knew why. Because she was perfect. Drop-dead gorgeous.

"And we've got a million places to show you," Parker said.

We've. So Ella would be with the entire time? "And I want to see it all—but I'm here to help find this ghost burglar too." Was Ella as close as she'd been today every other time Parker made his weekly FaceTime call?

Parker steered them back down Bearskin Neck toward the heart of town. "Mr. Steadman just outfitted the houses with nice security cameras. I'm not sure how much good your camera can do now."

Great. Like she wasn't needed at all.

The shops called to her. Each one welcomed her in—but she had to be content gazing in the windows as she pulled her roll-aboard past them. There would be a time to explore, but right now there was a bigger mission.

Parker stepped up between her and Ella. "I was just telling Ella that you two are going to be great friends. I just know it."

Like he really thought it would happen that easy. It had always been Parker Buckman and Jelly. PB and J. Something she thought of every time she ate a sandwich. But obviously something had changed. How had she been so naive to think everything would be the same as it had been when Parker lived in Chokoloskee? Living in a new town could change someone. She glanced at Ella's reflection in the windows. So could new friends.

A group of guys walked out of Roy Moore's—a place with a big lobster sign out front—laughing and slapping each other on the back. High school age—but definitely upperclassmen. Probably got their fill of lobster or clam chowder. One of the guys—with those ruddy cheeks that perpetually look like he's blushing—looked her way as they approached.

She turned to face the shop windows—and saw him do a double take as they passed.

He looked at me? For an instant her spirits soared. Not that she had any interest—because she didn't. But at this moment she appreciated that someone felt she was worth a second look.

Just as quickly, she realized he was probably looking at her roll-aboard. What kind of girl drags a suitcase when she walks through town, right? Instinctively she looked back to see if he was looking at her—or her luggage.

Neither.

He was looking at Ella.

Like an old habit, Angelica immediately turned to Parker—for help or encouragement. But he wasn't going to give her either one.

He was looking at Ella, too.

CHAPTER 54

Saturday, June 11, 4:15 p.m.

STEADMAN'S CAMERAS GAVE A CLEAR VIEW from the rental to the main house, and everything in between. He'd sent Parker a link for the app—El, too—so they could pull up the cameras on their phones. They could watch Steadman's places, too. Even though Rankin pronounced the Resistance as being dead, this was still a way to keep it alive.

Parker didn't know how much Steadman paid for the setup, but it was worth every dollar. The resolution? Amazing. Which meant Jelly's trail cam was pretty much useless. They didn't need it. Honestly, Steadman's gear had it covered. Anything her camera might capture would be a total redundancy.

Parker wished he hadn't made the dumb comment about how her camera wasn't needed, though, not after all she'd done to get it there. And in the end she found a spot to set it up in a small cluster of trees on the far side of the guest house—a tiny blind spot where Steadman's cameras didn't reach. Parker wasn't so sure there was a point to covering this small of an angle, but he kept quiet. She strapped it to a tree on the neighbor's property—and pointed it directly at the back door of the Houstons' rental cottage.

Jelly checked the angle. Readjusted. "Okay, Ella. Just walk to the back door. Let's test this."

El walked up to the house—then hurried right back. "The guests are inside," she said. "I wouldn't want to spook them."

Hopefully nobody else would either.

Jelly checked the images on her phone. She repositioned the camera slightly. "I've gotten pictures in the total dark with this."

El angled her head. "Spying on the neighbors?"

Jelly laughed. "Wildlife. Sometime I'll show you, if you want."

"Absolutely. We should do that. Soon."

There was something about the way El said it, like she didn't expect she'd be living here much longer.

Dad was still in the hospital—all the way in Boston because of the surgery. Mom was with him and was going to be there all night. So Parker would be on his own tonight. "You ladies want to grab dinner at Rockport Pizza?"

El shook her head. "You two go. I should stay here with Grams." She touched the cross hanging from her neck—like she wanted to be sure it was still there. "She says there's going to be vapors tonight. She won't be so nervous if I'm home."

Jelly looked from El to Parker. "Vapors?"

"Fog," El said. "Sea mist. Bad things happen when the vapors come to shore, according to Grams."

First El painting a coming storm. Now Grams had a premonition about fog? One way or another, both feared something bad was brewing.

Jelly nodded like El's explanation was totally logical. "Sounds like your grandma is superstitious?"

"You have no idea." El laughed like the whole "vapors" thing was silly. But she was holding the cross now, with both hands.

CHAPTER 55

Saturday, June 11, 5:20 p.m.

THE MINUTE HARLEY HAD THE SHOP SWEPT AFTER CLOSING, he wanted to make tracks for Gatorade's house and fix a mistake. But it was too early for that. He went to the Hangar instead. He'd spend some time with Kemosabe while he waited for darkness. If he went now, he might as well go there and ring the doorbell. He'd be spotted for sure.

He opened the Hangar doors wide, pulled out his key, and woke up Kemosabe. He sat there revving it, the volume from the straight pipes drowning out all distractions. He had to face the facts. Ella didn't trust him—but she sure trusted Gatorade. What if she discovered he'd bamboozled the facts when talking to Gatorade just to learn what was going on with her? Or what if the police found the light sticks in Gatorade's garbage—and Ella found out he'd planted the evidence? His chances of getting her to trust him would drop somewhere deep in negative territory.

And if Scorza followed the plan at all, he'd already dropped the light stick in Gatorade's garbage from last night. Harley had to make that disappear too.

The cops needed to find the real burglar, not be chasing down Gatorade. They needed to find that battering-ram Shadow-man that sent Harley flying into Rockport Harbor. *That* was the guy who was hurting Ella, forcing her to move. Harley had been so proud of his brilliant strategy to get Gatorade out of the picture with the stupid break-ins. But he'd missed his catch.

No. It was worse than that. He'd pulled off a regular "Wrong Way Marshall." He pictured the famous YouTube clip of the Minnesota Vikings defensive end who picked up a fourth quarter fumble back in 1964 and ran the ball some sixty yards to the wrong end zone, essentially scoring for the opposing 49ers.

Yeah, Harley had run the ball in the wrong direction. He'd actually helped the opposing team. The Shadow-man.

But no more.

Scorza had been texting him for the last hour. Pretty much acting like everything was normal. No apology for ditching him. And deep down, Harley wasn't totally surprised. That was the real Scorza.

Harley revved the motorcycle. Tonight he had to do a whole lot more than get rid of the evidence they'd planted. Ella didn't trust him enough to confide in him, so somehow he had to help her—even if she didn't know it.

The burglaries had hurt Ella and her Grams, right? The least Harley could do was help make sure their place didn't get hit again. He'd be joining up with Gatorade in a way. Hey, if Harley couldn't beat him, he'd join him, right?

Getting rid of Gatorade had been Plan A. But the real point had been to have a better chance of being friends with Ella. If Ella moved, it wouldn't make any difference if Gatorade was around or not. So that changed everything. It was like the goalposts had been moved. Yeah, Harley definitely needed to turn around and run the other way.

The way Harley saw it? Ella needed his help—whether she knew it or not. It was kind of an amazing thought, really. "Ella needs my help." Saying it aloud made it seem all that much more believable.

A text dinged in from Scorza.

`I say we hit Steadman's again tonight. You game?`

Not anymore.

`No point. Gatorade was helping Steadman. Staking out the place. They'll know it wasn't him.`

Scorza texted back immediately.

`Then let's do it for fun. It keeps us fast. Sharp. Call it our secret summer training camp.`

There were better ways to train that didn't involve breaking into houses and cracking guys across the face with a closet pole. A week ago Harley would have told Scorza his plan to watch Ella's place. But after Scorza's every-man-for-himself stunt from last night? Now he wasn't so sure that was a good idea. Actually, if Gatorade was right about Scorza's dad foreclosing? The less Scorza knew the better.

`Count me out. Busy tonight anyway.`

`Doing what?`

The guy just couldn't take a hint.

`Stuff. Gotta go.`

Harley rocked Kemosabe off its stand and backed it out of the shed. He dropped it into first gear and coaxed it back inside. A ten foot ride, but it was something. Medicine. Like the throttle was connected to an invisible IV. The longer he felt the vibrations throbbing through him, the better he felt. The Vikings had a setback in that game back in '64, but they still pulled off a win. Maybe he could make up for his own mess-up in this somehow, too.

He dropped Kemosabe into neutral, stepped it back outside again—farther from the shed this time—and sat there for a moment, revving. He looked over North Basin, the part of Rockport Harbor where the lobster boats were leashed to buoys inside the T-wharf area.

Gatorade was there—standing over on the granite block edge, turning to stare right back at him. A girl was with him. Red braids. Baseball cap. Hands jammed in her back pockets. She was watching Harley, too. It was an awkward moment—where Gatorade probably didn't trust Harley any more than Harley thought he could trust him. But if he just acted like he never saw them, how stupid would that look? And if he wanted to help Ella, he'd have to get used to the idea of being around Gatorade.

Whenever Harley locked eyes with a player on the other side of the line of scrimmage, to back away when the ball was snapped would be about the worst thing he could do. No, he'd slam into the guy. Hard. It was his little way of letting the guy know Harley couldn't be intimidated. He was sure Gatorade wasn't trying to stare him down, but Harley didn't want it to look like he was backing down, either.

He revved Kemosabe again, shifted into first, and swung the Sportster their way. He stopped near them and planted both feet on the ground.

"*Nice* bike." Gatorade looked like he meant it, too. "Your uncle lets you start it up—and drive it like this?"

"It's *my* bike. My uncle doesn't touch it. Doesn't even have a key to the shed." And he never would.

Gatorade squatted down. "The chrome looks fantastic. This isn't stock, is it? It can't possibly come out of the factory looking this great."

Obviously Gatorade had great taste. "It was a project bike my dad and I worked on."

Gatorade nodded like he'd heard Harley's backstory—or was smart enough not to ask any more questions. "This is Angelica Malnatti, my best friend from Florida. I call her Jelly."

Best friend? Okay, *that* was interesting. "Jelly." He pointed at her red hair. "Anybody call you *strawberry* Jelly?"

"Not unless they want to get on my bad side." She made a fist. Sort of in a joking way, but also in a way that he knew not to mess with her.

Harley raised both hands in mock surrender. "Good to know."

"Just ate at Rockport Pizza, and was showing her around town a bit." He took a step back, clearly admiring the motorcycle again. "This is one great ride. It looks like you just rolled it out of a showroom."

What was the deal with this guy? And it wasn't like he was putting on an act in front of the girl. The guy always seemed to treat others decent.

He couldn't say for sure what got into him, but before Harley thought about what he was doing, he showed Gatorade and Angelica the Hangar while he parked the bike. Gatorade seemed in awe of the place—like he'd just stepped into the Fortress of Solitude or something. So maybe the guy wasn't as stupid as Harley thought.

Even after Gatorade left, Harley watched him with that Jelly girl. They walked around the lobster trap stacks, heading toward the Motif. He couldn't quite figure Gatorade out. But Jelly was easy to read—and she didn't exactly act impressed, especially after Gatorade mentioned Harley was a running back. Whatever. But Gatorade had respected Kemosabe and the Hangar. That was something.

"Well *that* was interesting." Scorza's voice.

Harley didn't spin around. Didn't act startled one bit. He wished he'd closed the shed doors the instant Gatorade left.

"Looks like Harley Lotitto made a new friend." The quarterback stepped inside the Hangar. "So that's why you don't want to have a little fun tonight? Are you doing something with *Gatorade*?"

Harley grabbed the microfiber cloth and gave Kemosabe a quick wipe-down. It was a routine—not exactly needed. A speck of dust wouldn't dare cling to the chrome. "It has nothing to do with Gatorade."

"Okay." Scorza looked like he was enjoying this. "Then it's little miss Black Beauty."

Was the guy *trying* to get into a fight? He wasn't about to give him an answer.

"I've got news for you, motorcycle boy. You're wasting your time chasing after that girl."

"What's *that* supposed to mean?"

Scorza watched him—like he'd been hoping for the question—and couldn't wait to see Harley's reaction. "She's moving soon."

How on earth would he know that? "I haven't seen a For Sale sign on their lawn."

"You will soon. My dad called in her grandma's loan. But they don't got the money—so they'll be evicted. As in the sheriff knocking on their door and kicking them to the curb."

"How long have you known?"

Scorza smirked. "A long time."

And he'd never said a word, all those times Harley had talked to Scorza about wanting to be Ella's friend? What a jerk. "And your dad tells you confidential stuff about his customers? Nice guy."

"This little situation was special."

Harley's face was heating up—not something he wanted Scorza to notice. He flipped off the 12,000-lumen shop light. Scorza's dad was actually pushing the Houstons out? Gatorade wasn't exaggerating. "Why kick them out of their house? Wouldn't it be a better advertisement for the bank if they gave them some time?"

"Believe me, the bank won't lose any business with this move. Might even get some new customers."

"By running someone out of their home?"

"Some people think Rockport would be better off with a little less color."

Harley stared at him. "Sounds kind of racist."

"Not a racist. A realist." Scorza shrugged. "There was a flag on the play all those years ago when they bought the place. The way my dad heard the story? Old man Houston should never have gotten his hands on that property. The way my dad sees it—and plenty of others—my dad is fixing a wrong. He's a hero."

A hero? Yeah, right.

"My dad's got a buyer all lined up—one who knows how to treat his friends right."

"What's that supposed to mean?"

Scorza just smiled. Like he knew his jabs were hitting home no matter how hard Harley tried to hide it. Like he'd found another bruise, and wanted to drive his knuckle in a little deeper. "My dad is no realtor, but he's going to get a big, fat kickback on this deal, for sure. Maybe I'll talk him into buying me a Harley. But newer. Faster. Bigger."

And maybe Scorza was going to get a big, fat lip if he kept talking. "If you ran like you ran your mouth, you'd be in better shape. You wouldn't need Summer Football Camp."

Scorza laughed. "Not saying anything that isn't true. You'll see me with a bike better than this. And you can do lots better than Black Beauty for a friend. Move on. There's plenty of other warm bodies on the bleachers."

Harley was going to play it smart. Not lose it this time. He unfolded the blanket and draped it over Kemosabe.

"So one way or another Black Beauty is history. A total dead end. Maybe we'll get lucky and Gatorade will leave too. It'll be a two-fer. So what do you say, should we hit Steadman's again? Or a different rental?"

It was like a switch flipped in Harley's head. Right now he didn't care if Gatorade left. Scorza was the one he really wanted to see leave. He glared at Scorza. "I'm out."

"You're going to ditch me?"

"Like you didn't ditch me last night?"

"I thought you got out." He raised both hands and put on some kind of innocent angel face.

"You never even checked."

"Can I help it you can't keep up?" Scorza's smirk was back. "Fall behind, get left behind. You know that. And hey, I took a nasty fall last night. Tripped over something and totally hurt my knee—but you don't hear me complaining about it. Stop whining already. So are you coming—or not?"

"Not."

Scorza stood there for a few seconds. Staring at him like

he couldn't believe Harley wasn't dying to hang out with him. "Okay."

Honestly, he wanted to whack that smug look off Scorza's face.

"So that's how you want to play it?" Scorza nodded and took a step back. "I predict you're going to regret this."

"I doubt it." The one thing Harley really regretted at this moment? He didn't have a closet pole in the shed.

CHAPTER 56

Saturday, June 11, 7:30 p.m.

THE MOMENT PARKER GOT OFF THE PHONE WITH HIS DAD, he checked the security camera app from Steadman.

Dad appreciated the update, and was happy to hear Jelly made it safe to Rockport. Both he and Mom had been in on the plan—and they'd kept the secret well. Mom had the guest room all set for her, as it turned out. Parker explained the plan for tonight. Hang out with El and Jelly at the Houstons' house until Mom got home from the hospital. Maybe with enough activity at Grams's house, Shadow-man wouldn't show—and the renters would post a great review. Maybe Shadow-man would turn up at Bayview or Bayport—and Steadman would be waiting. That would be a win all the way around.

"Wish I could be there," Dad said. "Mrs. Houston is in a bad spot."

Maybe that's why he was giving Parker so much leash. "Do you think any of this will do any good?"

"Only God knows. Our job is to keep doing the next right thing . . . and leave the results to Him, right? What if God is the one putting these ideas in our head, have you thought of that?"

The thing Parker kept thinking was how there wasn't enough time. The loan was due the end of next week. Grams didn't have the money she needed. Even if they caught the guy, would any of that change? Maybe Mom could write an article, and some rich person would pay off her loans. It was a ridiculous stretch. "What's happening to them is beyond wrong. Grams is a widow, and El is sort of an orphan. They're in a hard place, and a bunch of rich people want to take the only thing Grams and El have? It feels . . . evil."

For a moment Dad didn't answer. Parker checked the screen to be sure they were still connected. "I'm glad you see it that way, son. Many don't."

"It just seems too big . . . how do we fight this—and is it even our fight?"

"Overcome evil with good," Dad said. "That's what the Good Book says. We do our part."

And hope God does His part. Parker didn't say it, but the thought was there. This whole thing seemed like just as much of a mystery as it ever did. From Devin's death to Shadow-man's attacks. He didn't say that either—but had a hard time thinking about anything else after ending the call with his dad.

Parker shook off the thoughts and focused on the security camera app. Right now he just needed to do something. Anything. Hopefully that next right thing.

Steadman's house popped up first. Bayview. Then Bayport.

Except for outside lights, they were dark. But Steadman was waiting inside one of them—hoping for a break. Or rather a chance to break someone's skull.

Ella's place had enough lights on—inside and out—to be seen from a satellite. Anybody stepping into that yard would be stepping onto a stage, whether they knew it or not. Parker needed to be there, just in case somebody did.

Jelly was waiting for him downstairs. She'd already moved into the guest room, and now she was studying pictures on the mantel. She set a framed print down the moment he walked in the room. "Ready?"

"You don't have to go if you don't want to," Parker said. "You know that, right?"

"So you're thinking I'd rather stay here alone—with some psycho, faceless, possibly paranormal nutcase breaking into homes?"

Parker smiled. "Well, when you put it like that . . ."

She grabbed him by the arm and tugged him toward the door. "Besides, who's going to keep you from doing something stupid?"

CHAPTER 57

Saturday, June 11, 8:45 p.m.

OVER THE NEXT HOUR Angelica stayed close to Parker. As in *between* him and Ella. It was like a game—and she was pretty sure Ella was catching on. The only thing Parker seemed to notice was the TV, where he had the app playing that monitored the two security cameras outside. He kept his eyes on the screen, looking for any movement.

If Ella was bothered by what Angelica was doing, she didn't show it. She seemed to be watching her Grams most of the time anyway. Talking to her. Coaxing her out of the rocker by the window and into an easy chair in the center of the room instead. She brought over a footstool and propped her legs on it.

"Land sakes, Ella Mae, you're treating me like an old woman here." Grams stood and marched to the kitchen. "We have guests." Minutes later she was back with a tray loaded with glasses of sweet tea, lemonade, and a plate of the best-looking scones Angelica had ever seen.

"Hold on." Parker was still glued to the screen. "I saw something."

All eyes stared at the security camera image. Patio furniture. Dozens of those solar-powered lights outlining the walkway, and an amazingly manicured yard . . . but nothing looked out of place.

Without taking his eyes off the screen, Parker squatted down and retied his shoes.

"Parker," Grams said. "Don't you be getting any fool ideas."

"Should we call the police?" Angelica whispered—as if whoever or whatever Parker saw could hear them.

Parker held up one hand. "There." He pointed at the shadows on the fringes of the image. "Something is there."

A figure stepped out of the darkness—dressed in black . . . head to toe. The hood was pulled up in place, so the entire face was shadowed. Suddenly a glow appeared, like he'd just activated a glow stick. This was it.

"Parker, we should call the police," Angelica said. "This thing is recording, right? I mean, we'll have the images, right?"

Ella nodded. "That's what Steadman said." She squeezed Angelica's arm. "The cop basically told us he didn't want to hear from us."

"Call Steadman," Parker said. "Put him on speaker."

Ella pecked at her screen.

The hooded figure stepped around the patio table—making his way closer to the house. "He's holding something." A brick?

"Ella? Everything okay?" Steadman was all business.

She held the phone up—as if that would make it easier for everyone to hear.

"We've got company," Parker said. "Check your app."

"Switching over," Steadman said. "And bingo . . . I see the bogey. I can be there in five minutes, tops."

Parker hesitated. "It'll be over before then."

Exactly what Angelica figured.

Steadman gave a frustrated growl. "You pray, don't you, Parker?"

His question took Angelica by surprise. *Why would he ask—*

"Actually, yeah. Not as much as I should, but—"

"Well, I never do." Steadman interrupted. "So you pray the bogey comes here to Bayview next. I've got a little surprise for him."

The figure turned and deepened his crouch a bit, like he heard something from the other side of the rental cottage. He held perfectly still for a moment, then focused back on the main house. He held the brick by his chest with both hands, tapped it twice, then hauled back and launched it at the house.

A window crashed above them—and something heavy thudded and bounced onto the floor overhead.

Without even knowing she'd done it, Angelica clutched onto Ella—who hugged her right back.

"Parker—no!"

Angelica turned the instant Grams shouted—but she was too late. Parker disappeared out the back door.

CHAPTER 58

THE INSTANT HARLEY HEARD THE CRASH OF SHATTERING GLASS, he scooted from his hiding spot for a better view of the backyard. Pressed against the shadowy side of the Houstons' rental cottage had been great for staying incognito, but not so good for seeing. The winter face mask didn't help—and made his face itch all over—but he was a whole lot less likely to be spotted this way.

Gatorade burst out the back door of Ella's place. "Hey!" He stopped in the center of the patio—looking one way, then the other—bouncing on the balls of his feet like he wanted to get moving but didn't know which way to go.

What was Gatorade doing in Ella's house? He had to remind himself again they were on the same team.

Gatorade ran to the far side of the yard, then cut and angled off to the other corner.

"Make up your mind, Gatorade." Whatever he was looking for, obviously it was gone.

Ella stood in the open doorway, along with Gatorade's red-headed friend, Jelly.

Suddenly Gatorade veered his way. Not at a hard run, but more like he was trotting back to a huddle.

Harley stood perfectly still. Fought the urge to run. There was no reason to run, right? He hadn't done anything wrong. Besides, his game plan was to guard Ella's place, not run and hide the first time something weird happened.

And that was the thing . . . he had to find out what was going on. And he wasn't going to do that by hiding. Harley stepped into the light. "Hey."

Gatorade stutter-stepped, then poured on the speed like Harley had a football in his hands. He plowed into Harley with surprising force—like the guy was totally juiced up on game-day adrenaline.

They both went down, and Harley used the momentum to roll on top of Gatorade. "What are you *doing*? All I did was say hey." He struggled to hold Gatorade's arms down, using all the leverage his weight gave him. He wouldn't hold him long. "Stop. *Stop*. Are you crazy?"

"Get off him!" Ella—with a garden hose. Clutching a pistol-grip sprayer nozzle in both hands like she was holding a gun. "Hands up!" Her face—dead serious. She sidestepped to a better angle. "I mean it."

He smiled. This girl was terrific.

"And I mean it, too." Strawberry Jelly coming at him from another angle. But she held a fireplace poker in her hands. The kind with the nasty-looking curved spike at one end. "I know how to use this."

She held it up like a Louisville Slugger—and her grip actually looked decent.

Harley caught a full blast of spray from the hose.

"I said—hands up!"

She was a dead shot—somehow got the thing right inside his hood. He squeezed his eyes shut too late. Ducked. It felt like he'd taken the full force in the eyes. She tracked him with the sprayer, somehow able to keep the jet of water trained on his head. The thing felt like a pressure washer. He shot both hands straight up. "Okay, *okay* already."

The waterboarding stopped. He couldn't see. Water filled one ear, making it sound like someone was holding a plastic cup over it. Gatorade wriggled out from under him. Broke free.

"Drop the hood—and pull off that mask." Even with his eyes closed he recognized Jelly's voice.

He'd barely grabbed the rim of his hoodie when Ella drilled him with the water again. "Hands up!"

"Hands up or hood down—make up your mind!" Harley was getting a little annoyed.

"Ah." Ella paused like she was coordinating with Jelly. "Hood down—with one hand. But no funny business or you'll need gills—got it?"

"Got it. I'm going to pull back my hood. Don't shoot." Harley lowered one hand as slow as he dared—not wanting to chance even the appearance of a sudden move.

"Let me help." It sounded like Gatorade was on his feet now. Gatorade yanked the hoodie back and whipped the ski mask off his head. "Harley?"

He drove his knuckles into his eye sockets and rubbed. It felt like the hose had spiked his lashes right into his eyeballs. He opened his eyes wide and blinked over and over. "Somebody better start explaining why I'm on the ground—soaking wet."

"My thoughts exactly." Ella stood with one hand on her hip, the other still aiming the hose. "Start talking, Mr. Harley Davidson 'you can trust me' Lotitto."

CHAPTER 59

THE GHOST SAW THE WHOLE THING. His rolling anticipation was a wonder. Not only did it give him a freaky sense of where his target was headed in a chase, but even here, tonight, his sixth sense led him to the Houstons' house much earlier than he'd originally planned.

Somewhere deep inside he possessed some kind of subconscious premonition that he'd needed to be here. How else could one explain how he'd been precisely in this spot when the kid busted the window?

And he had the bonus of seeing the other kid flushed out of hiding. So he was at it again tonight? The Ghost had let him off easy with the dunk in Rockport Harbor—and this is how he showed gratitude? The kid was going to seriously regret that.

Already it had been a really good night, and he hadn't even

started yet. He watched the four of them on the lawn. The confusion. The fact that he was here, for all this, was proof he should never doubt his instincts. It was almost as if he possessed something god-like. He had a power far beyond anything he was aware of.

His instincts were on target in another way, too. Stepping things up was the right thing to do—and right now. If the fat lady really believed kids were behind the strange goings-on, maybe she'd lose some of the fear that was driving her to the signature line. The fat lady needed to be convinced she was dealing with something otherworldly. Something too big for her. Time to remind her this wasn't kid stuff. By the time he scared off this group of renters, she'd be begging to sell the place.

The Ghost was on a roll, and he definitely needed to keep trusting his instincts. And right now his gut told him it was time to knock Do-Right back on his heels. Get him out of the way. It wasn't a change of plans. Not really. He was just accelerating what he'd already planned to do.

The knife and the note were already in his backpack. If he did this tonight, he'd need to slip the 3mil wet suit on under his hoodie—which was rolled up tight in his pack, too. Not really made for how cold the water would be, but he wouldn't be in long. The one-piece 3mil was flexible. Anything thicker would have been too bulky for the pack, anyway. He could quickly slip this one on. He had everything with him he'd need. It was like he really did have a subconscious sixth sense that had prompted him to bring the extra gear.

He hated the idea of leaving to change. Any time he was out in the open, he increased his chances of being spotted. But it was plenty dark behind the rental. Just a remote stand of trees. The Ghost could have his wet suit on in two minutes.

He lowered his pack. Decision made. Trust your gut.

The Ghost stripped down to his nylon basketball shorts. Stuffed his T-shirt into his pack. The night air felt good against his bare upper body. He flexed. Stretched. And slipped into the one-piece neoprene suit. He grabbed the zipper-pull strap and secured the back. He stuffed his shoes in the pack and pulled on dive booties. He slipped on a weight belt. A few extra pounds wouldn't slow him a bit—and would give him the help he needed later. He slipped the face-covering over his head. Black latex gloves. The hoodie was next. He didn't really need it—or want it—but it was all about keeping a consistent look. That was important.

He fished one of the giant light sticks out of his pack and tucked it in his waistband. He dug a little deeper in his pack until he found Do-Right's dive knife with the note he'd rubber-banded around it. All set. And in under two minutes.

He slipped to the corner of the rental in total stealth mode, staying with the shadows.

The fat lady wrapped a beach towel around the kid from the dive shop. Funny how he ended up wet again. And he'd be in some serious high water before the Ghost was finished schooling him. Do-Right, too. And who was that other kid? He'd find him before this was over.

The whole group of them walked to the house—and went inside. The Ghost couldn't have scripted it better himself. Getting so many of the players in one spot at one time? It was almost as if he could *will* something to happen—and it did. One thing he was certain of. His own powers were far beyond what he imagined.

CHAPTER 60

Saturday, June 11, 9:45 p.m.

ELLA ACTUALLY BELIEVED HARLEY'S CRAZY STORY—even though she wished she didn't. It was hard to stay angry with a guy after hearing his side of things. Grams believed him too, which was obvious by the way she encouraged him to take another scone. He spilled everything. Breaking into Steadman's. Planting evidence at Parker's. Going back to get rid of the light sticks—which he pulled out as proof. But it was what he said about his conversation with Scorza that clinched it for her.

"All that," Ella said, "because you wanted to be my friend? Why didn't you just buy me a pizza or something? We'd have all been your friends."

"It was stupid—and I'm really sorry," he said. "I had no idea how this was really hurting you—and Mrs. Houston."

Parker looked ticked. "So you were the one my dad was chasing when he got hit?"

"That was . . . somebody else. I'm the one who clocked you with the closet pole."

"Oh, that makes me feel way better." Parker was really laying on the sarcasm.

"I didn't know it was you. Honest. I thought it was that Shadow-man guy." He told them about how he'd been attacked at the boat launch.

"I made a mess of things, I know." He looked directly at Ella. "But after hearing how you needed the rentals, I thought I'd hang around and make sure nobody tried doing something to your place."

He seemed like he wanted to turn things around, but Ella wasn't about to pin a medal on his chest just yet. "Another one of your plans that didn't work out so well, eh?"

Harley angled his head and hit it with the heel of his hand—like he was still trying to get the water out of his ear. "I guess."

"I can take care of myself, Mr. Lotitto. Or do I need to get the hose to demonstrate again?"

Harley laughed. "No, I'm good. I'm just sorry I didn't get a look at the guy who smashed your window."

"I'll show you," Parker said. He had the app up on his phone, and was going back in the recorded footage. "Here."

Ella watched Harley's face as he viewed the playback.

"I know who this is, and it definitely isn't the real Shadow-man." Harley looked totally excited. "Look at the way he tapped the brick before he throws. That's Scorza's signature move every time he passes a ball."

Parker stared at him. "You're sure."

"I've seen it a million times," Harley said. "If he'd known he was being recorded, he wouldn't have thrown a pebble. I guarantee you that."

"So we show this to the police," Jelly said, "right?"

"I'm not sure how much good it will do." All eyes turned to Grams. "It may stop this boy, but that doesn't change our situation. Not really."

The room got really quiet. Like the truth of that statement was sinking in.

"Even if it won't change your situation," Harley said, his face dark. "I'm going to have a little talk with Scorza. I promise you, he won't be messing with your place again."

CHAPTER 61

Saturday, June 11, 10:05 p.m.

TIME FOR THE GHOST TO GO TO WORK. This was the moment for a little Element of Shock to come into play. The lights were off in the guest rental. Early-to-bed, early-to-rise kind of people, apparently. Now they were going to be early-to-leave people as well. Opening the back door of the cottage was easy. There were no security deadbolts or chains at all. Not that they would have stopped him. They simply would have delayed him for a few seconds more.

Once inside, he gave himself a full minute to adjust to the darkness. He knew the layout well enough, but still, having his full night vision could only help him. He'd done a little recon earlier. Two adults. Two kids—both likely under ten. Piece of cake. The security cameras covering the backyard and porch didn't scare him a bit, either. In fact, he'd use them to set a little trap for the do-gooder. It was the old trick of using an opponent's weapon to help defeat him.

Show time. He activated the light stick and stepped into the bedroom. They were asleep, just as he expected. The two kids were sandwiched between their parents like they'd been too afraid to sleep in their own beds. After tonight, he was pretty sure they'd be staying in their parents' bed until they left home for college.

But the fact that the kids were in the bed also told the Ghost that the man likely didn't have a handgun under his pillow, not with his kids so close. This was going to be easy.

In two quick strides he was at the foot of the bed. He grabbed the blanket and yanked it hard. The man came to—the full effect of shock registering on his face. His wife shrieked and threw her body half across the two waking kids at the same time. The kids screamed bloody murder, clutched their parents, and mirrored the sheer terror on the faces of both adults.

The Ghost held the light stick just above his own head. "Get! Out!" He conjured the voice up from deep inside. From his gut. It came as more of a roar. "Tonight!"

This was the moment. If the man was going to attack, he'd do it now. But he didn't. He just wrapped his wife—with the two kids between them—in his arms. Like pigs in a blanket. Honestly, it was all he could do to keep from laughing.

He backed toward the door. "I'll be back!" And he definitely would. But he didn't have to stand around watching to see if they'd leave or stick around. They'd load their car and be flying down the road in minutes—in their PJ's.

The Ghost left the same way he'd come in—but circled around the other side of the rental this time to the brightly lit backyard.

He got a quick visual on the security cameras. Perfect. He took a deep breath. The fun was only beginning.

Now he'd give the fat lady another visit. And he had a very special message for Do-Right. Then he'd go to the quarry—and see if the kid would take the bait.

CHAPTER 62

Saturday, June 11, 10:10 p.m.

MOVEMENT ON THE FLAT SCREEN caught Ella's eye. She pointed. "He's back."

In black from head to toe. But he moved differently. Confident. Strong. It was *him*.

"Shadow-man," Parker whispered.

In Ella's heart she sensed an evil presence like she hadn't felt with the brick-thrower.

She stood there, stunned. Unable to move. She couldn't take her eyes off the screen, but felt everyone else was just as transfixed as she was.

The figure set an envelope or something on the patio table, then drew out a knife and stabbed the thing—pinning it to the table. He set the most massive light stick next to it, like he wanted to be sure they saw it.

Shadow-man looked up at the security camera.

"No face," Grams wailed. "Sweet Jesus, help us!"

Slowly Shadow-man pointed into the lens.

"He knows we're watching," Jelly said.

Then he pointed at his empty hood—and back to the camera again.

"And he wants us to know he's watching us, too." A massive chill knifed through Ella. "Rankin?"

And just like that, the figure backed away and disappeared into the shadows.

CHAPTER 63

Saturday, June 11, 10:06 p.m.

PARKER WAS OUT THE DOOR and to the patio before anyone else said a word. There was no sense chasing Shadow-man. He was gone. The guy could appear and disappear whenever he wanted, it seemed—and he feared nothing. It was the note that had Parker mesmerized at this moment. The glow stick next to it washed it with a green tint—like the note itself had some kind of energy source inside.

Grams, Ella, and Jelly approached the table like they weren't so sure it was safe to be close.

Harley veered around them. "What's with the dive knife? I mean, why would he leave his blade?"

Parker stared at it in the green glow. The tip was driven through the folded piece of paper—right into the wood patio table. This wasn't just any dive knife. It was an Aqua Lung. Some invisible force grabbed Parker's stomach and wrestled it into a full nelson the moment he saw the inscription. "It's mine. From my grandpa . . . he had it laser etched." Parker pointed at it—still not sure he wanted to pick it up. "It went missing from my bedroom."

"That dude got in your *room*?" Harley scanned the yard as if he expected Shadow-man to return. "This is so messed up."

El had this look on her face as if she thought Shadow-man might materialize out of thin air. She and Jelly leaned in close to inspect the knife. The lights were blazing in the rental home now. Parker was sure they'd been off when they discovered Harley outside.

"He reveals deep and hidden things." El read the inscription. "He knows what lies in darkness." She rubbed down goose bumps on her arms. "If this is about God, and He knows so much, what is it with all the secrecy? I mean, it would be nice if He'd reveal it to *us*, while He's at it. Then maybe we wouldn't have to move. And maybe I could believe justice actually existed."

Parker wanted to say something about God's timing, but he caught himself. Sometimes he thought his go-to answers sounded ridiculous. The truth was, even Parker didn't understand what God was waiting for. "Somebody call Mr. Steadman," he said. "Tell him to be ready. Shadow-man may be there next."

"I'll handle that," Grams said. She disappeared back inside.

"You're sure this wasn't that other guy." Jelly glanced at Harley. "Your buddy, Scorza?"

Harley shook his head. "Positive. This guy was bigger. Moved different. This was the goon who put me in the bay."

"This was Shadow-man," Parker said. "The thing Devin chased. I saw him at Bayport."

"The one who wrote on our window," Ella said.

Parker tugged the knife free. "And this proves he was the one in my room." He stared at the folded paper Shadow-man had left for them. He wanted to know what it said, but dreaded it at the same time.

"Who is Rankin?" Jelly looked at Ella. "You said that name when you were watching Shadow-man."

"Did I?" She looked like her mind was trying to replay the image from the security cam. "Oh! It was the thing Shadow-man did at the end. Officer Rankin did that same pointing thing to Parker. The thought just popped into my head—but it was stupid. I'm not sure I believe Shadow-man is human."

Parker held up one hand. "Hold on a sec. I mean, think about it. What if it *was* Rankin? He was never around when Shadow-man struck. He always showed up later. And he didn't want us investigating, right? And what has he done to really help find Shadow-man? Nothing."

"Shadow-man might not even be flesh and blood, Parker . . . and Officer Rankin for sure is." Ella still looked spooked. "And we should be calling him right now."

"Police or poltergeist, whoever Shadow-man is," Harley said, "he can get to anybody . . . anywhere."

Parker couldn't get the idea of Rankin as Shadow-man out of his head. It was like a puzzle . . . and some pieces fit perfectly, didn't they?

"The knife, Parker. It's a warning," Grams said. "A warning."

Parker hadn't even seen her walk up—but he agreed. "Maybe we should read this note and find out." It might help them find—and stop him.

Jelly snatched the paper. "We can't just stare at the thing." She unfolded it carefully.

"Read it aloud," Harley said.

Jelly scanned the paper. She looked up at Parker for a moment, fear in her eyes.

"Just read it."

Jelly nodded. Cleared her throat. *"Remember the day you got this knife? I watched you open the package. You'll find me there."* She looked up at Parker. "He wants you to *meet* him?"

"You'll do no such thing, Parker," Grams said, "You do and we'll find you in the morgue. You kids get back in the house right now. The vapors are on the hunt."

Fog was definitely creeping in now. The fine mist hovered and glowed around the eave lights.

Ella and Jelly headed for the door immediately. Parker sheathed the knife and slipped it into his back pocket.

"So where *did* you open that package with the knife?" Harley's question seemed innocent enough. But he said it too quietly, like he didn't want the girls to hear.

"The quarry."

"Where Devin drowned?"

Parker nodded.

Harley rubbed his palms on his pants. "He's sending you a challenge, right? Daring you to go to the quarry."

Dear God Almighty . . . help me. "That's exactly the way I read it." Right now all he wanted to do was go home and lock the doors.

"So let's do it," Harley said. "You and me. Together."

Parker shook his head. "You know that's insanely insane, right?" He checked the time. Nearly eleven. He had at least another hour before his mom would be home, but she was under the impression Parker would be at Ella's—not creeping around some quarry. "I can't." Even if he begged his mom or dad, there was no way they'd agree to that.

"Scorza isn't the problem—we both know that. I'll deal with him later anyway." Harley locked eyes with him. "But we have to check this other guy out. Ella is going to move if something doesn't change—and fast. I, for one, don't want that to happen. And I don't think you do, either. You said you want to find this guy, right? Here's our chance."

Harley moved in closer. "Both security cameras recorded this, so right now we have a couple nice little clips to show the cops. But what do they show? A guy dressed like a ninja with a hoodie and no face. There was nothing to ID the guy. We need something more so the cops can catch this guy. They put him in the slammer where he belongs—and maybe Ella's problems go away, too."

Actually, Harley wasn't saying anything Parker hadn't been thinking. "How is going to the quarry going to help anything?"

"I have no idea," Harley said. "But maybe we get lucky. Find something that we can use to figure out who this guy really is."

It was a total shot in the dark. And it was sounding dangerously like Devin's logic . . . wanting to get so close, to figure out who Shadow-man was.

A police car barreled down the block—its blue and white flashing lights creating a frenzied glow in the deepening fog. None of them had called the police—so what was this all about? The car stopped at the Houstons' rental. A cop stepped out looking like he was ready for a fight. Younger than Rankin—about Dad's age. Friendly-looking face—but all business.

Actually, Parker was relieved it *wasn't* Rankin. And then again, the fact that it wasn't . . . didn't that fit? What if Rankin had been hired by BIG to scare homeowners into selling? He'd be the cop investigating . . . what better way to make sure he never got caught? Maybe Rankin was too busy pulling off his Shadow-man disguise to answer any 9-1-1 calls just yet.

The door of the rental flew open—and a man burst out carrying a whimpering kid in his arms. "Officer!" The wife stood in the doorway, clutching another child.

Parker and Harley inched closer—and got the picture real fast about what had happened. The family was leaving and wanted the police guarding them while they packed their car. Grams came back outside along with Ella and Jelly.

The policeman's name tag said Greenwood. He took notes from the rental dad—then went to the woman to get her story. The renter pointed at Grams. "I expect my money back. Every penny. And if I don't get it fast, I'll post a review that will guarantee you'll never get another rental. Not ever."

"I still have your check," Grams said. "You can take it with you." She hurried back to the house.

"We gotta do this," Harley whispered. "And you know that."

"Not without talking to my parents—who will never agree. And I know *that*." But even as he said it, he was torn inside. He wanted to do the right thing. But wasn't helping Ella—a friend in serious need—the right thing to do?

Harley nodded and backed away without another word.

Parker had never seen Ella look so . . . defeated. She stood there . . . head slightly bowed, eyes squeezed shut, tears streaming down her cheeks. In that moment he knew . . . she'd lost another bucket of hope.

Jelly stepped in close. "I feel terrible. They're going to lose the place, aren't they?"

Oh, yeah. They definitely were.

Wide-eyed, whimpering kids got buckled in car seats.

No sooner had Grams returned with the check than the man climbed in their car, locked the doors, and headed for who knows where. Likely where there was no fog.

Officer Greenwood watched the video from Parker's phone. The whole thing with Scorza and the rock through the window. And then the Shadow-man footage—from both angles. He slipped the note in an evidence bag. He went inside and came back a few minutes later with a granite block in a clear evidence bag. "With your permission, I'll take this to the station. Captain Rankin will want to look at this. He's in charge of the investigation."

Convenient.

"Where is Officer—or Captain Rankin?" Parker tried to sound super casual. "I thought he'd be here."

"He's off tonight. I left a message on his phone on the way over. He must have been too busy to pick up."

Parker imagined Rankin hustling to stash his Shadow-man suit. "I'll bet he was."

Greenwood took Grams off to the side, got her a patio chair, and talked with her so quietly Parker couldn't catch a word. Ella stood alone, hugging herself while still holding the cross necklace.

"What a mess," Jelly whispered.

"We should go," Parker said. "Grams and El are going to need time alone." It would still be a while before his mom came home, but the idea of having her pick them up at Grams's place now seemed like they'd be invading their privacy. Parker whipped off a quick text to Mom, letting her know what was going on and that he'd meet her at home, instead.

Officer Greenwood patted Grams on the shoulder like he really cared. He leaned down close, still talking—but his eyes were closed. Was he praying? A moment later he gave her a hug. "We'll get him."

Not if it was Greenwood's commanding officer.

"You rest easy tonight, ma'am." He patted her again.

She glanced at the broken second-story window and nodded.

Greenwood followed her gaze. "Mind if I run back inside one more time? I'll get a quick measurement of that window. I've got a piece of plywood in my shed. I'll cut it to size and swing by after my shift—which is almost over. If your light is on, I'll ring the bell and board up that window."

Grams stared at him.

"Won't take me five minutes, Mrs. Houston. You'll sleep better."

"I wish all officers were as kind as you."

"More are than you might think, ma'am." He disappeared inside.

Ella helped Grams stand, then hugged her arm and started walking with her to the house. "Did Harley go home?"

Parker gave a quick scan of the yard—but there was no sign of him. The guy who wanted to be near Ella so bad left without saying goodbye? Not a chance.

Parker's gut tightened. He was absolutely certain where Harley was headed—and it definitely wasn't home. "When's the last time anyone saw him? How long has he been gone?"

Nobody was sure. It could have been twenty minutes. No less than fifteen. There was no way Parker was going to catch him. It was like a nightmare that came back to haunt him all over again. Devin had asked Parker to go with him to the quarry—and now Harley had done the same. Devin had gone to investigate on his own—and never lived to tell what he'd seen. Would Harley end up the same way?

The policeman stepped back out on the porch.

"Officer Greenwood!" Parker hustled over and explained the situation. "Harley, that other guy that was here earlier when you came . . . he could be in trouble. I know where he's going—I'll lead you there."

"Why don't you just give me really good directions? I'll find him."

"There's no time for all that. Please."

Jelly gripped Parker's arm. "We'll both go. You're not leaving me behind."

Parker wasn't going to argue. There wasn't time for that either. "Officer, please. I have to make sure he's okay." Surely his parents would be all right with him getting a ride from a cop, right? "I'll send my parents a text and tell them exactly what's going on the moment we get in your car."

Greenwood gave a sideways nod of his head toward the police car. "Hop in."

Ella and Grams stood by the door, hugging each other. Both of them held the cross.

"Mrs. Houston, why don't you two go inside and lock up before I leave?" Greenwood said.

Parker yanked open the door of the police car and slid inside after Jelly. The instant Grams and El were in the house, Officer Greenwood swung into the driver's seat. As they pulled away, Parker gave a last glance toward the house and saw that Ella stood in the window, shaking her head like she thought Parker was insane.

Maybe he was.

CHAPTER 64

Saturday, June 11, 10:55 p.m.

PARKER SPOTTED HARLEY barely a hundred yards from the quarry. He had a good pace going, and only stopped when Officer Greenwood lit the cruiser up. Greenwood stopped alongside Harley and rolled down his window. "Get in."

Harley obeyed but didn't look too happy about it. Thankfully Greenwood was willing to drive the rest of the way to Parker's Pit to scope it out. The quarry looked like a giant, open grave—filled with a dark liquid. Thicker than water, yet less syrupy than oil. Honestly? It looked more like blood.

Greenwood did a slow drive-by. He swept the area with his searchlight. Crept along the gravel road separating the length of it from thick woods and smaller, unnamed quarries.

"I was there—on Humpback Rock." Parker pointed to the outcropping of granite that jutted out a good twenty feet into the quarry. "That's where I opened the package—that's the spot where Shadow-man said he'd meet me."

Greenwood locked his beam on the area. "Sit tight." He swung out of the car. "And don't touch anything." He checked the area—clearly on high alert. He walked out onto the granite peninsula and even shined his light into the black water. Then slowly around the perimeter of the quarry. He squatted down and appeared to be listening for what seemed like a couple of minutes.

Harley's leg was doing that bouncing thing. "I want to get out of this lousy cop car and do a little checking myself."

Parker wasn't sure what they would find, but he was itching to get out, too. "I can't believe you actually came here on your own."

Harley gave him a half-smile. "And I thought you weren't coming. Guess you changed your mind."

"Somebody had to make sure you didn't get yourself killed."

"Which is why he brought me," Jelly said.

Harley snickered. "Yeah, you look real tough, Strawberry Jelly."

"I had you on your knees, didn't I?" She pantomimed holding the fireplace poker like a bat again.

Harley raised both hands. "I stand corrected."

"Don't forget it."

He grinned at Parker. "Nice to know you've got *Jelly* when you're in a *jam*, eh?"

Jelly groaned.

Officer Greenwood eased back into the squad car. Turned off all the lights. Rolled down the passenger window. "Are you good with sitting here another few minutes—real quiet?"

They sat silently, straining to see out in the dark. When Officer Greenwood started the car again, Parker was pretty sure Shadow-man was long gone—if he ever was there.

"Okay, gang. One more pass and then let's get you home. I'd like to get that window boarded up for Mrs. Houston." He slowly drove the length of the quarry. At the far west end, he pulled a three-point turn, then crept his way back.

Harley's leg was bouncing again as they approached Humpback Rock. "Officer, would you drop me here? I've got to walk off this adrenaline or I'll never sleep."

The cop shot a skeptical look in the rearview.

"Don't worry. I'll go straight home."

Greenwood stopped the car. "Not really liking that idea, son. It's late. How about I get you home and you do some laps around your living room?"

"So, I'm under arrest or something?"

Greenwood laughed. "Nope. I can't hold you. If you tell me you want out, I'll—"

"Yeah, I want out."

Greenwood turned around to face Harley, staring him down as if he could change his mind. He sighed, "You're free to go."

Parker couldn't believe what he was hearing. "Why not just ride down to Beach Street?"

Harley shook his head. "I need to clear my head."

Jelly nudged Parker—and it wasn't hard to guess what she was thinking. Actually, he was relieved. Devin had promised he was going home, too—and Parker wasn't about to let what happened to Devin happen to Harley. "I think we'll all get out and walk together."

Officer Greenwood nodded like he knew he couldn't talk them out of it. "Two is company. Three is safer." He handed Parker a card. "Call if you see anything. I'll look around some more and then find you to see if you're ready for a ride."

The three of them watched the squad car drive away. Officer Greenwood tapped his brakes a couple of times as if saying goodbye. Seconds later his taillights melted into the fog.

Parker instantly wished the cop was still with them. Without a good moon, the place was way too dark, and the edge of the quarry felt too close.

"The creep factor of this place is off the charts," Jelly said. "We should go."

Harley snickered. "And here Gatorade and I were just thinking of taking a swim."

"Which is exactly what you'll be doing if you two don't turn around and walk me into town." Jelly stood there, hands on hips.

Harley stared toward the black waters. "I was thinking we could hang out for a few minutes. Just in case."

"We need to leave. Now!" Jelly hooked their elbows and walked between them—and not at a window-shopping pace. They hadn't walked more than ten feet before a heavy splash came from the flooded pit—ending with a thumping impact.

Instantly the three of them whirled around.

Jelly grabbed Parker's arm tighter. "*What* was that?"

Shadow-man was there. Standing on the granite peninsula. A giant glow stick held high over his head like he wanted to be sure they saw him.

"He's got no face," Jelly whispered. "We've got to get out of here."

But they couldn't. In fact, Parker found himself stepping forward. It was as if the green light was some kind of magnetic force. A tractor beam.

"Easy, Gatorade," Harley said. But he was moving closer, too.

"What are you two doing?" Jelly gave them a tug, but she didn't have a chance against the two of them. They half-dragged her to the quarry's edge.

Humpback Rock reflected the glow of the light stick like it had somehow come to life. Not forty feet away the figure stood, making no move to run, or hide, or give chase.

"If he takes one step this way," Parker said, "we bolt. Got it?"

"Roger that," Harley said. "This is what Devin saw, right?"

And what got him killed. "Dear God in heaven, protect us."

"Amen," Harley mumbled.

Jelly tugged harder. "Let's go. I mean it. I'm really, really scared, guys."

The giant light stick made the water of the quarry look darker. Deeper. Tiny ripples quivered across the black surface. Green reflections speckled the quarry's skin, like the pit itself was some awakening alien life form.

"Uh-uh." Harley shook his head. "I don't know what *that* is—but it wanted us to come here. I feel it."

The only thing Parker felt was a sense of present evil—and the need to get away. Still, he stood frozen, like he couldn't believe what he was seeing.

Shadow-man still faced them, but with no actual face showing. He pointed at them—like he'd pointed at the security camera at Ella's. Like he'd pointed at Parker on Steadman's back stairs.

"Back. Off." The voice was deep. Growly. Not quite human-sounding. "Final warning." And without another word, he stepped off the granite rock—into the oily blackness of the quarry.

"Whoa!" Harley jerked back a step. "What just happened?"

The glow stick cast a green circle of diffused light maybe ten feet across. Like a meteor from Krypton had fallen from space—and right into the quarry. But the giant glowing sphere grew smaller, and fainter, as Shadow-man dropped into the depths of the quarry, then disappeared completely.

Harley swore. And again. And again. "What on earth was *that*?"

"Whatever it was," Jelly whispered, "I'm not so sure it came from Earth."

Panicky ripples threw themselves against the granite edges of the quarry, like they wanted to get out. But still Parker didn't leave the quarry's edge. None of them did. It was as if his feet were vulcanized in place.

The ripples calmed. The surface evened out into one solid mass again. No sign of a green light. No bubbles. No sign of Shadow-man.

"He's not dead," Jelly said. "I feel it."

"I'm not sure Shadow-man was ever alive, either." Harley glanced at Parker. "I've never believed in zombies before . . . but that thing is making me wonder. He is coming back, isn't he."

Not a question. A statement of fact—and exactly what Parker was feeling. Like Shadow-man might burst to the surface in front of them. "Time to go. We've seen enough."

"You're wrong," Jelly whispered. "We've seen way too much."

CHAPTER 65

Sunday, June 12

PARKER DIDN'T NEED ANY KIND OF PARENTAL PUSH to get him to church Sunday morning. His parents weren't even around to do any pushing, anyway. Mom had returned to Boston to bring Dad home from the hospital. Parker and Jelly left the house early for the walk to church and he actually chose a pew closer to the front than he usually did. He felt safe there, and after what happened at the quarry the night before, that was a really welcome feeling.

Was he actually any closer to God when he sat in a church pew than he was last night at the quarry? No. Maybe it was just that he felt no presence of evil in the old sanctuary. Like demons had been prayed out of this place for so many years that they didn't dare return.

Jelly sat beside him, and just having her close brought another kind of comfort. It was like reinforcements had arrived—and Jelly was a great one to help sort out what was going on here.

Parker tried focusing on what the pastor was saying, but it wasn't easy. His mind was still caught in the tractor beam, pulling him to the quarry. Finally Parker stopped fighting it and just let his mind go there.

Officer Greenwood had come back minutes after Parker called. Nobody refused his ride that time. Even as late as it was when Parker got home last night, Parker wanted to give his parents a full update. Sure, it was part of the whole integrity thing he'd been working on from when he lived in Florida. But it was more than that. Parker needed his parents' input on this. And maybe their assurance that somehow this whole thing was going to work out for some good on this side of heaven. That God cared enough to bring justice to this world—not just the world to come.

Mom walked in soon after Parker and Jelly got home, and she sat across the kitchen table from them while he put Dad on speaker phone. It wasn't an ideal family conference, but it worked. His parents listened to every detail about what had happened at Ella's—and at the quarry. Usually the more worried Mom was, the quieter she got. And she was quiet. Even after Mom got Jelly settled in the guest room, and Parker went to bed, she kept talking with Dad. He couldn't hear their conversation, but he guessed that Dad's early release from the hospital wasn't due to him being a model patient. He'd insisted on leaving. Like he knew that whatever was going on with Shadow-man wasn't over yet.

Steadman's night hadn't been nearly as exciting as Parker's, but he did get a chunk of granite through the window at Bayport. Unfortunately he was at Bayview at the time—but he saw the whole thing on his surveillance camera. Same MO with a couple love-taps of the rock to his chest before he threw it. Scorza had been busy last night, too.

When Steadman heard about the rest of what happened at Ella's place, he sounded frustrated. "It's like he knows where I'm at. I need him to step inside the house when I'm there. I won't need a second chance."

Shadow-man's appearance at the quarry really got to Steadman. "You should have called me, Swabbie."

Everything had happened so fast when Parker realized Harley had gone to the quarry that he hadn't even thought of it. Mr. Steadman seemed to understand, but he was clearly disappointed.

Even though Rankin had told the Rockport Resistance to disband, Steadman called a meeting for that afternoon. Hopefully, Parker's Dad would make it.

El was absolutely convinced that Parker, Jelly, and Harley had seen a for-real ghost at the quarry. She wasn't even open to other possibilities—and couldn't understand why Parker wouldn't accept the obvious. It was hard to be sure over the phone, but she sounded an awful lot like she'd given up all hope of saving the house—or finding Shadow-man. "Let it go, Parker," she said finally.

Harley's reaction took Parker by surprise. He texted Parker maybe an hour after he'd gotten in last night . . . asking if Parker was having a hard time sleeping, too. And Harley started texting again early this morning.

I say we go down in the
quarry—have a little
look-see.

IN the quarry—as in
with scuba gear?

How else?

I thought you don't dive?

I said I don't like it—
not that I can't do it.

You think we'll find
Shadow-man at the bottom?

No idea. Not liking the
numbers on the score-
board. Ella's going to
lose the house. Just hate
doing nothing.

And that was exactly it. That last text so totally resonated with Parker. And he felt something else he would have never predicted. It was like some kind of uneasy alliance had started with Harley at Ella's—and then at the quarry for sure. But now it was clear that their bond was no fluke.

I'll think about it.

It was the best Parker could do. Honestly, the idea of diving a quarry . . . *that* quarry, just about had his stomach crawling up his throat. But there was something about the idea that wouldn't let him go, either. What if they found an answer? Something that would get the police involved? What if there was some kind of proof that Shadow-man was working for BIG? Would that bring in the FBI? Would it help the Houstons? What if by taking that single dive into the quarry, they were able to buy them some time? Wouldn't that be worth the risk?

Then again, what if they found Shadow-man himself . . . waiting for them on the bottom?

CHAPTER 66

Sunday, June 12, 5:00 p.m.

THE ROCKPORT RESISTANCE MEETING was well under way. Angelica had the entire couch to herself, which made her feel more out of place than ever. Parker stood, leaning back against the wall separating the family room from the kitchen. Uncle Vaughn made it at the last minute—and Parker's mom, too. Uncle Vaughn was on crutches and definitely moving slowly, and not very much. He was afraid he'd sink too deep into the couch, so Parker got him a kitchen chair instead. He winced when he sat. Angelica suspected he had skipped a dose of pain medication so he'd be clear-headed for the meeting. She feared he had checked out of the hospital way too soon.

Mr. Steadman paced. The guy was definitely a doer, not a sit-around-and-talk guy. Just watching him made Angelica antsy, like she ought to get up and do burpees or something.

Grams Houston sat in the rocker by the window. She had her chair positioned better for a view outside than in the room. Ella sat close to her, like she was her protector or something.

"I appreciate all you're doing for me," Grams said. "And all you've done. But I think we all know where this is headed."

Ella reached for her Grams's hand.

"Something evil is at work here," Grams said. "Something that we can't fight against. Every time we do, it seems somebody gets hurt." She nodded toward Uncle Vaughn—and Parker. "Last night we got as clear a warning as a body has a right to. A person's got to know when they've been licked. We're done here. I'm going to sell before they foreclose and take it from us."

There were many protests, of course, but in the end the room got really quiet. Like everyone knew this is where that train had been headed from the moment the meeting started.

"Tell me you're not selling to *them*." It was like Steadman couldn't bring himself to say *Boston Investors Group*.

Grams stared out the window. "The realtor might have found another buyer if not for the ghost. But there won't exactly be a bidding war now. There will be lots of questions. And we must have more than a signed offer to buy. The cash must be in our hands by Saturday to pay off the loan—or they take it and I get nothing. There just isn't time to do anything but sell to them. I've waited too long already. That Boston group isn't offering me nearly what the place is worth, but it's a good might better than foreclosure. I have all the papers from them. They aren't asking for a home inspection—no contingencies at all. I sign, and this is all over."

"Oh Grams!" Ella threw her arms around Grams's neck.

There was a gloom as thick as a Cape Ann fogbank. Nobody said a word. BIG had Grams right where they wanted her.

Steadman paced again—and then suddenly stopped. He turned to Grams. "Have you signed yet?"

Grams shook her head. "The hand is willing, but the heart is weak."

"Okay. Okay. I'm going to toss out a crazy idea, but hear me out, okay?" He hesitated for a moment like maybe he was looking for the right words—or deciding if he should say anything at all. "What if *I* bought it? We don't want the Boston Investors Group muscling in to Rockport, right? And I think we'd all like to throw Scorza, my ex-friend loan manager, a curveball. So I'll have papers drawn up. We'll make the deposit match the amount you need for the loan. You sign the agreement, and you'll have the money to pay off the loan immediately."

"But," Ella said, "we still lose the place."

"Maybe," Steadman said. "Probably. But we set the actual closing for another month down the road. It will buy you time to come up with another solution. If not, at least we keep the Rockport rental home business in the Rockport family."

"Just not in *my* family," Ella whispered, barely loud enough for Angelica to hear.

Uncle Vaughn didn't look convinced. "Can you realistically get that kind of money?"

Steadman took a deep breath and blew it out. "I've got two rentals and my own home. I can use the equity to leverage things. We all know how much the loan was. I can use that for the deposit."

"But you'll be vulnerable. They can do the same thing to you if this rental business doesn't turn around."

"Agreed." Steadman's face got this totally determined look. "I'm willing to roll the dice on it. We give them a toehold in Rockport and they'll push for more. Eventually they'll come after me anyway. If we keep them out now, maybe they'll look for another nice little town to take over in Maine or someplace else."

Angelica wanted to see BIG go a lot further north. Like somewhere above the Arctic Circle.

"I don't want to lose this place," Grams said, "but I'd rather you get it than let that Boston outfit run us out of town."

Steadman nodded. "So we're agreed?"

All eyes automatically gravitated to Grams. She nodded. "Agreed."

Steadman looked thrilled—and scared to death at the same time. "I'll get you a deposit that covers the entire loan. Now the bigger question. How much did BIG offer for the house . . . the property? I'll match it, and do better if I can."

Steadman's shoulders slumped when he heard the number. "I can't even do *that* much. I'd be at least forty grand short of that. Maybe fifty. You ask me, this is one of the sweetest pieces of property in Rockport. Three-block walk from the heart of town. Half-block walk to the Headlands. You deserve a lot more than they're offering—and a whole lot more than I am. Okay, it was a crazy idea anyway." He dropped on the couch like all his pent-up energy had drained away.

Angelica could see fresh tears in Ella's eyes.

"It's still more money than I'll get in foreclosure," Grams said. "And if I don't knuckle under to the animals responsible for scheming to steal my home, I can leave here with my head held high. Mr. Steadman, if you can scrape together a deposit that pays off my entire loan, you go ahead and get the papers drawn up. I'll sell Beulah to you—even at forty thousand less than the Boston offer."

Steadman looked stunned, just like everyone else in the room. "You're serious?"

"Do it," Grams said. "And you'll need to move fast. You've only got one week. Juneteenth is a Sunday—and the bank will be closed. But they'll own Beulah by then. I need to sign the papers and give the bank their money by Saturday . . . that's June 18."

Ella winced. Maybe nobody else noticed, but Angelica sure did.

The mood in the rest of the room changed instantly. It was like a celebration. Parker hugged his dad—and his mom. Grams smiled and rocked, and with every rock of the chair her smile got wider. Steadman's look of shock morphed into a slow shaking of his head as if in wonder.

The whole situation, the way Angelica saw it, was a loss. The Houstons were losing their home. They were going to be uprooted from the home they loved, but Grams still seemed to find some joy. "They may have won this battle with me," Grams said. "But they'll take no spoils of war with my retreat. This property will not be among their plunder."

Tears streamed down Grams's face as she spoke. Ella smoothed them away with her hand, not bothering to wipe away her own.

Angelica felt her heart softening toward Ella. She'd fallen in love with Rockport even before she'd arrived here, thanks to Parker. In two days, she'd come to love it even more. But Ella might lose the only place she knew as home. Why had she been so heartless toward Ella? Jealousy was an ugly thing. *God, forgive me. Please keep changing my heart.*

She'd arrived in Rockport feeling like she was going to save the world. Or Parker, anyway. The trail cam was going to show Parker how much he needed her around. Fat lot of good that did. Even after the Shadow-man incident in Ella's yard, nobody had wanted to check her camera. Mr. Steadman's gear was way better.

She hadn't helped at all. *God, help me make a difference. Help me make up for my lousy attitude.* Parker was hurting. Ella and Grams were, too. Angelica just wanted to ease their pain. Even if only a little bit.

CHAPTER 67

Friday, June 17

FOR HARLEY, the next five days trudged by. Since school was out for summer, Uncle Ray had him manning the shop open to close. By Friday, all he wanted to do was flip Rockport Dive Company's *Open* sign to the *Gone Diving* side. He had to do something. Anything that might make a difference—or help undo the damage he'd done.

Ella's grandma was going to sell to beat the foreclosure, and then Ella would be gone. Word on the street? They were already packing boxes. With each passing day, he felt like he was living some kind of launch countdown. Five. Four. Three. Two. One. He heard she'd be moving so far away, it might as well be the moon. Harley would never see her. And he wasn't exactly a talk-on-the-phone guy. *And would Ella even want to talk to him anyway?* Grandma Houston's sister lived somewhere in Connecticut, and that's where Ella and her Grams were going to live. Ella living with two old ladies? He couldn't imagine what she must be feeling.

His stupid break-ins hurt the rentals—and helped put Ella in the spot she was in. There had to be some way to fix things, but he had no idea how to change the scoreboard this late in the game. He wished there were a coach he could talk to. Someone who could call a play—and all Harley would have to do is run the pattern and make the catch. He'd had that kind of coach, once upon a time. "I need you, Dad." He'd whispered those four words a hundred times this week.

Kemosabe had been in bad shape when Dad bought it. But Dad had always known just what to do every step of the way. He knew which tool they needed next until they'd restored the bike to better-than-new condition. If only there were a tool in the Hangar that could restore the mess Harley had made out of Ella's life—and his own.

Harley had paid Scorza that little visit he'd promised. His ex-friend wouldn't admit he'd thrown the granite through Ella's window, but he didn't deny it, either.

"My theory? Someone gave her a going-away present to show how little they'd miss her." Those were his exact words. Scorza just couldn't resist grinding his knuckle into that bruise again.

There'd been pushing and shoving. Yelling. Threats. But nothing had been permanently broken—except a friendship that hadn't been all that strong anyway.

Gatorade somehow convinced Officer Greenwood to check out Parker's Pit again—but with divers this time. Mr. Steadman himself led the fire department's search and rescue dive team to the bottom of the quarry. No body. But there hadn't been another burglary either, so it was anybody's guess as to what became of Shadow-man. Harley hoped he was gone forever, but he wasn't so sure.

Ella and her Grams were more convinced than ever that

Shadow-man was some kind of spirit. Not alive, but not exactly dead either. Grams insisted he'd be back with the next fog, the way Harley heard it.

Even though there was no real estate sign in Ella's front yard, there was already a buyer. Parker wouldn't say who, but that didn't really matter. Harley was pretty sure Parker still didn't trust him. Whether Harley knew who the buyer was or not wouldn't change the outcome anyway. The papers were to be signed tomorrow. Game over.

No . . . worse than that. Season over.

They needed more time.

One idea kept gaining more yardage in his mind. He couldn't ditch his earlier idea to search Parker's Pit. He hated the thought—because it would mean strapping on scuba gear himself. He'd rather do back-to-back practices—or wind sprints for an hour. And the rescue team had already checked the quarry, right? He'd texted Gatorade about it again, but he didn't exactly seem excited to pick up the ball and run with it.

Fifteen minutes after he closed the shop, Harley was out in the Hangar—with the doors wide open. Kemosabe faced the back wall. He straddled the bike and started it up. He thought better out here—especially with Kemosabe running. He hoped the bike's vibrations would wake up any sleeping cells in his brain. He needed every one of them.

If they didn't find a way to put this game into overtime, he'd never have to bribe someone to buy Ella's watercolors at the Farmer's Market again. He'd never have to rearrange things on the shed walls to hang them. The thing was he wanted more watercolors with Ella's name smiling at him from that bottom right corner of the canvas. The way he saw it, there was always room for more "windows" in the Hangar. Heck, he'd attach them to the ceiling as skylights if he couldn't find a spot on the walls.

"Harley."

He whirled to see Gatorade standing at the open shed doors—with Jelly and Ella right behind him. He cut the motor. "Hey."

"We were on the T-wharf and heard the engine," Jelly said. "Thought we'd say hi."

That was something. *If Ella was totally angry with him, she wouldn't have come, right?*

Ella scooted around Gatorade, staring inside the shed like she was slightly confused. "These paintings are all mine. Every one of them." She stepped inside to look closer.

Busted. "Are they?"

"I had no idea you had such an appreciation for art."

"I don't know much about it. But the paintings are mostly of the harbor." Harley couldn't believe he was telling her this. "They're my windows."

Ella raised her chin slightly. "Uh-huh." She walked around the bike, scanning the walls. "Nice place you've got here. I like your decorator." She stopped at the framed picture of Harley and his dad with Kemosabe. She looked at it for what seemed like a half minute. Nodded like she understood how much he missed his dad.

She turned her attention to the bike. Actually dropped on one knee to look at the engine. She pointed to the name on the gas tank. "*Kemosabe*. Trusted friend. Faithful scout. Great name for a bike."

"Uh-huh." Most people didn't even know how to pronounce it right—much less what it meant. "Your dad must have loved westerns too."

"It was my grandpa, actually." She pointed at her boots. "We both did."

Jelly drifted outside and stared out toward the harbor, like she couldn't get enough of the view.

"So," Ella said, "where's your friend?" She went through the motions of passing a football. "The one who likes to throw bricks."

"That friendship is over. Permanently benched." Scorza wasn't the kind of friend Harley wanted. Not anymore.

She looked at him for a long moment. "I'll bet your dad would be proud of that decision."

Harley swallowed down a lump in his throat. She was probably right. "Is there anything we can do to keep you from moving?"

Tears welled up instantly. "I don't want to talk about that."

She strode out of the shed, hooked Jelly's arm, and the two of them walked out of sight.

"Why do I always say stupid things?" He stared at Gatorade. "What is *wrong* with me?"

"You didn't say anything stupid," Gatorade said. "This whole thing is just messed up. That's all."

"We have to do *some*thing," Harley said. "We're diving that quarry."

Parker shrugged. "The rescue team combed it themselves. Didn't find a thing."

"But they were looking for a body."

"And what are *we* looking for?"

That was the big question. "Honestly? I don't know. Something they missed. Something that might lead us to who is behind all this. Something hidden."

Gatorade seemed to snap to attention. "He reveals deep and hidden things."

"What?"

"Part of that verse my grandpa had etched on my dive knife, remember?"

Harley nodded.

"You're really serious about this?" Gatorade looked at him like he was crazy.

Diving the quarry was *not* a good idea. Harley knew that. But he already had enough regrets about all this. He didn't want to always wonder what might have happened if he'd made the extra effort. "Look, we've got a lousy field position, I get it. It's late in the fourth quarter. Fourth down and a long way to go. But we can't just punt the ball. Let's run the ball, Gatorade. You and me. The game is already lost—so we can't make our situation any worse, right?"

"Um, I'm not really into football, but I get what you're saying. I just don't see how anything we do now can make a difference. The papers for the sale—"

"Get signed tomorrow. I know, I know. So let's try one more play. We go down into that quarry. We check it ourselves. Maybe we find nothing, but at least we know we tried, right?"

Gatorade seemed to be thinking about that for a moment. "We go down swinging."

"Exactly."

Gatorade squatted down like he was studying the chrome on Kemosabe. "I'll talk to my dad. Maybe he'll let me."

Harley grinned. Couldn't help himself.

"He'll probably say no. All I said is that I'll ask."

"I really, really hope he says yes."

"But he might not. What then?"

Harley knew exactly what would happen. "Then I'm still going in. Even if it's alone."

CHAPTER 68

Friday, June 17, 8:10 p.m.

ELLA PICKED HER WAY ALONG THE STORM-WORN ROCKS of the Headlands. Parker and Jelly had still wanted to hang out with her. Like they thought she'd be too depressed about losing the home to be left alone. But right now, alone was the only place she wanted to be left. Finally, they'd relented and gone back to Parker's.

There was no justice in this world. Not really. Crooks cheated and connived. Lawyers worked the system to their advantage. People in politics got corrupted. Used their position to push their own agenda or those of campaign contributors rather than serve the people who had elected them. Too many people with money craved more—even if that meant taking the home from somebody barely scraping by.

Was the foreclosure legal? Completely. But that didn't make it right. It was as if someone or something had been plotting against them for longer than they'd realized. They'd been caught in the bear trap set for them. And the cost of getting free from its jaws? Grams's home. Ella's home. Beulah.

Mr. Steadman's offer was nice and all, but in the end—how was it doing anything other than helping himself? So he'd save Rockport from the big city investors. But Grams would still have to rent a moving truck. And now Steadman would have four places to rent out while they didn't even have one to live in. Where was the justice in that?

The papers would be signed tomorrow, June 18. She'd get them to Mr. Steadman. They'd shoot a photo of the check to deposit it into their account—and then use it to pay off their loan. Mr. Scorza—and the bank that gave him the cushy office and paid for his flashy suits—would have their money. And that next day, June 19 . . . the day they were to celebrate their freedom, they'd be grieving their loss of independence.

It was cruel.

Had Mr. Scorza known the significance of the date . . . that it was Juneteenth? He couldn't possibly. Why would he bother learning about Black history? He'd probably laugh to know he was robbing them of freedom—on a day that celebrated their release from slavery.

Scorza's dad was the type who wielded power over other people's lives. And if those other people weren't his friends or weren't the right color, well that just made his job that much more enjoyable, she'd guess.

The wind fought her dress, pulling it this way and that. Like her spirit. So torn.

She raised her face to the sky. Marveled at the clouds jostling each other like they were fighting for better placement on the canvas. She'd never be able to capture the beauty of that view with all the watercolors in the world.

"God . . ." Did she really expect Him to hear her? "How come You can make this world such a beautiful place, but You can't seem to do a blessed thing with the heart of man?" Mr. Scorza's heart had to be a horribly dark place. A windswept desert. With scorpions. Venomous snakes. "Where's the justice? Why do You let people hurt others like this? Don't You see what he's doing to Grams? To me? Don't You care?"

Relentless, slate-gray swells rolled to shore, seawater erupting from a fissure in the rock just below and soaking the granite around her. But still the water receded—as if drawn by an unseen force—back to the ocean it came from.

The water was like her Grams. How she and Gramps had fought for Beulah. Worked and scraped to own a tiny piece of Cape Ann. But in the end they couldn't hold on to the ground they'd gained. Grams would still be dragged back to her "rightful" place, the way some saw it. And Ella was getting torn from her home right along with her.

"Why don't You *do* something?" How *could* a God who made so much beauty in the world allow such ugly hatred a place on the same canvas? She raised her hands to the sky. Pinched the skin on her arm. "You made me—You chose this color from Your pigment palette. And I love it. I do. But why don't people see the beauty in color . . . all color?"

There was no answer, and she expected there would be none coming. But she'd spoken her mind and hadn't been swept out to sea by some divine rogue wave. That was something, anyway.

The waves thudded and thundered into the rocks with a concussion-type force she could absolutely feel, even standing on solid granite. She watched breaker after breaker rise up and charge the shoreline. Like doomed soldiers landing for an invasion—but always retreating before really taking any new ground.

For some reason the picture in Harley's shed haunted her. Harley's dad, to be specific. Working on that bike with Harley. Arm around him. A protector. But suddenly gone. Another kid without a dad. Where was the justice in that?

At least Harley had known his dad for all those years. What would it be like to have a dad in the picture? One who truly cared? One who was there for her? One like Parker had. He was there for Parker—and maybe even for her and Grams, it seemed. Mr. Buckman was different that way. Different from any man or dad Ella had ever known. She liked being around him. There was a strength she didn't understand. And now he would be taken from her, too.

Darkness was descending on Rockport—something far beyond a simple sunset. Something wicked. Evil. Grams would worry if she didn't get home before dark tonight. Grams was already going through so much, Ella had no intention of adding one more thing.

Ella closed her eyes. Filled her lungs with the sea air. Turned and climbed back up to where she'd left her boots. She slid them on and hurried for the trail.

She was home in less than ten minutes. Grams was on the porch, likely watching for Ella. She took the steps two at a time, kicked off her boots, and kissed Grams on the cheek.

"Ella-girl." Grams squeezed her. "I'm so sorry. So very, very sorry. I love this place. And I know you love it just like I do."

Ella knelt in front of her. "You did good, Grams. You and Gramps. You fought hard. And you gave me this wonderful home for all these years."

"We wanted you to always have it."

No matter how hard she told herself not to cry, there was no stopping the tears. "I know, Grams. I know."

"My sister's place . . ." Grams shook her head. "It's nothing like here. Nothing."

Ella stroked her Grams's arm. "We'll get by. And I'll be fine. You'll see." She hoped it would be true.

"Parker's dad, and Mr. Steadman . . . they both believe this is some kind of scare tactic by some big-city outfit. But that *being* we saw on the cameras . . . I don't believe it had a soul. We're better off moving, to get out from its reach. Its clutches."

Goose bumps raised on Grams's arm. Ella smoothed them back down again, hoping that would do something for her own arms as well.

"I think that thing came in with the vapors, Ella-girl. It's an evil spirit on a devil's errand."

Ella had felt that too, hadn't she?

"When I looked at those camera images . . ." Grams's whole body shuddered. "I felt I was looking at the angel of death himself. And I do believe this will end in death if we don't get you out of here. I'm not just selling because I have to, Ella Mae. I'm doing this for your protection. Lord Almighty . . . deliver us from evil." She reached for the cross necklace she'd given Ella. "You don't take this off, Ella-girl. Not when you shower. Not when you sleep. Understand?"

"I absolutely do." Ella leaned over and kissed her on the forehead. "Let's get you inside."

With one more look toward the sea, they stepped into the house. Ella closed the door and slid the dead bolt in place. Grams set herself to turning on the lamps. Ella gripped the cross necklace.

Read and reread the inscription on the back. *Deliver us from evil. Deliver us from evil.*

"Check the other locks, honey," Grams said. "Windows, too."

Exactly what Ella planned to do. Although if Grams was right about what was haunting their little town, locks wouldn't do any good.

CHAPTER 69

Friday, June 17, 10:15 p.m.

PARKER FIGURED HIS DAD was about the most understanding dad in the world . . . but still. What Parker had just asked was a massive stretch. Like, a bungee-jump-to-the-bottom-of-the-Grand-Canyon type of stretch. Mom, Dad, Jelly. All of them were crammed in Parker's bedroom.

The later it got, the easier it was for Parker to talk. And some of the best talks took place in his bedroom. He'd started with a one-on-one with his dad, but he should have closed the bedroom door. Mom had passed by with Jelly—and now they were all in the room.

"You want to dive the quarry. The one where your friend died." Dad shook his head. "With Harley Lotitto—who used to be your enemy—as your dive buddy?"

Parker nodded. "He's certified."

"And you're certifiably insane," Jelly said.

Mom stood and motioned Jelly over. "Let's give the men some space to talk, honey." She gave Dad an I-can't-believe-you're-even-considering-this look.

Parker locked eyes with Jelly for an instant. He was pretty sure she was sending him the same message.

Parker waited until Mom and Jelly left the room before saying any more. "You'll be right there with us, Dad. Right at the edge of the quarry."

"And helpless. If anything should go wrong," Dad pointed at his leg, "I couldn't get down there in time to help. And if you say nothing can go wrong—then I *know* you're not thinking clearly enough to do any dive, not even in a pool."

Good to know. Parker crossed that argument off the list he had going in his head.

"You want to help Ella. And so does Harley. I get that. You really think he'd go it alone?"

Parker nodded. "There's nobody to stop him. The shop closes at four tomorrow. He'll go right after that."

"I'll still be in my physical therapy session. They'll be doing a full assessment—and it's not like I can reschedule this. My commander will be there too, just to hear firsthand what I can and can't do on the job—and for how long. I won't get out until closer to five."

"You could come over right after that," Parker said. "We'll get all set—and go down when you get there. There'd still be plenty of daylight."

"Between the trees around the quarry—and the walls of the pit itself—do you have any idea how dark that quarry will get? You'd need the sun directly overhead to give you any decent light in that place. At five it will be more like a night dive by the time you reach bottom."

Actually, Parker didn't want to think about it. But the idea was already creeping him out. "Harley says he can get lights. They rent them at the shop. And we'll limit our bottom time to fifteen minutes. We won't go anywhere near decompression limits. All we want to do is check that area where we saw him go down—not the whole quarry."

"You'd need a man topside—one with the gear, ready to go in if something goes wrong. Even if I could be there at four, I can't be that guy to help. Not with this." Dad pointed at his leg again. "Tell me why you want to check the quarry so bad."

How could he explain it? "Because I can't think of anything else we can do to try to help. The bank isn't going to suddenly grant mercy. The police aren't going to do anything either. Not unless they have some kind of proof that Shadow-man has been hired by BIG to intimidate the Houstons—and Mr. Steadman. And sometimes I still wonder about Rankin, anyway." He didn't need to run his theory by Dad for a second time.

"So you think *you* need to save Rockport from some Boston Investors Group? Don't you think that's something God would have to do?"

But God wasn't doing a thing. Or maybe that was just the way it looked. Maybe God was waiting for someone willing to take a chance . . . someone willing to trust Him to do the impossible? "Sometimes God uses ordinary people to do big things, right? He helps them do it . . . so they learn to trust Him. You've told me that." Moses. Daniel. Joseph. David. Gideon. Peter. Esther. The list was endless. Parker had grown up with Dad telling him great stories of people who got in spots so impossible that they knew they'd die if God didn't show up.

Dad looked at him for a long moment. "Saving Rockport

from BIG? That's not what's driving you. How about you tell me the real reason? The one that comes from right down here." Dad tapped his chest.

Parker wanted to get this right. He breathed a silent prayer that he would. "I want to go down in the quarry because a friend is going to lose her home. I like her, Dad. And Jelly is going to need a friend. And Harley? He's got nobody . . . he needs new friends more than anyone. It's like we've all got this connection. I can feel it. And it's about to be taken away. Besides, the way it's coming down isn't right. They worked so hard to get the place. Fought the system that only pretended to be color-blind. And I want to fight it somehow. But everything we've tried has been a dead end. Even Mom couldn't find anything on this BIG organization."

Dad sat on the edge of Parker's bed. "And you think going down in the quarry can help somehow?"

Parker shrugged. Looked at the deliberately misspelled INTEGRITTY sign on the wall his grandpa had carved months ago. "Doing the right thing takes some courage, right? I learned that in Florida. And honestly, Dad? I'm not wild about diving the quarry without you. But we've tried everything else. I don't know what we might find down there. What if we picked up Shadowman's wallet or something? I know, it's stupid. But if we find one thing that points the police to that BIG outfit, maybe we can stall the sale of Beulah until we figure something out."

Parker was on a roll—and his dad hadn't interrupted with a firm *no*. Not yet anyway. He took a breath. "It's a shot in the dark, Dad. I know. It's beyond a long shot. But Ella is going to move. Her family is going to take a giant step back from everything they've fought for. I just want to feel like I tried to throw them every lifeline I could before they go."

Dad sat quiet for what seemed like a long minute. "Standing up for the oppressed. Helping a friend in need. That's good stuff. Those are principles God Himself wants us to develop. I'm proud of you."

This is where the big *but* was coming. Parker could feel it. *But you're too young. But this is too dangerous. But your mother would be worried sick. But something bad could happen.* Yeah, there was a *but* coming. Dad was setting up for it.

"I know it's risky," Parker said. "I know the quarry isn't like a swimming pool . . . with a really, really deep end. But I'll be careful. I'll keep my head on the dive. I'll stay focused on everything you taught me."

Dad looked deep in thought.

"And look at the bright side of me diving a quarry, Dad. You won't have to worry about sharks, right?"

Dad smiled. "It's just that I've never taken you down in a place like that. I'd feel a whole lot better if I could go with you the first time."

If Dad's leg wasn't stitched up from the surgery, he'd definitely be going in. Parker knew that. "Pull up some quarry dive on YouTube. We can do that together—and you'll still be prepping me for the real thing."

Dad actually looked like he would do that. "We'd need an experienced diver topside. I mean somebody who could throw on a tank and get down there if something didn't seem right."

Parker's heart did a double take. *Dad was actually considering this!* He held his breath. "Maybe Harley could recommend someone. He sees divers all week."

"Okay, let's start there," Dad said. "He's got to know somebody who would be qualified."

Parker leaned and slammed into his dad, giving him the strongest, tightest bear hug he'd ever given.

Dad winced. "My leg."

Parker jumped back, "Oh, sorry." He couldn't stop grinning. "Can I tell Harley I can go?"

"Pump the brakes, Parker. Let's wait until we get a solid spotter, okay?"

But they would find somebody. Parker just knew it.

"You'll be in deep water, Parker—and I'm not just talking about the actual depth. This quarry can be totally unforgiving. Dangerous. You know that, right?"

Parker nodded.

Dad took a deep breath and blew it out. "I'm trusting God with this, son. And I'll be praying like crazy. But you're a good diver. I know you are. You'll be okay."

Just like his dad to encourage him when he needed it most.

Dad stood and stretched. Grabbed his crutches and tucked them in place under his arms. "And right now your dad is going to do something he'd rather not do. I'll be in some deep water myself."

Parker tried to read his face.

"I'm going to try to explain my decision to Mom."

Both of them laughed. Even then, a crazy chill flashed through him. Deep water, indeed. *High water.* Parker couldn't help but believe they were both going to be in way over their heads before this was over.

CHAPTER 70

Saturday, June 18, 3:00 p.m.

ELLA CRINGED when Grams took the paperwork from Mr. Steadman. She didn't know whether to be grateful or not that the guy was true to his word. He'd pulled in some favors or something. He had two copies of a signed offer to buy, a certified check for the deposit big enough to pay off Grams's entire debt, and all the documents to prove he had the approval for the loan to close on the property. And he was right on time. Three o'clock.

And Grams had sweet tea and lemon scones for Mr. Steadman. Like she was determined to be a good hostess—right up until the day she lost the house. That's just who she was. And Ella knew she'd have every corner of Beulah sparkling and neat when she handed him the keys at the closing, too.

The only bits of sunshine were that the Boston Investors Group wouldn't get their hands on Beulah. And Scorza's dad couldn't foreclose and resell the property. Grams wished she could see his bloated face when he learned he'd been outmaneuvered.

"The closing is set for July 27," Mr. Steadman said. "That gives you time to find a way to come up with the money to pay back the deposit. If you do," he held up the legal document, "we'll just tear this up."

There was no way they'd come up with that money. But it was nice of Mr. Steadman to make the offer. No bank would give them another loan. Not with all the black marks on their recent credit history. Those kinds of breaks just didn't happen for people like Grams.

Grams picked up a pen and leafed through the legal document. "I should read this."

Mr. Steadman took a swig of tea. "Definitely. Your lawyer too, if there's time."

"Don't have a lawyer, Mr. Steadman."

And there wouldn't be time, anyway. Grams would need to get that deposit check in the bank before four o'clock so she could pay off the loan.

"Then call my lawyer if you've got any questions. We'll tell him to put it on my bill."

The guy couldn't have been nicer. He wasn't just "all business." But Steadman was still getting a phenomenal deal—and he knew it. He should have brought Grams a couple of dozen roses or something.

A series of texts came in rapid-fire from Parker. They still hadn't found a topside man. Parker was already waiting at the quarry, getting everything set. His dad had dropped him off with his gear and then left for his appointment. If they didn't find a man, Parker wasn't going down. Ella wanted to stand up and cheer. But Harley would be there soon—and he insisted he'd go down alone if he had to.

A flash of panic swept through her. Deep in her heart, she absolutely knew Harley would do it. As risky as the quarry was for two divers, she couldn't imagine the danger Harley might face by going down alone. And if Parker had any suspicion that Harley was having trouble, wouldn't Parker go in after him? It was a disaster waiting to happen. Both of those boys had been way too casual in the Old First Parish Burying Ground. She couldn't shake the sense that they'd brought some kind of curse on themselves . . . and there'd be no outrunning it. She reached for her cross.

"What is it, Ella Mae?"

Even as she explained, she sensed the fear rising in Grams.

"It's not good, child," she said. "My heart tells me this is the thing I've been fearing. They mustn't go down in that demon quarry."

Steadman looked more concerned than she'd ever seen him—which wasn't helping Ella keep it together one bit. "Have they lost their minds? The rescue team checked it. I was with them. If there was a body, we'd have found it. The entire team is trained for that."

"He's not looking for a body," Ella said. "He's obsessed with the idea that there might be something the team missed."

"He has no idea what he'd be getting himself into. Quarries can be tricky," Steadman said. "Harley would really go down . . . alone?"

Ella nodded. "I'm sure of it."

"And Parker's dad can't stick around?"

Ella shook her head.

Steadman thought for a few seconds. "Look, I'll go over there and talk some sense into those boys. And if they won't listen, I'll stay topside and be their spotter." He whipped out his phone. "I can keep the boys out of trouble. I'll work it out with Parker's dad."

Mr. Steadman made the call on the front porch, pacing the whole time. When he returned, Grams was still staring at the papers.

"I've got to run." Steadman pocketed his phone. "You take your time, look over the agreement. I'll be back in a couple hours to pick up my copy—and another glass of that sweet tea."

"That is a godforsaken quarry, Mr. Steadman."

"I'll be fine, Mrs. Houston."

"It's the boys I'm worried about," Grams said. "I'm afraid they'll end up like that poor Catsakis boy."

He smiled and patted her arm. "Then I'd better hurry over there to make sure that doesn't happen."

Grams smiled back, like her mind was at ease. Ella reached for the cross again. Slipped her fingers around it . . . and wished she felt the same way.

CHAPTER 71

Saturday, June 18, 4:30 p.m.

PARKER SAW THE RELIEF ON HARLEY'S FACE the moment after he read the text out loud from Dad.

"So you're going down with me—and Steadman is our topside guy, right?"

Parker reread the text. "That's the way it looks—and he's on his way." It was a good thing, too. A battalion of clouds had formed just offshore. A fogbank waiting for the order to storm the beaches and invade Rockport. Other than cutting their light even more, the sea mist wouldn't bother them underwater. But would the heavy fog make it harder for Steadman to spot their bubbles—or know if they were in trouble?

Harley stared out over the quarry. "Lots of ground to cover if we're going to give it an honest search. Deep, too. We won't have much bottom time."

He was right. The quarry was nearly two hundred yards long and choked by woods on all sides. Humpback Rock jutted out like a rock peninsula.

"We don't need to search the whole quarry," Parker said. "Just where we saw the Shadow-man go down."

Parker and Harley readied their gear. Parker looked at the knife from Grandpa, reading the inscription:

"He reveals deep and hidden things;
he knows what lies in darkness."

Harley read over Parker's shoulder. "Let's hope your God reveals something to us that everyone else missed, right?"

Parker totally agreed. *Show us those hidden things, God . . . bring some justice here, please.* He sheathed the knife. Slid it into his BCD vest pocket and smoothed the Velcro seal back in place.

Steadman showed up ten minutes later. By the time he swung out of his pickup, Parker and Harley both had their wet suits on, regulators secured to the tank valves, and the BCD vests attached. They'd set their fins, masks, lights, and weight belts at the lip of the quarry.

"You two look like you're all set." Steadman pulled an oversize duffle from the bed of his truck.

"Thanks for doing this, Boss." And Parker really meant it.

"Don't thank me yet." He hefted the duffle to the edge of the quarry and whipped open the zipper. His tank, wet suit—all his gear was stowed neatly inside. "First I'd like to try talking you out of it."

"Save your breath," Harley said. "I'm going down."

Steadman smiled. "That's what I was afraid of." He stepped to the edge of the quarry. "A dive here is way different from any place you've gone down before. Neither of you has quarry experience, right?"

Parker looked into the still water. He was definitely wishing Dad was here.

"I'll take that as a no." Steadman folded his hands across his chest. "So how about *I* go down instead, look for anything unusual, and report back to you two?" He glanced up at the sky. "Looks like our ceiling is dropping, too. I'll be quick, thorough, and we'll all get out of here before we can't see ten feet in front of us."

"I'm doing this," Harley said. No one was going to talk him out of this. He gave his mask a squirt of the no-fog solution and smeared it around the entire inside surface of the glass.

"Okay," Steadman said. "Plan B. How about *I* take you down? We'll let Swabbie be our topside guy. I've logged a thousand more dives than the both of you combined. I'll lead—and I'll get you down and back in one piece. When we're done, I'll even treat you two to dinner at Top Dog. How's that?" He looked to Parker.

Honestly, Parker would have loved to sit this one out. But wouldn't he be ditching Harley? And Parker didn't want any regrets. If Steadman and Harley did the looking for Parker, would he wonder someday if they missed something *he* might have seen? Steadman had already scouted the quarry out earlier in the week anyway. Could Parker really expect him to notice something he didn't see the first time?

And there was more, wasn't there? Hadn't he prayed—asking God to help him make a difference somehow? Didn't he feel he was *supposed* to do this dive? If he backed away from this, might he miss what God had planned for him?"

"Mr. Steadman, part of me would love that. Honest. But I'd feel you were doing my job."

"Taking a late afternoon dive is no big deal to me, Parker. I'll just be working up a bigger appetite for dinner."

The water looked black now. Parker *really* wished he could take Steadman up on his offer. But if Harley went in—and Parker stayed back? That still didn't feel right. "Look, you're helping Ella and her Grams plenty. You're going the extra mile with them. I guess I just want to feel like I've helped in some way, too. I know we'll probably come up with nothing, but I need to do this."

"Sounds like someone wants to step up and be a man. Roger that." Steadman shrugged. "I can respect that. But let me go over a few things with both of you before you go down, okay?"

He warned about the cold—how they'd hit a thermocline layer where the water would turn icier than it already was. He put the fear of God into them about the dark, too. Especially now that the sun was no longer overhead. The quarry floor was covered in a fine silt—which was another hazard.

"Stay off the bottom if you can," Steadman said. "You stir up that silt, and you'd better not stop moving—not for three seconds. You do and that silt cloud will swallow you whole, blocking out what little light you have."

Steadman let that image percolate in their brains for a moment. "Look, boys, I've seen good men get caught in a silt cloud and lose it. A light won't help—it will actually make it worse. If you get caught in a silt cloud, what are you going to do?"

"Don't panic," Parker said. "And start moving."

Steadman nodded. "Forward—or up until you get clear of it. The stuff spreads fast, and as you move you're creating a current. The cloud will follow you. You'll need to go farther than you think to clear it, but you *will* get past it."

He looked down into the quarry like he really wished he was

going in. "I'm going to ask one more time. How about you stay topside, Swabbie, and I'll take Harley down? I'll make sure we stay on course—and off the bottom."

But wasn't the whole idea of diving the quarry to *get* to the bottom . . . to look close to see if there was any clue Shadow-man left behind? "I really have to do this," Parker said.

Steadman raised both hands in mock surrender. "Okay, okay." He lowered his hands and his face got that serious look again. "Now, if you see any old quarry equipment down there, steer clear. I don't want one of you getting tangled up in rusty steel cables. They're down there, and it's a real devil to see them. Even harder to get free if it snags your gear."

Parker hadn't thought about that. And didn't want to think about it now. He explained that their focus would be the bottom of the quarry at the base of Humpback Rock. He had no desire to go past that point.

Steadman looked toward the granite peninsula. "Humpback Rock. When you get in the water, swim far enough out to get a clear visual on that peninsula. Set your compass for the rock before you go down. Doesn't look far, but it's easy to lose your way in the dark. Once you're at depth, follow that compass. At the halfway point, you'll see a car. A 1966 Plymouth Valiant, to be exact."

"There's a *car* down there?"

"Sitting on all four rims like someone parked it. And it's no wonder the guy pushed it into the quarry. I would too if I had a total dweeb-mobile like that."

Harley was staring into the water like maybe he thought he could see it if he looked hard enough. "Still got the plates on it?"

"Don't stop for souvenirs, hotshot. The silt, remember? It will gobble you up faster than you could pull out a screwdriver to get the plate off. The driver's door is jammed in a full-open position. But don't even think about going inside the car. It's tighter than it looks—and turning around to get back out of the car with all that gear? You're asking for trouble—especially when the silt cloud rolls over you. Stick to your mission. By the time you get there, you won't have much bottom time."

Parker was feeling even less confident about the whole thing than he had felt just a few minutes earlier.

"The car itself works like a compass. The open driver's door points you to the south wall of the quarry. You won't be able to see the wall, but it's close. There are some nasty rock formations on the south wall. I'd steer clear of it at all costs."

"Avoid the south wall. Check," Parker said. "Humpback Rock is where we want to search."

Steadman nodded. "Good." He looked at the sky, then back at the quarry. He tapped the lip of the quarry. "You follow the Valiant's nose and it will point you in the right direction. You'll run smack-dab into another rock wall. That's the base of Humpback Rock. You'll have a few minutes to search the bottom, but don't lose sight of that granite tower. You make your ascent, right up that rock wall, and you'll surface right there. Put some air in your BCD and swim right back here on the surface. Got it?"

Yeah, they got it. And right now Parker just wanted to get going. It was getting darker by the minute. What if his dad got back early and decided the dive looked too risky after all?

Steadman spun the dial on his watch. "You have twenty minutes. From the instant your head disappears below the surface to the moment I see your smiling faces bobbing at Humpback. Deal?"

Parker and Harley both set their watches.

"Ten seconds late, and I'll be gearing up and following your bubbles down. And you will not like seeing me down there." As if to make his point, he pressed his mask against his cheeks and made a mock angry face. "Now move out."

Parker and Harley sat on the edge of the quarry, their feet dangling in the cool water. Fins. Tank with BCD vest. Weight belt. Mask. Gloves. All went on quick—like the clock was already ticking.

"I'll take lead on the descent, and to the car," Harley said. "You can lead us home."

Parker nodded.

"Stay together," Steadman said. "If you lose sight of the other for more than thirty seconds, you abort the mission and surface. You got that? You get to the surface and tap out. I'll go down to pick up the stray. You do *not* want to be alone at the bottom of this quarry, and you don't want to wander anywhere near the south wall. Are we clear?"

Parker and Harley both gave Steadman a thumbs-up.

"Here we go." Harley settled the mouthpiece in place, boosted himself off the granite lip, and splashed into the quarry.

Parker did the same. Both bobbed at the surface for a moment. Parker set his compass. Rinsed his mask and reseated it on his face. Unclipped the light from his weight belt and secured the lanyard around his wrist. He flashed Harley an "OK" sign and turned on his flashlight.

"Stick to the plan," Steadman said. "Don't make me come in after you."

Parker raised the release valve on his BCD as Harley did the same. Together, they slipped below the surface on their feet-first descent to the bottom. Parker squeezed his nose and gently forced air into his ears and sinuses to equalize the building pressure. Diving the quarry already felt different from any ocean dive Parker had experienced. The biggest thing was the overwhelming silence. The ocean was full of sounds. A motor from a hundred yards away sounded like it was overhead. Here in the quarry, the only thing Parker heard was his own breathing. A Darth Vader sound as he sucked air through the regulator, and the bubbles tumbled past his hood.

Parker had never been on a night dive, but he imagined it would be something like this. The bottom wasn't visible. Only a blackness that appeared to have no end.

Even at twenty feet below the surface, water was still trickling inside his wet suit. Looking for a dry spot of skin to torture with its icy fingers.

The temperature took a definite plunge at the thermocline layer. Not a gradual thing, but more like a literal line. Parker slowed. Slid his hand above the thermocline, then below it again. It was like pulling his hand from a bucket of somewhat chilly water and thrusting it into one filled with ice water.

Parker slowed as the bottom loomed into sight. A lunar landscape kind of place. No seaweed. Eerie lack of life. Everything about it reminded him that they didn't belong here. For a moment, they both hovered above the bottom. Even as they did, great plumes of black silt billowed up from the quarry floor, reaching hungrily for them, gobbling up their fins.

Harley checked his compass and pointed. Parker verified the direction with his own compass. They struck out side by side.

Parker's beam found the Valiant first. Sure enough, the driver's door stood wide open, like someone had just been inside. Harley swept off a bit of the back window and shined his flashlight inside.

From where Parker floated, the light cast eerie shadows from inside the car that looked like hulking figures were waiting inside, ready to pounce on anyone foolish enough to venture in. Harley hovered over the driver's door for a moment. *Oh, man!* Parker just remembered how Harley's dad died. This had to be a tough reminder.

Harley turned back to make sure Parker was still there. He pointed ahead—then pointed at Parker. A quick compass check confirmed the nose of the Valiant definitely pointed toward Humpback Rock.

They kept off the bottom by three feet. Close enough to see anything that might have been dropped, but not so close to stir up the deadly silt. Parker took the lead, but not by much more than a couple of inches. They swam shoulder to shoulder—and stayed so close their fins often sideswiped each other. Parker didn't mind. He couldn't imagine doing this alone. *Would Harley have really gone in by himself?*

The bottom was way darker than Parker would have guessed. Huge chunks of granite stood here and there—like some quarryman had them all cut to size right before the quarry flooded.

Silt covered everything, just like Steadman said. A bicycle was covered with the gray-black stuff. It looked like pictures he'd seen of the debris around the Titanic.

Suddenly Harley gripped Parker's forearm and pointed. His beam was locked on a pipe-shaped object—close to two feet long—just lying on the bottom.

Parker kicked harder and glided down to see it. It wasn't a pipe. It was a massive light stick—the kind Shadow-man had been carrying. There wasn't a speck of silt on it. Was this the one that went down with Shadow-man the night before? Parker tucked it in his vest.

They hadn't gone six feet before Parker saw a second one. A fine layer of silt covered it—but not nearly what he'd seen on the car and other things down there. Parker knelt on the bottom. Was this the light stick that had lured Devin Catsakis to his death? The thought totally creeped him out. He picked it up and held it out to Harley. He nodded, like he knew exactly what Parker was thinking.

Parker added this one to his vest as well. How many light sticks were down here? Suddenly a cloud of silt caught up to them. Surrounded them. Hugged them close. Everything went black in the most suffocating way. How could their fins have kicked up this much muck?

Parker reached for Harley. Found his arm. He didn't let go but yanked him forward, kicking with all his might. It seemed like it took ten strokes to clear the black cloud, and the moment he did, he kept pushing for another ten before slowing up.

The light sticks were still tucked in his vest. He was sort of treading water—suspended at sixty-five feet, with Harley doing the same. Parker concentrated on steadying his breathing. Checked the time. They were good. Still had a solid ten minutes before they needed to be at the surface.

Harley pointed at his compass and raised both hands, palms up. Parker checked his own compass. Okay, the retreat from the quarry dust got them off course a little. Actually a lot.

He could just get himself pointed in the right direction and move—but how far out into the quarry had he gone to get away from the silt cloud? What if he missed the Humpback Rock tower wall and headed farther out into the flooded old pit where there might be rusty steel cables and equipment?

Parker held his flashlight out and did a slow 360-degree turn.

Black. Black. Black. Black. Granite. Black. He backtracked a few degrees. Definitely a rock wall. He checked his compass. Clearly this wasn't the deep base of Humpback Rock. It would be the south wall of the quarry—where the passenger door of the Valiant pointed. Exactly where Steadman had warned them not to go.

Keeping his beam locked on the granite wall, Parker motioned to Harley, using the best sign language he could manage. Should they go to *that* wall, and just go to the surface—or keep looking for the wall they'd originally planned to ascend? They could still check the bottom all the way there. But the truth was, now that he'd seen the bottom, his hopes of finding anything significant had dimmed as much as the light from overhead. If a wallet had dropped, the silt would have swallowed it up.

Harley pointed at the wall in the beam. Which was a relief. The idea of following the compass into blackness was totally creeping him out. Maybe it was finding the light sticks. Maybe it was the cold. The tomb-like darkness. Or the unnatural metallic sound of his regulator as he drew in the compressed air, and the bubbles as he exhaled. He'd seen enough.

Together they kicked for the granite wall. Harley swept the bottom with his light as he went. Parker kept his light trained on their target. At the very base, where the granite wall jutted up from the bottom, another light stick.

Harley angled down to scoop it up.

Three light sticks. Parker didn't know how they would prove anything that would help Ella. In fact he was pretty sure they wouldn't. But still it was something to bring to the surface, if nothing else, to prove Shadow-man had been there. To prove Devin Catsakis hadn't imagined the light . . . that he really had seen Shadow-man—just like Parker, Harley, Ella, and Jelly had. At least they wouldn't end the dive empty-handed.

Parker checked his watch. They still had time on the clock, but he'd seen enough. What he really wanted now was to get out of here. He pointed up the wall toward the surface. Harley nodded and gave a thumbs-up. They ascended side by side at an even pace, careful to keep breathing—and not to get ahead of their bubbles. Too fast and the compressed nitrogen from the scuba tank mix would actually bubble in their bloodstream—which wouldn't bring a happy ending to their quarry dive.

Parker didn't look down. His imagination was already conjuring up Shadow-man rising from the blackness below them. Dragging them down.

The surface was nothing more than a distant light smudge—but it looked good. And passing above the thermocline *felt* good. They kept close to the wall, both of them using their hands more than their fins now. There was something about being weightless like this. Grab a handhold, pull yourself up. It was as easy as Spider-Man made it look to climb buildings. Parker checked his depth gauge. They'd stop at fifteen feet for three minutes, just to give some of the nitrogen buildup an extra chance to leave their body naturally.

At a depth of twenty feet the rock wall ended—as in there was nothing there. Parker swung his light. A cave. Five feet across, maybe. Five or six feet high. As if a block had been extracted from the side of the quarry like a bad tooth. How far back did the cave go? Parker wasn't sure. And the idea of going deeper inside the rock wall to find out absolutely wasn't going to happen.

Something bright reflected off the floor of the alcove. Parker swung his light that way—and stared in stunned silence. Two scuba tanks sat side by side—and not a speck of silt on either one. Each had deflated BCD vests and complete regulator kits with a weight belt draped across them. Parker moved closer. Shined his light on the pressure gauges. Both tanks at a full 3,000 pounds of pressure. Wait, the tanks were ready to go, with the air turned on? To be sure, Parker pressed the purge valve on the regulator. Bubbles gushed out of the mouthpiece.

Parker picked his way deeper into the man-made cave—Harley right behind him. A mesh dive bag rested on the rock bottom between the two tanks. Inside sat a mask, snorkel, and fins. Everything a diver would need—all right there. Suddenly it was all coming together.

Oh, God, this is it. This is how Shadow-man did it. When he disappeared into the quarry he went to his little cave and had plenty of air. He could sit here for an hour and just wait for everything to calm down on the surface if he wanted. Even his bubbles would be trapped in the cave . . . not escaping to the surface to betray him. Shadow-man was no ghost. No supernatural being. Shadow-man was a living, breathing human being who wanted others to *think* there were ghosts—or whatever—at work.

Wouldn't this prove to the police that BIG was behind this? He'd bypass Rankin and call Officer Greenwood the moment he got to the surface. Could this discovery somehow delay the foreclosure—and the sale—from happening until a full-scale investigation was mounted?

Hidden things—just sitting here in the darkness. Oh, God . . . You are the revealer of mysteries!

Harley tapped his shoulder. His eyes alive—like he'd figured out exactly what this meant, too. He motioned to the tanks and pointed to the surface.

He was right. They needed to get back to the surface pronto. The cops needed to see this evidence. They'd caught a break. But still, an uneasiness clung as tight to him as the wet suit he was wearing. Parker couldn't explain how he knew what he felt, but they had to get out of this quarry with the evidence—and fast.

CHAPTER 72

Saturday, June 18, 5:15 p.m.

ANGELICA SHOULD HAVE GONE WITH PARKER. *Could she have talked him out of diving the quarry?* Probably not. And Harley was just as stone-stubborn as Parker. She'd come up from Florida because she knew Parker needed protecting, right? Why hadn't she stuck with him?

But she knew why. Even though she felt she had to be the voice of reason with these boys, she didn't want them to know that. She'd taken a little gamble that they'd never actually find a topside dive spotter at the last minute . . . and she'd lost.

At least there would be no alligators in the quarry. No Ella-gators either. So that was good, right? In fact, Parker had asked her to hang out with Ella a bit while the guys went to the quarry. But with the whole losing-the-house thing, being with her and her Grams right now was way beyond awkward. And Angelica had no idea what to say . . . or how to really help.

Was that why she'd stalled going to Ella's place until now—or was it something more?

A twang of guilt played deep in her spirit somewhere. She'd been so protective of her friendship with Parker that she'd looked at Ella as a threat from the first time she'd heard her name. A rival, maybe. Competition in a tug-of-war for Parker's time and attention. The trail camera hadn't done a bit of good. Honestly, Angelica didn't even have the heart to look at the images it had captured. But maybe it gave Angelica an excuse to stop by Ella's house.

Even as she walked into Ella's backyard, she still had no idea what to say. Or what to do.

Ella sat on the porch swing behind her house. Head down. Shoulders slumped. A sheaf of papers sat on her lap. Little "Signature Here" tabs clung to the margins. Obviously the selling agreement for Beulah.

Angelica picked her way closer, torn between not wanting to disturb her and legitimately wanting to help.

Ella's shoulders moved in rhythmic, silent sobs. Angelica stood there, not wanting to stare, but not able to look away. This was a girl whose family had fought an uphill battle all the way. No real mom or dad in the picture. But a grandma who loved her and had adopted her—and had worked to give her something she could truly call her own. A place. A home.

Now she was losing it all. As far as Angelica knew, Parker was the only real friend she had. And Angelica, deep down, had wanted to take that from her too, hadn't she? Parker had been so excited for the two of them to meet . . . trusting she'd be good for Ella. Thinking the two would hit it off somehow.

If Angelica had heard a month ago that Ella was going to move, she'd have had a private little celebration. A victory party. Didn't that make her just a little bit like that banker dude who'd forced Grams to sell? Scorza preyed on a nice family, taking the only home Ella had. And Angelica had wanted to rob her of her only friend.

"God in heaven, I already asked you to forgive me . . . but I am soooo sorry for how selfish I've been," she whispered. The more she saw Ella and her Grams—and reflected on their story—the more she wished none of this had happened to them. Angelica hadn't just been protective of her friendship with Parker. The word *protective* made her attitude seem noble or something. She'd been possessive. And she'd been wrong. So very, miserably wrong. "And God? May the boys find something in that quarry that makes a difference."

A whimper escaped Ella's lips. A helpless-sounding thing—like she'd been trying desperately to keep it bottled up, but a little bit of the pain broke free anyway.

No pain, no gain. Why that stupid saying passed through her mind at that very moment, she had no idea. There was nothing wrong with a person making personal sacrifices—feeling a little pain—to get something they wouldn't have gotten otherwise. It seemed like Grams did a whole lot of that. But Ella's pain had been brought on by someone else. A heartless person. A cowardly person who created pain for others—so that he'd gain something for himself. Warm tears glossed her own cheeks now. "God of justice . . . please . . . make this right somehow."

Suddenly Ella looked up—like she'd sensed someone was there. "Jelly!" She looked relieved. "I thought you were my Grams." She took a handful of her sleeve and wiped her cheeks. "Wouldn't want her to see me like this."

Angelica sat on the swing and put her arm around Ella's shoulders. "Cry all you want with me. Just let it out."

Ella pulled her into a hug. "This move is going to sap the life right out of Grams. I can't bear to see that."

"I'm so sorry." For her horrible attitude. Her lack of concern.

"Living with her sister . . . in the city . . . it won't be good for her. I know it."

Not a word about Ella's own fears. Not a mention of the hard changes she'd absolutely go through with a new school and living someplace that didn't seem like home. "Oh, Ella." She hugged Ella back. "I'm praying to God that He brings some justice to this mess."

Ella released Jelly. "You do that. We need a little Almighty intervention here."

Angelica's phone chirped with an incoming text. Uncle Vaughn.

`You still want me to pick you up on the way to the quarry?`

She whipped off her answer.

`Definitely. I'm at Ella's.`

She pecked out another message and held it up for Ella to see.

`Ella's coming with.`

Ella smiled. Just a quick flash. "I'll tell Grams. She worries whenever the vapors come inland," she said as she motioned at the fog, "but she'll be okay knowing Parker's dad will be with us." Her phone dinged again. `ETA 15 minutes. Be ready.`

She wished Uncle Vaughn could get here even sooner. Angelica fired off another text. `We'll both be waiting at the curb when you get here.` He probably wanted to get to the quarry even more than she did—and she did not intend to slow him down.

Ella read the exchange and nodded in approval.

"I'll get my trail cam and meet you by the street." There was no sense keeping the camera strapped to a tree any longer—now that the papers were signed. Shadow-man would be Steadman's problem now. Which hopefully meant Parker would leave it alone. Maybe he'd actually give her a proper tour of Rockport now.

The camera was right where she'd hidden it a week earlier. A fat lot of good it did bringing it up from Florida. She slid her pack off her shoulders, placed the cam inside, and hustled for the front of the house just as Grams walked Ella down the porch steps.

"I have a bad feeling about this, Ella Mae." Deep worry lines creased Grams's face. "The vapors are especially thick—and that doesn't bode well. Something wicked this way comes. You get up to that quarry and get those boys home right now, you hear? I'll not have those fine young men walking right into harm's way on my account."

Something wicked. Harm's way. The words chilled Angelica like an ice cube down her shirt.

Ella sent Grams inside and walked Angelica to the street.

"Is your Grams always this way with the fog?"

"Always. But it's worse this time. I haven't seen her this bad since . . ." She held the cross necklace and stretched to look down the block. "Where *is* he?"

Uncle Vaughn's pickup wasn't in sight—and probably wouldn't be for another ten minutes. "You haven't seen her this bad since *when*?"

Ella looked at her for a long moment. "Since the night Devin Catsakis died."

CHAPTER 73

Saturday, June 18, 5:20 p.m.

PARKER GRABBED THE BLACK TANK. Harley the silver. Both of them backed their way out of the cave. Parker stuffed one of the weight belts in the mesh bag and wrapped the drawstring tie securely around the tank valve.

Harley stood on the lip of the cave. Tested the weight of the tank, and added a shot of air to his BCD. He gave Parker a thumbs-up to be sure he was ready to go to the surface. Parker flashed the sign back, and Harley started his ascent.

Parker launched right behind him—but too close. Harley clipped him with his fin, partially knocking off Parker's mask. He grabbed it just in time—but lost his grip on the mystery air tank in the process.

The tank—with the mesh bag and weights—plunged toward the bottom. Parker quickly cleared the water from his mask, but it was too late to save the tank. The gear had already disappeared into the darkness below him.

For a moment he stayed suspended there. Harley was a good ten feet above him now—totally unaware as to what had happened. To swim all the way back down to the bottom to find the tank? Not a chance. Not without his dive buddy—and there was no time to change their dive plan even more.

Harley looked back—as if he sensed Parker had stopped. Parker motioned toward the bottom and shrugged. Harley shook the tank in his own hand and pointed to the surface.

He was right. One tank was all they needed. If the police wanted the second one, Parker would tell them where to find it. Parker kicked off for the surface. Caught up and swam alongside Harley. Grabbed hold of Shadow-man's tank to share the load. Harley gave him an "OK" sign and grinned.

Steadman was there waiting for them the instant they surfaced. Obviously he'd seen their bubbles and figured out their course change. Together they handed Shadow-man's tank to Steadman. He grabbed it and looked at it for a long moment before laying it on the ground beside the rim of the quarry.

"There's a cave with gear inside—another tank too," Harley said. "This is the evidence we need. This is how Shadow-man did it. He's not a ghost at all!"

Parker spit out his mouthpiece and gave his BCD a couple shots of air for flotation. "The whole Shadow-man thing was just a scheme to get people like you and Ella's grandma to sell."

Harley sat on a natural granite ledge a foot below the surface.

Parker joined him and peeled off his mask. "We found these, too." He set the giant light sticks on the ground. "We need to get Officer Greenwood out here. Maybe the police can do something to stop the foreclosure thing and start an investigation." This had to prove someone had deliberately been sabotaging the rental home business. It only made sense that BIG was behind this. He shrugged off his BCD vest and tank.

Steadman lifted their gear onto shore. "I was just about ready to gear up myself. Another minute and I would have. You didn't follow the plan to surface at Humpback Rock."

Parker explained how they'd gotten off course. "But it was meant to be—us finding the cave and all. God works in mysterious ways—and reveals hidden mysteries. Find the owner of this tank—we've got Shadow-man. And if he works for the Boston Investors Group?" Parker slapped his hands together. "Bam. The police will probably call in the FBI."

Steadman just wasn't getting it—or wasn't convinced. Maybe he was still trying to put the pieces together, but he didn't look one bit excited.

Harley inspected the silver tank from the cave. Ran his gloved hand over the serial number stamped at the base of the valve.

"Hey, Harley, the other day in the dive shop, you claimed you can tell who owns each tank just by the markings and stickers and stuff." Parker took a closer look at a Rockport Dive Company visual examination sticker. The thing had passed the inspection—this year. "This one has been in your shop. See anything here you recognize?"

Harley turned the tank over and stared at a sticker just above the boot. *Black Ops Coffee. High Caliber Caffeine.* He tensed. Flipped the tank back over like he wanted to hide the sticker. "Nothing. Just like any other silver tank. I don't think I've ever seen it before." He glanced up at Parker—something desperate in his eyes. "I'm sure of it."

"Really?" Steadman stepped closer. "Take another look."

Parker's gut twisted. Something was wrong here.

Harley pushed the tank away from him. "No, I'm positive. Never seen it before." His voice cracked.

Harley shot Parker another look. A warning. And Parker knew. *Help us, Lord. It's Steadman!*

"You say you've never seen the tank before." Steadman toed the silver tank. "But your body language is telling me something very different. Actually, this looks like one of my tanks, don't you think?"

"Hey, look," Harley said. "I don't know nothing about nothing. I just want to get home and take a hot shower."

Parker needed to get some distance between him and Steadman. Maybe if Harley ran one way and Parker ran another. He slipped off his fins and boosted himself onto the rock ledge.

"Hold on, Swabbie." Steadman drew his Glock 19 from his holster. "There's a round in the chamber, boys, and a band of brothers lined up behind it. Fifteen to be exact."

Both boys froze.

"You two just *had* to take the dive today. Wouldn't let me do it for you. Wouldn't let me take one of you down to keep you on course. And sure enough, you didn't follow the plan. I warned you, too. Go straight to Humpback Rock. But you wouldn't listen."

Parker raised both hands. "Mr. Steadman, we don't—"

"Want any trouble?" Steadman shrugged. "Well, it's too late for that." He glanced down the fogbound gravel road. "Daddy's going to be coming soon, so we need to hurry—or he gets hurt, too. And that pretty little redhead friend from Florida—if she's with him. You copy?"

Parker nodded.

"Empty your tanks. Like you're in a race."

Parker turned off the air. Removed the regulator. Cranked the valve wide open. Harley did the same. Pressurized air whooshed out.

"So it was you. The whole time?"

Steadman smiled, but he didn't lower the Glock.

"But that first night—when I was chased. How did you . . ."

"I left you at the Old First Parish Burying Ground—right after you ditched your T-shirt. Ran for my truck. Your phone call worked perfectly as an alibi, don't you think?"

Parker was still trying to wrap his head around this. "You're part of BIG?"

Steadman looked smug. "There was no Boston Investors Group. War is all about deception. You ever read about the Ghost Army in World War II?" Their faces must have looked confused, so Steadman continued. "I love this story. The US Forces had this idea of appearing bigger—and in more places—than they actually were. So they had giant inflatable tanks made—not scuba tanks, but looking like real armored tanks. Their artists made them look totally legit. The Ghost Army would pack them up in trucks outfitted with big speakers. Then they'd drive past towns in the dead of night—all the time playing a recorded soundtrack of a big convoy on the move. It sounded like an invasion."

Steadman was so confident he was taking the time to tell them a story? Parker and Harley exchanged sideways glances.

"So then the Ghost Army would set up camp and inflate those tanks," Steadman said. "The enemy would get wind that there had been some big movement. Maybe send over a recon plane—and what would they see? Rows of tanks. They'd divert their troops or change their battle plan—and when they got to where they'd spotted the tanks? Poof! They'd disappeared like ghosts. It kept the enemy reinforcing the wrong positions—leaving the right ones unprotected. The enemy never figured it out—and we won the war, right?"

"Mr. Steadman, I—"

"So I became my own Ghost Army. Deception is a powerful thing, boys. And you ate every bit of bad intel I fed you. I used BIG to drive the price way down. And then I got it down even more."

Harley looked confused. "Scorza's dad . . . was he in on it, too?"

"I usually work alone . . . but he did his part . . . and got a nice little gift from me for calling in the loan."

"All this . . . just to get a piece of property?"

Steadman shook his head. "I didn't *just* buy a piece of property. I bought a money tree. I get two rental homes in one bargain buy. I'll more than double my income—which means I'm sitting pretty. I'm set for life. Just sit back and let the money come to me. Bayview. Bayport. I'm thinking of sticking with that theme. Baybreeze for the big house. Bayside for the smaller. What do you think?"

Steadman was out of his mind. *Now he was asking their opinion about house names?*

The air flowing from the tanks lost force and escaped with more of a whisper now. Like most of its fight had drained. Parker knew the feeling.

"Okay. Close the valves. Regulators back on. Disconnect the BCD hose. Air on."

Both boys did as they were told.

Steadman checked the pressure gauges. Both tanks deep in the red danger zone. "Tanks on your backs. Hurry."

Parker shrugged on his pack. Clipped in. Harley did the same.

Careful to keep the gun on the boys, Steadman unzipped a side panel on his gear bag and pulled out a handful of oversized nylon ties. "Now I want to see you tie yourself in so that vest can't come off—even if you release the clips. Right here." He motioned to the padded straps on the BCD vest.

Parker looped it through and snugged it. Steadman reached over and cinched it tighter. There was no way Parker could take the tank off if he wanted.

Steadman did the same to Harley. "You're going to the bottom again. But you'll run out of air within a minute or two. Everyone will think it was another tragic accident."

He grabbed a nylon mesh bag from his duffle and stuffed two entire weight belts inside. "Zip-tie this to Harley's valve stem."

Parker obeyed. Harley struggled to keep his balance with the awkward placement of the weights.

Steadman grabbed a hunk of granite the size of a brick and dropped it in a second nylon bag. He motioned to Harley. "Zip-tie this to Parker's valve stem."

Harley obeyed.

"Now nylon strap yourselves together." He pointed at the BCD vest shoulder straps. "Make it tight."

Hardly any air. Too much weight to do anything but go straight to the bottom. And now tied together so they couldn't even maneuver? "Mr. Steadman—please."

"Life is a survival of the fittest, boys. And that would be me."

Parker couldn't believe this was really happening. "So you're going to survive . . . by killing us?"

Steadman smiled apologetically. "I never wanted this to happen. You two just wouldn't leave it alone." He waved the Glock at Harley. "I gave you a chance. A solid warning. I normally only do that once. But I warned you both right here at the quarry again."

"And you." He locked eyes with Parker. "You're a do-gooder, Swabbie. Mr. Do-Right. Always trying to help others out and not paying attention to the danger you put yourself in. Like a soldier who throws himself on a live grenade to save someone else. You brought this on yourself. Quick news flash? The moment you brought my tank to the surface the grenade detonated. You're already dead . . . you just don't know it yet. It's too late to put the pieces back together."

"I *trusted* you."

"A tactical error. War is about deception . . . and you didn't even consider I could be involved?" He shook his head. "You're way too trusting for your own good."

Maybe he was, when it came to people. But he hadn't trusted God enough in all this, had he? At first he didn't trust God to bring justice . . . and had tried to make things happen somehow on his own. He'd had things upside down. But he'd prayed . . . and definitely felt like he was supposed to go into the quarry today. And he'd obeyed, even though he'd felt afraid. *God . . . please . . .*

"When we don't come up—they'll look for us," Harley said. "You were our spotter. How will you explain the nylon ties? No one will believe this was an accident."

"I won't have to. When you two don't come up on time, I'll call the police myself, and the water rescue team. I've got my gear here. I'll be ready, and as soon as they come, I'll go down to make the heroic rescue. It'll be ten minutes before the team gets ready. I'll have the nylon ties cut long before they get to the bottom. And the nylon bags will disappear in a crevice. It will look like two inexperienced boys ran out of air and panicked."

It was brilliant, in a sick-minded way. If he'd tied their hands and feet, there'd be bruising that would show—even with the nylon ties gone. But with the vests tied together? There'd be no telltale marks at all.

"Give me your knife, Swabbie." Steadman waved the gun. "With its sheath."

Parker's heart spiked. Did Steadman know he had two knives on him—or one? *God, please don't let him check my vest pocket.*

Staying on his feet was incredibly hard with all the extra weight and them tied together like they were. There was no way he'd be able to keep his head above water. He reached down to his calf and unclipped the straps to his dive knife. Held it out.

"Toss it. Nice and easy."

Steadman caught it with one hand. "I'll give you a few minutes and then toss it down after you. No need for the police to see that."

Parker had to stall for time. Think of something. "God, help us!" He said it right out loud. "I know you can do it. Don't let him get away with this!"

"Calling in the big guns?" Steadman held out his hand. "Gee, I'm shaking, Parker. But are you sure God sees—or hears—any of this? The fog is pretty thick."

"Mocking God? You don't know who you're messing with."

Steadman shook his head. "Actually, I was mocking you."

"Devin Catsakis," Harley said. "That drowning was no accident, was it?"

"Ah, Mr. Catsakis. You've heard the saying, 'Curiosity killed the cat,' right? That's what got *Cat*sakis. His dumb curiosity. Like I say, some people don't know when to stop. That stupid kid should have left when he had the chance. I waited underwater a good ten minutes. I was sure the kid had left and wouldn't stop running until his head was under his covers. But he came back. Saw me surface—and take off my hood. I really had no choice."

Parker shook his head. "There's always a choice. And you've got one right now."

"Prison? Not much of a choice, Parker."

"You could run," Harley said. "Just disappear somewhere. No prison that way, right?"

"Or I could stay." Steadman shrugged. "I've got a really sweet setup here. The money from the rentals is too good to walk away from. Look around. There are no witnesses. Don't tell me I can't get away with murder. I already have."

"Don't you fear God—even a little bit?" Parker's mind went to the letter from his grandpa. "He's a God of justice. A revealer of mysteries. The exposer of every hidden thing."

"Thanks for the Sunday school lesson, Parker. And if your god is as powerful as you seem to think he is, he can rescue you, right? So I'll have a clear conscience on this. If he doesn't save you, it's on him. Not me."

Parker didn't know how to respond. *Would God save them?*

"Now, fins on. Masks in place. Better have your mouthpiece in hand." Steadman acted like he was going down a checklist. "I'd deploy those flashlights, too."

Parker and Harley used each other to steady themselves as they donned their gear. Parker toggled on his light. *God, help us. God, help us.*

"Looks like you boys are set." Steadman checked the road behind him. The fog had set in thick and heavy. But no signs of headlights. "Now, I've decided to give you a fighting chance. Take a step back—right to the very edge."

The boys obeyed, trying not to get tangled up with the other's fins.

Steadman holstered his Glock.

If they weren't wearing fins—and strapped together—they could have rushed him. But right now it was all they could do to keep from tripping over each other and falling into the quarry. Harley gulped. "This is a fighting chance?"

"Mr. Lotitto . . . you're the star football player." He held up Parker's dive knife. He wrapped the nylon straps around the sheath and snapped them to form a tight bundle. "I'm going to toss you this knife in the sheath. You catch it, and you'll easily cut free from the weights once you hit bottom."

"Seriously?"

"Dead serious." Steadman backed away. Ten feet. Fifteen. Glanced over his shoulder down the empty road again. "This will be the biggest catch of your life. But if you miss it? Look on the bright side. It'll be the last miss of your life."

"You can do it, Harley," Parker said.

Harley shifted his weight from foot to foot. But they were tethered too close for him to move freely. "If I jump, you jump with me, got it?"

Steadman grabbed the knife like he'd just been snapped the ball. He rolled back a bit, cocked his arm. "Hey, Lotitto . . . go *deep*!" He threw the knife—but high.

Harley lunged up and slightly backward—Parker tried to move with him. Harley's fingers must have grazed the sheath because suddenly the thing deflected end over end and behind them.

They were terribly off balance. "Har—ley!"

Too late he realized his mistake. Back they went, hitting the surface of the quarry with a mighty splash even as Parker slapped his mouthpiece in place.

Steadman was visible through the sheet of water for a split second, waving goodbye.

Instantly the water closed over them, and the weights dragged them toward the rock bottom of the quarry.

CHAPTER 74

Saturday, June 18, 5:31 p.m.

THE WEIGHT PULLED PARKER headfirst and backward at a crazy fast speed. He tried to right himself, to stop the plunge, but it was impossible with the way Harley was hog-tied to him. Harley slammed into him in a tangle of arms and legs and lights. Like two skydivers hopelessly tangled in their chutes, tumbling toward earth—and certain death.

Parker held his mask from being ripped off—constantly grabbing his nose and equalizing the pressure that hammered his ears and forehead like a battering ram. No sooner would he force air into his sinuses for an instant of relief than the pressure would threaten to crush his head again. If either eardrum ruptured, he'd lose all equilibrium—all sense of what was up and what was down.

He clenched the mouthpiece in his teeth, desperately fearing he'd lose it. He needed more air—and sucked hard—but it felt like it was coming through a straw instead of a hose.

Deeper.

Darker.

He passed the thermocline.

Colder. So awful cold.

They slammed into the bottom of Parker's Pit tanks-first. Instantly storm clouds of silt enveloped them—massive, menacing thunderheads that swallowed their light. Parker couldn't see Harley—but he was there. And he was absolutely sure Harley was still alive . . . because he was still screaming.

CHAPTER 75

THE GHOST STOOD AT THE EDGE OF THE QUARRY, watching the surface of the water morph from panicked to absolutely serene. His own breathing evened out, too.

He had to congratulate himself. He'd handled this like the soldier he was. Met each attack with a countermeasure. His rolling anticipation had served him well yet again. The moment the boys surfaced at *that* wall, he had been ready. And when Mr. Football Hero handed up the tank from the hidden quarry stash, the Ghost knew he'd simply execute his backup plan.

Adapt and execute. It was his way, and he was good at it. It was all about knowing when to make a course correction . . . finding a way . . . and finishing the mission. Always. Aborting wasn't an option.

All of life was war. Steadman's MO was to gain trust with

everyone and make allies whenever possible. Then if one of those allies got in the way of a mission, that ally's first reaction would be to trust him—which, of course, was a fatal miscalculation. That simply gave Steadman the easy edge to do what he needed to do. Deception was an effective weapon.

And the boys had made it *too* easy. They should have kicked off their gear and run—and taken their chances that he wouldn't shoot or that he'd miss. Stupid on their part.

"Rule number one, fellas, if a guy has a gun on you, don't get fooled into thinking he intends to let you live if you just do what he says. That kind of against-all-logic trust is a great way to get yourself killed." He looked down into the dark quarry. Case in point.

And he'd employed the element of shock flawlessly. Shock had a way of handcuffing someone as effectively as a set of real steel bracelets. The surprise on the boys' faces as they plunged backward was priceless. Too bad he couldn't tell anyone about this little black ops he had going. He'd adapted to the change of plan and executed his mission perfectly, but couldn't tell a soul. Mr. Big-shot Banker Scorza would figure it out, but wasn't man enough to give him trouble. And if Steadman even got a whisper of pushback from him, maybe he'd arrange for him to take a ride in the Valiant.

Oh well.

Now to focus on what needed to happen next. He suspected the boys had already panic-sucked their tanks dry. Likely it was over. But another five minutes should do the trick.

The Ghost unclipped his concealed carry holster and locked it in the safe under his driver's seat. He wouldn't be needing that now, and he didn't need any extra steps to slow him down once the rescue team arrived.

He slipped out of his pants. He'd worn his swimsuit underneath, and this just got him one step closer to ready. There was a balance to this. To get in the water ahead of the dive team, he'd need to get ready in little ways that wouldn't be noticed. He didn't want to appear overanxious—or that he'd had any indication of the boys having trouble. The main thing was to simply have his gear ready—which would make him look all the more like the perfect spotter.

Steadman took his fins, mask, dive knife, and the rest of his gear from his dive bag. Set them on the lip of the quarry. He brought the silver tank next. Checked to be sure the air was on and the regulator was working. He unrolled his wet suit. All he'd have to do is slip in, zip up, and add his hood. He'd be set to be the hero who'd find the boys. He took the light sticks they'd brought to the surface and threw them far out into the quarry. They'd never be found. And even if they were, what would they prove?

So far, so good. He was ready for the next stage, but he'd really like an audience. Parker's dad, to be specific. Mr. Park Ranger would be a witness to the heroic efforts he'd make . . . starting with jumping into the quarry alone to save the boys. That would build more trust, and complete the deception. Vaughn Buckman would never guess Steadman was really going down to hide all evidence of what he'd done. Maybe Steadman would call Rankin, too. He'd make a great witness to all this if Parker's dad didn't get here soon. He pulled out his phone and hit Rankin's number.

And by now dear Mrs. Houston would be dashing to the bank with the earnest check to pay off her loan before closing.

He was certain the fat lady wouldn't be singing on her drive to the bank, but by now she'd definitely signed. He pictured Beulah and the cozy little rental house. Baybreeze and Bayside. They were his now. Spoils of war.

CHAPTER 76

Saturday, June 18, 5:36 p.m.

HARLEY DIDN'T WANT TO DIE. Wasn't ready to die. Was Gatorade already gone? He swung his flashlight around. The silt clouded everything. Zero visibility. Gatorade squirmed to free a hand trapped underneath Harley.

Okay, so Harley wasn't the sole survivor. He shifted his weight until he felt Gatorade's hand pull free from its pinned position. Still, they were tethered together so close their masks had to be almost touching. With the silt it was impossible to tell.

Harley reached over his head. Found the line to the bag of weights. Pulled on it with all his strength.

Gatorade groped frantically for something at his ribs. His BCD vest pocket? Harley heard the Velcro release.

The knife. Gatorade had a knife in his pocket! He'd seen him stuff it in his vest, right?

A moment later Gatorade was tugging at his vest—sawing the nylon tie holding them together—and the tie keeping him from ditching his gear.

Go faster, Gatorade. Faster. Harley swallowed down the panic. Fought the urge to claw past Gatorade and out of the black cloud. Gatorade and his knife were their only hope now, and Harley knew it. Harley was sucking on fumes here. His tank was dying. And if Gatorade didn't cut them free quick enough, they'd be dying too.

CHAPTER 77

Saturday, June 18, 5:37 p.m.

ANGELICA HAD SEEN FOG A MILLION TIMES, but never this thick. It looked more like a fine mist in Uncle Vaughn's headlights. He hunkered over the wheel, as if being that much closer to the windshield might help him see better—or avoid missing a turn.

Ella rode alongside her in the second seat of the extended cab, clutching her backpack on her lap.

She's lost. Why those words popped into Angelica's head, she had no idea. But Parker's friend definitely didn't look like an Ella-gator. Not at all. She wasn't a threat. And Angelica realized she never had been. Actually, Ella looked how Angelica felt month after month while she waited for her dad's transfer to come in. Like she'd lost her footing. Had no place to call home. Like her whole future was in a fog.

Angelica stretched to look out the windshield. How Uncle

Vaughn could drive this fast with all the sea smoke was beyond her. He braked hard and made a sharp turn off Beach Street. Almost there. *God . . . protect Parker and Harley. They're in trouble. I feel it.*

Maybe it was the fog—or the fact that so many bad things had happened to Parker in the Everglades. But the tangle of dread in Angelica's stomach was growing more knotted. "You think the boys are okay, right?"

Ella hesitated, then nodded.

"Good. I wish I felt the same."

Ella angled her head slightly. "I used to get all scared watching some movies—just knowing something bad was about to happen."

Angelica totally got that.

"But now I listen to the movie soundtrack. It always changes just before something bad happens. It gets more ominous . . . off-key or something. When I get tense, I check the music. If it hasn't changed, I can relax."

That actually made sense. "So, when it comes to the guys . . . you don't sense the music changing right now?"

"Exactly. The soundtrack of my life has been pretty horrible all week, but it's not getting worse at the moment. So I think they're okay."

"This is it," Uncle Vaughn said. "We're here."

Angelica and Ella rushed out of the pickup the moment Uncle Vaughn stopped.

Mr. Steadman was there, pacing along the quarry's edge, but he was alone.

"The boys are *still* down there?" Angelica couldn't believe it.

He nodded. "They were really focused on finding some evidence, even though I told them I already searched the quarry. My guess? They haven't found a thing—and they're sucking their tanks dry to find something that isn't there."

Uncle Vaughn growled. "Parker knows better than to push it like that."

Angelica thought it sounded very much like Parker. She should have been here. Then again, what could she have done? Tied a rope to him so she could pull him up?

"I put in a call to Rankin," Steadman said. "If the boys got lucky and found something, it would be good for the police to witness it. He said he'd have a car swing by."

Obviously Steadman was giving Parker and Harley the benefit of the doubt, which was a lot more than Angelica was doing. She stared into the black water. There was no way somebody could pay her to strap on a tank and dive to the bottom of that abyss. Not for a million bucks. She wasn't so sure Parker would do it for money either. But he'd do it for a friend. Apparently so would Harley. And now they were pushing the limits of safety and sanity. She was going to kill them when they surfaced. Actually, she'd hug them first. *Then* she'd kill them.

Uncle Vaughn swung over on his crutches. "How long has it been?"

Steadman checked his watch. "They've got a few minutes before I told them I'd be going down after them."

Angelica walked along the south rim of the quarry—with Ella beside her. The stark lines of the granite. The fog. The black mirror surface of the water. Nothing but shades of black and gray. Totally eerie. She pulled her trail cam from her pack. The camera wasn't ideally designed for handheld use, but she had to capture the spooky feel of the place.

Angelica took a half dozen pictures, changing her angle each time. She sat on a granite slab and scrolled back through the pictures. They actually looked pretty good.

That's when she saw the other images—from when the trail cam had been strapped to the tree. The renters pouring out after Shadow-man made his creepy visit Saturday night. Shadow-man leaving the rental house and circling to the side of the house where he'd been picked up by Steadman's surveillance camera.

Angelica's images were okay—but didn't offer anything new from those captured by the high-tech security cameras. There was nothing here that would have helped them figure out who Shadow-man was. Black hoodie. Black pants. Black everything—but nothing distinguishing about any of it.

Ella sat beside her. Angelica angled the screen so they both had a decent view.

"That was the worst night of my life," Ella said. "That's when I knew we were finished. I was right . . . and here's the proof." She pulled the legal papers from her backpack. "Signed copies for Mr. Steadman. Grams asked me to deliver them to him so he won't have to stop by later. Guess there's no point stalling this."

Ella motioned Mr. Steadman over. "I have something for you." She held the documents up like a white flag. "All signed."

Steadman hustled over and took the papers. Checked the back page. Nodded. "*Now* it's over."

Weird. Angelica had no idea what that was supposed to mean.

Steadman gave Ella a pat on the head. "You'll both have a new start now."

She pulled back. "Not a new start, Mr. Steadman. It means we have to start over. There's a big difference."

Angelica put her arm around Ella's shoulders. Ella reached up and squeezed her hand.

Steadman rolled the selling agreement like a relay baton and tapped it on his open palm. "I'll just run these back to the truck." A moment later he tucked them under the front seat.

Angelica focused on the trail cam again. She scrolled back more frames—then froze. She'd captured images of Shadow-man breaking into the guesthouse.

She backtracked further through the images—like she was seeing the night unfold in reverse. She'd actually captured pictures of Shadow-man *watching* the house. Standing with his back to the camera, but really close. His upper body dominating most of the foreground. From the time stamp he'd been standing there a good ten minutes or so. Watching. Listening. Totally creepy.

She did a rapid scroll backward another dozen images or so. Shadow-man was still there—but something was different. No hoodie. A baseball cap instead. Long-sleeved T-shirt. Gray, maybe? His back was still to the camera—so not much to go on—except for the fact Shadow-man had light skin. It was something anyway—but not much. Shadow-man was a white male . . . like 90 percent of the other men in Massachusetts. So the guy had been watching the place—and changed into his Shadow-man garb right there in that little patch of woods?

It made sense. If the guy was seen walking through the neighborhood with a black hoodie, the cops may pick him up for questioning. But wearing a T-shirt and a backpack over one shoulder, he'd look totally normal. He didn't put on the hoodie until he was sure he was going in.

"We've got a visitor." Ella pointed to a dim set of headlights approaching on the gravel road. Moments later Officer Greenwood swung out of the cruiser. He talked with Mr. Steadman for a few seconds, then walked over to the lip of the quarry.

Greenwood looked their way and caught Angelica's eyes. There was something about his face. A quiet confidence—yet kind. She felt better knowing he was here.

Angelica went back to the camera. So she had images of Shadow-man when he was in his hoodie outfit—and she had images of him before he'd changed. What was in the middle? She flipped through the images. The hat was off now. He was still wearing the T-shirt—but he was stepping into some kind of one-piece thing . . . like a wet suit. When he had it pulled up to his waist, he reached back and pulled off his T-shirt.

For one image his bare back dominated the screen. Angelica sucked in her breath. A giant tattoo covered his back. What looked like a Navy battleship—bearing down straight at her through heavy seas. Humongous cannons bristling off both sides—all belching fire and smoke. Above the ship were the words CLEAR THE WAY. And below the ship—OR HELL TO PAY.

They could use this to absolutely identify Shadow-man, right? Her hands trembled. She struggled to steady her breath. This was hard evidence—the most concrete thing they had.

"Mr. Steadman." Ella looked out over the still surface of the quarry. "Shouldn't we see some bubbles or something?"

Angelica motioned Officer Greenwood over. He held up one finger—his eyes back on Mr. Steadman like he needed to hear his answer first.

Greenwood was right. There was time for him to look at the images later, when the boys were out of the quarry . . . standing around with towels over their shoulders.

Steadman studied the water. "At the depth they're at, the bubbles may be dissipating a bit before they reach the surface."

But even if the bubbles rose from sixty or seventy feet,

shouldn't they see a little movement? A bubble gasping at the surface?

Uncle Vaughn looked antsy. He crutched along the rim one way, then back. Scanning the surface. "How long has it been?"

Steadman checked his watch before answering. "They should have been up by now. They're probably ascending as we speak."

But if they were on their way up, the bubbles would be more obvious, right?

"I don't like it," Uncle Vaughn said. "They're pushing it. The quarry is too dark. Parker wouldn't cut it that close on the air."

Angelica got a sick feeling in her stomach. Parker wasn't cutting it close. He was in trouble. Ella clutched the cross pendant with both hands and backed away from the quarry until she was nearly beside Angelica.

"Bad feeling, Jelly," she whispered. "The music. It's changing."

Exactly what Angelica was sensing.

Uncle Vaughn pointed to Steadman's tank. "That thing filled?"

Steadman seemed like he was one step ahead of him. The man sprang into action. "Officer, call in the water rescue team. The moment they get here, send them down. I'm not waiting."

Greenwood whipped out his phone. Angelica stared at Ella. Fought a sense of dread. "You pray much?"

Ella shook her head.

"You may want to start." Angelica sure was kickin' it into gear.

"Please," Uncle Vaughn said. "Hurry."

Steadman peeled off his T-shirt. "I'll be on the bottom in two minutes."

Uncle Vaughn nodded. "How can I help?" Without waiting for an answer he propped Steadman's tank up.

Ella stood. Angelica did too, but her knees felt like they could collapse. All she knew was that Parker was somewhere deep in the quarry—and three grown men were getting nervous. "Dear God, help Parker . . . Harley too."

She studied the water. Still no sign of bubbles.

"Rescue team is on the way." Greenwood pocketed his phone and joined the others. The men were moving fast now, silently focused on getting Steadman geared up.

Steadman bent to get his hood—and turned just enough to reveal a massive tattoo on his back. A battleship.

God, no. Sweet Jesus . . . no.

Suddenly it felt like one of the battleship cannons fired a live round below the waterline—and right into Angelica's heart.

CHAPTER 78

Saturday, June 18, 5:39 p.m.

WITH ONE LAST SAW OF HIS KNIFE, the final nylon tie broke loose. Parker felt the bag of weights drop off Harley's tank. They were free! Instinctively Parker grabbed Harley. He wasn't about to lose him now.

Parker tugged on Harley's arm. They had to get away from this silt. He kicked desperately, sucking so hard on his regulator that his chest hurt. Harley kept up, with a death grip on Parker's forearm.

Suddenly the water cleared, and the two faced each other. They weren't ten feet from the Valiant.

Harley drew one hand across his throat and jerked his thumb toward the surface.

God, help us—what do I do? They could make the seventy-foot ascent, couldn't they? But if they surfaced now, what was to stop

Steadman from picking them off like fish in a barrel? He shook his head. Held his hand out like a gun.

Harley looked to the surface, like he was ready to take his chances with Steadman.

And in that instant Parker knew what they had to do. He held his palm up for Harley to see, and drew on it like he was sketching a pass pattern. He pointed at the Valiant, then motioned sharply away from it at a hard angle.

Harley pointed at himself, then at Parker—like he understood Parker was telling him to follow.

Parker nodded and kicked off for the Valiant with Harley following close. Even as he reached the drowned car, Parker's chest already felt like it was going to cave in. He checked over his shoulder once to be sure Harley was still behind him. *God, help us. Help us.*

Parker pushed off the Valiant at a right angle, trusting the line of the open driver's door to point the way to the south wall. Swam hard into the darkness, staying just low enough to see bottom but high enough to not disturb the silt.

I pray I got this right. There would be no second chance. Cutting a straight line was iffy underwater. One leg would pump stronger than the other, and he'd angle off course. He focused on steady strokes. *Jesus, we need a break here!*

His tank was basically empty—and slowing him down. He unbuckled the BCD and wriggled out of the harness. The tank hit bottom, sending up a silent plume of silty smoke. Harley was beside him now—he'd shed his tank as well.

His light picked up the wall of the quarry. *Thank you, Jesus! Now the tank, the tank!*

Parker's lungs burned and did that convulsing thing. Desperate for air, his body was trying to take over. He clenched his teeth and fought the urge to breathe. His body would go on autopilot soon and force him to inhale—even if it meant sucking in water. The craving to breathe grew stronger by the second. The instant it caused him to draw in water—he was dead.

His beam reflected off something shiny. He swept the area again.

There! He pointed at the black scuba tank lying on the bottom.

Harley saw it too—and the two of them raced for the cylinder, kicking hard and clawing the icy water.

Parker grabbed both mouthpieces—shoved one in Harley's hands. Jammed the other in his own mouth. Had no air left in his lungs to blow first and force the water out of it.

He sucked hard—taking in a mix of water from the mouthpiece and air from the tank. He coughed. Gasped in more air—but no water this time. Coughing, gulping in air, repeating. Over and over he hacked to clear the water from his windpipe. But he had air—and his breathing evened out.

Wide-eyed, Harley held his regulator to his face with both hands, and by the volume of bubbles tumbling out the exhaust, he was absolutely gorging himself on air. He gave Parker an "OK" sign, but didn't let go of the regulator.

Parker wanted out of this quarry. Fast. Just get to the surface and never come back. But Steadman would be up there. Waiting to make sure they were dead. And if they surfaced now? There'd be no mercy. He'd find a way to finish the job.

CHAPTER 79

Saturday, June 18, 5:43 p.m.

ELLA DIDN'T KNOW HOW TO HELP other than stand off to the side and stay out of the way. She clutched the cross necklace and tried to swallow an unexplainable fear slithering up her throat. Maybe it was the vapors that unnerved her. Maybe it was the desperate way Parker's dad peered into the quarry. Steadman's face was a little harder to read. He had that search-and-rescue focused look. She didn't have much occasion to be around men—so she was no expert on reading them. But even the cop seemed to be in red-alert mode. Oh, yeah, the music had definitely changed.

"Officer Greenwood." Jelly's voice . . . just a ghost of a whisper.

Actually, she looked like she'd seen a ghost. *What was going on?*

The cop held up one finger. "Give me a minute. Reinforcements." He pointed down the gravel road at the muted flashes of approaching rescue vehicles.

Mr. Steadman seemed totally cool. He strapped a nasty-looking dive knife to his calf, moving quickly. Ella's theory? It was the tattoo. A guy with *Clear the Way or Hell to Pay* permanently etched on his back *should* be calm, no matter what was going on—at least the way Ella figured. But then what did she know about men, right?

"Ella!" Jelly whisper-shouted, frantically motioning Ella back to her, and pointing at her trail cam.

Just one more knot in a total string of weirdness, but the music was getting louder, too. More ominous. Ella hustled over, but glanced over her shoulder once. She didn't want to miss a thing. Steadman's hood was on now. He tucked it under the collar of his wet suit top.

"Ella," Jelly hissed again. She pointed at her screen. "Shadow-man. The ghost—gearing up that night. Look."

One image dominated the display. Partial image, really. A man's back—with a massive Navy ship tattoo—and the words that looked anything but cool now. Shadow-man wasn't a ghost—but he wasn't a man either. He was a monster. Ella locked eyes with Jelly. "The moment Steadman goes under, we show this to Officer Greenwood."

Steadman stood on the edge of the quarry—fins, mask, weight belt: all in place. Officer Greenwood lifted the tank and BCD rig for Steadman, like he was about to help somebody on with their coat.

Jelly gripped Ella's arm. "The guys are still in the quarry. Do we really want a murderer down there with them?"

Ella's mind flashed to Devin Catsakis's funeral. "Stop him!" Ella pointed at Steadman. "He's the ghost. He's Shadow-man!"

"We've got pictures!" Jelly held up the trail cam. "The tattoo on his back—we have proof he's the Shadow-man."

Greenwood pulled the tank back. "Don't move!"

Steadman lunged for his gear and jerked hard to free it from Greenwood's grip.

The cop held on like a gorilla. "Let me see your hands!"

The wrestling match ended as quickly as it started—as if Steadman knew he wasn't going to get that tank or fight off the firemen already stepping out of the truck. He stepped back, hands raised—but only to chest height. Reflections from the red flashing lights pulsed off his body. He drilled Ella and Jelly with steely eyes.

"On your knees." Greenwood dropped the tank to one side.

"The boys," Parker's dad cried. "Are they—"

"Collateral damage." Steadman took another step back—on the very edge now. "They figured it out. You're too late."

"No!" Parker's dad roared, his face twisted in agony. "NO!"

Jelly dashed to the lip of the quarry. "Parker!" She screamed at the water. "Parker!"

"Knees, Steadman!" Greenwood reached for his gun.

Steadman leaped for the quarry just as Greenwood cleared the Glock from its holster. He didn't fire. Maybe he feared Parker or Harley might surface at any moment. Or maybe he thought Steadman couldn't go far without a tank.

Steadman disappeared in a geyser of white water as rescue workers raced to the quarry's edge. Vapor mists swirled and danced where Steadman went down.

Somehow the cross pendant was in Ella's hands again. She stared into the black water through hot tears. "What did he do to the guys?"

But she knew. They all did.

Hell to pay.

CHAPTER 80

Saturday, June 18, 5:45 p.m.

PARKER HEARD THE MUFFLED *WUMPH*, like someone had rolled another Valiant into the quarry. Instinctively he cringed and looked up—but saw nothing. Harley must have heard it too by the way he was hugging the granite wall.

Steadman. Coming down to make sure they were dead, one way or another.

He pointed ahead—along the wall toward Humpback Rock. Harley gave a frantic nod.

Each of them wrapped an arm around the tank, holding it between them as they kicked off. They followed the face of the granite around as it jutted out and tucked in like a giant, corrugated fortress wall.

Got to go faster. Parker pumped his legs and kept the circle of his light straight ahead. Granite outcroppings followed by black valleys, like there were a whole series of caves in the stone. Deep blackness where anything might be waiting to drag them in. What if Steadman saw their light? He'd find them in seconds. But going dark wasn't an option. They'd be lost instantly—or swim headfirst into a granite wall. They needed a place to hide.

Looking back was out of the question, but he imagined Steadman closing in. Ripping the regulator from his mouth. He clenched his teeth tighter.

The wall angled out sharply in front of them. The peninsula . . . Humpback Rock. It had to be. They circled all the way around it. Steadman would expect them to be tangled on the bottom near the Valiant. Not all the way over here. And definitely not alive.

Part of him wanted to keep going. Just follow the wall to the remote end of the quarry—as far away from where they went in as possible. They could widen the distance between them and Steadman until the tank was empty and they were forced to surface. On the other hand, the idea of running out of air again didn't sound at all appealing.

He motioned to Harley. They'd hide where they were. For a couple of minutes anyway. Harley nodded. They stayed a good ten feet off the bottom so they wouldn't kick up silt. Parker pointed at his own light and toggled it off. Harley gave a thumbs-up and did the same.

El had once said the quarry was as dark as a basement closet. And it was . . . but infinitely more scary. The basement would have to be flooded to be anywhere near what Parker felt.

They huddled close, Harley actually gripping Parker's forearm. At least Parker knew he was still there. Parker listened, but the only thing he heard was the hiss and rumble of his regulator and bubbles. The air still came easily from the tank, but it wouldn't for long with both of them sharing it.

God, don't let him find us.

The darkness totally distorted any sense of time. It seemed like they'd been clinging to the rock and each other for ten minutes. It probably wasn't half that. But the cold was taking its toll. He was pretty sure Harley was shaking—but with the way Parker was shivering now, it was impossible to tell. And he knew—for certain—if there was any living thing in this quarry . . . it was sneaking up on them now.

Harley gave Parker's arm a double-squeeze. Not a panic thing, but he definitely was trying to tell him something.

Parker flipped on his light. Harley squinted and pointed his thumb toward the surface. He was right. Parker would rather face whatever was waiting for them topside than stay in this black hole for another minute. He flashed Harley an "OK" sign.

They made the ascent slowly. Maybe at half the speed their bubbles rose. He glanced down once, but the unending darkness below wasn't doing a thing to keep his breathing steady.

Seeing light above them—even though it wasn't exactly bright—made him want to kick hard for the surface. He switched off his light.

Harley motioned to him and tapped his finger across his lips.

Absolutely. He'd be quiet all right. He broke the surface without a splash. Got his bearings. They were definitely on the backside of Humpback.

Parker's jaw muscles were cramping from biting down so hard on the mouthpiece. He spit it out, then leaned over and whispered to Harley. "We climb to the top. Scope it out." He checked the air pressure. "If he's there—we go back down?"

Harley shook his head. "I'll take my chances on foot." Harley hoisted the tank on shore, then kick-boosted himself onto the edge. "I'm *never* going in this quarry again."

Parker climbed up beside him. The rock gave them perfect cover. They shed their masks. Fins. Weights. Mapped out their escape route if it came to that.

Both of them looked toward the top of Humpback. Parker took a deep breath and let it out slowly. Trying to calm the jitters. They had to know if the coast was clear—or if Steadman was still waiting for them.

The moment Parker peeled off his hood and shook the water from his ears, he heard voices. Lots of voices. Together Parker and Harley army-crawled to the top of Humpback and peered over the edge. Rescue divers in the water. Some still gearing up on shore. Dad. Officer Greenwood. And Jelly clutching tight to Ella.

Steadman's truck was right where it had been parked, but no Steadman.

Harley elbowed him and grinned. "We made it."

"Thank you, God," Parker whispered.

"Hey, Gatorade." They locked eyes for a moment. "You were pretty good down there."

Parker smiled. They made a good team. "You weren't so bad yourself."

Together they stood up on the top of Humpback Rock.

"Jelly!" Parker waved.

"Ella!" Harley slung his arm around Parker's shoulders.

A shout rose from the rescue workers. Dad raised both crutches over his head and said something Parker couldn't make out. Jelly and Ella screamed—hugging each other and jumping and shrieking.

"Officer Greenwood!" Parker pointed at the pickup. "Steadman is Shadow-man. He has a gun. He killed Devin Catsakis—and he tried to kill us."

Greenwood nodded and gave a thumbs-up. "He did a flying leap right into the quarry—without a tank. But he never came up. It's been like ten minutes."

A diver surfaced, raised his mask, and spit out his mouthpiece. "He's not down there. Totally disappeared."

"Well, he ain't no ghost," Harley said. "He's got to be somewhere."

"The south wall," Parker shouted. "There's a cave at about twenty feet. That's where he had tanks hidden."

Greenwood motioned to the diver, and the man disappeared beneath the black waters.

"I'd like to have seen Steadman's face when he realized his getaway oxygen had gone MIA," Harley said.

A police car roared up and slid to a stop. Rankin boiled out, looking like he wanted to be the cop slapping cuffs on Steadman. Another police car barreled down the road toward them. Between the cops and rescue workers, Steadman would never get at Parker and Harley—even if he was the world champion for holding his breath and somehow surfaced. "They'll find him," Parker said.

"I'll rest easier," Harley said, "when I see them haul his body out of the water. But we're alive—thanks to your quick thinking—Gatorade."

"Not me, Harley. That was all God."

Harley gave him a little shake. "Whatever. But we made it! I feel like we just won the Super Bowl."

Dad crutched his way toward them faster than he probably should, but Parker wasn't about to tell him to slow down.

Ella ran along the edge of the quarry—passing Dad—with Jelly close behind. "Looks like the girls are happy to see us, Parker."

"A little too happy. Brace yourself."

Ella ran right down the spine of Humpback and bowled into Harley. He obviously hadn't expected her to hit with such force. He staggered backward—arms flailing.

"I've seen those moves before," Parker said. "Go deep!"

Harley was still laughing when he plunged into the quarry.

Jelly steadied Ella so she didn't fall in after him.

Dad stood at the edge of the quarry, leaned on his crutches, and grinned, just taking it all in.

The moment Harley thrashed to the surface, he struck out for the quarry lip. Parker scanned the water, still somehow fearing Steadman might surface and take his revenge.

El wagged her finger. "If you boys ever—and I mean ever—scare us like this again, we're going to send both of you for another swim in this quarry, right, Jelly?"

Jelly gave a single nod, her chin held high. She linked elbows with El as if that sealed the deal.

Harley struggled to hoist himself up on the side of the quarry, but the lip was too high. He held on to the edge, just grinning up at them.

Had Harley forgotten there was still a killer on the loose? Parker just wanted to see him get out of the quarry, but honestly, he'd never seen Harley happier.

"Did you hear what I said?" El stood there, hands on hips. "Even if it's in the dead of winter, we're going to break the ice and toss you right in the quarry."

"We heard you," Harley said. "And we're shakin'—right Parker?"

"Well, that's the first smart thing I've heard one of you boys say in a long time," El said.

A diver surfaced and whipped off his mask. "It's not a cave—it's a tunnel. No telling how far it goes back, but I'm not going in without backup."

A tunnel? There was no way he could hold his breath long enough to go all the way through it, right? Immediately Parker looked to his dad.

If Dad was worried, he hid it well. "They'll get him, Parker." It was as if he read Parker's mind. "But even if they don't, God's got this. I think He's already proved that."

Oh, yeah. And then some. But still, Parker would feel better once Harley was out of the water. "Time to get out, Harley." He eased down Humpback and stretched out his hand to him. "Thought you were *never* going in this quarry again."

Harley gripped Parker's hand, but planted his feet on the rock wall and yanked Parker into the quarry instead.

Parker scissors-kicked back to the surface.

Harley was still grinning. "I meant I'd never go in without you."

EPILOGUE

Saturday, July 2

IF EVERY WEEK OF THE YEAR were ranked in order of how good they turned out, the two weeks following the incident at the quarry would have topped the charts. Totally blown the lid off, in fact. That's the way Parker saw it, anyway.

Ella, Jelly, Harley, and Parker. They hung together most of the time Harley wasn't working—and plenty of times at the dive shop when he was. Jelly got the tours she wanted. Pebble Beach. Good Harbor Beach. Half Moon Beach. The Gloucester Fisherman's Memorial.

They gave her guided tours of the docks in Gloucester Bay. Halibut Point State Park. Eastern Point Lighthouse. Annisquam Light. Wingaersheek Beach. The Headlands. And of course Bearskin Neck.

Jelly ate spaghetti at Rockport Pizza. Fries at Top Dog. Chowder at Roy Moore's. Chocolate-covered Oreos at Tuck's. Strudel at Helmut's. Coconut shrimp at The Fish Shack. The apple fritters at Brothers Brew coffee shop had her addicted at first bite.

The four of them explored the shoreline at high tide, low tide, and everything in between.

They climbed the rocks. Tooled around the bay in the *Boy's Bomb*.

Even when Jelly wasn't with Parker and Harley, she could usually be found with Ella—unless El was out watercoloring somewhere. Jelly probably spent more time at Grams's home than she did at Parker's. Her connection with Grams was almost as magnetic as Jelly's was with Ella.

Jelly talked to her dad a couple of times every day. Only once Parker asked her the question he'd been dreading since the day she arrived in Rockport.

"Not that I want to rush you or anything." Actually, he'd wanted to brace himself for the hard news. "When do you have to go home?"

She looked at him and smiled. "I *am* home."

He never asked again. He knew it would have to end—like a vacation—but it was nicer not to have the end in sight.

It had definitely been the best two weeks of the year. Maybe his life.

And Officer Greenwood. The guy made a regular habit of checking on Grams—and within days she started calling him Dave. He even came on his day off to install a new window. Actually, Grams hated to see the plywood go. The night Officer Greenwood put it in place over the shattered window? He'd drawn a cop's head and shoulders on the plywood with a marker—complete with a shield name tag with *Greenwood* printed in neat letters. "Now, I've deputized this plywood to keep an eye on things while I'm gone," he'd said. Night and day, Greenwood's deputy stood in the second story window, keeping watch over Beulah. Grams had Officer Greenwood hang the plywood in the living room after the new glass was installed.

Grams had treated Parker, Harley, Jelly, and El to her famous homemade Blueberry Hill Pie. Even the crust was made from scratch. The taste? Unreal. She'd cut it in six slices. One for each of the girls. Two for Harley and two for Parker. In one sitting . . . the whole pie was gone. By the time they'd finished their second piece, they'd be groaning in agony—which absolutely energized Grams. It seemed she always had something coming out of the oven for them.

Harley was hungry for so much more than pie. Jelly was too. Grams seemed to know that, and somehow, without the need for any legal document, Grams adopted two more grandkids. El said Grams was happier than she'd remembered seeing her in a long, long time.

El had her own way of saying thanks. Exactly two weeks after Steadman's escape, she'd invited all three of them to meet her at the end of the Rockport Harbor breakwater—and then go to her house for dinner. Jelly and Parker met Harley at the Rockport Dive Company right at closing. Together they helped him sweep up and straighten the displays. Within fifteen minutes the three of them were on their way to meet El.

Harley leaped from rock to rock on the jetty, occasionally stiff-arming an invisible tackler. "What's this surprise all about?"

"No idea," Jelly said. "She's been really secretive."

"Huh. I thought you two talked about everything."

"True. But we spend soooo much time talking about you boys

and whatever idiotic things you two did that day, there's hardly time to talk about anything else."

Harley laughed and shook his head.

El stood all the way at the end by the signal light, motioning them to hurry. Three easels stood on the rocks—each with a canvas propped on it . . . covered by a pillowcase.

"About time you three got here," El said.

For a moment Jelly leaned in close, whispering in El's ear. El nodded. Rolled her eyes. Glanced at the boys and laughed.

Parker pointed to the easels. "You giving us watercolor lessons?"

"Tell me you didn't do portraits of us." Harley turned to strike a profile pose.

"I thought about it," El said. "But I didn't have a canvas large enough for that big head of yours."

Harley reached for a corner of one of the pillowcases. "So are you going to show us, or what?"

El swatted his hand away. She sat down on the rocks, facing town. "In a minute. First an announcement." She patted the granite next to her and motioned Jelly over.

Parker and Harley found nearby rocks that made perfect granite chairs.

"Grams has been talking to the bank." Her eyes were more alive than ever. "That certified check from Steadman—the deposit for the sale?"

She scanned their faces like she was milking this for all it was worth—or maybe waiting for a drumroll. "We've paid off the entire loan with it. We've got no debt. Zero." She squealed and clapped her hands. "The way they explained it, that money was Grams's the moment Steadman handed it to her. If Steadman doesn't show up for closing—he breaches his contract. The money is legally ours. Nobody can contest it."

Cheers. Whistles. And Parker said a silent prayer of thanks.

"We've even got some rentals on the books. We're going to make it—as long as Steadman doesn't come before the thirty days to get his money back."

Steadman. Would he come back? Parker was pretty good at pushing the thought out of his head during the daylight. But at night? He checked and double-checked his bedroom window lock.

"There's no way he'll show up," Jelly said. "He knows exactly what'll happen if he does."

"Wham." Harley clapped his hands together. "Into the slammer he goes—for the murder of Devin Catsakis."

"And attempted murder of two of my three best friends," El said.

"*Best* friends?" Harley raised his eyebrows. "We're you're *only* friends, Miss Houston."

"Which is all I need, Mr. Lotitto," El said. "And my friends call me Ella. Or El."

Harley gave a quick nod. "I can do that."

Parker still couldn't believe Steadman escaped without a trace. "Officer Rankin had every inch of that quarry searched," he said. "No body. The tunnel was empty too."

Jelly looked out over the harbor. "Who'd have figured there was a tunnel that led to a little quarry hidden on the other side of the road?" Buried in the woods the way it was, no wonder nobody paid any attention to it.

"At some point the quarry workers must have hit a spring," Harley said. "The tunnel was probably dug to run hosing from the quarry to a pumping station to keep the pit from filling with water."

"I still can't imagine how he could have gone all that way . . . holding his breath," El said.

Harley shrugged. "He was a Navy Seal. Or maybe he had another tank stashed that we didn't see. Farther back in the tunnel. He's probably in the Bahamas by now."

"I hate the thought of him being"—Jelly waved her hand in the air—"out there someplace."

"Better than him being around here," Harley said. "Hopefully he's smart enough never to come back."

Would Steadman risk coming back, bent on revenge? Payback for them totally messing up his dark plans? Parker didn't want to think about that.

"He's not coming back. Ever." Jelly gave a determined nod. "But likely you boys will do a lot of looking over your shoulders for a while. Especially at night."

"Just us boys?" Harley laughed.

"Don't you worry, though, tough guy," Jelly said. "We'll help protect you. Right, Ella?"

"As long as they stay out of the cemetery."

"I think Parker and I can watch our own backs," Harley said.

Actually, Parker didn't need to be constantly watching his back. What he really needed is what he'd needed all along . . . to work at trusting God more. He got that now.

"June 19," El said, "was looking like it would be the darkest day of my life. I was losing everything I loved. Home. Friends. Honestly, I couldn't even look at the flag waving outside Mr. Scorza's bank. Liberty and justice for all? Right. Not unless you're white."

"He's going to get a lot paler, too," Jelly said. "He won't be getting much sun if he ends up in jail."

Harley snickered. "Scorza's dad got what was coming to him—and I hope he gets more."

The way Parker heard it, he'd already lost his cushy job—which he needed to keep up his payments on his humongous house. "The guy who was going to foreclose on your Grams might well face foreclosure himself. There's some justice for you." Not to mention an investigation to see how deep his partnership with Steadman went. Did Mr. Scorza know about what Steadman did to Devin? Holding that information back from the police was serious stuff, right? If that was the case, the guy was going to find himself in a deep quarry of sorts—without an air tank *or* an escape tunnel.

"The man who digs a pit to trap someone else will fall in it himself," El said. "That's what Grams says."

Parker wasn't sure, but it sounded like that came right from the Bible. Proverbs? Grams was certainly an interesting mix of Scripture and superstition.

"All those things . . . those secrets." El shrugged. "Steadman's real plan. Scorza's part in that. All the injustice . . . all the vile things they tried so hard to hide. It all came out."

Immediately Parker pictured the knife Grandpa sent him . . . and the verse etched on the blade. About God exposing the hidden things. How people can't get away with doing wrong without God noticing—and doing something about it at just the right time. Payday someday.

"So Juneteenth became a really, really special day to me all over again," El said. "I feel like Grams and I were truly set free from two evil men and their hidden—absolutely *clandestine*—plans."

"Speaking of hidden things," Harley said. "Are you ever going to show us what's on those mini scoreboard thingies?"

"Easels, Mr. Football." El stood. "Yeah, I guess it's time."

She lifted the pillowcase off one of the canvases. "For Jelly."

The granite rocks of the very jetty they were standing on made up the foreground, but closer to the circle at the end of Bearskin Neck. Shops in the background. And there in the middle stood a girl with red braids and a baseball cap. A roll-aboard suitcase stood next to her.

"I titled it *Finally Home*."

Jelly touched the corner of the canvas, like she was afraid the paint was still wet. "Oh, Ella. I love it."

El nodded. "For Harley." She held the corner of the pillowcase, but didn't pull it off. "You've changed a lot in these last couple weeks, you know that?"

"Someone once said I needed to make new friends."

"Sounds like you got some really good advice." El smiled. "You ought to listen to that person more often."

"Yeah, I think it was my Uncle Ray."

El slugged him in the arm. "Better stop before I decide to keep this watercolor for myself."

"Okay, okay." Harley pretended to lock his lips with an invisible key. "I'll stop."

"Much better," El said. She pulled off the pillowcase.

A shed. Harley's, to be exact. The doors stood open wide. A guy with a Harley T-shirt straddled a black motorcycle with lots of chrome. One boot on the ground. One on the foot peg. Hands on the grips like he was revving it up. A second boy squatted down beside the bike—like he was totally admiring it.

Harley touched the edge of the canvas—almost with a reverence. "Me. And Parks."

Funny how he didn't call him Gatorade anymore. And the "Parks" thing . . . it kind of made sense when Parker thought of all the national parks where his dad had been stationed before.

"Unreal," Harley said. "It's fantastic . . . your best ever. Did you title this one?"

"Check the back," El said.

Harley ducked around the backside of the easel. "*Kemosabes.*" He looked at her. "Plural—as in the three of us . . . Parks, me, and the bike?"

El nodded. "Trusted friends. Faithful scouts."

Harley gave Parker the side-eye. "Works for me."

Oh yeah. That definitely worked.

"Think you'll have room in your shed?" El had a teasing look to her.

"I have just the spot."

"And Parker." El raised the covering halfway up the canvas and paused. "This one was the hardest to do."

"Is that . . . the quarry?" From the sound of Harley's voice, he was just as surprised as Parker.

Parker's heart sank. The quarry may have been hard to paint—but it was harder to look at. Not a memory he'd want hanging on his wall.

She raised the cloth the rest of the way to reveal two guys in wet suits standing on Humpback Rock. Parker with one hand raised. Harley with his arm slung around Parker's neck. The moment they truly knew they'd been saved. The moment their friendship locked them tighter together than those nylon ties ever could. Actually, this would look great in his bedroom.

"Title?"

"Look for yourself."

Parker lifted the canvas off the easel and flipped it so they all could read it.

"*Liberty and Justice for All.*" When Parker looked up, there were tears in El's eyes. "Does this mean you've changed your views on justice in this world?"

Ella shrugged. "Not a lot. But when it comes to your God . . . I'm definitely beginning to see things differently."

Jelly hugged her. Harley looked like he wanted to, but he drove his hands in his pockets instead.

"And now," El said. "You're all coming to my place. Jelly has a super important announcement, and Grams is making a special dinner for all of us. A real Juneteenth celebration. A little late, but worth the wait."

Harley tucked his canvas under one arm like it was a football. "I'm starving. What's she making?"

El smiled. "I'm not saying. But there will be Blueberry Ghost Pie afterward."

"*Ghost* pie?" Parker couldn't tell if El was serious.

She nodded. "Grams renamed it. Now, don't worry, we're sure Rockport has no mysterious ghost. But the pie sure disappears like one."

The four of them probably looked like idiots. Laughing. Carrying paintings and easels along the granite breakwater.

Parker gave Jelly a sideways glance. "And what's this announcement of yours? You promised me a long time ago you wouldn't be keeping any secrets."

"Hey, every hidden thing is going to come out anyway, right?"

Harley looked at Parker like he needed backup. "So how about you girls just telling us everything now?"

"Not going to tell you what's on the dinner menu no matter how much you beg," El said. "But Jelly's news—that's up to her."

Jelly looked like she was thinking about it for a moment—then she stopped abruptly and faced them. "Okay. Here it is. I'm not going back to the Everglades. Ever. I'm staying in Rockport."

"Your dad's transfer . . . it finally came?"

Jelly grinned. "He'll be here in four weeks."

"So I have to put up with you stealing my Frosted Mini-Wheats in the morning for another month?" Parker groaned.

She shook her head. "I'm moving in with Ella and Grams. Until my dad gets here anyway."

The way the two of them had been hanging out, Parker probably shouldn't have been surprised. "I knew you two were good for each other."

Jelly reached up, snatched his cap, and slapped it on her own head. "Don't get a big head on that one, buster. I don't want you stretching out my hats."

"*Your* hats?" Parker wasn't even going to try getting it back from her. And it probably wouldn't be the last one she snagged from him.

"I've already talked to your mom and dad about me moving to Ella's," Jelly said. "They felt a lot better when I assured them I'd still be looking out for you."

"What?" To Parker, it felt like a setup.

Jelly motioned to Ella. "We both will. We've determined to protect you boys in case Steadman shows up again."

Harley snickered. "I feel safer already."

In some ways it seemed insane to joke about Steadman when

the possibility of the guy returning was still real. Maybe they were still in that phase of giddiness that follows a brush with death.

"Make fun all you like," Ella said, "but Steadman wasn't tough enough to stand up to us girls."

"*Really*?" Parker wanted to hear the logic on this one. "Try backing that up with facts."

Jelly smiled at Ella like they'd hoped he'd say something like that. "Steadman hog-tied you two amateurs and sent you to the bottom of the quarry—with empty air tanks. Am I right, Ella?"

Ella nodded. "And what happened when these two girls—"

"Strong girls," Jelly said. "And brave."

"Right." Ella raised her chin in mock pride. "When these strong, *brave* girls blew the whistle on Steadman, the big, tough ex–Navy Seal? Did he even *try* to mess with them?" She glanced at Jelly.

"He didn't dare," Jelly finished. "The *fact* is, he jumped into the quarry himself. *Without* a tank. So I think Ella and I are just the bodyguards you need."

Harley grinned. "Are you hearing this crazy talk, Parks?"

"I am." Was Steadman still lurking in the shadows of his mind? Sure. Was there a tiny bit of fear that he may come back someday? Roger that. But in the daylight of this moment, the concerns about Steadman shrank in the company of his friends. "I only have two words for you, Jelly."

Jelly hooked elbows with Ella. "Girls rule?"

Parker shook his head and grinned. "Welcome home."

Special thanks to . . .

Blackwood BBQ, Chic-fil-A, Culvers, Five Guys, and Portillo's: Thanks for a friendly smile and great atmosphere whenever I came to work. And the fries went down really easy too!

Tina at Dunkin: For making the coffee just right to fuel my writing.

Dave and Cyndi Darsch: For providing me with just the writing retreat I needed when the deadline loomed like a storm on the intercoastal. You gave Cheryl and me a place to stay that was off the grid and out of this world, a place where my heart soared with the joy of writing. God truly used the quiet waters and wildlife surrounding your dock to restore my soul.

Eddie Jones: For being one more voice to encourage me to make that trek to Florida for the writing retreat—and for praying for me when I was there.

Nancy Rue: Mentor, friend, and for the quiet confidence you give that says "you can do this."

Larry Weeden and Danny Huerta: For making the decisions that made this series possible. For your vision to reach this audience.

Vance Fry: For solid, tactful editing suggestions. For your easygoing manner that I so appreciate. The novel is stronger for your insights.

Edwina Perkins: For opening my eyes to a need, for valuable input that helped strengthen this story.

Dawn Johnson and Charlie Ball at Scuba Quest: For clear and helpful instruction when I was getting re-certified as a scuba diver. You helped me write with more experience and accuracy, and your love for diving was obvious and contagious. Dawn, you kept the dive class relaxed and fun. Charlie, you've got a gift for teaching. Thank you for sharing it with me.

Art at Sea Level Diving: For taking the time to show me the behind-the-scenes world of your great dive shop so I could make Rockport Dive Company more real!

Fran Linnehan of Down Under Diving Ventures: For letting me tag along on a dive excursion out to the Dry Salvages—and for answering dozens of questions on the way. If I ever take a dive trip in the Cape Ann area, you're the captain I'll call!

Scott Story and Rosemary Lesch: Rockport Harbormasters who gave hours of their time and expertise answering my questions, telling me stories, and making me feel that much more at home in the town I can't seem to get enough of.

Christine Burke: For taking the time to show me your school. I loved it!

Dave Greenwood: For insights on how a good cop would react in various situations.

Cheryl: To the woman who knows every hidden thing about me and still loves me: I love you, Babe! You've encouraged me every step of the way. Without your support, *Every Hidden Thing* would have remained hidden on my computer.

My Lord and God: I wouldn't be who I am, and I couldn't do what I do without You. Thanks for the countless times You gave me the words, the ideas, the boost, and the direction I needed.

"My soul clings to you; your right hand upholds me."

PSALM 63:8

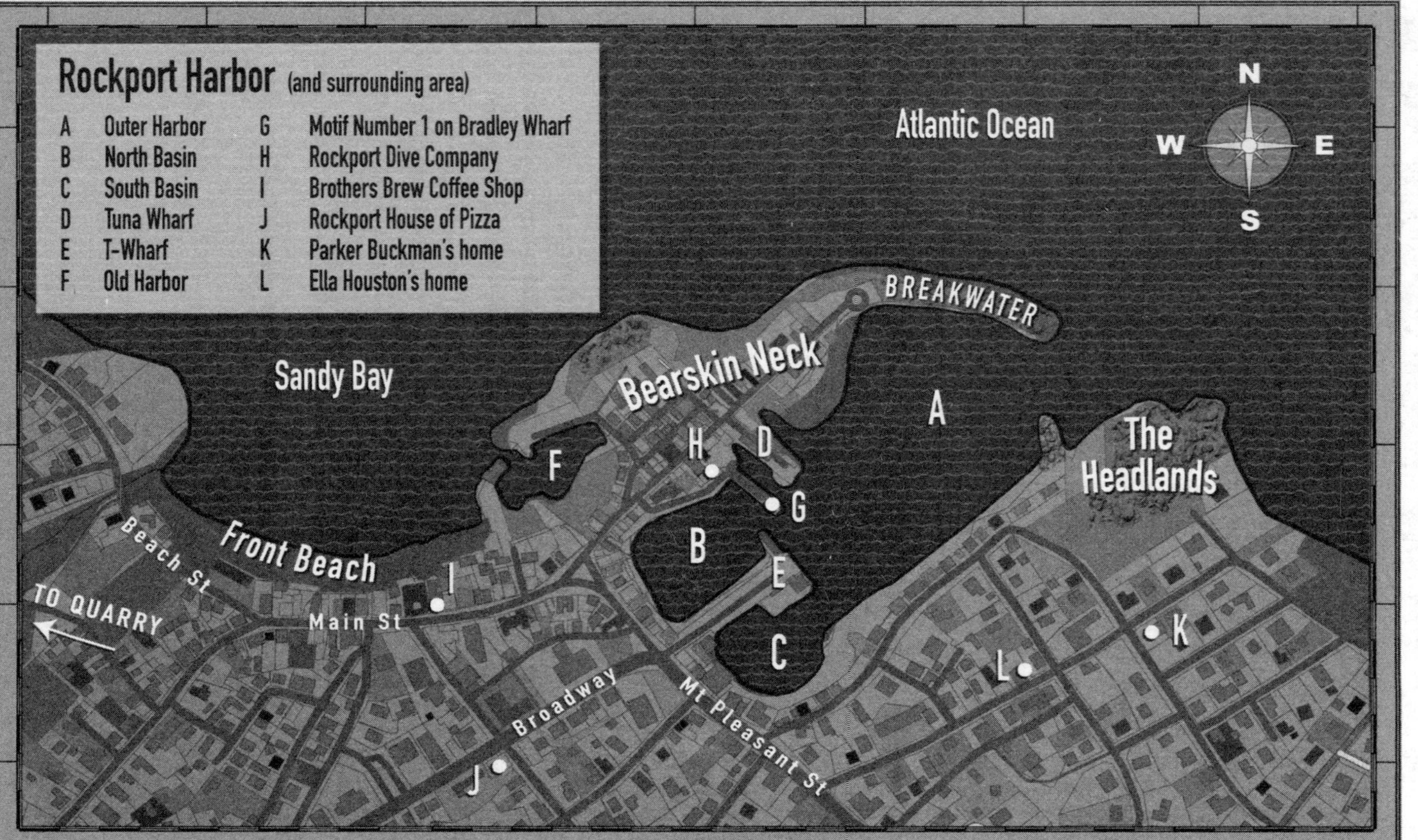
Rockport Harbor (and surrounding area)
A Outer Harbor
B North Basin
C South Basin
D Tuna Wharf
E T-Wharf
F Old Harbor
G Motif Number 1 on Bradley Wharf
H Rockport Dive Company
I Brothers Brew Coffee Shop
J Rockport House of Pizza
K Parker Buckman's home
L Ella Houston's home
N
W
E
S
Atlantic Ocean
BREAKWATER
Sandy Bay
Bearskin Neck
The Headlands
Front Beach
Beach St
TO QUARRY
Main St
Broadway
Mt Pleasant St